Jane Frances Mary Carter, Thomas Thellusson Carter

Nicholas Ferrar

His Household and His Friends

Jane Frances Mary Carter, Thomas Thellusson Carter

Nicholas Ferrar
His Household and His Friends

ISBN/EAN: 9783744649117

Printed in Europe, USA, Canada, Australia, Japan

Cover: Foto ©Raphael Reischuk / pixelio.de

More available books at **www.hansebooks.com**

NICHOLAS FERRAR

HIS HOUSEHOLD AND HIS FRIENDS

EDITED BY THE

REV. T. T. CARTER, M.A.

HON. CANON OF CHRISTCHURCH, OXFORD

LONDON

LONGMANS, GREEN, & CO.

AND NEW YORK: 15 EAST 16th STREET

1892

INTRODUCTION

BY THE

REV. T. T. CARTER, M.A.

THE following pages represent a very remarkable personality, and one of a wide and enduring interest. They also illustrate an important epoch in the later history of the Church of England.

It might, perhaps, seem unnecessary, and, as the author herself fears to be possible, even presumptuous, to put forth a fresh biography of Nicholas Ferrar, considering how much has already been made public in the lives previously written, and most especially the interesting details given by the Rev. J. E. B. Mayor. But the preface shows that, while a great debt is due to previous writers, fresh materials of importance have come to light since their works were published, and there seemed room for a different treatment of the whole subject. The author of this volume desires to withhold her name, and it is, therefore, left to me to give the assurance that great care has been taken to gather together and test the value of the materials now available for the elucidation of the facts stated, and that this has been done with a warmth of enthusiasm that will, I think, be felt to give life to the narrative, replete as it is with important principles.

It would not be true to say of this volume that it could be entitled, "Nicholas Ferrar and his Times." Many most important forces were then at work, or growing into power, influencing both the nation and the Church, acting and reacting the one on the other. But there is no attempt here to enter into such general questions, or to describe the course of events. There is but the portraiture of the one family and its surroundings. Yet Nicholas Ferrar was a marked character; he had relations with many other interests besides his own special objects in life, and he was in friendly intercourse with leading men of the time, some of whom are still cherished in the grateful memories of Churchmen.

Moreover, Nicholas Ferrar's life coincided with one of the most momentous periods of our Church's history. It fell in the period that intervened between the closing years of Elizabeth and the Great Rebellion. The life-and-death conflict with Rome had closed with the defeat of the Armada. The Puritan movement was gaining strength, but as yet was under restraint, and its tremendous influence unsuspected. The Church had the full support of the State, unconscious of the injury to its spiritual interests which such patronage involved. The popular feeling was settling down upon the lines on which the Church, as reformed, was intended to continue, preserving the old Catholic traditions, free from what had been rejected of mediæval development. During this interval lived and taught Andrewes and Overall, Bramhall and Hammond, George Herbert and Jeremy Taylor, Laud and Cosin. There was, indeed, in the general temper an acute sensitiveness as to anything that seemed to savour of a return to past abuses, real or supposed, as is sufficiently shown in this volume, from the suspicions aroused by the establishment at Little Gidding. But, allowing for such exceptional instances, the sense of the continuity of the Church with the Church of the past was as yet undisturbed, and the old customs were generally held to be as true to its life, as they had been before the rupture with Rome. We may, therefore, fairly look at this period as indicating the character of Church life, which was intended for us as the result of what has been generally considered the Elizabethan settlement. It was, in fact, an interval of comparative peace, during which the Church had a fair opportunity of putting forth her true principles. Afterwards followed the prostration of the Church, and on its restoration most unhappily the currents of higher thought were diverted aside from the Church's main channels by the secession of the Nonjurors. They ran comparatively underground for upwards of a century, only appearing here and there in individual cases, witnessed to by a few, of whom Robert Nelson and Bishop Wilson are prominent examples, but destined not to rise again to the surface, nor indeed to be regarded as the Church's true inheritance, till the Oxford movement. John Keble had Nonjurors for his progenitors, and this may partly account for the fact, that to him, as to Pusey, the great revival, now spreading more and more throughout the length and breadth of the land, was seen at once to be the natural and legitimate aspect of the Church of England.

It is not that this volume attempts to portray the state of the Church at the time here spoken of—the interval preceding the Great Rebellion; but it has, as I believe, its value in illustrating the currents of thought prevailing at the time, and thus marks the characteristic tendencies then acknowledged to be the groundwork of future progress. Nicholas Ferrar's life and work give the most detailed view we possess of the religious feelings and habits of a private family, and thus serve to paint in some degree the character of the period.

From its bearing, therefore, on the history of the Church of England at a very critical time, as well as for the sake of the records it supplies of a deeply religious life, bent not only on personal holiness, but also on practical usefulness, I venture to recommend the work, hoping that it may tend to promote and deepen the interest now happily felt more and more widely in tracing throughout the records of the Church of England the continuous life of the higher forms of devotion, which have ever characterized the Catholic Communion.

T. T. CARTER.

CLEWER,
 October, 1892.

b

AUTHOR'S PREFACE.

IT is with sincere diffidence that this volume is offered to the public. It aims at presenting the history of Nicholas Ferrar in somewhat fuller relation to the life of his times, than was permitted by the scope of previous biographers; but a sense of the inadequacy with which this aim is fulfilled has deepened with the writing of each succeeding chapter.

The chief excuse for its publication lies in the fact than on two points of interest —the dedication of the " Maiden Sisters" and the history of the Concordances of Holy Scripture, the making of which formed so large a portion of the occupations of Gidding—additional information has come to light since the appearance of the most recent of the Lives of Nicholas Ferrar.

Most grateful thanks are tendered to A. G. Peskitt, Esq., Librarian of Magdalene College, Cambridge, for his kind permission to see and make extracts from some of the deeply interesting letters (hitherto unpublished) which have been lately found among the Ferrar manuscripts in the library of his college; to Harold Mapletoft Davis, Esq., for the loan of a manuscript volume of extracts from the Life of Ferrar by Francis Turner, the non-juring Bishop of Ely, and of transcripts from the Gidding "Conversation books," of which the originals are now in Australia; to Captain J. E. Acland, for permission to use his Catalogue of the Gidding Concordances, printed in the

Archæologia for 1888 ; and to others who have kindly helped in various ways, not least to the present owner of Little Gidding, the Rev. William Hopkinson, and Mrs. Hopkinson, to whose kindness the author is indebted for the sight of the fields amid which Nicholas Ferrar lived, the church in which he prayed, and the grave close by in which he now lies.

The Lives of Ferrar already issued are five in number. The first is the "Memoirs of the Life of Mr. Nicholas Ferrar, by P. Peckard, D.D., Master of Magdalene College, Cambridge : Cambridge, Archdeacon, 1790," founded on an unpublished Memoir of Nicholas Ferrar by his brother John, and other family papers, of which Dr. Peckard became possessed through his wife, a descendant of the Ferrars. The value of this work is somewhat impaired by the author's obvious wish to tone down the peculiarities of his subject to suit the taste of his own day.

Next comes the "Brief Memoirs of Nicholas Ferrar, M.A., and Fellow of Clare-Hall, Cambridge, Founder of a Protestant Religious Establishment at Little Gidding, Huntingdonshire. By a Clergyman of the Established Church," published at Bristol by J. Chilcot in 1829. This book passed through two editions, in the second of which, published by Nisbet in 1837, is given the name of the author, the Rev. T. M. Macdonogh. It is founded, as stated in the preface, on an unpublished Life by Bishop Turner, or rather on extracts from that Life, printed in the *Christian Magazine* for 1761. This magazine is now difficult to find, but the manuscript Life, belonging to Mr. Mapletoft Davis, which has been for some time preserved in his family, is evidently either the draught or a copy of these extracts. It is entitled " Life of Nicholas Ferrar, by the Right Rev. Dr. Turner, formerly Lord Bishop of Ely." In a short preface the transcriber of the manuscript states, that " the following curious and instructive Life was drawn up by Bishop Turner, whose manuscript papers are now before us." He adds that " as the Life is rather too long for our pamphlet" (qu. the *Christian Magazine*), " even divided, we have taken the liberty to abridge some particulars in the Bishop's account, and now and then to alter a phrase or two of his language, which through length of time is rather in some places become obsolete." On comparing this manuscript with Mr. Macdonogh's book, it appears that he has followed it almost word for word, even to assigning February

1st as the day of Ferrar's birth, a transcriber's error for 21st, the date given in another copy of Turner's Life to be mentioned presently. The incidents omitted from these extracts are also omitted from his memoir, except in a few instances, in which Peckard's Life has obviously been made use of to fill up gaps.

In 1852 Messrs. Masters published an abridgment of Peckard's " Life of Nicholas Ferrar," to which is appended particulars of the state of Gidding Church at that time.

Last in order of publication, but earliest written, and incomparably first in interest and value, is the " Two Lives of Ferrar," edited in 1855 by the Rev. J. E. B. Mayor for his " Cambridge in the Seventeenth Century " (Macmillan, Cambridge), to which are added selections from the Collett Letters, and " Some observations that happened upon these fore-named works done at Gidding," containing an account of the last days of Nicholas Ferrar, Junior, by John Ferrar: reprinted from Wordsworth's "Ecclesiastical Biography." The original manuscript of the "Observations" is in the Library at Lambeth. The first of the "Two Lives" consists of extracts made by the Rev. Thomas Baker, the celebrated antiquarian and Nonjuror, from the original memoir of Nicholas Ferrar by his brother. The second is entitled by Mr. Mayor, "Life of Nicholas Ferrar, by Dr. Jebb," because it is so called in the manuscript from which it is printed; but he says, "What is certain is, that the Life is in substance, and generally in expression, Turner's." This life by Dr. Jebb is identical except for the occasional alteration of a single word or short phrase, with Mr. Mapletoft Davis's manuscript as far as the two go together, but it contains many passages omitted in the latter. It is not, however, a complete copy of Turner's life, for some points are left out, *e.g.* the account of the night watchings, and of the setting up of old Mrs. Ferrar's tablet, both of which are given in the manuscript. It is curious that both the Life by Turner, and the Memoir by John Ferrar, have been lost sight of in their original form, and are known to us by extracts only.

From the " Two Lives " and the copious notes with which they are illustrated, these pages are, with the Rev. J. E. B. Mayor's kind permission, chiefly drawn. The author feels unable sufficiently to express her obligations to Mr. Mayor's work. She owes to it not only the rich store of material accumulated in the Notes and Appendix, to much of which she could have gained access in no other way, but also guidance and suggestions as to further search.

The frontispiece has been engraved with much care by Mr. C. J. Tomkins, by the kind permission of the Rev. the Hon. L. Neville, Master of Magdalene College, Cambridge, from the portrait of Nicholas Ferrar by Cornelius Janssen in Magdalene Lodge, with some assistance, the picture being in parts indistinct, from the engraving published by P. W. Tomkins in 1791, which is to be found in some copies of Peckard's Life of Ferrar. The view of the church of Little Gidding, with the grave of Nicholas Ferrar, facing page 277, is from a drawing made on the spot by the author.

CONTENTS.

CHAPTER V.

1626–1628.

CHAPTER VI.

1628–1632.

CHAPTER VII.

CHAPTER VIII.

CHAPTER IX.

CHAPTER X.

1633.

CHAPTER XI.

1633–1637.

CHAPTER XII.

1634–1637.

CHAPTER XIII.

1637–1642.

CHAPTER XIV.

1642—1660.

CHAPTER XV.

1660–1720.

CHAPTER I.

CHILDHOOD AND YOUTH.

A.D. 1593—1613.

A KEEN interest attaches to periods of growth and reconstruction, and to none more than to that time, so remote from our own day, and yet so closely linked with it, in which the English Church, just recovering from the struggle and shock of the Reformation, gathered its strength together, and, resting for awhile from the heat of battle, gave itself to the task of building up once more the devotional life of its people.

No doubt reform had been sadly needed, but quiet people, indisposed for controversy, who only longed to serve God in peace, must often have found their lives very cold and bare during those first years of separation. The old forms of piety in which their parents had been trained were broken up ; the daily Sacrifice was no longer offered; the Religious Life was wholly swept away; the very churches themselves were often suffered to go to ruin. "The people," says Clarendon,[1] "took so little care of the churches, and the parsons so little of the chancels, that, instead of beautifying and adorning them in any degree, they rarely provided against the falling of many of their churches, and suffered them at least to be kept so indecently and slovenly, that they would not have endured it in the ordinary offices of their own houses ; the rain and wind to infest them, and the sacraments themselves to be administered where the people had most mind to receive them." When Bishop Williams became Dean of Westminster in 1619, he found the Abbey Church in such decay "that all that passed by and loved the honour of God's house shook their heads at the stones that dropped down from the pinnacles."[2]

If we try to picture to ourselves the daily life of England in the beginning of the seventeenth century, it seems at first sight as if men had grown so weary of the controversy and persecution which had so long

[1] Clarendon, " History of Rebellion," Book I.
[2] Hacket's "Life of Archbishop Williams," i. 55.

been associated with the name of religion, that they tried to put the subject from them, and to forget everything that could recall the fires of Smithfield, or the fierce vengeance that followed the Rising of the North.

When we endeavour to trace the features of this perplexing time in the pages of its greatest writer, we find in his vast gallery of portraits every type of character save one—the religious enthusiast. The plays of Shakespeare burn with a passion of patriotism. We find in them the intellectual difficulties of the time, and its strange superstitions, its lofty refinement, its love of state and splendour, side by side with its pleasure in coarse buffoonery. There, too, we see the keen and new delight in outward nature, the wild spirit of adventure, the thirst after fresh fields of thought and knowledge, which mark the century; but we look in vain for a trace of the spirit which made Latimer rejoice, while the faggots were heaped round him, that he was about to light a candle in England which should not be soon put out; and prompted the dying words of the Jesuit Campion, "To be condemned with these old lights, by their degenerate descendants, is both gladness and glory to us."[1]

For a while, overwhelmed by the splendour of the State, by golden dreams of the New World, the

---

[1] Quoted in *Church Quarterly*, April, 1879.

religious question seemed to vanish out of sight;
but underneath the magnificent England of the
Court and of literature there lay another England—
the England of the people. Impatient of change,
unforgetful, indifferent, for the most part, to the
charm of high culture; sober-minded, dutiful, religious
to the core, this inner England grew in silence and
shadow, slowly gathering to itself some of the
choicest spirits among those who felt that the thirst
of their soul could not be quenched at the fountains
of the Renaissance.   One of the finest scholars of the
time has recorded, in well-known verses, his pursuit
of the learning and the splendour of the world, and
his sense of its insufficiency to fill the heart.

> " I know the ways of learning; both the head
>   And pipes that feed the press, and make it run;
>   What Reason hath from Nature borrowèd,
>   Or of itself, like a good housewife, spun,
>   In laws and policy; what the stars conspire,
>   What willing Nature speaks, what, forced by fire;
>   Both the old discoveries, and the new-found seas,
>   The stock and surplus, cause and history:
>   All these stand open, or I have the keys—
> 			Yet I love Thee.
>
>   .   .   .   .   .   .
>
> " I know the ways of Pleasure, the sweet strains,
>   The lullings and the relishes of it;
>   The propositions of hot blood and brains;
>   What mirth and music mean; what love and wit
>   Have done these twenty hundred years and more;
>   I know the projects of unbridled store:

> My stuff is flesh, not brass ; my senses live,
> And grumble oft, that they have more in me
> Than He that curbs them, being but one to five :
> Yet I love Thee." [1]

So wrote George Herbert when, after a long struggle, he put aside his dreams of Court favour and devoted himself to the priesthood ; and no doubt he spoke the thoughts of many silent students in the Cambridge of his day. Gradually the life of the English Church, as we know it, grew into shape.

Among the contemporary records from which we obtain glimpses of this growing life, few are more interesting than the " Memoir of Nicholas Ferrar," by his brother John, from which the biography here attempted is chiefly drawn. [2]

The father of the family, Nicholas Ferrar the elder, is a fine type of the great merchants of London ; well-born, loyal (he " was written Esquire by Queen Elizabeth " in return for liberal assistance), hot-tempered, generous-hearted, a man of wide sympathies, gathering many of the notable men of the day round the hospitable table of his fine house in the City ; a zealous Churchman, repairing and seating, at his own expense, his parish church of St. Sythe, [3] and providing

---

[1] G. Herbert, "The Pearl."   [2] See Preface.

[3] Commonly called "St. Bennet Sherehog," in honour, according to Stowe, of an earlier restorer, one Benedict Shorne or Shrog.   Later authorities consider this derivation as doubtful.

a morning preacher for the same, the congregation
having apparently gone sermonless until he brought
Francis White, afterwards Bishop of Ely, to town, and
made him their first lecturer.   Mr. Ferrar's portrait,
by Janssen, is to be seen at Cambridge in the Masters'
Lodge at Magdalene College—a fine open face, with
uprightness and honesty in every line.

His wife, Mary Woodnoth, of the ancient family of
the Woodnoths of Shavington, was a remarkable
woman, gifted with the same singular power of im-
pressing her own personality on those around her,
which was one of the most marked characteristics of
her son Nicholas.   Her portrait hangs beside her
husband's.   The firm delicate lines of her finely cut
features, the exquisitely fair complexion, the noble
and serious countenance, suit well with the description
which is given of her in the memoirs of her son.

We are told that she was beautiful, bright-haired,
and fair, upright even to her eightieth year; highly
educated, of a strong judgment, a wise and even
temper, so that her choleric husband declared that in
their five-and-forty years of married life she had never
given him cause for anger; a woman who did not
talk much, but whose word was a law in her little
world, and whose discreet, careful, charitable life was
grounded in deep love and study of the will of God.

Nicholas and Mary Ferrar were the parents of seven
children, of whom the fourth is the subject of this

sketch.   His affectionate brother and biographer tells us that the little Nicholas was a lovely child, with his mother's bright hair, the petted favourite of the family and their many friends.   Of the other children, some died young.   One, Richard, a merchant like his father, grew up careless and unthrifty, the black sheep of the household, and passes out of sight. Susannah only, and John, stand out clear and distinct in the family records.   We read Susannah's character in her letters, of which a number have been preserved. She appears in them as an energetic, affectionate woman, a wise counsellor to her many children, falling, as every one else did, under the strong influence of her mother and her brother Nicholas, but not always, as we gather, fully agreeing with them, though she gives in dutifully to their wishes.   John, short and dark—following the Ferrar side of the house probably—an excellent man of business, clear-sighted and upright, humble above all things, and self-effacing, seems to have been one of those men who live only for others.   Not brilliant, remarkable in no way, little spoken of, he is yet the member of his family whom no one can do without.

Dr. Lindsell, Bishop of Hereford, the lifelong friend of Mrs. Ferrar (whom he held in such affectionate regard that he was himself accustomed to call her " mother "), and the tutor of her son Nicholas, gives a pleasant picture of the household in its happy early time, when the mother was constantly to be found sitting at work with her children and maids around her, singing psalms with them, and hearing them read chapters in the Bible, and stories from the " Book of Martyrs," the *Acta Sanctorum* of those days. They had family prayer twice a day, a clergyman generally residing in the house to act as chaplain. Even on a journey this was not omitted, and they were careful to attend the church services on Wednesdays and Fridays, as well as on Sundays. The good bishop rather quaintly computes that Mrs. Ferrar must have heard, in the course of her life, as many as twelve thousand sermons, adding, "What good use she made of all these things, let the world speak of it ; her deeds will praise her in the gates of the City, and in the country, in the open fields abroad."[1]

In this atmosphere of religion and good works, Nicholas Ferrar was born on the 22nd of February, 1593, and baptized in the small parish church of St. Mary, " called Stayning because it standeth at the north end of Stayning Lane " (a little street once chiefly inhabited by paper-stainers, which turns out of Mark Lane), on the 28th of the same month, a day " which he registered as more memorable than his birthday, esteeming it, as he ought, a greater favour

[1] " Life of Nicholas Ferrar," by his brother, p. 64, the first of the two lives of Ferrar, edited by Rev. J. E. B. Mayor, in the first vol. of " Cambridge in the Seventeenth Century."

to be received into the Catholic Church than to come into the world." [1]

He was an active, graceful child, quick-witted, gifted with a strong memory, and great perseverance (he had the Psalter by heart at seven or eight years old), and the precocious love of books which often accompanies delicate health. His brother relates that he would often forget his meals while he pored over the " English Chronicle," or the "Book of Martyrs," quaint old folios which were new then, and of which the last had a touch of personal interest. The little boy learnt by heart the story of Robert Ferrar, Bishop of St. David's, burnt at Carmarthen in 1555, "for his name's sake," though it does not appear that there was any relationship.

His keen and eager spirit broke forth on occasion in these childish days, showing itself sometimes in an oddly original fashion. When about six years old he was brought to be confirmed, and having duly received "the laying-on of hands," and, it is to be supposed, returned to his place with his companions, he contrived to slip away and again present himself to the bishop, who, naturally thinking that he saw before him a new candidate, confirmed him afresh. "I did it because it was a good thing to have the bishop's prayers and blessing twice; and I have got it!" said little Nicholas, triumphantly, when called to account for this irregular proceeding.

[1] Life, by Dr. Jebb.

His childish fancies seemed to foreshadow his future vocation. "Make my bands little and plain, like those of Mr. Wotton, for I would be a preacher as he is," he said one day to his mother, when she was making for the children the dainty lace-trimmed collars with which we are familiar in the portraits of the time.

He was not eight years old, when it was resolved to send him to join his elder brothers at Emborne, near Newbury, where was a school famous for its healthful situation and the careful and religious discipline maintained therein.

Stirred, no doubt, and excited by the prospect of this new life, his sensitive nature wrought up to the highest point, he underwent an experience singular in such a young child, and remarkable for its abiding influence on his mind and heart. One night as he lay alone in his little bed, he was tempted to doubt the existence of God, and whether it were possible to render Him an acceptable service. Unable to shake off the horror of these thoughts, and perhaps unwilling to be found weeping by the other children, he got up, went downstairs, and stole out into the garden, and then threw himself on his face on the grass, in an agony of prayer and tears, and " earnestly, with all his strength, humbly begged of God that He would put into his heart the true fear and awe of His Divine Majesty, and that this fear and love of God might never depart out of his mind, and that he might know how he must serve Him. After much bitter weeping he felt his heart much eased, and comforts began to come to it, and to have an assurance of God, and the doubt began to pass away and his heart was much cheered. He then rose up and went up to his chamber to bed again, but could not sleep but little ; yet he found daily more and more confirmation in his soul, and so had all his lifetime after a more than ordinary fear of God in him, and His presence, which continued till his dying day." "Two things," says Dr. John Worthington, "in that night's holy exercise were so imprinted in the heart and mind of the child, that they came fresh into his memory every day of his life. (This he told me more than once two or three years before his death.) The one was the joy and sweetness which he did in that watching night conceive and feel in his heart; the other was the gracious promise which God made to him to bless and keep him all his whole life so that he would constantly fear God and keep his commandments." "This invocation," adds the writer just quoted, "and fervent prayer of this child, stirred up in him by the Spirit and grace of God, was so followed by the same Spirit in an evident effectual vocation of him, that it resembleth the calling of Samuel when he was yet a child." [1]

[1] Account by Dr. Worthington, printed in Hearne, "Caii Vindiciæ."

Mr. Brooke, the headmaster of Emborne, seems to have been a born schoolmaster; he loved his work, and "forsook the noise of a great city to preside over children in a country retirement, believing his charitable pains amply rewarded by the prayers of such happy innocents." He appears to have bestowed equal care on the religious and secular instruction of his pupils. The children had set times for learning the Psalter and the Epistles and Gospels, as well as the Catechism, and we are told that none of the scholars "performed their tasks of this kind (nor indeed of any kind) so constantly, carefully, and easily" as did Nicholas Ferrar. The work of the school would seem to have been hard, and the discipline severe, but the child had the true scholar's temperament, which loves learning for its own sake, and his retentive memory made his tasks the easier, though perhaps his frail health and high-strung nerves (he would steal away and cry when praised) may be partly traceable to overwork.

In 1606 his master declared him fit for the University, saying that he would lose precious time by remaining longer at Emborne, and he was entered at Cambridge, as a pensioner at Clare Hall, before he had completed his thirteenth year.

This does not appear to have shown extraordinary precocity; at that time boys commonly went to the Universities at a much earlier age than is now usual.

Laud, when Chancellor of Oxford, forbade the establishment of a riding school, "for the gentlemen there are most part too young and not strong enough." Lord Herbert of Cherburg, the elder brother of the poet, was sent to Oxford at twelve. Bacon entered Trinity at the same age, and probably Nicholas Ferrar found other undergraduates as young as himself among his fellow pensioners at Clare.[1]

The discipline of the colleges was suited to the age of the students, the tutors exercising a close supervision over their studies and conduct. "What pains he would take with those under him," was said by an old pupil of a famous scholar[2] of that time; "and among other things what excellent lectures he would deliver to them of piety and instruction from the chapter that was read on nights in his chamber," —and Mede gathered his pupils in his chamber each evening "to satisfy him that they had performed the task he had set them," and before dismissing them to their lodgings "by prayer commended

---

[1] Instances may be found much nearer our own times. Both Mr. J. Keble and the late Dr. Copleston, Bishop of Llandaff, were elected scholars of Corpus before they were fifteen. —Coleridge, "Life of Keble."

[2] Henry More, quoted by Mr. J. B. Mullinger, "Cambridge Characteristics in the Seventeenth Century," to which book the writer is indebted for the notices of Cambridge life in this chapter.

them and their studies to God's protection and blessing."[1]

Ferrar's tutor was the senior Fellow of his college, Augustine Lindsell, afterwards Bishop first of Peterborough, and then of Hereford. The close and kindly relationship begun at Clare lasted through the life of Ferrar, and had a strong influence on his character. "Nick," the bishop would sometimes say to his old pupil when he saw the austerities of his later years, "whither will you go? what example will you give us?" "Nay, tutor," he would reply, "you are to answer to God for this. Why did you commend unto me, and made me (being so young at college as I was) to read the lives of all the holy men of old time, and saints of God, the good fathers of the Church, and of those good men in our later times even in the Church of England, the saints and holy martyrs? Was it that I might only know the good things that they did? And what was that to me, if you intended not, or that I should not endeavour to fit and frame my lips, in all I could, by the assistance of Almighty God's good grace and spirit, to do and to live as they did, as much as was in my poor power to do?"[2]

He spent seven years at Cambridge, winning golden opinions. The "sweet mixture in him of gravity with

[1] Mr. Mullinger, ibid.

[2] "Life of Nicholas Ferrar," by his brother, p. 92.

affability, and modesty with civility," is affectionately remembered long after his death by a senior member of his college, Dr. Byng. " His comportment was such in all respects as that it was exemplary, not only to his puisnes and compeers, but to many who were much his ancients, who were all so much pleased with his company as that they thought themselves happiest who most enjoyed it," he writes in 1654 to a mutual friend, also a Fellow of Clare, Barnabas Oley.[1]

Chief among these " ancients " were his friend and physician, Dr. Butler, and the " excellent comedian," Mr. Ruggles, author of a Latin play which was performed by the Fellows of Clare for the amusement of James I., on one of his frequent visits to Cambridge. Of his " puisnes and compeers " one would like to know more.

One whose name was afterwards closely linked with his own, George Herbert, came up to Trinity in 1608, but there is no sign that the two young men formed any acquaintance. Herbert was a year younger, and combined with his brilliant scholarship " a genteel humour for clothes and courtly company," keeping carefully out of the way of his inferiors, among whom he would probably have reckoned the merchant's son at Clare.

There is indeed no trace of friendships formed by Ferrar at this time among his contemporaries. Per-

---

[1] Quoted by Mr. Mayor in his notes to " Two Lives."

haps the boy, though so greatly beloved by his elders, was considered rather old-fashioned and sententious by his young companions. There was a precocious gravity about him ; his natural seriousness was deepened by family sorrows. He writes to his parents of his "dearest brother Erasmus, and your other children that are departed in the Lord ; " and we have glimpses of deep melancholy of an inward strife that rose at time to anguish. "My soul hath been almost rent," he writes ; " I may truly say that from youth up Thy terrors have I suffered with a troubled mind." His talents were of a sort to delight his teachers more than his equals. He was thoughtful rather than brilliant or original, and though he possessed in a high degree the magnetic influence which enables some men to draw their fellows round them and rule them as by right divine, the current was not so much an intellectual as a spiritual force, and acted mainly on those whose hearts were awake to spiritual influences.

He worked so hard that his window was known by the light which glimmered earliest in the winter mornings, and was last put out at night ; and he was constant in his attendance at the chapel services, "officiating" (by reading the chapters?) " as regularly as if he had been the college conduct," a regularity which implied more effort than in our more luxurious days, as the chapel bell rang at five in the morning, and prayers were sometimes followed by a homily from one of the fellows.

His principal recreation (it is the only one of which his biographers make any mention) was found in visits to his eldest sister, Susannah, married in 1600 to Mr. John Collett, and now settled at Bourne, about ten miles from Cambridge. He took from the first a deep interest in her children, "catechising and giving them fatherly counsel." He was not more than seventeen or eighteen when he assumed this position, as adviser in the gravest matters ; and it is a striking proof of the influence which he already possessed over those who knew him best, that Mrs. Collett, a woman of strong character, with the experience of several years of married life, seems from the first to have accepted his aid in the training of her family with unquestioning gratitude.

His studies were broken by frequent fits of ague, then one of the commonest of English illnesses, and the system of starvation by which his friend Dr. Butler tried to keep it down, "though very agreeable to his patient, who was so great a lover of abstinence" proved, when added to the lowering effects of the damp air of Cambridge, a very inefficient cure.

In 1610, after the commendable performance of his acts "in scholis publicis," he was made Bachelor of Arts, and soon after elected Fellow of his college, where he continued to reside until the end of the winter of 1612–13.　　He was to receive his M.A. degree in the following midsummer, and had already performed "all private and public acts"—which no doubt included the disputations maintained in the College Hall, and also in St. Mary's before the University, then customary before the taking of each degree (and which until the establishment of the Tripos were the only public tests of proficiency)— "with approbation of the college and University, and to his own high commendation," when his attacks of ague, which had for some time been increasing in severity, became so serious, that Dr. Butler advised him to leave Cambridge at once, without waiting to take his degree, and try if he could recruit his health by foreign travel.

His parents were greatly averse to this step, and it needed strong representations from his tutor to induce them to give their consent.　A journey on the Continent was then a serious matter, and it is not wonderful that Mr. and Mrs. Ferrar shrank from exposing their delicate young son to the difficult journeying and wild license of the time; but Lindsell had full confidence in his pupil.　"We may hope comfortably to see him again," he assured the anxious parents, "not only improved in learning, but grown in grace; a stock few of our young travellers increase abroad."

Nicholas himself felt the long journey, the distance and separation from his friends, to be a serious crisis in his life; his heart was wrung by the pain of parting, and he was probably too much depressed by illness to take pleasure in the prospect of novelty and excitement which opened before him.

The "pathetically kind" letter, addressed to his parents, which was found in his study three days after his departure, gives a picture of his feelings. He makes a solemn vow that "if the good Lord God be merciful to me and bring me safe home again, I will all the days of my life serve Him in praising His Holy Name and exhorting others; yea, in His tabernacle and in His holy sanctuary will I serve Him, and shall account the lowest place in His house better and more honourable than the greatest crown in the world." But he writes as one who had little hope of a happy return to home and friends; the keynote of the letter is his tender wish that his parents should have comfort in his death. "If I go before," he says, "you must come shortly after; think it is but a little forbearance of me. It was God that gave me to you, and if He take me from you, be you not only content but most joyful that I am delivered from this vale of misery and wretchedness. I know that, through the infinite mercy of my gracious God, it shall be my happiness, for I shall then, I know, enjoy perpetual quietness and peace, and be delivered from those perpetual combats and temptations which afflict my poor soul." In a postscript he assures his "dearest brothers and dearest sisters," [1] that " If I live, you shall find me a faithful loving brother unto you all. If I die, I beseech you by the fear of God, by the duty to our parents, by the bond of nature, by the love you bear me, that you all agree in perfect love and amity, and account every one the other's burden to be his; so may plenty and prosperity dwell among you." And he ends with a request that in case of his death £5 of his books may be given to the college; some to his "worthy tutor Lindsell and Cousin Theophilus;" and if any of my sister's sons prove a scholar, the rest may be given to him." [2]

The letter is dated, " This tenth day of April, 1613, being Sunday," just a fortnight before he left England.

[1] His own sister, Susannah Collett, his brother John's first wife, who died in the following summer.

[2] Copied by Jebb from John Ferrar's MSS. Peckard has omitted several passages.

CHAPTER II.

FOREIGN TRAVEL.

A.D. 1613–1618.

"The mind of man is this world's true dimension,
    And knowledge is the measure of the minde ;
    And as the minde, in her vast comprehension,
    Contains more worlds than all the world can finde,
        So knowledge doth itself farre more extend,
        Than all the minds of men can comprehend.

"A climing height it is without a head,
    Depth without bottome, way without an end,
    A circle with no line environed ;
    Not comprehended, all it comprehends ;
        Worth infinite, yet satisfies no minde
        Till it that infinite of the God-heade finde."
        FULKE GREVILLE, LORD BROOKE, 1554—1628.

WHILE Nicholas Ferrar, with a sinking heart, prepared to leave Cambridge, his friends were exerting themselves to make his departure as pleasant and honourable as possible. The University, by a special grace, granted his M.A. degree three months before the customary time ; and Dr. Scott, the Master of Clare, procured for him a place in the household of the

Princess Elizabeth, then newly married to the Elector Palatine, so that he might begin his foreign life under distinguished patronage.

In the beginning of Lent the bridegroom visited Cambridge, accompanied by Prince Charles and a " comely concourse" of gentlemen, both English and German, and received a splendid welcome from the University. It was probably on this occasion that the young Fellow of Clare was first brought to his notice.

Bishop Hacket gives an amusing description of the public disputation which formed one of the most important features of the entertainment. This academical tournament took place, according to the usual custom, in St. Mary's, which was scaffolded for the occasion, and filled with " the most judicious of the whole island," who listened with delighted interest while Mr. Samuel Collins " stood in the gap, to maintain the truth in three theses against all assailants." " No flood," cries the bishop, rapturously, "can be compared to the springtide of his eloquence, but the milky river of Nilus with his Seven Mouths all at once disembogueing into the sea. Oh, how voluble, how quick, how facetious he was ! What a Vertumnus when he pleased to argue on the right side or on the contrary ! These things will be living in the memory of the longest survivor that ever heard him." [1]

[1] " Life of Archbishop Williams."

No doubt Nicholas Ferrar, who, though not of sufficient age or importance to figure on such a great occasion, was himself an adept in these affrays, was among the admiring crowd, who listened while the combatants plied each other with "as many turns and twists of argument as ever greyhound following a hare on Newmarket Heath," and looked with interest and curiosity on the learned Germans in the Pfalzgrave's train, whose nearer acquaintance he was soon to make.

The prince and princess sailed from Margate on April 23. Nicholas Ferrar, no longer in his plain scholar's garb, but splendidly dressed as befitted the attendant of a royal bride, was in their retinue, and with him probably another young Cambridge scholar, Francis Quarles, author of the " Pious Emblems." [1] The voyage to Flushing lasted four days, and in the course of this time, Ferrar lost his ague, cleared away perhaps, as Dr. Butler had predicted, by sea sickness, perhaps also by the keen salt breezes, and the novelty and liveliness of the gay company among whom he travelled—so great a change from the damp air of the fens, and the grave talk of the common-room at Clare.

From Flushing the bridal party crossed the grey levels, brightened here and there by vivid patches of spring blossom (for the Dutch were already famous

[1] Quarles, who was about a year older than Ferrar was in the princess's service in his early life.

gardeners), to the Hague and Amsterdam. Ferrar's attendance does not seem to have been very onerous, for he is said to have made during his stay in the low countries, a careful study of the manners and habits of the Dutch, their polite inventions and ingenious manufactures, their modes of provision for the poor and infirm, and their forms of worship, which were so numerous, that a contemporary traveller tells us that in the street where he lodged " there be near as many religions as houses."

He won the favour of the princess, and hopes were held out that he might become her secretary (a place subsequently held by Quarles), but a courtier's life was unsuited to his taste, and when she quitted Holland for the Palatinate, he resigned his place in her suite, and continued his journey alone and untrammelled.

No doubt the grave young scholar was far happier when the first novelty was past, wandering about the quaint crowded streets, " having ever his Dutch book with an English translation in his hand, that he might not lose a moment "[1] in the study of the language, than in following the princess to all the splendid entertainments provided for her by the States of Holland. One would give a good deal to see the diary which he diligently kept during his years of

[1] The account of Ferrar's travels is taken from "Life of Nicholas Ferrar," by Dr. Jebb.

travel. It does not appear that he was greatly attracted by the wonders of painting and architecture. He " did not make it all his business to see sights or to measure the height of towers," being chiefly interested in the new customs, the varying forms of government, the jarring medley of sects among which he found himself, all the confused and dazzling stir of life into which he had come suddenly from his study at Clare.

He spent some time at Hamburg, where the English merchants, correspondents no doubt of the prosperous Ferrar house, received him warmly. Indeed, their hospitality was so overwhelming, that he was obliged, much to their surprise, to avoid all wine and strong drink, finding moderation impossible at their overflowing tables. Not content with this silent protest, he tried to elevate the tone of his hosts' conversation, in a way that would now seem rather priggish for a youth of twenty, but which was then perhaps considered suitable in a Cambridge scholar. He " would lead the conversation to some considera- tion of virtue and vice, and would so delicately array the one and disrobe the other, that his conversation was no less pleasing than it was instructive, ever embracing some pertinent and remarkable passages out of sacred and civil history." There must have been some great charm in the manner in which all this youthful wisdom was poured forth, for the kindly merchants were "strangely taken" with this "new way of conversation."

From Hamburg Ferrar proceeded to Leipsic, and there, in the familiar atmosphere of a university town, he settled down to studies so many and so various, that it is no wonder his father wrote to him "not to destroy himself with too much diligence." Besides his attendance at the exercises in the public schools, where his fluent and elegant Latin was much admired, he "made inquiries for the ablest masters in every art, whom he would gain entirely, if gold and good words would gain them, to teach him their mystery." Nothing seemed to come amiss to him, and we are not surprised that he found it desirable to learn a system of artificial memory. "Painters, weavers, dyers, and smiths were much at his lodgings, and at his service, which enabled him to treat with artisans in their proper terms; he could maintain a dialogue with an architect in his own phrases; he could talk with the mariners in their sea terms, knowing the word for almost every rope and pin in a ship. Such was his curiosity in all the fine parts of learning and knowledge; an affection which is last mortified in a polite and a capacious mind, that now made the great world his other book."

Among other arts in which the Germans greatly excelled the English at that time, was that of engraving, and the large collection of prints which

Ferrar brought home, and of which he afterwards made so much use in the illustration of his Scripture harmonies, was probably begun during his stay in Germany. His talent and industry attracted attention, and his acquaintance was much sought; but he loved a quieter life than could easily be had among the crowd of students who lodged, unbound by any rules of discipline, around the lecture halls of the University, and after a time, no doubt with many longings for his rooms at Clare, for the quiet garden in the shadow of King's, and the noiseless river gliding past, he retired to a neighbouring village where he spent his leisure in the study of the best German writers.

The duration of his stay at Leipsic is uncertain, but it seems most probable that he set out again on his travels in the early summer of 1614. From Leipsic he went to Prague, where he stayed some time; he then visited Nuremburg and Ulm, Spires and Augsburg, noting everything, and saw the splendours of the Imperial Court at Vienna; but the plague was raging in Southern Germany, and it would seem that he hastened his journey on that account, for it was still winter, apparently the January or February of 1615, when he crossed the Alps.

We are not told which course he took, but as he came first to Venetian territory travelling by way of Padua, it seems most likely that his route was through the valleys of the Brenner, from Innspruck to Trent, a road which must have been frequented at all seasons of the year.   One incident only of this mountain journey is recorded.   " Riding one time over some narrow and dangerous passages of the Alps, his guide being but a little way before him, out comes an ass from the side of a hill between him and his guide, laden with a large piece of timber lying across her back, running upon him down the hill, where the way was extremely strait and narrow and steep, as having a wall on the one side and a dreadful descent on the other.   His guide, not hearing the tread of his mule, looked behind him, and seeing the ass thus laden and now near him, he cried out, ' *O Lord ! O God ! the man is lost if he had a hundred lives !* ' "   Overhearing the guide's voice, he was amazed, and, looking up, he saw the ass coming down hastily upon him, so that, the wood lying athwart her, he thought it must tumble him and his mule headlong into the dismal valley beneath him ; therefore he instantly called upon God to preserve him, and by His infinite mercy to find some means of delivering him.   Just as the ass came upon him she tripped, and with that bowing and sudden violent motion the timber swayed away from him and only gave him a brush on one side as the ass passed quickly by, while he and his mule stood still.   Immediately alighting and falling on his face, he made his most humble acknowledgments to Almighty

God for his preservation, while the guide and the owner of the ass—who, coming up, told how she broke away as they were loading her—stood crossing themselves, and crying *Miracolo.*

How fair and smiling the sunny slopes of the Southern Alps must have seemed to the traveller now come from the plague-struck German towns over frozen mountain paths ! In some green valley on the edge of the Venetian territory he was detained, not unwillingly, for a quarantine of thirty days. The period of his detention coincided (possibly he had so pre-arranged it) with the Lent fast, "so that he was forced to do penance both under a restraint from company and from flesh,[1] though neither of these was any great constraint upon one already so mortified. Here he had leisure enough to recollect his thoughts, to revise his notes, and to reduce his observations into method. He spent his time of fasting and sequestration from the world very agreeably. In the morning he went up to a neighbour mountain, where abundance of wild thyme and rosemary grew ; there with a book or two, and with his God, whom he met

---

[1] An entry in the diary of Sir John Oglander shows how strictly the Lent fast was still observed by Englishmen. In 1610 " Abbot, Archbishop of Canterbury, granted a dispensation to Sir E. Conway, his wife, and two others whom he might choose to eat flesh at prohibited times, as fish did not agree with him, provided that he did so privately to avoid scandal, and paid 13*s.* 4*d.* per year to the poor of his parish."

in the closest walks of his mind, having spent his
day in reading, meditation, and prayer, he came down
in the evening to an early supper (his only set meal)
of oil and fish. He omitted not his offices and exercises of devotion morning and evening and at midnight in his travels, for to serve and please his Maker
was the travail of his soul. He needed not many
books, who was his own concordance and had the
New Testament in a manner without book.[1] And if
the time and place would not serve him to kneel, yet
then and there he made the lowest prostrations of his
soul and spirit." [2]

This month's retreat, for so it may be called, must
have been the utmost gain and refreshment to Ferrar's
spiritual life. From the time he left England, he had
lived in a ceaseless whirl of new ideas, fresh faces,
differing manners, conflicting creeds, and he must
have greatly needed time to retire into himself and
prepare in quietness to meet the rush of thought, the
keen religious difficulties, and the learned unbelief,
which awaited him in Italy. On the mountain-side,
withdrawn from the bustle and worry of the quaran-

[1] It would seem that he was afraid to carry a Bible about
with him, for it is said that the Psalter, Epistles, and Gospels
learnt in his childhood "served him to good purpose and his
great consolation when, many years after, he travelled and fell
grievously sick among those who count it a mark of heresy in a
traveller to carry about him an English Bible."

[2] Jebb, ii., "Two Lives of Ferrar," p. 187.

tine station, where no doubt plenty of impatient travellers were fretting their hearts out over their enforced delay, he found a solitude more complete than in his study at Clare, looking over the great lawns and quiet river. Steeped in calm, and a silence that could be felt—

> " No sound of worldly toil ascending there
> Mars the full burst of prayer."

We may believe that in after days he often loved to recall this peaceful time. Of all the noticeable scenes he passed through in his five years' travel, this mountain resting-place is the only one to which his biographer adds a descriptive touch, and it is characteristic that the point which struck Ferrar's fancy, here on the threshold of Italy, is no beauty or strangeness of the foreign landscape, but the fragrant growth of thyme and rosemary, familiar flowers in every English garden.

About Easter Ferrar proceeded to Venice; but though he was kindly received by Sir Dudley Carleton, the English ambassador, an introduction that must have opened to him the best society, he did not linger in that gayest and fairest of cities. Probably he longed to be again absorbed in study, for we soon find him settled in Padua.

For travellers from beyond the Alps, the chief attractions of the Italian Oxford now lie in the picturesque cathedral on the river bank, and the silent garden, where, among long lines of mulberry trees, stands the deserted chapel which Giotto painted while he listened to the talk of Dante.

It was very different in the seventeenth century.[1] The city was then crowded and overflowing with youths who came from all parts of the civilized world, eager to study in its famous schools of law and medicine. The students in the great University of Law were classed in twenty-three " nations," each of which had its own officers[2] and its own rules, and was permitted under the sole condition of not interfering with the government or religion of the State of Venice, to live according to its own customs. Its humbler sister, the University of Arts, could number but seven " nations," five of which belonged to the States of Italy, the foreign students being grouped as " oltremonte," or " oltremare," but the *artisti* enjoyed equal independence with the aristocratic *qiuristi*, or law students.

Neapolitan and Tuscan, Frenchman and German, Pole and Dalmatian, Englishman, Scot, Hungarian, Spaniard, Cypriote, each, when he came forth from the magnificent palace (once the dwelling-place of the

---

[1] This account of the university is taken from " Galileo Galilei e lo Studio di Padova," by A. Favaro, and some notices in Evelyn's Diary.

[2] In 1644 John Evelyn was elected " Syndicus Artistarum," probably of the " Ultramontane nation," or students from beyond the Alps.

Dukes of Carrara), which is still the home of the university, and went to his lodging in the fresco-painted streets of the student's quarter, found himself in the midst of a little world of his own countrymen, where he might unmolested practise the manners and profess the religion of his own land, a toleration possible at that time in no State of Italy, or perhaps of Europe, but the territories of the Venetian Republic, which, owing its importance mainly to its wide commercial relations, used every means in its power to make foreigners feel at home on its soil.[1]

Quarrels of course were of constant occurrence in this mixed crowd of unruly young men, and the luckless "birro" who might rashly venture to interfere was often ill-used and even stabbed with impunity. It was very dangerous, says Evelyn, to traverse the streets after dark. When St. Francis de Sales, who was a student in the University of Law from 1587 to 1591,[2] irritated his companions by his refusal to join in their evil ways, they attacked him with blows, and the future bishop was forced to defend himself with his sword.

[1] " The commodity which strangers have
With us in Venice, if it be denied,
Will much impeach the justice of the State
Since that the trade and profit of the city
Consisteth of all nations."
Merchant of Venice, Act iii. sc. 3.

[2] " Life of St. Francis de Sales," by Mrs. Sidney Lear.

D

This was the world in which Ferrar found himself, when, some time in the spring of 1615,[1] he entered the University of Arts, in which was taught medicine, geometry, philosophy, and rhetoric. Ferrar, who held the Physic Fellowship at Clare, seems to have devoted himself chiefly to medicine, for which the schools of Padua were becoming famous. They already possessed an anatomical theatre, and a " garden of simples rarely furnished with plants," to which was attached a school of pharmacy, which had been in existence for more than sixty years. There were also two hospitals for the study of clinical medicine, furnished with " the greatest helps and most skilful physicians," and most miserable and deplorable objects to exercise upon, " very carefully attended, and with extraordinary charity."[2]

He also became a proficient in geometry. Galileo, who quitted the Chair of Geometry, " leaving his heart in Padua and taking with him the hearts of his friends," only four years before Ferrar's arrival, specially recommended this study to medical students. " Hippocrates," he is reported to have said, " when writing to his son, warmly exhorted him to the study of geometry, because it would render his mind clearer and more acute in gathering fruit from the study of

[1] As Sir Dudley Carleton left Venice in 1615, Ferrar's arrival cannot be placed later. See Mr. Mayor's notes to Ferrar's Life.
[2] Evelyn's " Diary."

medicine." By the physicians of the day the science was valued for another reason. It formed a needful introduction to the study of astrology, which was still considered an important branch of the medical art.[1]

It was probably at this time also that Ferrar first became acquainted with some of the Oriental languages, a printing press having lately been established at Milan, by the liberality of Cardinal Federigo Borromeo,[2] for the publication of books in Hebrew, Chaldee, Arabic, Persian, and Armenian.

The thirst for solitude, for space and silence, still haunted him, and from time to time he broke away from his studies and took refuge in one of the pleasant villages which lie among wide and fruitful fields on

[1] A manuscript book on astrology, believed to have belonged to Nicholas Ferrar, is now in possession of Mr. Bowes, of the firm of Macmillan and Bowes, Cambridge, who kindly lent it to the writer for examination. This "wyse boke of fylosophy and astronomie" gives an account of the virtues of the seven planets and the twelve signs of the Zodiac, each of which have their influence on different parts of the body, as Aries on the head and face, Aquarius on the legs, etc.; and the transcribers (it is written in different hands), having apparently become weary of their task, it ends abruptly in the midst of an enumeration of the advantages of the "ouz" (house) of the moon.

[2] Cousin and successor to St. Charles. Readers of the *Promessi Sposi* may remember the description given by Manzoni of this saintly man, as one of those "rare in all ages, who devoted a great intellect, all the resources of a large fortune, all the advantage of privileged rank, with continual application, to the practice of that which is most excellent."

the banks of the river Brenta.[1] What thoughts did he take into these quiet places, as he wandered alone among the green entanglement of trellised vines, mingled with little tracts of rye and feathery Indian corn, which make an Italian field-path the most fascinating of walks—what were the plans, the hopes, the dreams which filled his soul?

No letters or journals have reached us to give an answer to this question.

That his life was ever pure and holy we have abundant evidence. It made a deep impression on the careless and often dissipated youths around him, who "would often ingenuously confess that he was in the right way, and that they could not but wish that they could live as he lived." The name of one friend, to whom his advice and example were of priceless service, has been handed down to us. "Mr. Edward Garton had been forced to fly from England to escape a trial for murder, having killed his antagonist in a duel; and being a stranger at Padua, he was noted there as a man desperately melancholy, till in a good hour for him, he fell by

[1] "At other times I repair to a village of mine, seated in the valley, which is therefore very pleasant, because many ways thither are so ordered that they all meet and end in a fair plot of ground, in the midst whereof is a church suitable to the condition of the place. This place is washed by the river Brenta, on both sides whereof are great and fruitful fields."—L. Cornaro, "Treatise on Temperance," translated by George Herbert.

chance into company with Mr. Ferrar, and found so much goodness in him that he made him his confessor. He, finding the poor soul's hearty repentance and sorrow for what he had done, so applied the mercies of God to him, that he was well satisfied and much comforted ; yet he would say 'he was never well but in Mr. Ferrar's company,' whom henceforward he loved and esteemed above all the world." [1]

Among his friends at Padua there were not wanting some who strove hard to win so devout and thoughtful a youth to the Roman Obedience. "By what I have seen in manuscript of Mr. Ferrar," says Barnabas Oley,[2] "and heard by relation of his travels over the western parts of Christendom, in which his exquisite carriage, his rare parts and abilities of understanding and languages, his morals more perfect than the best, did tempt the adversaries to tempt him and mark him for a prize if they could compass him. And opportunity they had to do this in a sickness that seized on him at Padua, where mighty care was had by physicians and others to recover his bodily health with design to infect his soul. But neither did their physic nor poison work any change in his religion, but rather inflamed him with a holy zeal to revenge their charity by transplanting their waste and misplaced zeal to adorn our Protestant religion, by a right renouncing

[1] "Life of Nicholas Ferrar," by Dr. Jebb, p. 71.
[2] Oley's "Life of George Herbert."

the world with all its profits and honours, in a true crucifying the flesh with all its pleasures, by continued temperance, fasting, and watching unto prayers."

Oley seems unduly severe in ascribing the assiduous care with which the good Paduan physicians tended Ferrar in his illness solely to their controversial zeal. It is not likely that they who showed such charity to the sick in their hospitals would be less kind to their pupil. They watched over him with the greatest attention ; but he owed his life not so much to their skill as to his own dread of bleeding. He felt sure that this remedy, to which they wished to resort, would hasten his end, and one very old physician, with insight born of long experience, advised that his prejudice should be respected. The vein was not opened, and in a few days he began to recover, to the great joy of his good old friend, who had doubtless passed some anxious hours, and endured much silent criticism from his learned brethren.

There was very much no doubt in the Church life of Padua to awaken Ferrar's deepest interest, and often his admiration. He carefully collected books on religion and the retired life, and one such, the "Spiritual Combat" of Lorenzo Scupoli—a work which was so popular that, in the thirty years which had elapsed since its publication, it had gone through fifty editions—must have been well known to him, and can hardly fail to have awakened his interest in the austere order to which its author belonged ; it was, perhaps, in the Theatine house at Padua that he first saw realized that life of retirement, prayer, and fasting for which he seems to have longed from his boyhood, with a longing which struggled for mastery with his keen thirst for knowledge.

Another form of the devout life must have come before him in the congregation of the Oratory. This society, composed of laymen and secular priests living under a strict rule, had for one of its chief objects the promotion of holiness among men living in the world. With this view, instructions and addresses open to all who would attend, were given daily in every house of the society, and these were often followed up by some practical lesson in good works, such as visiting and succouring the sick in some hospital. A letter from a priest, who afterwards became a member of the congregation of the Oratory,[1] thus describes the method followed in these exercises. "Since that time, I go to the Oratory at St. Giovanni of the Florentines, where they deliver every day most beautiful spiritual discourses on the Gospels, or on the virtues and vices, or ecclesiastical history, or the lives of the saints. There are four or five each day who discourse, and persons of distinction go to hear

---

[1] F. Giovinale Ancina. The letter is taken from the "Life of St. Philip Neri," published by Richardson in 1849. Father Ancina was a friend of St. Francis de Sales.

them—bishops, prelates, and the like. At the conclusion there is a little music to console and recreate the spirits, which are somewhat wearied by the preceding discourses. They have gone through the life of the glorious St. Francis and some of his disciples, and of St. Antony of Padua. I assure you it is a most delightful entertainment, and a most consoling and edifying thing altogether; and I regret very much that neither you nor I knew last year of this excellent and laudable exercise. You must know, too, that they who deliver the discourse are in holy orders, and of most exemplary and spiritual lives. Their superior is a certain Reverend Father Philip, an old man of sixty, but wonderful in many respects, and especially for holiness of life, and for his astonishing prudence and dexterity in inventing and promoting spiritual exercises, the author also of that great work of charity, which was done at the Trinità de' Pellegrini [1] during the last Jubilee. Father Toledo, Possevino, and others attribute much to him. In a word, they say he is an oracle, not only in Rome, but in the far-off parts of Italy, and in France and Spain, so that many come to him for counsel ; indeed, he is another Rusbrochio, or Thomas à Kempis, or Taulero."

One of these oratories had been opened in Padua,

---

[1] St. Philip here founded a confraternity for the care of poor pilgrims. The house which served for their reception was also used for convalescents from the hospitals.

and we may well imagine that Nicholas Ferrar, seeking some peaceful retreat from the noisy crowd which streamed to and fro through the narrow streets, would meet, as he threaded the dim arcades echoing with gay talk in half a dozen languages, with some like-minded friends on their way to join in the " excellent and laudable exercise," and having once followed them into the quiet chapel, would come and come again. We can even fancy that we perceive in the pious conversations, interspersed with music and with stories from history and the lives of the saints, which he instituted long afterwards at Gidding, some reminiscences of this Oratorian exercise.

Another influence which strongly affected him, was connected with the teaching of the Spanish mystics who made so deep a mark on Italian thought in the seventeenth century. He was so much struck by a once famous book, the " Hundred and Ten Considerations " of Juan de Valdes, an early writer of this school, that some years after his return to England he published a translation of it.

If Ferrar may have learnt something of rule and the practise of devotion, from the more zealous among the religious houses of Italy, the study of Valdis may have deepened his meditative and inward tone of mind, the uncontroversial, it might be almost said the undogmatic, spirit, which in a most controversial age made him so averse to strife, that he " would scarce venture to opine even in points wherein the world censured him possessed." [1]

But neither Roman zeal nor the charm of mystic thought had any power to shake his dutiful unquestioning attachment to his Mother Church. The foundation of that love had been laid too deep in his earliest years.

When Nicholas Ferrar had completed his studies at Padua, he visited Malta and travelled through a great part of Italy. Scarcely any record of his travels remains except a scanty mention of his ten days' visit to Rome, a visit made secretly, for the English Government was suspicious of possible intercourse with the Roman Court, and the Roman authorities were not less keenly on the watch to stamp out what they deemed heresy, in the stronghold of the Church. Ferrar stole into the city privately on foot on the Monday in Holy Week, and visited, with what feelings we can but conjecture, the tombs of the apostles, the sacred sites where the modern world grows dim beside the vivid memories of the past. For fear of discovery by the Inquisition,[2] he changed his lodging

[1] Oley, Preface to " Country Parson."

[2] Such fears were not causeless, even for an English subject. In 1607 one Mr. Mole, tutor to Lord Roos, being in Rome with his pupil, was arrested on a charge of circulating heretical books, and confined for thirty years in the prisons of the Inquisition.—Aiken's " Memoirs of the Court of James I.," quoted in Macdonough's " Life of Ferrar."

every night, but, in his extreme eagerness to see everything, he pushed one day in the crowd into one of the long Vatican galleries to watch the Pope pass, and being probably ignorant of the etiquette observed on such occasions, and forgetting all precaution in the interest of the sight, he ran the risk of arrest by remaining erect among the kneeling throng, and was only saved by the rough kindness of one of the Swiss Guards, who, with a hand on his shoulder, forced him to his knees, crying, " Down, rascal, down ! "

After this adventure he avoided public places, and, getting safely out of Rome, returned to the more liberal air of Venice.

From Venice he went to Marseilles, meaning to sail thence to Spain; but here he was seized by an old enemy, harder to escape than the Roman inquisitors—an attack of fever, from which he nearly died.

On the first day of this illness he wrote to his dear friend, Mr. Garton, " entreating him to take a charitable voyage to visit the sick in a place where he was a perfect stranger, where he was obliged to be his own priest, his own cook, and was able to endure no light but from his own memory; wherefore he prayed him to come immediately, if ever he would see him alive, or else procure him some corner for a Christian burial."

Garton, with a grateful recollection of that sickness of the soul of which he had been cured by Ferrar's means, set off at once, travelling night and day, and arrived to find the crisis of the fever safely past, and to nurse his friend back to health.

Ferrar was so deeply touched by this proof of affection that he would not allow Garton to return alone to Venice, but insisted on accompanying him. There he stayed till his health was recruited, and then, taking a last leave of Mr. Garton and the other good friends who had gathered round him during his years of study, he embarked in a little English vessel bound for Spain, and sailed down the Adriatic in search of " fresh fields and pastures new." [1]

The pleasant monotony of a summer voyage on the shining Mediterranean was broken by an adventure which was still common in the seventeenth century.[2] The little vessel, overladen and lying deep

---

[1] So Peckard. Jebb says that he sailed from Marseilles.

[2] Evelyn was chased by a pirate in the Straits of Dover in 1649. Piracy was by no means confined to the Turks, and was not thought a disgraceful occupation. " Sir Henry Mayneweringe, that quondam famous pirate, my wyfe's cosen germain, was then Surveyor of the Navy," writes Sir John Oglander, calmly, without the least expression of surprise. And this sea Robin Hood, who, though he "always respected his own flag," plundered every Spanish ship he could lay hands on, was actually selected—after his pardon—to bring home Prince Charles from Spain.—" Oglander Memoirs."

in the smooth water, was chased by a great, swift-sailing Turkish pirate. The big ship gained rapidly on the small merchantman, and officers and men held hasty council whether to yield or to stand at bay and fight the matter out with their ten guns. Ferrar, the only passenger, stood silent among them. "This young man has a life to lose as well as we," said one of the seamen; "let us hear what he thinks of the matter." Landsman and student as he was, Ferrar had plenty of courage. "Let us fall into the hand of God, and not into the hands of men," he said, as the great vessel, its speed aided most likely by the oars of Christian captives, loomed larger and more threatening on their view; and then, remembering no doubt the tales which he had heard in his childhood from Sir Francis Drake and his fellows, he strove to kindle the enthusiasm of the crew with stories of the gallant deeds of Englishmen at sea. He gave active help also, and everything was made ready for an engagement, when, just as the master was giving the signal for a broadside, the Turk fell off and steered away with all the sail he could, to the inexpressible joy of the crew, who, gazing anxiously over the poop, saw that a much larger ship had come in sight, and that the pirate had turned to chase this more valuable booty.

They continued their voyage without further incident, and Ferrar on landing made straight for Madrid.

For some unexplained reason he concealed his name during his Spanish travels, perhaps finding secrecy as needful for Protestants in Spain as in Rome. He would not even make himself known to his fellow-countrymen in Madrid, and when he went to inquire for the letters and bills of exchange which he expected to find awaiting him, asked as if on behalf of a friend. The bills had not arrived, his father thinking that he would not reach Madrid so soon, and to this inconvenience was soon added another and more serious anxiety. He fell in with a Mr. Wyche, the son of an old friend of his father's, who, though not knowing his name, was so pleased with his manners that he introduced him among the English residents in the capital, and he then learnt, apparently from chance conversation, that his family was involved in great distress, and that his return was necessary to extricate them from their troubles. On hearing this bad news he at once gave up his intention of visiting France, and settled to return home as quickly as possible.

No money having come for him, and being unwilling to accept the loan kindly pressed on him by Mr. Wyche, he sold his cloak and a few jewels, and with the small sum thus obtained started on foot for St. Sebastian. He soon became footsore with this unaccustomed travel on sandy paths, at the hottest season of the year, and would scarce have been able to get on but for the remedy prescribed by the hostess

of a roadside inn where he rested for the night, who
brought him a bowl of sack in which to steep his feet.
By the help of this application, to which he had frequent recourse, he plodded on, meeting with no
hindrances but weariness and bad accommodation.
Once, indeed, he was stopped and closely questioned
by the governor of a town through which he passed,
who was so delighted with his costly rapier (a parting
gift from Mr. Garton) that he was near taking it from
him by force ; and once, trying to find his way through
a rocky pass, he followed a hog, which he supposed
must belong to some farm, through a subterranean
passage, and found himself in a cavern inhabited by
men whom he took to be robbers. But from both
these dangers he escaped safely, and, after a fatiguing
walk of some five hundred miles, arrived at St.
Sebastian. Here he had to wait some time for a
favourable wind, and, his resources being quite exhausted, was glad to accept a loan of £10 from
a friendly English factor. With the first fair wind
he sailed for Dover.

He had been five years absent from England, and
more than once had cause to think that he would
never again look on those white cliffs. The sight
filled him with such rapture that, leaping ashore, he
flung himself down, with his face pressed close to the
dear English earth, and, thus prostrate, gave humble
thanks to God for his safe return. From Dover he

travelled post to his father's house in London.   The
door stood open, and Nicholas went in unannounced
through the familiar rooms till he found his father,
and, kneeling at his feet, asked his blessing.   In the
first moment of surprise Mr. Ferrar, who thought him
still far away, did not recognize his son in the travel-
stained figure before him, in foreign dress, his fair
complexion browned by the sun of Spain.   "Who
are you?" he asked, bewildered, while the young
man looked up to him with a heart perhaps too full
for speech.   It is easy to imagine his answer, the
father's fervent blessing, the mother's entrance, all
the confused, tremulous joy of this loving family reunited after so long a separation and so many
anxieties.

CHAPTER III.

" Where can he busy himself better than in those new plantations and discoveries, which are not only a noble, but also, as
they may be handled, a religious employment ? "—GEORGE
HERBERT, *A Priest in the Temple*, chap. xxxii.

THE nature of the family trouble which brought
Nicholas Ferrar home in such haste does not appear.
It may probably have been connected with the affairs
of his eldest brother Richard, who seems to have
been, through life, a constant source of anxiety.
John Ferrar passes over his brother's misdeeds in
kindly silence ; but in his father's will, made in 1620,
the administration of the family property is left to
John and Nicholas, Richard having his debts forgiven
and receiving a younger son's portion, which he
apparently squandered, for Mrs. Ferrar in her will,[1]
dated March, 1628, desires that, "if he deserved,"

---

[1] Both wills are given in Mr. Mayor's appendix to "Two
Lives of Ferrar."

his brothers should, out of their love, make provision
for his "great necessities."

When the crisis, whatever it may have been, was
past, Nicholas wished to return to Cambridge, and,
once more taking up his abode at Clare, continue
the study of medicine; but his parents would by no
means consent to part again with their beloved son.
A flattering offer was made to him about this time
of the Chair of Geometry at Gresham College, the
late holder of that office, Mr. Briggs, who had just
been appointed to the newly-established Savilian
Professorship at Oxford, recommending him for the
post, as being "like, if he set to it, to be the ablest
man in the world therein."   This also was put aside.
Nicholas Ferrar thanked the master and wardens of
the Mercer's Company (in whose hands the appointment lay) for the great honour they did him, but told
them that "he must not undertake that which he knew
he was at best but a novice in; nor, in truth, did his
studies bend that way.   He had, indeed, some other
good ends, if God thought fit to bring them to pass."[1]

If these words allude to his desire for a life withdrawn from the world, he had still long to wait for its
fulfilment, and, before he had been two months in
London, he had flung himself heart and soul into a
new interest.

For the next six years his energies were almost

[1] Letter from Peck to Ward, quoted by Rev. J. E. B. Mayor.

entirely given up to the work of assisting in the guidance and government of the rising settlement in Virginia, on which so many hopes were already placed.

It is so impossible to give any idea of the life of Nicholas Ferrar during this period, apart from the history of the vast undertaking in which he was engaged, that readers will perhaps pardon a digression, which may be readily skipped by those to whom that history is already familiar.

In 1606 a Company had been formed for the purpose of establishing a colony in that part of the New World visited by Raleigh, and named by him Virginia. This work, which was taken in hand not for gain only, but in the hope expressed in the noble words of the patent, that the work of colonization "may, by the providence of God, hereafter tend to the glory of His Divine Majesty in propagating the Christian religion to such people as yet lived in darkness and miserable ignorance of the true knowledge and worship of God, and may in time bring the infidels of those parts to human civility, and to a settled and quiet government."

The first expedition sent out by the new Company sailed on December 19, 1606, and, after long battling with unprosperous winds, reached Cape Henry, in Virginia, on April 26, 1607.[1] They were accom-

[1] This sketch of the Virginian settlement is taken from Peckard's "Life," Anderson's "History of the Colonial Church,"

panied by a chaplain, chosen under the advice of Archbishop Bancroft—the Reverend Robert Hunt. Much of the success of the expedition seems to have been due to this holy man. During the stormy, tedious voyage, when the adventurers, anxious and over-weary, broke out into quarrels which threatened to bring the enterprise to an untimely end, he, "with the water of patience and his godly admonitions (but chiefly his true, devoted example), quenched these flames of envy and dissension." When the voyage was over he gathered together the little band of settlers, and, on the northern shore of the James River, a few miles below the place where now stands the town of Richmond, he administered to them the Holy Communion. It was the birthday of the American Church.

On that spot was soon raised a little cluster of huts, with a reed-thatched church in the middle, and some rude protection of palisades about it, to which the settlers gave the name of Jamestown.[1] The infant colony had a hard struggle for existence. Sickness, fire, and the treachery of the Indians, cost many lives and much property. The settlers, in their eagerness

and Hawk's "Contributions to Ecclesiastical History of United States." The Ferrars' share in the work is gathered from Peckard and Jebb.

[1] "In 1836 a ruined church tower and surrounding graveyard still marked the site of Jamestown."—HAWK.

to grow tobacco for export (at one time they planted it even in the streets of Jamestown), neglected to sow sufficient corn, and they passed through a period of fearful destitution, remembered long afterwards as the "starving time." Through all this trouble Mr. Hunt's patience and courage never failed; and it is a touching proof of his influence with his flock that in this hour of their extremest need the whole remaining stock of wine was put aside to be used for the Holy Eucharist alone.

In the early summer of 1610 the distress became so great that the survivors resolved to abandon the settlement. They gathered together their scanty remaining possessions, buried their ordnance, and having, "by their peale of shot, taken a last and woeful farewell of this pleasant land," they embarked in three vessels rudely made of cedar wood, and dropped down the James River. The next morning, while they waited for the tide to bear them out to sea, they saw, coming up the stream, an English boat. It brought the news that Lord De La Warr, with a squadron of relief, was already in the Chesapeake; and on Sunday, June 10, his ships arrived off Jamestown.

The famine-stricken settlers drew up to receive him on the river bank, outside the gate of the palisade. On landing, he knelt down, and remained long in private prayer; then, before addressing himself to any business, he went straight to the dismantled church, followed by all the rescued people, to give thanks to God.

The settlement, thus saved from utter ruin, continued to grow slowly, and with varying success. Among those who watched it with intense interest, both as merchant and as Churchman, was Mr. Ferrar.

When Nicholas returned to England in 1618 his father was a shareholder both in the Virginia Company and also in the New Bermuda Company, which had grown out of it; and his brother John was on the Council of Virginia. Nicholas's academic studies— perhaps also, to some extent, his spiritual yearnings— were swept out of view by this rush of vivid life. He had been surveying, with the eyes of a keen dispassionate observer, the laws and manners, the social and political life, of foreign lands; now, without crossing his father's threshold, he found himself a witness of the making of a nation.

The Virginian Council met every week in Mr. Ferrar's great parlour, and in that hospitable house in Sythe's Lane were laid the foundations of the first free state of America. Sir Edwin Sandys, the treasurer of the Company, a pupil of Hooker, and himself a distinguished scholar, was at once struck with the ability of Nicholas; he was constantly in his society, and so frequently asked his help, that Ferrar, though he held no office in the Company, did most of the work of secretary.

Under Sandys's able management the little colony began to flourish; during his year of office its population rose from six hundred to more than three thousand souls, and with large-hearted foresight he gave a representative government to this small community. The first Legislative Assembly of Virginia met at Jamestown in June, 1619. He and his colleagues were as careful for the Church as for the State.[1] They founded a college for the Christian education of the Indians, and of the colonists' children, and, at the suggestion of Sandys, the Company set apart ten thousand acres of land for its support. The interest taken in this college was great and general. The king issued a letter to the archbishops and bishops desiring them to make collections in their dioceses for its benefit; and the Bishop of London alone raised £1000 for this pur-

---

[1] The following extract from one of the appeals put forth by the Company shows how zealously they urged the cause of religion :—" Oh! all ye worthies, follow the ever-sounding rumpet of a blessed honour; let religion be the first end of your hopes, *et cetera adjicientur*, and other things shall be added unto you; ye shall be registered to posterity with a glorious title. . . . Doubt ye not but God hath determined and demonstrated that He will raise our State and build His Church in that excellent climate, if the action be seconded with resolution and religion."—HAWK.

pose. An unknown benefactor sent £500 more; another, also anonymous, gave Communion plate. Mr. John Thorpe, a gentleman of the king's bedchamber, gave up his place at Court, to go out as head of the new college, which was established in Henrico, a settlement which had been raised not far from Jamestown, on the opposite side of the river, and named in honour of Henry, Prince of Wales.

The colonists résponded warmly to the efforts made on their behalf; one of the first acts of the new Legislative Assembly was to establish a fixed payment of corn and tobacco for the support of the clergy, who were to be sent out by the Bishop of London, and to set aside a hundred acres of glebe in every borough, for each of which the Company at home provided six tenants at the public cost.[1]

The Company were so well satisfied with their treasurer that, when Sandys's year of office expired, they resolved to choose him a second time. "Very great was the reputation of the plantation and company," says John Ferrar, "by the most wise, prudent, and industrious management of it by that most eminent man."

---

[1] Sandys, though so good a Churchman, was far from intolerant. During his treasurership the Company granted a patent permitting the Nonconformist emigrants of the *Mayflower* to form a settlement in Virginia, and it was by an accident that they landed north of that territory. See S. R. Gardiner, "History of England," vol. iv. chap. xxxvi.

But Sir Edwin Sandys, though "a wise patriot" according to the view of the Ferrars and their friends, was but a factious leader of opposition in the eyes of the king, who was determined, by any means he could command, to oust him from his post. Peckard's account of the election is full of interest.[1]

It was the custom of the Company to name three persons, one of whom was then chosen by ballot. In a court of near five hundred persons, three names having been agreed on, that of Sir Edwin Sandys was being put first to the vote, when a gentleman of the royal bedchamber entered the room, and, interrupting the ballot, announced that the king forbade the election of Sir Edwin Sandys; he added that his Majesty, *being unwilling to infringe the rights of the Company*, would himself nominate three persons on whom they might vote.

This speech was received at first in deep silence, which was soon broken by murmurs, in which were heard the words "invasion of rights" and "tyrannic power." Some of the Company moved that the courtiers should retire while they considered what to do, but the Earl of Southampton desired that they should remain and hear the rules of the Company publicly discussed.

"Let the patent be read," said Sir Laurence Hyde.

[1] Peckard, p. 100.

"The patent! the patent!" cried many voices. "God save the king."

"Gentlemen," said Hyde, when the reading was concluded, "by the words of the patent the election of a treasurer is left to your own free choice. No doubt these gentlemen will undeceive the king on this point."

Sir Edwin Sandys, anxious to prevent an open break with the Crown, whispered to Sir Robert Phillips, who sat near him, that he desired to withdraw his claim; and Sir Robert, rising, proposed that the king's messengers should nominate two persons, while the Company preserved their privileges by naming the third. This was accordingly done. The Company named the Earl of Southampton.

When the ballot was taken, the nominees of the Crown had but three votes between them, and the earl was chosen by acclamation, the court-room echoing with the cries of "Southampton! Southampton!"

John Ferrar was at this time elected deputy treasurer, and Nicholas succeeded to his brother's vacant place at the Council Board.

Since Southampton made it a condition of taking office that he should have the advice and assistance of Sir Edwin Sandys, it seemed at first as if all might still go well; but clouds soon gathered thick and fast over the fair prospects of the colony.

Before the bad news reached England, one of the

warmest friends of Virginia had passed away. Old Mr. Ferrar died in April, 1620, and was buried, on the 12th of that month, in the church of St. Bennet Sherehog. "Like a merciful Father, He calleth us unto him," says the good merchant in his will, signed a few days before his death. "Therefore being called, O Lord, I come unto Thee; receive me graciously, for Thy mercy's sake, into Thy hands, O Lord. For my body, I leave it to be buried in the place where it shall please God to appoint; and, further, that there be a sermon made at my burial, if it may be that thereby all men may be admonished to fear God sincerely, and truly remember what they are, and whither they shall, for death is the end of all flesh." On his sick-bed the true-hearted, humble, affectionate man entreated the friends who stood round him to comfort his dear wife, and commanded his children in all filial duty to love and obey her. "Never, I think," said the dying husband, "man had the like in all kinds; and these forty-five years we have lived together, I must say of her, she never gave me cause to be angry with her, so wise and good she is. You all know," he added, "I was by nature— which God pardon—both quick and choleric and hasty, which she also will forgive."

The funeral sermon was preached by his old friend, Francis White, then Dean of Carlisle, in the church which the good merchant had repaired and reseated.

" I never came into old Mr. Ferrar's company," he said, " but that saying of our Saviour Christ came into my mind, ' Behold an Israelite indeed, in whom is no guile.' "

Mr. Ferrar left careful and liberal provision for his wife and family, with gifts and legacies to his grandchildren, Mrs. Collett's daughter Mary, who had lived with him from her cradle, being specially provided for; he also made many charitable bequests, among which the first and largest is to the new Virginia College, to be paid " when the said college is erected, and to the number of ten of the infidels' children therein placed to be educated in Christian religion and civility ;" and until that time he desired that " Sir Edwin Sandys and John Ferrar shall yearly pay by eight pounds a year to any three several persons in Virginia of good life and fame, that will undertake therewith to procure and bring up each of them one of the infidels' children, and intreating them in all things so Christianly, as by the good usage and bringing of them up, the infidels may be persuaded that it is not the intent of our nation to make their children slaves, but to bring them to a better manner of living in this world, and to the way of eternal happiness in the world to come."[1]

The peace of the good man's deathbed was un-

[1] " Two Lives," Appendix.

troubled by any knowledge of the cruel blow which had fallen on the colony in which he took so deep an interest; but he had not long departed when London was horrified by the news of the massacre of Henrico. The colonists had lived among the natives on terms of unsuspicious friendship, but the Indian chief grew jealous of their inceasing numbers, and in perfect secrecy a plot was formed for the entire destruction of the colony. On the night of Friday, March 22, a horde of savages broke on Henrico, and in a few hours the flourishing village was left desolate. The rector of the college, Mr. Thorpe, lay dead among his murdered scholars. Men, women, and children, the whole population of Henrico, and of the scattered settlements in the forest round it, to the number of 340 souls, fell that night by the Indian knife. The remainder of the colony was saved by the loyalty of a Christian convert, Chanco by name; he was servant to one of the settlers, who loved and treated him as a son. His brother, a heathen, tried to persuade him to join the attack, but the bonds of religion proved stronger than those of race, and he warned his master of the coming danger. The master hurried to Jamestown to give the alarm to the governor, and the settlements on that side of the river gained time for defence.

The colonists can scarcely be blamed if they took a fierce revenge, but when " the savages had been driven far away, many destroyed of them, their towns and houses ruinated, and their cleer grounds possessed by the English to grow wheat in," it was impossible to bring back the former friendliness, and the cause of Indian Missions was thrown back for many years.

The settlers were full of courage and endurance; they revived with wonderful quickness from the awful stroke. "Yesterday came again good news from Virginia, that the colony will subsist again; hath driven Oppockanknogh (the Indian chief) far off; slain many of his men, in revenge for his last year's murdering of the 340 of ours, and have got much corn from them," we read in a letter of 1622.[1]

Southampton and the Ferrars did not relax their efforts in the cause of Christianity and civilization, in spite of this bitter experience. Mr. Copeland, the chaplain of a homeward-bound East Indiaman, had prevailed on the crew to subscribe £70 towards building a church or free school in Virginia. The Company allotted a thousand acres of land as endowment, and a school, named, in honour of its founders, the East India School, was founded at Charlestown, as a dependency of Henrico College, to which its more promising scholars were to be transferred. A new rector was appointed for the college in place of the murdered Thorpe, and it is natural to suppose that the Copeland designated for

---

[1] Letter to Rev. J. Meade, " Court and Times of James I."

this office was the same who had already shown so much interest in the mission.[1]

The Dean of St. Paul's, Donne, who was a member of the council, urged the cause of the mission with his most passionate eloquence. "Before the martyrs under the throne shall be silenced, before all things shall be subdued to Christ," he exclaims in a sermon which has been preserved to us, "His kingdom established, and the last enemy destroyed, the gospel must be preached to those men to whom ye send, to all men. Farther and hasten you this blessed, this joyful, this glorious consummation of all, and happie reunion of all bodies to their souls by preaching the gospel to those men. Preach to them doctrinally, preach to them practically; enamour them with your justice and (as farre as may consist with your securitie) your civilitie; but inflame them with your gentleness and your religion. . . . We shall have made this island, which is but as the suburbs of the old world, a bridge or gallery to the new; to joyne all to that world which shall never grow old, the kingdom of heaven."[2]

---

[1] Owing to the dissolution of the Company, Mr. Copeland was never sent out, and the college remained in abeyance till Dr. Blair, who was appointed by the Bishop of London in 1685, restored it under the name of the "College of William and Mary."—Bishop Wilberforce, "History of the American Church."

[2] Donne's "Sermons," quoted by Anderson.

But many things conspired to delay the good work. The treachery of the Indians was not the only difficulty which beset the Company and its settlements. They had also to meet the jealousy of Spain, and to meet it with divided counsels. Gondomar, the Spanish ambassador, told his friends that he was commissioned by his sovereign to do his best to ruin the English settlement. "If it is permitted to gather strength," he is reported to have said, "my master's Indies and his Mexico would shortly be visited both by sea and land by these planters." It was currently believed that "our statesmen, when time was, had store of Gundemore's gold to destroy and discountenance the plantation of Virginia."[1]

The quarrels at the council board were as mischievous to the colony as the possible gold of "Gundemore," and more distressing. Sir Thomas Smith, a former treasurer, with his brother-in-law, the Earl of Warwick, and sundry officials who had been rebuked or dismissed by the council, did their utmost to stir up dissension. Accusations of mismanagement were freely exchanged, and the town rang with stories of the quarrels of the rival parties. "Guelphs and Ghibellines were not more enemated against each other."[2] Sandys and Cavendish fell foul of Warwick; Warwick told Cavendish that he lied; there was a

---

[1] "A Perfect Description of Virginia," 1649.
[2] Chamberlain to Carleton, "Court and Times of James I."

talk of duels ; their supporters " brabbled " when they met in the streets. To add to the difficulties of the council, the king took the side of Smith and Warwick. James could not abide the " country party " to which Sandys and Southampton and the Ferrars belonged ; and he wished above all things to preserve the Spanish alliance. To this end he was quite willing to sacrifice the interests of the Virginian plantations. He discouraged the importation of tobacco, which was their most valuable product. The planters complained piteously. They had never, they said, had any help from England, except through Mr. Sandis (Sir E. Sandys), and since, " by the sinister practises of some principal persons " of their own Company, his Majesty had been persuaded to prohibit the importation of tobacco, " the only commodity we have hitherto had the means to raise towards the apparelling of our bodies and other needful supplements," they feared to be worse off than ever. They implored the king, as he valued his word, ratified by the Great Seal, " than which we could account no earthly thing more firm," either to restore their former liberties or send for them home to England.[1]

---

[1] " Petition of the Governor and Colonists in Virginia," quoted by Peckard. The king, hearing that mulberries grew in Virginia, wished the settlers to cultivate silk instead of tobacco, and Nicholas Ferrar, while deputy treasurer, procured skilled workmen from France to instruct the colonists in the care of

Their entreaties were in vain. James only said that smoking was an extravagant and pernicious practice; but he sanctioned the importation of the objectionable article from the colonies of Spain.

The confusion had nearly reached its highest point when Nicholas Ferrar was called to fill one of the most important offices of the Company. His brother John, either because his term of office was expired, or under the necessity of attending to his private affairs, which the failure of his partner had reduced to the verge of ruin, resigned his post, and Nicholas became deputy treasurer in his place. The vast stock of miscellaneous knowledge which he had delighted to pick up during his travels, now came into use. His office was no sinecure. He had to lay in the stores needed for exportation to the colony, to superintend the lading and provisioning of the ships, probably also to assist in the selection of suitable emigrants, a matter in which the authorities of the Company took great pains, being specially anxious to provide good wives for the colonists.[1] In addition

the worms. But this industry was not successful; the worms were eaten by rats, and the stock seems never to have been renewed.

[1] Here is a specimen of the recommendations sent with emigrants; it is one of several given by Peckard. "The bearer hereof, Abigail Downing, widow, hath paid for her own passage, so that she is free to dispose of herself when she cometh to Virginia; but if she think good to live with you, the adventurers

to these labours, he drew up all the instructions sent by the treasurer and council to the Colonial Government. His cares were not confined to Virginia; he was also deputy for the Bermudas. The Church in those islands had been greatly neglected, and the clergy had grown careless, but during the administration of Nicholas Ferrar there was a happy change in this respect. There was no native population in Bermuda, but Nicholas and his brother John gave shares of their estate in the islands, to found a free school for the children of the colonists, and sent out a great supply of Bibles and Psalm-books for their use.

For a time all went well, and the colony grew and developed on the lines laid down by Sir Edwin Sandys. The Earl of Southampton established trial by jury, and with wide-hearted statesmanship made the Colonial Assembly independent of the Company at home. But the days of his rule were numbered. Urged on by Gondomar on one side, and the factious minority in the Company on the other, the king determined to find a pretext for withdrawing the charter. Commissioners were appointed to inquire into the manner in which the Company's affairs had

are content that you allow her victual and diet, as to your other people; and further, they desire you to have a care of her, and let her have your good counsel and advice for bestowing her upon some honest man. Her kindred are honest people of good fashion, well known to the society."

been conducted, and the treasurer was not permitted to employ counsel for the defence of himself and his colleagues.

The chief burden of maintaining the interests of the council fell on Nicholas Ferrar. He was frequently summoned before the commission to give evidence as to the government of the colony, and the eager "adventurers," whose affairs were at stake, pressed in after him in such numbers, that an order was issued forbidding him to present himself at the board with more than twelve persons attending him.

"In the management of this weighty cause, wherein he had the advice of the ablest lawyers, he discovered such great integrity, with such a presence of mind, and yet with so much deference and profound submission to his Majesty, that even they whose interest it was to decry the merits of his cause would acknowledge the merits of his person, and were pleased to say he well understood State affairs, and that it was fit he should be taken off that business and employed on higher;" and, with the hope of depriving the council of his services, a diplomatic appointment was pressed upon him, and also the situation of clerk of the Privy Council. Both offers were refused.

The commissioners grew angry at the persistence of the Company in defending its rights. "Your interest and advice might prevail on the Company to lay down the patent," said the Lord Treasurer Cranfield, hotly. Ferrar answered by an appeal to the king's good faith. "A very considerable number of the English nobility and gentry," he said, "besides all the planters, were engaged upon the royal word, and under the broad seal; they had ventured their estates, and many of them their lives, upon the most religious accounts and the most honourable action in its kind that England ever undertook; that now they had brought the plantation, if not to perfection, yet into a very thriving condition; that he could only speak for himself and in behalf of some others there present, in whose names he laid his and their private interest at his Majesty's feet; but he would not abuse his trust to hurt the public."

Since Ferrar could not be persuaded to quit his post, an attempt was made to drive him from it by false accusations. "A lie," the Spanish ambassador is said to have remarked on this occasion, "might be worth a good deal if it would hold water but a few hours." It was said that since the inquiry began, Ferrar had drawn up and despatched letters of very evil counsel to the Governor of Virginia, advising the planters to insist stiffly on the patent. A pursuivant was sent to fetch him to court with all haste, and he was ordered to produce the despatches. He replied that all those papers were in the secretary's hands. The papers were sent for, and read before the Privy Council, "not only to their entire satisfaction concerning his integrity, but even to the admiration of his politics, piety, and eloquence."

"Who draws them up?" inquired one of the lords.

Ferrar replied modestly, "The Company."

"No," said another Privy Councillor; "it is all one hand, and you have the chief hand in it. They are very rare pieces."

A copy of one of the letters was shown to the king, who joined in the admiration of the Privy Council. "It is a master-piece indeed," his Majesty condescended to observe; "the man hath much worth in him."[1]

But Ferrar's efforts brought nothing but empty compliments; the Company was already doomed. "The Virginian Company," Gondomar told the king, "is but a seminary to a seditious parliament;" and James was not likely to love it better for any proofs of the ability of its leaders.

The examinations dragged on through the early spring of 1623, and at last, on the Thursday in Holy Week, a lengthy accusation, directed against the whole government of the Company, was presented to the Privy Council. The Lord Treasurer sent notice of the presentation to Ferrar, as deputy of the Company, and demanded that a complete answer

[1] Jebb.

to all particulars of the accusation should be sent in by the following Monday afternoon. Ferrar protested against this haste, which pressed with peculiar hardship at such a season, but Cranfield "austerely refused" to grant an hour's delay. Finding himself unable to gain time, he at once assembled such of the Company as could be got together, and read the charge to them. It was so voluminous that the reading occupied three hours.

The Company referred their concerns entirely to Lord Cavendish, Sir Edwin Sandys, and Nicholas Ferrar. "These three made it midnight ere they parted; they ate no set meals, they slept not two hours all Thursday and Friday nights; they met to admire each other's labours on Saturday night, and sat in judgment on the whole till five o'clock on Sunday morning; then they divided it equally among six nimble scribes, and went to bed themselves, as it was high time for them." The transcribers finished their task by five o'clock on Monday morning; the Company met at six to review their labours, and by two in the afternoon the answer was presented at the Council Board.

This answer gave complete satisfaction to the friends of the Company, its enemies, as might be expected, remaining as dissatisfied as before. They sent two Commissioners to the colony to examine into its condition, and rake up, if possible, fresh grounds of accusation, and meanwhile the case was transferred to the Court of King's Bench, Ferrar and about thirty more of the directors and principal members of the Virginian Company being served with a writ of *Quo Warranto*, and commanded to show by what authority they claimed to exercise a power over the plantation, and send a governor thither. The deputy and the other officials were compelled to conduct their defence at their private charge.

The case was decided against them, and the court gave sentence "that the patent or charter of the Company of English merchants trading to Virginia, and pretending to exercise a power and authority over his Majesty's good subjects there, should be thenceforth null and void."

The Company were not disposed to submit tamely to the ruin of all their hopes and projects, but nothing more could be done for the present.

The party opposed to the extension of the royal prerogative was watching, in deep discontent, the progress of the negotiations for Prince Charles's marriage with the Spanish Infanta; and when, in 1624, James reluctantly summoned a Parliament, to be opposed to the policy of Spain was in itself a recommendation to a majority of the electors. The new House of Commons contained more than a hundred members of the dissolved Virginia Company, with Sandys and Ferrar [1] at their head. The king vainly tried to prevent Sandys from taking his seat by offering him an appointment in Ireland.

When the prince returned home, he was welcomed with a tempest of rejoicing, and the popular feeling with regard to Spain was shown even in the anthem selected for the thanksgiving service held in St. Paul's on the occasion. It was " *When Israel came out oj Egypt.*" On the day when Buckingham stood up in the House, with Prince Charles by his side, to explain the reasons for breaking off the marriage contract, he became for the time the most popular man in England.[2]

Buckingham was determined not only to break off the Spanish marriage, but to wreck the Spanish party at the Court, and to this end he made up his mind to separate the Lord Treasurer Cranfield, now Earl of Middlesex, from the king. The weapon he chose for this purpose was an impeachment by the House of Commons.

The king struggled feebly to save his minister. " You will live to have your bellyful of Parliamentary impeachments," he said with prophetic shrewdness

---

[1] Ferrar was one of the members for Lymington.—Parliament Roll for 1624.

[2] S. Gardiner, "History of England," vol. v. chap. xlvii. Buckingham "is now a favourite with Parliament, people, and city, for breaking the match with Spain."—Howell's "Letters."

to his son, who took Buckingham's part. The Lord Keeper Williams, the duke's "creature and bedesman,"[1] who feared lest his own turn should come next, advised the king to give in. "If you suffer not your old and perhaps innocent servant to be plucked from the sanctuary of your mercy," said the official "keeper of the king's conscience," "you foil your son. Necessity must excuse you from inconstancy or cruelty."[2]

The impeachment proceeded. The members of the Virginia Company had their own quarrel to settle with the treasurer, and it is probably for this reason that Ferrar, though so young a member, was joined with Sandys and Cavendish in bringing the impeachment before the House of Lords. We have no record of the "long, but not tedious," speech which Ferrar delivered on this occasion,[3] but in the opinion of his friends it was a main cause of the condemnation of Middlesex.

---

[1] Williams signs himself thus in a letter to Buckingham, through whose influence he had (at his own request) been made Dean of Westminster.

[2] Hacket, "Life of Williams."

[3] "Many desired to have his speech, but he craved pardon."—"Life of Nicholas Ferrar," by his brother, p. 18. The writer hoped to have discovered some notice of this speech in Sir E. Nicholas's "Notes of the Parliament of 1624" (Domestic State Papers, clxvi.), but was baffled by the extremely difficult handwriting.

For eight weary hours the treasurer stood at the bar of the House to listen to the charges against him. He was quite worn out, and when a deputation from the Lords was sent to his house, they found him in bed, and complaining bitterly of the treatment to which he had been subjected, in being made to stand for so many hours, and to defend himself without the aid of counsel. He met with little pity. Lord Southampton, who was one of the deputation, told the House that "his voice seemed strong enough," and it was agreed that when he was next summoned before them he should be allowed "a stoole, but no counsel." Middlesex defended him bravely—in the opinion of Clarendon he cleared himself from blame; but his enemies had no mercy on him. "The faults of Bacon," said Southampton, passionately, "were few to the faults of the Lord Treasurer;" he had been guilty of "extorsion and tyranny," was unfaithful to the king, "and a wolfe to all the kingdom."[1]

He was found guilty, imprisoned, fined, and rendered incapable of again sitting in the House; and so violent was the feeling against him, that in spite of that severe sentence, we read in a contemporary letter that "it is marvelled they proceeded no further to degrade him upon so many just reasons."[2]

Very different was the feeling of Nicholas Ferrar

[1] Elsinge's "Notes" (Camden Society).
[2] Chamberlayne to Sir D. Carleton, "Court of James I."

when, in calmer days, he looked back upon the thing which he had helped to do. Middlesex may have been wrong, very wrong according to a high standard of honour, wrong even according to the standard which prevailed among the public men of his time, but he had not deserved the treatment which he received ;[1] and Ferrar's sensitive spirit repented long and bitterly for the course, which loyalty to his party, and perhaps also some personal anger against the man who had done so much to destroy his work in Virginia, had led him to take. "I would I were assured of the pardon of that sin," he was heard to say, stretching out his right hand, "though on that condition this right hand were cut off."

If the members of the Virginia Company thought that either the failure of the Spanish alliance or the condemnation of Middlesex would restore their fallen hopes, they were cruelly mistaken. A great effort, in which Sir Edwin Sandys and Nicholas Ferrar again took a leading part, was made to procure a confirmation of their rights by Act of Parliament.

The Journals of the House briefly record the struggle.

---

[1] On the question of Middlesex's guilt, see Mr. S. R. Gardiner : "Some things which formed the subject of accusation were even to his praise. But after all allowances have been made, there remains enough to show that he had done things which he ought never to have done."—"History of England," vol. v. chap. xlviii.

" Lunæ, 26 April :

" Mr. Ferrar delivereth a petition from the Treasurer, Council, and Company of Virginia.   Read.

" A Committee of several and all that will come. Those that are of the company to be present to inform, but to have no voice."

" 20 Maii.   Sir Edwin Sandys moves for a select commission to peruse the draught he and Mr. Ferrar have made for grievances on trade."

" May 24.   Petition of grace, not grievances, upon questions ordered to be drawn by Sir Ed. Sandys and Mr. Ferrar."

" May 25.   The Committee thought fit a petition of right, etc.   Sir Edwyn Sandys and Mr. Ferrar to do it."

But on this same day a message from the king was delivered to the committee.   His Majesty " thought the House need not meddle with it this session . . . will have the honour himself of recalling the patent." He added, that " by the next Parliament they should all see it; he would make it one of his masterpieces. as it well deserved to be."   The Virginian charter was withdrawn by the king under the Great Seal ; and shortly after, by letter merely, he suppressed the Bermuda Company.

The king's promises " were but fair words, as the event showed, for all was let loose, and to go to six and seven," writes John Ferrar, with natural bitterness, in concluding the story. The colony was " never looked after, whether sinke or swimme, and hath now these twenty-four yeares since laboured for life, and only to subsist with much adoe, . . . in all these many yeares no more people in it, and they having little incouragement and great uncertainties whether even to be continued a colony ; whereby men have had no heart to plant for posterity, but every man for the present, planted tobacco to get a living by it."[1]

But the work of Southampton and Sandys, the work to which the Ferrar brothers devoted some of the best years of their lives, was not thrown away.

" The Earl of Southampton, Sir Edwin Sandys, and the patriot party in England, unable to establish guarantees of a liberal administration at home, were careful to connect popular freedom so intimately with the life, prosperity, and state of society of Virginia, that they never could be separated."[2]

They had planted with as firm a hand the Catholic Church, according to the English rite.[3] The colony continued to bear " a great love to the stated constitutions of the Church of England, in her government and public worship, which gave us (who went

[1] " Perfect Description of Virginia " (1649).

[2] Bancroft, " History of the United States."

[3] " The last act of the Colonial Legislature, while still under the company, provides that in every settlement a house should be set apart for the worship of God, according to the Church of England."—Hawk.

thither under the late persecutions of it) the advantage of liberty to use it constantly among them, after the naval force had reduced the colony under the power, but never to the obedience," [1] of Cromwell.

The ruin of the Company must have been a deep sorrow and disappointment to Nicholas Ferrar, but he had still before him the possibility of a brilliant future. He was an active member of the popular party, the trusted friend of its most distinguished leaders. "Every parliament man was very willing to be acquainted with him." [2] He might have become, as the stirring years went on—

> " A potent voice of Parliament,
> A pillar steadfast in the storm."

He deliberately chose instead to spend his life in prayer and fasting, and in the training of a little group of relations and friends in devotion and good works.

[1] " Virginia's Cure," quoted by Bishop Wilberforce, " History of the American Church."

[2] " Life of Nicholas Ferrar," by his brother.

CHAPTER IV.

FERRAR PREPARES FOR A LIFE OF RELIGIOUS RE-
TIREMENT — THE PURCHASE OF GIDDING — HIS
ORDINATION.

A.D. 1625, 1626.

> " Thee sovereignly my will shall chuse ;
> My love shall to Thy love aspire,
> The sole desirable desire.
> Thou wilt have all my heart or none,
> The world I for Thy sake disown."
>
> BISHOP KEN, 1637–1711.

> " They carry music in their heart
> Through dusty lane and wrangling mart,
> Plying their daily task with busier feet,
> Because their secret souls a holy strain repeat."
>
> *Christian Year*, " *St. Matthew's Day*."

THESE lines express the attitude of Ferrar's mind throughout the busy years which he spent in London, filled as they were with business, anxiety, and the heat of political conflict.

It was thought that he took a vow of celibacy on recovering from his illness at Padua. Whether this be so or not, it seems certain that the desire to devote his life to religious retirement sprang from no sudden impulse, but was the secret growth of years.

His refusal of the Professorship at Gresham College, and of Government employment, has been already mentioned. A rich merchant, one of his friends of the Virginian Company, made him a proposal which sounds strange to us, but was permitted by the manners of the time; he "courted and wooed" him to take his only child in marriage, with ten thousand pounds to her portion.

He put all these flattering offers gently aside. He said that he was not worthy of so much honour; that he had other intentions and aims. To the merchant only, in his eagerness to avoid discourtesy to the proffered bride, he confessed his secret purpose—to lead, with God's help, a retired and single life.[1]

But though "he had formed his resolutions, he had not yet shaped his occasions" for the retirement he longed for. He could not leave his father's affairs unsettled, and his tender love and regard for his widowed mother kept him constantly near her. In the absence of private letters or journals, we have no means of learning how the peculiar form of religious life which he afterwards adopted, formed itself in his mind; but it was apparently the result of circumstances, and was probably due, in great part, to the influence of Mrs. Ferrar.

He himself seems at one time to have cherished the idea of devoting himself to mission work among

---

[1] " Life of Nicholas Ferrar," by his brother, p. 93.

the Indians in the Virginian colony which he loved so well. This wish he frequently expressed to Mr. Copeland, the rector designate of Henrico College, who told Sir Edwin Sandys that he verily believed Mr. Ferrar was determined to spend his life in the conversion of the infidels or others in that country, adding, "If he should do so, I will never leave him, but wait upon him in that glorious work." [1]

The sorrow which he expressed on his death-bed for his "great neglect in almsgiving," perhaps points to some struggle between his high sense of family duty and affection, and the desire to give up everything, even those tenderest and most sacred bonds, for the love of God alone. "It had been my part to have given all I had," he said to one who spoke of his deeds, adding, "The Lord God forgive, I most humbly beseech Him, my too much carnal love to my friends on this kind." [2]

During these early years he observed very strict rules of life, preparing himself, by acts of increasing austerity, for whatever form of devotion he might eventually be called to embrace.

In the course of his travels he had collected a quantity of choice books in various languages ; many of these books treated of prayer and the spiritual life, but there were also among them a great number

----

[1] " Peckard," p. 106.
[2] " Life of Nicholas Ferrar," by his brother, p. 81.

of " comedies, tragedies, love-hymns, heroical poems, novels, and the like," in which he had formerly taken great delight. With Puritan severity, he cut himself off from this world of imagination and poetry.[1] He could not make up his mind to destroy his cherished volumes, but he put them under lock and key—three great hampers full—and left them to gather dust and mildew undisturbed. The hours which he could secure from business were so frequently spent in prayer and fasting, that his seasons of retirement passed unnoticed in his family.

While on the Continent his opportunities of joining in the worship of the English Church must have been scanty and infrequent, and we can fancy how eagerly he would return to the habits of his youth, how devout and constant would be his attendance at the divine service.

---

[1] Bishop Ken, lover and writer of poetry as he was, seems to have taken the same line. In the catalogue of his books, given by the late Very Rev. E. H. Plumptre, no poems occur except some of the works of Milton and those of Herbert, Donne, Crashaw, and Sandys. Read in the light of this fact, the lines—

> " The heavenly fire Jehovah sent
> Was only on His altar spent,
> And all poetic heaven-born flame
> Should be devoted to His Name,"

would appear to mean, that all poetry should be distinctly religious, not only in tone but in subject.

That " strong north wind coming out of Scotland," which was said to have blown Abbott across the Thames to Lambeth, had reduced the ritual of our churches to the coldest depth of desolation which it has ever reached. The archbishop forbade his household to bow at the Holy Name. King James showed open disregard for public worship, seldom entering his chapel till the prayers were nearly over.[1] With such examples before them, it is not wonderful that the careless young court noblemen tilted on Good Friday, that the clergy sometimes ministered without surplices, and their congregation received the Holy Communion standing or sitting.

But new life was springing up. In one diocese, at least, and that one of the most important, Catholic teaching and devout ritual were enforced. Of the work of the great and saintly Bishop of Winchester, the venerable Lancelot Andrewes, it would be presumptuous for the present writer to attempt any description ; yet, since the training of a Churchman in King James's time without the teaching of

[1] " I desired his Majesty King Charles that he would please to be present at prayers as well as sermon every Sunday ; and that at whatsoever part of the prayers he came, the priest then officiating might proceed to the end of the prayers. The most religious king not only assented to this request, but also gave me thanks. This had not before been done from the beginning of King James's reign unto this day. Now, thanks be to God, it obtaineth."—Laud's " Diary," November 14, A.D. 1626.

Andrewes would have been as incomplete as that of our own generation would be if Dr. Pusey or Mr. Keble had never existed, it may be allowable to give some account of that teaching in the words of one who can speak on such a subject with authority.[1]

" Without departing from the position or the lines of the original Reformation," Bishop Andrewes " greatly enlarged its field of teaching. In the outskirts and fringes of its system, where it had been characteristically reticent, he was not afraid to supply from the authorities, to which it had all along appealed, what was wanting to complete the harmony and fulness of its doctrine. Thus, with respect to the idea of the Christian sacrifice in the Eucharist, on which the language of the ancient Church was so clear and strong, and on which, from the superstitions and errors of the Mediæval Church, the English Prayer-book was so reserved, Andrewes, without hesitation and as of full right, recurred, both in controversy and in teaching, to the language of the Liturgies, familiar to the early writers from Irenæus to Augustine. So, again, with respect of those forms and offices for special occasions not provided for in the general office-book of the Church, he threw himself, as an ancient bishop would have done, on his inherent

---

[1] " Masters in English Theology : Lancelot Andrewes," by the late Very Rev. R. W. Church, Dean of St. Paul's.

episcopal authority to supply the want.   It is mainly
according to the model used by him that our churches
are even to this day consecrated.   Full of discrimi-
nation for what really had the authority of the ancient
Church, he was the most fearless of English divines
where he had that authority.   English theology would
be in danger of being much less Catholic, much
more disconnected with that of the earlier ages,
much more arbitrarily limited in all directions, except
towards Geneva or else towards simple latitude, but
that a man of Andrewes' character and weight
had dared to break through the prescription which
the Puritans were trying to establish against the
doctrinal language, at once more accurate and more
free, of the ancient Church."

Ferrar had been mainly left to form his own
opinions, for he was little more than a boy when he
was launched on the Continent to steer his way alone
amid the conflicting claims of the Roman Church,
the Protestant sects, the scepticism and the indif-
ference which met him on every side.

It must have been an infinite gain to him to hear
the teaching of his own Church put forth in all
its strength and fulness by an authority so weighty.
We can fancy him hanging on the lips of Andrewes,
his keen mind following the great preacher through
all the windings of his condensed and rapid thought,
undeterred by the quaint abruptness which makes

those famous sermons appear difficult and unattractive to modern readers. They were not unattractive then. The chapel at Whitehall was crowded whenever the " matchless bishop," "the oracle of our present times," occupied the pulpit; and a great school of men was rising up to carry on and develop his teaching.

Among these men were Dr. Lindsell, Ferrar's old tutor, and his father's friend, Dr. White, Dean of Carlisle; and closely linked with them were Laud, lately made Bishop of St. David's, and Cosins, still young, but already so highly regarded that both Andrewes and Overall had offered him posts in their households, the so-called "families" with which bishops surrounded themselves in those stately days.

The directions given (under the advice of Laud) to the chaplains who attended Prince Charles in Spain [1] show both the progress which had been made in reviving a decent and orderly ritual, and the great need of enforcing the most ordinary reverence; it was even thought necessary to direct that those

---

[1] These instructions direct that in the room set apart for prayer there should be "an altar, fonts, palls, linen-coverings, demy-carpet, four surplices, candlesticks, tapers, chalices, pattens, a fine towel for the prince, other towels for the household, a travese of water for the Communion, a bason and flaggons, two copes ; and also that water should be mixed with the wine, and smooth wafers used for the bread."—Heylin's "Life of Laud," vol. i. p. 106.

present at the services should be uncovered, and should stand at the Creeds and Gospel.

There was in London another remarkable preacher, who, though he has left no such mark as Bishop Andrewes, was yet of great influence in his day. Dr. John Donne, Dean of St. Paul's, did not form a school of theology, but he stirred men's hearts to their innermost depth.

"His own heart was possessed with those very thoughts and joys which he laboured to distil into others; a preacher in earnest, weeping sometimes for his auditory, sometimes with them; always preaching to himself, like an angel from a cloud, but in none; carrying some, as St. Paul was, to heaven in holy raptures, and enticing others by a sacred art and courtship to amend their lives; here picturing a vice so as to make it ugly to those that practised it, and a virtue so as to make it beloved even by those that loved it not; and all this with a most particular grace and an inexpressible addition of comeliness." [1]

We are reminded of the St. Paul's which we know and love to-day, when we read of the "organs, cornets, and sackbuts" which rolled their waves of sound through the aisles of the perished cathedral, "accompanied and intermingled with such excellent voices that seemed rather to enchant than chant," and picture to ourselves the crowds gathering from all

[1] Walton's "Life of Donne."

parts of the city—from Westminster and Southwark, and across the fields from quiet suburban villages, Kensington and Paddington, and others long since swallowed up by invading London—to hear the sermons of the great dean, "lit up by the genius of of a poet, and heated by the zeal of an evangelist."[1]

We can even distinguish individuals as the streams go by and disappear in the open doorways, names familiar to us as the names of those who were alive but yesterday. There is Donne's college friend, Sir Henry Wotton, stately and gracious, with the sweet and polished manner that made his company "one of the delights of mankind," and with him, perhaps, Isaak Walton, just settled in his new shop in Fleet Street. The keen eye of the practised scholar and diplomatist must have detected some rare gift in the young linen-draper whom he honoured with his companionship, but he could little have foreseen that his fame and that of the preacher whom he admired and loved were in the keeping of this modest friend ; that by his portraits, alive with insight and tender sympathy, their features would be chiefly known.

Here, too, George Herbert, still wearing the silk clothes and sword of a courtly layman, would come from time to time to listen to the old friend of his childhood. He was going through a sharp conflict.

[1] "Donne, the Poet-Preacher," by Bishop Lightfoot, in "Classic Preachers of the English Church."

It was long before he could decide to give up "the painted pleasures of a court life" for the service of the Church. He tells us himself that—

> "Whereas my birth and spirit rather took
>   The way that takes the town,
> *Thou* didst betray me to a lingering book
>   And wrap me in a gown.
> I was entangled in a world of strife
> Before I had the power to change my life."

Was it in some crisis of this struggle that he first met Ferrar, and formed with him in that one interview—

> "A friendship that hath conquered Time"?

Since Arthur Woodnoth, the goldsmith, the valued friend of Herbert's family, was also Ferrar's cousin, what more probable than that these three, coming forth from the twilight aisles of the cathedral, their hearts pierced by Donne's fiery eloquence, should meet and walk together through the darkening streets to Woodnoth's house in Foster Lane?

The young poet and the young member of parliament steeped to the lips in business seem to have understood one another at once. After their first, and, as is thought, only meeting, wherever it may have taken place, Ferrar became George Herbert's "exceeding dear brother," his "entire friend and brother."[1] Shortly before his death he desired to

[1] "I know they" (Herbert and Ferrar) "loved each other most entirely, and their very souls cleaved together most intimately;

exchange Bemerton for a living near Huntingdon, for no other reason but to be within reach of his friend; and in Ferrar's care he left his poems, at his absolute disposal, to be burnt or printed as he might see fit. Herbert had been for eight years public orator at Cambridge; he had been a courtier; he had older friends, friends more highly placed than the recluse of Gidding. This display of confidence and affection for a man of whom he had seen so little, marks a deep sense of admiration, perhaps also of personal obligation, and a conjecture forces itself on the mind as one thinks of the brief intercourse of these fervent spirits, that the influence of Ferrar, more practical, more determined, less swayed by imagination, may have helped to decide the wavering mind of Herbert in his resolution to lay aside all hopes of rising in the state, and devote himself to the service of God at the altar.[1]

and drove a large stock of Christian intelligence together long before their deaths; yet saw they not each other in many years."—Oley, "Life of George Herbert." "As I take it, having but once had personal conference with each other."—"Life of Nicholas Ferrar," by his brother.

[1] There are many traces of this struggle in Herbert's writings. For one of the most striking, see the poem entitled "Affliction" (No. 63).

> "Broken in pieces all asunder,
>   Lord, hunt me not,
>   A thing forgot;
> Once a poor creature, now a wonder—

Nicholas Ferrar did not take his final leave of London life till the summer of 1626, but during the winter of 1624–25, after the collapse of the last hopes of the Virginia Company, though his family affairs, owing to the failure of John Ferrar's partner, were still seriously embarrassed, he felt free to consider the place and manner of his retirement from the world.

The scheme of life which he then formed, displays a remarkable union of determination and flexibility. He accepted the situation in which he found himself, which was not perhaps that which he would have chosen, with the calmest common sense, and at the same time with undiminished fervour. He was the chief support of his mother, the virtual head of the family, and he made up his mind to carry out to the full all the varied duties imposed on him by this position, and yet to abate nothing of the ascetic ideal to which he had so long desired to conform his life. The result was a compromise, as so many things must be, but a compromise which he turned to the loftiest purpose.

Mrs. Ferrar entered heartily into her son's plans,

> A wonder, tortured in the space
> Betwixt this world and that of grace.
>
> My thoughts are all a case of knives,
> Wounding my heart."
>
> .　　.　　.　　.　　.　　.　　.

which she may indeed have helped to mould, and agreed to leave London and fix her abode in some retired part of the country, where Nicholas might without interruption lead the life of his choice.

In May, 1625, she completed the purchase of the lordship of Little Gidding, a depopulated parish turned entirely into pasture land, with a large ruinous mansion, a single shepherd's cottage, and a small church used as a hay barn, situated in a solitary neighbourhood twelve miles from Huntingdon. The house required considerable repair and alteration before it could be made a fit dwelling-place for Mrs. Ferrar and her family, which included, besides Nicholas, her granddaughter, Mary Collett, a girl of twenty-two, who had lived with her from early childhood; but circumstances compelled her to leave London and take up her abode at Gidding at an earlier date than she at first intended.

The summer of 1625 set in wet and gloomy, and unhealthy mists crept up from the river, carrying the seeds of illness from the ships in the Pool into the narrow streets of the city. The solemnities of the funeral of James I., the rejoicings for his son's marriage, lost their importance in the presence of a great fear. By Ascension Day, people began to whisper to each other that the plague had come. In the course of that week a friend of the Ferrars, living in the next house, died. His relations were doubtful as to the cause of his death, or desirous to conceal it, and some of the Ferrars were invited to the funeral, but on Whitsun Eve another member of the family sickened, and Nicholas Ferrar took the alarm.

He at once procured a coach and sent his mother and her household to Hertford that night; on Whit Monday Mrs. Ferrar proceeded to her son-in-law's house at Bourne, taking with her, as it would seem, her grandaughter Mary and John Ferrar's wife and children, while John himself went on to Gidding to make the newly purchased house fit for habitation as speedily as possible, and Nicholas remained in town to attend to his own affairs and those of his brother. The wet weather still continued, and the fear of famine began to be added to that of pestilence. By the middle of July the plague was raging throughout London and Westminster, and four thousand persons died in one week.

Nicholas stayed in the sorrowful city till he had wound up his business connected with his father's estate, paid off all debts, and cleared his family estate from the encumbrances resulting from the failure of his brother's partner, and probably also from the ruin of the Virginia Company—a task which he could only accomplish at considerable personal sacrifice. The sum left by his father to the college at Henrico he made over, now that the restoration of the college seemed indefinitely postponed, to the Governor of

Bermuda, in trust for the Christian education o
" three wild young infidels."

When his family affairs were at last brought into
order, he joined his brother John at Little Gidding,
entreating his mother to remain a month longer at
Bourne, lest he should have brought infection with
him.

But the mother's heart would not suffer this delay.
Within three days of his arrival, she rode, though now
seventy years of age, the fifteen miles from Bourne to
Gidding, through miry lanes impassable for a coach.

" Their greeting was like that of old Jacob and his
son Joseph, after his father had given him over for
lost, while he was providing for the support of the
family. Such an interview must needs be passionately kind and zealously devout, both of them blessing God, and she again and again blessing her son.
He prayed her to enter the rude house and to re-
pose herself after her journey. ' Not so,' said she ;
' yonder I see the church ; let us first go thither, to
give God thanks that He has brought me to this good
place and has restored me my son.' It was told her
there was no getting into it, for as yet there had not
been time to empty the hay that was in it, which was
intended shortly to be done. By the sacrilege and
profaneness of the former inhabitants of Gidding the
house of God was turned into a hay-barn and a
hog-stye. But this good woman had somewhat of

Augustine's mother, Monica, in her devotion, of whom
that Father affirms, that 'if a dragon stood between
her and the altar, she would have stept through him
to advance thither.'　So this divine soul persisted in
her ardent resolution, and, thrusting into the church a
little way, she kneeled and prayed and wept there
about a quarter of an hour.　Then she charged her
son to send instantly for all the workmen about the
house, which were many, and commanded them to
fling out the hay at the church windows, and to
cleanse it as well as they could for the present.[1]　She
was obeyed, and she saw all this done before she
would stir or set her foot in the house."

Under the energetic rule of this devout and high-
spirited lady, the renovation of both church and
house proceeded so quickly that in a month's time
she was able to send for some of her family from
Bourne, though the old mansion still required much
repair and alteration before it could be properly fitted
to the needs of a large household.　Mrs. Collett was
the first to rejoin her mother, and she was followed
in the course of the summer by the whole of her
numerous family, as well as by Mrs. John Ferrar and
her children.　The spendthrift eldest son, Richard
Ferrar, though a constant object of anxiety, is scarcely
mentioned in the memoirs, but Mrs. Collett's letters
show that he was an occasional visitor at Gidding,

[1] " Life of Nicholas Ferrar," by Dr. Jebb, p. 29.

and it is hardly likely that he was left uncared for in this time of dismay and trouble.

Through the remainder of that dreary summer and the long winter that followed, the reunited family remained at Gidding. All, following the mother's example, took a deep interest in the repair and decoration of the desecrated church, working at it with their own hands. They made it their oratory, and there daily recited the Litany on behalf of those suffering from the plague. On Sundays they attended the neighbouring church of Steeple Gidding, and when the repair of Little Gidding was sufficiently advanced, the friendly vicar of that parish would sometimes come over, followed by his flock, to perform service in the restored sanctuary.

During this time Nicholas Ferrar, freed from all labour but the congenial task of fitting house and church to be the home of his little community, worked out in his mind a scheme which should combine the rule of a Religious house with the ordinary routine of domestic life. At what time he first proposed this manner of life to his relations, by what persuasion he won them to adopt it, how far the union of the different branches of the family under one roof grew out of this plan or was the result of accident and convenience, is matter of conjecture only.

Probably the anxieties which they had gone through

H

together, the sadness which hung over the land, the hours of united prayer when they knelt in intercession for the " deplorable city " to which they were bound by so many ties, drew the hearts of the little company nearer to each other and to God. In this green and pleasant solitude, their minds were free to rise undisturbed by the thousand influences of business and society which are too apt to choke devout aspirations. " They began already to taste the delicious fruits of peace and quietness," and when Mrs. Ferrar, after nine months' experience of this quiet life, made up her mind " by the grace of God to take livery and seizin of her new purchase by laying her bones there," John Ferrar and his wife and Mr. and Mrs. Collett determined to remain with her. From this time we hear no more of the house at Bourne, and Gidding remained the home of the entire family.

After Easter, the plague having at length ceased, they all went up to London, " that the good old gentlewoman might take her last leave of all her friends, expecting to see them no more till the great Easter morning at the Resurrection."

They remained in town for several weeks, arranging for the letting of the great London house, and settling their remaining affairs ; and, this accomplished, Nicholas Ferrar felt that the time was at last come when he might solemnly dedicate himself to the exclusive service of God.

He kept his resolution secret, fearing, for what reason it is not easy to understand, that his friends might still oppose it. It is possible that his mother, though herself desirous to live a retired life, still clung to the hope of some brilliant destiny for her favourite son. He passed the week before Whit Sunday in prayer, fasting, and watching, but his family, accustomed to see him spend much time in devotion, observed nothing unusual in this retirement. On Whitsun Eve he watched the whole night through. Dr. Lindsell, the only person to whom he had confided his intentions, was "ravished with joy" to find that his beloved pupil was now about to enter on the profession which he had so long desired for him; yet even he did not fully sympathize with the life to which Ferrar felt called. "If he could but be prevailed on to ascend the pulpit," the good man was sometimes heard to say, "he were then in his proper orb, and would shine among those who turn many to righteousness." It was perhaps in order to avoid all possibility of preferment, perhaps only from the intense humility which underlay his somewhat authoritative ways, that he made known to his old tutor his resolve never to pass beyond the diaconate.

Early in the morning of Trinity Sunday he went, accompanied by Lindsell, to Henry VII.'s Chapel in Westminster Abbey, and there Laud, still Bishop of St. David's, ordained him deacon, he being then in his thirty-fifth year.

It was towards evening when Ferrar returned home on that, to him, memorable Sunday. He went straight to his mother, who was seated among her children and friends—a little gathering, of those from whom she was to part so soon—and, drawing from his breast a roll of vellum, he begged her to allow him to read to her what he had written. It was a formal and solemn vow, written and signed with his own hand, to devote himself to God's service as an act of thanksgiving for his preservation in so many dangers of soul and body, and the deliverance of his family from the brink of ruin. He added his resolution to be "the Levite in his own house," and make his own family his cure of souls.

The assembled friends seem to have been over-whelmed with amazement at this declaration, remem-bering perhaps how short a time had elapsed since Nicholas had stood in the forefront of the parliamen-tary battle, and did service to Buckingham which the all-powerful duke might now be both able and willing to requite. They stood silent, looking at him ; but the mother, falling on his neck, wept and blessed him, praying that he might be filled with the Holy Spirit daily more and more. " I also," said she, " will, by the help of my God, set myself with more care and diligence than ever to serve our good Lord God, as is all our duties to do, in all we may." [1]

[1] " Life of Nicholas Ferrar," by his brother, p. 25.

All Ferrar's friends seem to have shared in the astonishment caused by his ordination. So reserved had he been, and so completely had his inner life been concealed during his six years of work in London, that even Sir Edwin Sandys, who had known him intimately from the first, was amazed. Offers of benefices were immediately showered upon him, it being apparently inconceivable to the imagination of the time that anybody should wish to live without preferment of some kind. Sir Edwin, through whom these offers were made, pressed him to accept them, but Ferrar was fixed in his determination.

He told his friend that he had parted his worldly estate among his family, and meant to devote his " half-talent," as he modestly called it, to make them partakers of spiritual treasures.

There was now nothing more to do but to return to Gidding, and there settle down in the strict way of life which Nicholas had mapped out. That he should have induced not only his devoted mother, but his brother and brother-in-law, both married men of middle age (Mr. Collett had sixteen children), to submit to this austere rule, and to bring up their families in the same, is a remarkable proof both of his extraordinary personal influence and of the recoil of feeling which was drawing back Churchmen more and more towards the lost Religious Life. This feeling meets us again and again in the writings of the century which lies between the period of the Elizabethan Settlement and the period of the final separation of the Nonjurors; the hatred and terror of Popery was still so great that few ventured openly to propose the foundation of a Religious Order, but their minds dwelt on the subject, and here and there, singly or in little groups, they strove after some fashion to live the life.

Bishop Andrewes, in his " Devotions," gives thanks for—

> " The ascetics and their tears,
> The virgins, flowers of purity,
> Celestial gems,
> Brides of the Immaculate Lamb." [1]

It was the cherished hope of Lettice Lady Falkland, a hope which her early death in the midst of the civil war left unfulfilled, to aid in the foundation of houses " for the education of young gentlewomen and the retirement of widows," "hoping thereby that learning and religion might flourish more in her own sex than heretofore, having such opportunities to serve the Lord without distraction." [2]

Sir George Wheler,[3] in the preface to his " Protes-

[1] "Devotions of Bishop Andrewes," p. 33. Oxford edition. 1848.

[2] "The Holy Life and Death of the Lady Letice Vicountess Falkland," by John Duncon, Parson (sequestered). See also Note at the end of this chapter.

[3] Sir George Wheler, or Wheeler, was in his youth a traveller of some note. He afterwards took orders and became Rector of

tant Monastery," published in 1698, writes that "Convents for single women seem convenient, if not very necessary for all times and countries," and if duly ordered, "would undoubtedly be both a reputation to the Church and advantageous to the nation." "Yet," he adds, "considering the great decay of Christian piety, and especially of devotion in this age, there seems but small hopes that anything of this nature shall be brought to pass. Therefore, till it shall please God to send such unprejudiced times as may bring such commendable works to perfection, the pious conduct of private families shall be the monasteries that I shall most earnestly commend to all devout masters of them."

Of such devout and strictly ordered households,

Houghton-le-Spring. "The Protestant Monastery; or, Christian Æconomicks," is a manual of devotion compiled originally for his own family, and used, as he tells us, in his household for twenty years before its publication. It consists of four day hours, and four night watches, matins, sext, and the second night watch, or compline, being intended for the use of the whole household, and the five remaining offices for such of the family as have more leisure. These offices are formed from those in the Common Prayer-book, with paraphrases and "enlargements," among which is a very beautiful "Litany of Praise" for use on festivals. Sir G. Wheler adds minute directions for setting apart the best room in each house as an oratory, or, if this be not practicable, for a careful arrangement of the family sitting-room before prayer-time, and suggests that the reader and all his family should face the same way, and that men should be placed on one side of the room, and women on the other.

the family of Gidding is perhaps the most remarkable and certainly the most conspicuous example.[1]

NOTE.

A plan of a college for the higher education of women, which should be at the same time a religious house, was put forth half a century after Lady Falkland's death by Mrs. Astell. After deploring the ignorance and frivolity of the ladies of her time, she proposes as a remedy " to erect a *monastery*, or if you will (to avoid giving offence to the scrupulous and injudicious by names which, though innocent in themselves, have been abused by super-stitious practices) we will call it a *religious retirement. . . .* Here such as are willing in a more peculiar and undisturbed manner to attend the great business they came into the world about, the service of GOD and improvement of their own minds, may find a convenient and blissful recess from the noise and hurry of the world, . . . and all that *acme* of delight which the devout seraphic soul enjoys when, dead to the world, she devotes herself entirely to the contemplation and fruition of her Beloved ; when, having disengaged herself from all those lets which hindered her from without, she moves in a direct and vigourous motion towards her true and only good. . . . Your retreat shall be so managed as not to exclude the good works of the active, from the pleasure and serenity of a *contemplative* life."

Daily service " in the cathedral manner," frequent communion, and a careful observation of the precepts of their " holy mother the *Church*, whose sacred injunctions are too much neglected even by those who pretend to the greatest zeal for her," were like part of the rule of the house, and " care shall be taken that our

---

[1] Cf. the account of the Ladies of Naish Court in the 24th chapter of the " Life of Bishop Ken," by the late Very Rev. E. H. Plumptre.

religious be under the tuition of persons qualified to minister to all the spiritual wants of their charge, watching over their souls with tenderness and prudence, applying fitting medicines with sweetness and affability."

The ladies were to spend some time in study as well as prayer, Mrs. Astell holding that they had as much right as men to improve their minds, and that learning would assist them in the practice of devotion; "for even the men themselves," she remarks, "if they have not a competent degree of knowledge, they are carried about with every wind of doctrine."

Their special work was to be the education of girls of the higher class, and also, if their means would admit, of the daughters of poor gentlemen, who must otherwise remain untaught; but all works of mercy, both spiritual and corporal, were to be practised among them as opportunity might offer.— See "A Serious Proposal to the Ladies by a Lover of her Sex" [Mary Astell], 1694.

Mrs. Astell's scheme roused considerable interest, and an unnamed lady (supposed to be the queen) was ready to give £10,000 for the foundation of such an institution; but Bishop Burnet, who seems to have been consulted in the matter, put an end to the plan, saying that it would be too much like a nunnery. —See "Life of Mary Astell," Dict. Nat. Biog.

CHAPTER V.

THE FAMILY ESTABLISHED AT GIDDING—MANNER OF
LIFE AND OCCUPATIONS.

A.D. 1626-28.

> " Slight those who say amongst their sickly healths,
>   ' *Thou liv'st by rule.*'   What doth not so but man ?
> Houses were built by rule, and commonwealths.
>   Entice the trusty sun, if that you can,
>   From his ecliptic line ; beckon the sky.
>   Who lives by rule, then, keeps good company."
>
> G. HERBERT.

THE estate of Little Gidding consisted, and consists to this day, of an upland pasture divided into small irregular fields, of which some still bear names which recall the memory of its old proprietors. The air blows freshly on these green heights. There is a sense of space, of quiet, and pleasant wildness. All around are lower hills, half covered with trees, which open and sink down into wide valleys, rich with hidden streams, through which the eye travels till the grey distance melts into the sky.

The little church stands on the highest level, sheltered by a wood, which has sprung up among the roots of ancient trees, remnants of the grove which shaded it when first Mrs. Ferrar rode up the muddy field track which, until a few years ago, was the only access.

The Hall has disappeared so completely that its site can only be conjectured from John Ferrar's statement that it was about forty paces from the church. It stood, probably, a little in front of the present farmhouse, facing south ; a ridge still visible in the grass is supposed to mark the line of the path which led to the west door of the church. The little churchyard has been somewhat enlarged. Some large box trees, apparently of great age, now within its boundary, may have formed part of the hedge formerly dividing it from the garden ; these, with a single holly, are the only remaining traces of the old plantations. In a neighbouring field, the dried-up hollows of fishponds are still to be seen, and the name of the " Dovehouse Close " commemorates the site of the pigeon-house.

The place is as retired and still as when the Ferrars first came to it, yet it is not lonely. At the foot of the hill, deep buried in trees, lies Glatton, and, half-way up, the houses of Great Gidding cluster round their ancient church. Steeple Gidding is scarce a quarter of a mile off, and Coppingford but a little way to the westward.

The road that goes through Huntingdon to Stamford and the north, passes the foot of Gidding hill, and an older highway, the " bullock road," used until lately by drovers bringing herds of cattle from Scotland, runs along the crest of the ridge on the further side of the valley. From this upper road the great house at Gidding must have been plainly seen.

When fully repaired and completed, the mansion must have been of considerable size, for it gave ample accommodation to a household of above thirty persons. The men and boys (three schoolmasters lived in the house) were lodged at one end of the building, the women and girls at the other, Nicholas Ferrar having his chamber and study in the midst, so that he might keep watch over his little community. The ground floor was occupied, besides the necessary offices, by the large dining-parlour, by rooms for the reception of guests and of the neighbouring poor who came to seek assistance, and by alms-rooms for poor widows. These last were handsomely wainscoted, with four beds in each, "after the Dutch manner in their almshouses." There was also a dispensary for the compounding of medicines and ointments, and a large room set apart as an infirmary, in case of sickness in the family. The centre of the home life was in the "great chamber" upstairs, where Mrs. Ferrar, seated in her armchair with one of her daughters near her, was usually to be found. This room, hung with tapestry and glowing in winter with cheerful firelight, was at once oratory and community room. Here, till the work grew so large as to require a separate room, the famous Harmonies were compiled. Here the maidens practised embroidery and "fair writing," while the little children, too young for school, sat by, silently working or learning their simple lessons; and here, at the upper end of the room, before the eastern window which looked towards the church, the whole family assembled for the daily offices. For private devotion they had two oratories, one for men, the other for women, each at their own end of the house.

A schoolhouse was fitted up in the grounds; the great dovecote (probably one of the large beehive-shaped stone buildings still sometimes found attached to ancient houses)—which they had cleared out because, their own land being all in pasture, they thought it unfair to keep a flock of pigeons to feed on their neighbour's corn—being utilized for this purpose.

The house was furnished with the utmost plainness and simplicity, and had a grave religious aspect, befitting the life which its inmates had chosen. "Even the walls are not idle, but something is written or painted there which may excite the reader to a thought of piety."[1] A brass plate affixed to the outer door bore the words, "FLEE FROM

---

[1] G. Herbert, "A Priest to the Temple," chap. x. Many passages in the "Country Parson" remind us of the customs of Gidding.

EVIL AND DO GOOD, AND DWELL FOR EVERMORE;' and in the parlour, in which it was the custom of the family to receive strangers,' a tablet was placed, admonishing all comers in what temper of mind they should visit this devout household. It ran as follows:—[1]

I.H.S.

He who (by reproof of our errors and remonstrance of that which is more perfect) seeks to make us better, is welcome as an angel of God.	And	He who by a cheerful participation and approbation of that which is good confirms us in the same, is welcome as a Christian friend.

But

He who any way goes about to disturb us in that which is and ought to be amongst Christians (tho' it be not usual in the world) is a burden whilst he stays, and shall bear his judgment, whosoever he be.	And	He who censures us in absence for that which in presence he made show to approve of, doth, by a double guilt of flattery and slander, violate the bands both of friendship and Christianity.

MARY FERRAR, *Widow,*
MOTHER OF THIS FAMILY,
AND AGED ABOUT FOURSCORE YEARS,
(WHO BIDS ADIEU TO ALL FEARS AND HOPES OF THIS
WORLD, AND ONLY DESIRES TO SERVE GOD),
Set up this Table.

---

[1] Bishop Turner, "Manuscript Extracts." The copy in Lenton's letter gives "charity" for "Christianity."

The care and cost which the Ferrars saved in the simple furnishing of their dwelling were spent freely on the church. It was hastily put in order on their first coming, but when they were finally settled at Gidding they beautified it to the utmost of their power.

It is a tiny brick building consisting only of nave and chancel, without aisles. It is very narrow, and is now somewhat shorter than formerly, about seven feet at the west end having been pulled down, and a new west front built, in 1714.

Mrs. Ferrar had the church new floored, and the walls wainscoted for warmth. It was seated after the fashion of a college chapel, with stalls and benches running east and west; a pulpit and reading-desk of equal height (to show that prayer was an ordinance of equal value with preaching[1]) were placed on each side of the entrance to the chancel, and between them stood a brazen eagle[2] of great beauty, still preserved, as are the curious small brass font, with its

---

[1] A point on which protest was much needed. "One beauty hath beat out another; the beauty of preaching (which is a beauty too) hath preached away the beauty of holinesse; for if men may have a sermon, prayer and church service, with the ornaments of God's house, may sit abroad in the cold."—Shelford, "Five Discourses." Cambridge: 1635.

[2] This eagle was discovered about the time of the restoration in 1853, in a pond on the estate, where it is supposed to have lain since the pillage in 1646. The claws, which were probably of silver, had been carried off.

crown-shaped cover, three brass tablets engraved with the Creed, Lord's Prayer, and Ten Commandments on the east wall, and an hourglass stand, of a pattern resembling the font cover.

The chancel was raised a step above the rest of the church, and the floor covered with tapestry; on each side were stalls, which seem to have been reserved for clergy or visitors. The altar, which still remains, is a massive table of cedar wood. It was covered with rich silk, green for ordinary days, on festivals blue with gold embroidery, and furnished with silver candlesticks. It seems to have been placed length-wise,[1] a point on which Bishop Williams, the diocesan, would probably have insisted.

The whole chapel was " fairly and sweetly adorned with herbs and flowers,[2] natural in some places and artificial upon every pillar " of the stalls, and lit by wax tapers affixed to each stall, after a convenient and

[1] " Upon that half-pace stood the communion table (not altar-wise as reported), with a rich carpet, hanging very large upon the half-pace, and some plate, as chalice and candlesticks with wax candles."—Letter from Edward Lenton to Sergeant Hetley, describing a visit to Gidding in 1634, published by Peckard and subsequent biographers.

[2] So common was then the custom of decking churches with flowers, that even the little reed-thatched church at Jamestown, on some occasion of special rejoicing, was " neatly trimmed with the wild flowers of the country."—Purchas's " Pilgrims." quoted by Bishop Wilberforce, " History of the American Church."

picturesque fashion which may still be sometimes seen.

The church seems to have shared in a measure the decay of the house, but in 1853 [1] it was repaired by reverent hands, and as far as possible restored to the condition in which it was placed by the Ferrars.

Such was the home in which Nicholas Ferrar and his family lived their strict and devout life. The rule which they observed is minutely described by John Ferrar.[2]

The whole household rose at five o'clock in winter, and four in summer, old Mrs. Ferrar herself never getting up later than five; [3] and, having said their morning prayers in their several chambers, went as soon as they were ready to the great chamber, where Nicholas always awaited them. Here the

[1] By the late William Hopkinson, Esq., of Sutton Grange, Northamptonshire, who purchased the estate of Gidding, and restored the church, out of respect for the memory of Nicholas Ferrar.

[2] "Life of Nicholas Ferrar," by his brother.

[3] Compare the practice of Mrs. Hopton (1627–1709), the "devout gentlewoman of quality," who arranged the "Devotions in the Antient Way of Offices," edited by Hickes. She kept up a constant course of devotion, "setting apart five times every day for religious worship, from which she would not suffer herself to be diverted by any business that was not very extraordinary. Even in her old age and the cold winter season she would be up, and in the closet at her Mattins, by four of the clock in the morning."—Ballard's "Lives," p. 389.

I

younger boys and girls repeated to him such chapters and hymns as each had been set to learn ; and, the recitation finished, all returned to their own rooms. At six o'clock they met again in the great chamber, and said the first office of the day. These offices, which appear to have been said by heart, consisted of Psalms, a portion of the " Harmony of the Gospels " compiled by Nicholas, and a hymn, the whole occupying about a quarter of an hour. An office was appointed for each hour,[1] and as it would have been impossible for the whole family to meet so frequently, they were divided into companies, each company being responsible for certain hours, and coming at the sound of the bell into the great chamber, where they found Mrs. Ferrar and such of the others as were able to be present. Three times in the day, at seven, ten, and four, all went to church, assembling first in the great chamber, and going thence in order, two and two.[2] The three schoolmasters, followed by their pupils, all in black gowns, led the way ; then came John Ferrar and Mr. Collett, and Nicholas leading his mother ; Mrs. John Ferrar and Mrs. Collett, with their daughters, followed their mother, the ladies

---

[1] " Eight, nine, ten o'clock come ; those hours had their several companies, that came and did as at the former hours ; psalms said, and a head of the concordance, the organs playing, the hymn sung at each hour, as the clock struck.—" Life of Nicholas Ferrar," by his brother.

[2] See the letter of Edward Lenton.

being dressed plainly in black, with veils on their heads; the little procession was closed by the servants. All, as they entered the church, made an obeisance[1] and took their places, the masters in the chancel, the boys kneeling on the chancel step, and Mrs. Ferrar, with her daughters and granddaughters, on the north side of the aisle, where sat all the women. Nicholas Ferrar, in surplice and hood, said Matins and Even-song according to the Prayer-book, and at ten o'clock recited the Litany, of which, by permission of the bishop, they continued the daily recitation that had been begun during the plague.

The schoolmasters and children breakfasted directly after Matins, and then went to the school-house; but the others appear to have taken nothing until eleven o'clock, when they dined with strict moderation on the simplest fare.[2] To prevent un-

[1] "The fourth sort of reverence . . . is at the entering in, before we take our seat, to bend the knee and bow the body to Him in the more usual and special place of His residence or resemblance, which is the high altar or the Lord's table usually standing at the east end of God's house. . . . But many of our people come to God's house as the horse goes into his stable, without any reverence at all."—Shelford, "Five Discourses." 1635.

[2] "They had the more leisure to work because they fasted so much. . . . It was not by fits, but by constancy, that they subdued their bodies by sobriety. Their bread was coarse, their drink small and of ill relish to the taste."—Hacket, account of Gidding in "Life of Archbishop Williams," part ii.

The Ferrars retained, or returned to, the hardy habits of an

profitable talk, the meal was eaten in silence, enlivened by the reading of some pleasant book. "Chronicles of nations, journeys by land, sea voyages, and such like," were read aloud by the younger members of the family in turn, and that all might remember and profit, one of the elders made an abstract of the most interesting or instructive points, to be afterwards fairly copied out and studied by the children. After dinner, all went to their several occupations, broken only by the summons to prayer, until supper-time, which was usually at five in summer and six in winter. While the table was being set, they sang a hymn accompanied by the organ (this also was their custom before dinner); a chapter of the Bible was read during the meal, followed by a story from the "Book of Martyrs." In the summer evenings they went out after supper, walking abroad where they pleased, and in winter they gathered round the fire, and the elder people "found some good discourse or other to pass the time with," while the younger ones, if they would, "had candles and went away," perhaps to some livelier amusement. At eight o'clock the bell again called them to prayers in

earlier time. "These od repasts—thanked be God—are verie well left, and eche one in maner (except here and there some young hungrie stomach that cannot fast till dinner-time) contenteth himself with dinner and supper onlie."—Harrison, "Description of England," 1577, quoted in *Church Times*, March 18, 1892.

the great chamber, and after prayers the children and grandchildren came to Mrs. Ferrar, and, kneeling, asked her blessing. Then they wished each other good night and went to their own rooms, no one being allowed to go about the house, or into each other's chambers after they had retired for the night. After a time, at the suggestion of George Herbert, Nicholas Ferrar added to the day offices a constant night watch ; but this severe rule was not imposed on all the family, but on such only as voluntarily accepted it, and it was arranged with great care and consideration, lest any should be over-wearied.

The watch was kept every night, from nine o'clock till one in the morning, either by two men or two women, in their own oratory.   During these four hours they recited, kneeling, the whole Psalter, occasionally rising to rest and warm themselves at the fires which were always provided in cold weather.   Ferrar himself usually watched twice in the week, but he would not permit any one else to take more than one night in seven.   At one o'clock on the nights that he rested the watchers knocked at his door, and at that hour, till his last illness, he always rose and spent the rest of the night in prayer and meditation.   Sometimes the monotony of the long watches was broken by singing and soft organ-playing, low and gentle, so as not to disturb the sleeping house.   The children and servants would beg to join in these watches, and two of the boys, young Nicholas Ferrar, John's son, and another "towardly youth," Ferrar Collett, joined their uncle in his watch as often as he would permit. In the summer, Nicholas Ferrar often spent the time in church, and his boy companion would lie down at one o'clock on a bench to sleep, while he remained in prayer till the morning bell called him to the first office in the great chamber.

Day and night through the years, so fair on the surface, so anxious and troubled below, which preceded the civil war, this ceaseless offering of prayer [1] went up from the quiet house among the Huntingdonshire meadows—

"A kind of tune which all things hear and fear."

"Our calling is to serve God, which I take to be the best," said Nicholas Ferrar, when asked if such continual prayer did not interfere with other duties; but he did not wholly forget the activities of life. He devoted a large portion of his time and thoughts to the careful education of the

---

[1] "Note the word *continually*, for there was no intermission day nor night. . . . By night they kept watch in the house of the Lord, and two by turns did supply the office for the rest, from whence they departed not till the morning. . . . This was the hardest part of their discipline, that they kept sentinel at all hours and seasons to expect the second coming of the Lord Jesus."—Hacket, account of Gidding in "Life of Williams," part ii. pp. 30, 31.

children of the house. Mr. and Mrs. Collett had eight sons and eight daughters—Thomas (already a barrister of the Inner Temple), Nicholas, Edward, Richard, Ferrar (the little companion of his uncle's night watch), John, and two others whose names are not given; Mary, Anna, Susanna, Hester, Margaret, Elizabeth, Joyce, and Judith, all still at home.

John Ferrar had one son,[1] Nicholas, his uncle's godson, and a little daughter was born on the first Christmas Eve after he came to Gidding. She was baptized on Christmas Day, and her uncle and grandmother, "out of their affection to the remembrance of the plantation of Virginia, which they so dearly affected, and that John Ferrar might daily more and more have the memorial of it, so as not to cease praying for it, and doing all the good he could otherwise to it," named her Virginia, "so that speaking unto her, looking upon her, or hearing others call her by her name, he might think of both at once." "Let me say," her father adds, "both grandmother and uncle loved her, and liked her much the better for her name; and what further insight they had in giving her that name let others conjecture."[2] These last words seem to point to some hope or intention of bringing up this little Christmas gift to the Religious

[1] Another son, John, was born two years later, and a daughter, Mary, who seems to have died in infancy.

[2] "Life of Nicholas Ferrar," by his brother, p. 83.

Life ; but Nicholas by no means contemplated educating all his young charges for perpetual seclusion from the world, though he may naturally have hoped that some of them would be drawn to follow his own example, and his eldest niece, Mary Collett, seems from very early days to have felt the desire for a lifelong dedication.

All the children were taught with extreme care. One of the schoolmasters instructed them in English and Latin, another in arithmetic and writing, and the third in music. Nicholas constantly examined the boys himself in their various studies ; and he was also careful to train them for intercourse with the world, accustoming them to produce their knowledge on occasion, and to speak freely and easily. To this end they were constantly called upon to repeat what they had studied, aloud, before the rest of the family. "This practice brought the youths to deliver any speech with a becoming assurance, and not only taught them a graceful pronunciation, but inured them to express themselves handsomely and without affectation, when they spoke or wrote after such excellent copies of a chaste and clean style as Mr. Ferrar had set them. This made them men betimes, and even acquainted the women with the histories, ancient and modern. And thus a family sequestering itself from the world could not be thought to despise the world from want of understanding, for they knew

the past and present state of empires, and were more
learned in the great affairs of human life than many
that live in the throng of business, yet have little
insight into things, and less into themselves, notwithstanding the great scuffle in the dark which they are
ever engaged in, and never the wiser."[1] The
children of the neighbouring gentry were permitted
to share the teaching of the Gidding school, "where
they might learn virtue as well as grammar, music,
and arithmetic, together with fair writing;" and the
Ferrars also took charge of the sons of one or two
friends at a distance. A letter from Mrs. Collett to
her cousin, Mr. Arthur Woodnoth, in 1628, on
receiving his son Ralph into the house at Gidding,
shows the spirit of their training. From the allusion
at the end, it would seem that Mary Collett was to
have the care of Mr. Woodnoth's niece.

"DEAR COUSIN,

"I am glad we have received such a pledge
of you, whereby, though we cannot make requital, yet
we shall strive to make proof of that thankfulness and
love which we owe you for your care of ours. Believe
it, Ralph shall not want what lies in our power, and
as we shall truly love him with the selfsame kind of
affection which we do our own, so shall we endeavour
to train him in the selfsame dispositions of mind

---

[1] "Life of Nicholas Ferrar," by Dr. Jebb.

which we desire to see in ours, which although at beginning they will seem a little harsh, yet by practice they will grow easy, I doubt not, to him, and the end will be full of joy and comfort to himself and friends, which God grant. My brother hath told us of many new kindnesses (the fruit of your old love) towards my children, besides those to himself, which I esteem the first and chiefest; they be so many and great as passing the ordinary bounds of affection in you, one not with words to be requited on our parts; and therefore I say nothing, but that we owe you more in all this than we can pay, save in love. My daughter Mary hath not been well of late, but I hope in God she mends, and though we all hope to see you shortly, yet she prays me to write you. She hath with much joy embraced her uncle Nicholas's proposition, and though she cannot sufficiently answer your expectation touching your niece, yet she will not fail in the truth and height of affection towards her good, if you think fit. And so, with all our best prayers, I commit you to God." [1]

[1] Collett Letters. These letters were found in pulling down a house in Huntingdon. In 1855 they were in possession of the late Mr. Samuel Buckle, of Leamington, by whom they were lent for the use of the Rev. J. E. B. Mayor. I have been unable to ascertain where they now are, and have only been able to use those already printed by Mr. Mayor in the appendix to " Two Lives."

The Ferrars provided teaching for the poor as well as the gentry of the neighbourhood. Sunday schools were at that date an almost unknown institution ; but Nicholas Ferrar, mindful perhaps of those schools established by St. Charles Borromeo, which gathered (as they gather still) in the chapels of Milan Cathedral, invited the children from the surrounding parishes to come to Gidding every Sunday morning, and set his elder nieces to teach them to repeat the Psalter. As a penny was given for every psalm learnt by heart, and the children had dinner before going home, the new school became very popular, and the careful teaching and gentle care of the young ladies produced a great effect for the better on their little scholars. "Their parents, who were mostly plain country folks, were extremely pleased and obliged by it, and quickly, not only their parents, but the adjoining ministers, when they came to Gidding, protested that a mighty change was wrought, not only on the children, but on the men and women who sat hearing their children reading and repeating at home. And whereas heretofore their tongues were exercised in singing either naughty or lewd or else vain ballads, that much estranged their young minds from the ways of virtue, now they heard the streets and doors resounding with the sacred poetry of David's harp, which drove away the evil spirit from Saul."[1] Some of the parents

[1] "Life of Nicholas Ferrar," by Dr. Jebb.

begged that their children might be taught the Catechism as well as the Psalter, but this Nicholas Ferrar refused to allow.   He told them that " bringing children to learn their Psalter was a thing by itself, but catechising belonged to their minister and their parents," adding that "by doing something good in appearance, one might do very ill by encroaching on other men's offices, and that they should have a special care of this fine-trimmed and hidden snare which the devil every where lays in the way of well-meaning people.   When he cannot persuade them to ugly known sin, then he tempts them to do some handsome thing which it is not their parts to act, but presumption for them to do it "—a sound principle, though it may appear somewhat overstrained in its application.

The house at Gidding was well known to the poor of the neighbourhood for its charities as well as its teaching   Its inmates visited and comforted the sick and poor in their own homes, and Nicholas used his medical knowledge for the instruction of his nieces, teaching them to dress wounds and prepare salves and balsams, "all which being as freely given by them to the poor as themselves freely received them all from God and their kind uncle, they were sure not to want customers, which every year cost them a good round sum.   None of them were nice of dressing with their own hands poor people's wounds, were they never so offensive; but as for prescribing physic, their uncle understood it well himself, yet he never practised it, and he forbade them to tamper or meddle with it. And together with helps for the body, the virgins were expert and ready to administer good counsels, prayers, and comforts to their patients, for their souls' health." [1]

The large family of girls had many occupations. "A mean in all things," Ferrar was wont to say, "was the only way with good order to effect great things with ease and delight," and he laid great stress on a constant interchange of employments. The four elder nieces took charge of the housekeeping. All were taught embroidery [2] as well as household needlework, and music also was much studied. Mr. and Mrs. Ferrar had all their children taught music carefully, and Mrs. Collett played admirably on the lute. The young people no doubt inherited the taste of their parents, and they were diligent in the practice of singing and playing on various instruments. "Fair writing" was also made a great point of, not only the ordinary current hand, but a delicate and beautiful kind of writing, a survival of the days before

---

[1] "Life of Nicholas Ferrar," by Dr. Jebb.

[2] A small piece of tapestry, the work of one of the sisters, still preserved in Gidding Church, where it is used as a kneeling-mat, is so exquisitely fine and delicate, that a facsimile embroidered by Mr. Hopkinson's niece, cost that lady six months of diligent and patient labour.

printing, used in formal writings and in copying books, which, according to a curious fashion very prevalent in the seventeenth century, were often circulated for years in manuscript before their authors made them over to the printer. To add variety to their occupations, Ferrar also had his nieces taught bookbinding. The daughter of a Cambridge bookbinder lived in the house for a year to give the young ladies lessons in binding and gilding, and he himself also acquired the art, with which he had probably gained some acquaintance while living in Germany.

But the characteristic works of Gidding were the Harmonies or Concordances. The first of these was undertaken entirely for their own use, and but for the interest and admiration it excited, it might have remained the only specimen. It was a " Harmony of the Four Gospels," so arranged that the four books could be read either separately or in one continuous history, the printed text being cut out and pasted on large sheets of paper, and every page illustrated with engravings.

This first book was finished in 1630. It was followed by many others, several of which may still be seen.[1] So ingeniously and delicately are the printed slips of paper, some of which are very small, united

---

[1] A descriptive list of such of these works as are known to be still in existence, was published by Captain Acland in the *Archæologia*, 1888, vol. ii. See Chap. VIII.

together, that at first sight the pages might be supposed to be printed in the ordinary way. The headings are written in a fine clear hand, and the pages surrounded with ruled lines, generally in red ink. The books are usually richly bound by the hands of the ladies of Gidding, and each has a short preface, with the name of Gidding, and the date of the year, but only one has the name of its maker. This is a " Harmony of the Four Gospels," bound in leather and illustrated, now in the possession of the Bishop of Bath and Wells. It originally belonged to Thomas Harvey, who married the daughter of Sir Thomas May, vice-chancellor to Charles I., and has always remained in the Harvey family. At the end of the preface to this book is written—

" Thanks be to God.
" Done at Little Gidding, Anno Domini 1640, by Virginia
Ferrar, an. 12."

It is easy to imagine the pride and pleasure with which the little girl's work was contemplated by the elders of the house, and how John Ferrar, who has never a word for his own labours, could not refrain from inscribing his daughter's name in the great book before sending it to Mr. Harvey.

In the midst of all their occupations, time was set apart for recreation. On Thursday and Saturday afternoons the young people were allowed to amuse themselves with "running and vaulting and shooting

at butts with bows and arrows."   Their elders, though
they kept up some acquaintance with the neighbouring families, and received courteously any visitors
who chose to come, made it known from the first
that they had settled at Gidding for retirement, and
avoided all visits of ceremony and the social gather-
ings of the county gentry.

Thus the weeks passed in a grave and cheerful
monotony marked only by recurring Sundays.

> " Thou art a day of mirth ;
> And where the week days trail on ground
> Thy flight is higher, as thy birth.''

Then the lesson-books were closed, and the busy
hands rested.   They rose on Sunday at the same hour
as in the week, but after the early morning office they
-retired again to their own rooms, and remained in
privacy till nine o'clock, when the bell called them
to Matins.   Having sung a hymn together in the
great chamber, they went, as on week days, in procession to the church, all dressed carefully in their
best clothes ; and after the service, which was read by
Nicholas, they returned to find the " Psalm-children "
awaiting them.   The time till half-past ten was spent
in instructing them, or hearing them repeat their
former lessons, and at that hour the Vicar of Steeple
Gidding, having already said Matins in his own
church, arrived accompanied by his parishioners, who
apparently followed him straight from the church door,

a pleasant quarter-of-an-hour's walk across the fields. The Little Gidding family, bringing with them the Psalm-children, met him at the church, and Nicholas Ferrar read the ante-Communion Service. At its close a psalm was sung, and then the vicar preached. Once a month, and on great festivals, the Holy Communion was celebrated.[1]

On returning from church their first care was for the Psalm-children. A long narrow table supported on trestles was laid in some convenient place, round which the children stood expectant, while Mrs. Ferrar with her own hands set the first dish on the table, the servants following. When grace had been said for the children, the old lady and her family went to their own dinner, leaving only one or two to superintend the Psalm-children, who, when they had finished their

[1] It need not be supposed, because the Holy Communion was celebrated after Matins, according to the usual custom of the time, that this devout family failed to keep the ancient rule of fasting Communion. Shelford, writing in 1635, puts among the preparations for the Sacrament " to come fasting when men are able," quoting St. Augustine's saying that " it pleaseth the Holy Ghost that, in honour of so great a sacrament, the Lord's body should first enter into the mouth of a Christian."—" Five Discourses."

Dinner was usually at eleven or twelve, and the early breakfast now universal appears to have been considered rather as a luxury than a necessity. Lessius, author of a book on temperance, translated by Nicholas Ferrar, speaks of those who "provide breakfast betimes in the morning " as " miserably beguiled."

K

meal, were sent home to go with their parents to their own parish churches.

When the family had dined they went to their own rooms, or refreshed themselves with a quiet walk in the gardens and orchards as they pleased, and at two o'clock all met together again and went to Steeple Gidding church for Evensong. On Sunday the private offices were not said at the usual hours, but all together on returning from evening service, after which the remainder of the day was given up to rest and recreation. The servants of the house were carefully considered. Nicholas Ferrar " so ordered that what was for dinner should all be performed with the least and speediest loss of time as might be ; that was, by causing ovens to be heated, and all the dinner to be set into them before church-time, and so all the servants were ready to go to church, not any left at home. And for supper, church ended in the evening, then the spits were laid for meat to be roasted at the fire. And one thing else beside will not be amiss to be recounted concerning the servants. It was the custom of that family that, having a Communion the first Sunday of each month throughout the year (besides the great festival times, Christmas, New Year's Day, Easter, and Whitsuntide), they stood at lower end of the board where the old gentlewoman sat, and there they dined that day." [1]

[1] " Life of Nicholas Ferrar," by his brother.

This peaceful and useful life flowed on unbroken till Gidding Hall was plundered by Parliamentary soldiers in 1646, and was resumed when the surviving members of the family ventured back to their ravaged home. The monthly thanksgiving instituted by Nicholas Ferrar in 1625, of which a few clauses here follow, was continued until John's death in 1657,[1] if not longer.

"Thou hast given us a freedom from all other affairs that we may without distraction attend Thy service. . . . That holy gospel which came down from heaven, with things the angels desire to look into, is by Thy goodness continually open to our view; the sweet music thereof is continually sounding in our ears; heavenly songs are by Thy mercy put into our mouths, and our tongues and lips made daily instruments of pouring forth Thy praise. This, Lord, is the work, and this the pleasure, of the angels in heaven; and dost Thou vouchsafe to make us partakers of so high a happiness? The knowledge of Thee and of Thy Son is everlasting life. Thy service is perfect freedom; how happy, then, are we, that Thou dost constantly retain us in the daily exercises thereof!"

[1] "Two Lives of Ferrar," by Rev. J. E. B. Mayor, Appendix.

CHAPTER VI.

"O happy you, that have subdued
The force o' the world's desire !
And in th' fort of solitude
For safety do retire.

"You fled from freedom so supposed
In straitness freedom find,
Because true freedom is enclosed
I' the circuit of the mind."
Song by the "Submiss," "Gidding Conversation Book."

THE house, strictly ordered as it was, was bright with youth and movement. The hours passed evenly, full of cheerful work, measured by ringing of bells, and organ music, and the continual recitation of psalms. The life set to these grave melodies was an active life; the younger members of the family coming and going, carrying the result of their devout training into the world outside, and bringing new joys and wider interests to the old home; in some cases throwing off the restraints which had wearied them, and causing anxiety and heartache to the loving friends who watched and prayed for them in the great chamber and the church hard by.

Nicholas Ferrar took the keenest interest in all these young people, and towards the Colletts he acted the part of a father. Mr. Collett must have been a man of singularly passive, not to say apathetic, temperament, for he seems to have taken no trouble at all about the disposal of his children. Every arrangement was made by his energetic wife, under the advice of her brother.

When the eldest son, Thomas, is about to marry, it is Nicholas who goes up to town to see about the affair. Mrs. Collett writes to her aunt in February, 1628—

" I suppose you may have expected to have heard from me upon occasion of the late business touching my son ; and indeed I had performed it, but that answering my son's letters every week hath taken up that space of time which the carrier affords us between the delivery of his letters and the calling for an answer. And now my brother Nicholas being to come up, I think it superfluous, for he is able and hath full authority to give satisfaction in all things, and if my son cheerfully submit his judgment and affections to his directions, I shall not doubt of a happy issue." [1]

[1] Mrs. Collett to her aunt Collett, February, 1628.—Appendix, " Two Lives."

Some time in this same year, 1628, Susanna, the third daughter, married the Reverend Joshua Mapletoft, and settled at Margetting, or Margaretting, in Essex. From this time Mrs. Collett's letters are full of the interests of the young home. She often visited Margetting, and during her absence Nicholas kept her fully acquainted with all that went on at Gidding. He certainly did not deserve the reproach often cast on him in later years, of wishing to make nuns of all his nieces ; on the contrary, he seems to have been most desirous of getting them well married. His efforts in this direction were not always judicious, and the anxious mother, in the midst of her cares for young Mrs. Mapletoft, appears to have been cruelly divided between habitual submission to his judgment and a very natural doubt whether he were really qualified to settle such important and delicate matters. The following letter explains itself.

[Mrs. Collett to Nicholas Ferrar.]

"Margetting, August, 1629.

"I applaud it as most judiciously resolved on neither to send for Hester nor offer two to the choice.[1] For the other part of your letter, I can say

[1] To what this refers is not explained, but apparently it had been proposed by somebody that two of Mr. Collett's daughters should be offered to the choice of some eligible suitor. It appears to have been not unusual in that time, when marriages

little to it, only I will persuade myself, since you have done it (and with such consent), that you are able to show better reasons for it than my present apprehensions are capable of; and as my continual prayers shall be that all may prove for the best, so shall my hopes be that it will. Let this, I beseech you, satisfy for answer to that which is past, and for the future I would have said nothing, had not you likewise desired my opinion, but left it to yourself and my dearest friends with you, both to consider and determine of, as those whose judgments are not by me to be questioned, and whose love to me and mine I am most confident cannot be paralleled by any in the like kind. Give me leave only to say, that such is my affection to my dear Anna, that it would be most heavy to me to see her bestowed on any man that did not willingly, nay, most *desirously*, make choice of her. But doubting neither of your love nor wisdom, I dare leave it to God and yourselves to proceed in or suppress the motion as you shall think fittest, and God, I trust, shall direct you." [1]

As far as Anna was concerned, these cares were needless. Another aim was shaping itself in her mind—an aim which could be best fulfilled within the walls of Gidding. It would appear that her elder

were arranged chiefly by parents, for the lady's family to take the first step.

[1] Appendix, "Two Lives."

sister, Mary, who had lived with the Ferrars from infancy, had long shared her uncle's aspirations, and had dedicated herself, if the expression may be allowed, to the Religious Life from the first days of the settlement at Gidding. She was then twenty-three years old, and Anna twenty-one. If we may judge from the reliance which the elder members of her family evidently placed on her, Mary must have inherited much of the strength of character, the calm sweetness and discretion, which distinguished her grandmother.

She would naturally have had much influence with her younger sister, the more so, perhaps, that they were not brought up together, and that Anna came freshly, at an impressionable and thoughtful age, under the spell of her earnestness and the high enthusiasm of their uncle Nicholas, of whom she could have seen but little since the time when, in her early childhood, he had been accustomed to come over from Cambridge to spend a few days of rest and recreation in her father's house at Bourne.

Among the Ferrar manuscripts lately brought to light in the Library of Magdalene College, Cambridge, there are letters from Anna to her uncle, from which, by the kindness of the authorities of the college, a few extracts are permitted to appear here.[1]

---

[1] These manuscripts, left by Peckard to the college, were lost sight of for many years. It may be hoped that, when fully

These letters show a deep religious spirit, and many of them are evidently answers to letters of advice and instruction from Nicholas Ferrar. In the winter of 1629, she paid a long visit to Mrs. Mapletoft, and writes from Margetting, January 27—

" To the worshipful Nicholas Ferrar, my most dear Uncle, these.

" MY MOST DEAR AND HONOURED UNCLE,

" Or rather may I tytel you my tender father, . . . for your care hath not rested only in providing a temporal portion, but it hath reached for the procuring for mee an eternal habitation, by your often instructions of mee in the way of holinesse."

In March, 1630, Nicholas himself went to Margetting, and Anna writes to him from Gidding, addressing him as—

" My dear father and soules instructor," asking his help " to stir up my frozen mind . . . to performe this work which is every moment due from mee," and asks his prayers " that I may in some measure be accounted worthy of that fountain of living water that floweth to every one that thirsteth, and that without Price."

From Margetting Nicholas seems to have gone to

examined and catalogued, they will throw much fresh light on the history of Gidding.

London, and while he is there Anna writes, expressing her thankfulness to God for having not only delivered her from fears, but also granted her " joy and comfort more than I could wish or desire, whilst I behold your exuberante love to mee. But whereas you are pleased, dear father, to engadge yourself to performe your . . . to me by deserte, I must wholly renounce it from myself and wholly attribute it to God, and your owne free love, whatever Benefit I have or doe receive."

" P.S.—I beseech you, dear Unckel, remember my duty to my Aunt Collett. My sisters' and owne best love to our Deare Cosin Arthur." [1]

Anna seems to have thought over her vocation for some time before taking a decisive step, and Nicholas was not likely to encourage a hasty resolution on a matter of such grave importance. It was not till September, 1631, she being then in her twenty-seventh year, that she wrote the letter from which the subjoined extracts are taken. It is in "fair writing," which, indeed, she frequently uses in her correspondence with her uncle, and is endorsed (by Peckard ?) "Anna Collett to her father," but the note which accompanied it shows that it was really addressed to Nicholas.

[1] Mr. Woodnoth.

"September 22 [1631].

"My most dear and honoured Father,

(The letter begins by stating that the writer thinks it needless to repeat what she has said previously as to her wishes) "Which, if not deceived in mine owne heart, were and are still at present my earnest wishes, but I rest on God and you, my dear father, for the accomplishment of them when and how He pleaseth.

"Touching my condission of life, such content do I find, I neither wish or desire any change in it; but as God may please, with my Parents' leave, to give me grace and strength, that I may spend the remainder of my days without greater encumbrances of this worlde, which doe of necessitie accompany a married Estate;

"But dare not trust my own judgement in this waity matter; but first beseech you, dear father, to let me know your opinion of it and counsel according to your faithful love." She goes on to answer some questions as to her fortune, expressing a wish for "if God so please, such a portion as may be helpful to others."

This letter is signed "Anna Collett."

Anna still shrank from making known her resolution to her family, feeling perhaps the natural dread of hearing her deepest and most sacred desires made a subject of discussion and questioning.[1]　It was not till a month later that she summoned up courage to let her uncle have the letter, and she then sent it to him by the hands of her sister Mary, together with a little note, addressed—

"The Worshipful Nicholas Ferrar, our much honoured father, this.

"MY DEAR AND HONOURED FATHER,

　　　"It hath not only brought me delay [illegible].　To my dear and worthy sister Mary my Futyer love and thanks are ever obleiged to her for the true and loving affection herein expressed to mee.

　　"Your bounden obedient daughter,

　　　　　　　"ANNA COLLETT."

"October, 22, 1631."

On this note is written, evidently by Nicholas Ferrar—

"This letter, together with the declaration of her choice, Anna gave her sister for me, to read them in her presence."

On the declaration itself, in the same hand, is written—

---

[1] Mrs. Collett was in much distress at this time owing to the misconduct of her son Edward.　This may have been the reason for postponing the mention of her own wishes.

"This enclosed declaration, Anna desired her sister Mary to give mee on Saturday, the 22nd October, but I willed her to lay it by till this present 23rd, in the afternoon, when I read it in Mary's presence ; only I willed her, and not by word but by writing, to show to her Grandmother and Unkle Ferrar, and so [words illegible]. But without any speed."

There is among the Magdalene manuscripts another paper, a fragment without date, signature, or endorsement, which, if the writing be Anna's, would appear to have been written subsequently to the letter given above. It is as follows :—

"I.H.S.

"In the Name of God. Amen.

"Mine honoured Parents and dearest friends, that I may not be wanting in what I am able to performe, I beseech you accept of my humblest thanks, which I tender to you, for it hath pleased you freely to give me your love and consents to that I have soe much desyred both from God and from you—that is, that I may end my days in a Virgin Estate. And this desyre, I hope, hath been of and from God, although mixed with much corruption ; and further beseech that none would judge it to proceede either of persuasion by any one to it, or contempt of the Estate of Marriage, or to think it inferior to that which I

choose, for I here professe in the sight of Heven that
the choice be freely my own, not any . . . further
than their leave ; nor out of contempt for that of
Marriage, for . . . honour it, but have not the herte
. . . myne own choice, wherefore . . ."

The lower corner of the paper is scorched, and the
second sheet, on which the signature would have
been, torn away.   It is in a hand much resembling
Anna's ordinary writing, but larger and more rambling,
and until the manuscripts have been fully examined,
and the handwritings compared by some qualified
judge, it must remain doubtful whether this is
Anna's final declaration, or if, as the writer ventures
to think, we have here the act of dedication of her
sister Mary.   In either case, a deep interest attaches
to this piece of torn paper in which across the gulf
of two hundred years the " maiden sisters of Gidding "
hold out their hands to the growing company who
in happier times and with fuller completeness have
given themselves to the Religious Life in these days
of its revival.

A letter from Anna Collett to her parents, also in
the Magdalene collection, seems to belong to this
time, though it has no date of year.   It is apparently
written at some time anterior to the declaration given
to her uncle, in answer to a permission to decline
some project of marriage, and an assurance of provision for her in a single life.

"In the Name of God. Amen.

"Therefore, as I have your consents to be freed from it, soe I humbly abide in prayer that I may continue soe in my desires, and that blessings may rest on mee . . . thereby, for that Lardgeness of Estate which you, my dear friends, are pleased to bestow on mee, I acknowledge it to be not only above my deserts, but even my desires; I durst not expect so great a favour, and being so given me leave to make Brother a partaker of it, I esteem it a singular blessing of God, and pledge of your great love to mee, that I have leave for to pro . . . it with such gayne as I wish was greater. For this and all other . . . from God and you, I humbly prayse His holy name, and pray ever to approve myselfe

"Your most obedient and faithful

"ANNA COLLETT."

(Endorsed, "Anna Collett to her Parents. July.")

That Mary and Anna Collett considered themselves absolutely pledged to a single life there can be no doubt. One of their sisters speaks of "the virgin estate, whereof our chief hath made profession," and Nicholas Ferrar, in 1634, in answer to an inquiry about the "nuns" of Gidding, replied that "the name of nuns was odious," but that "two of his nieces had lived, one thirty, the other thirty-two years, virgins; and so resolved to continue, as he hoped they would, the better to give themselves to fasting and prayer, but had made no vows." [1]   This last statement must be understood to apply to formal vows.

Whether they desired to seal their resolution by such a vow is a difficult question, as we have on this point two different and contradictory statements. Hacket, in his account of Bishop Williams' visit to Gidding in 1634, of which more will be said farther on, after warm praise of the devout life of the family, goes on to add that " nothing is so sound but in time it will run into corruption. For I must not hold it in, that some persons in Little Gidding had run into excess and incurred offence, if the bishop had not broken the snare which they were preparing for their own feet. For after he had spoken well of the family in the pulpit, and privately to divers, some of them could not see when they were well, but aspired to be transcendants above their measure. For two daughters of the stock came to the bishop, and offered themselves to be veiled virgins, to take upon them the vow of perpetual chastity, with the solemnity of the episcopal blessing and ratification, whom he admonished very fatherly, that they knew not what they went about. That they had no promise to confirm that grace unto them ; that this readiness, which they had in the present, should be in their will, without repentance, unto their life's end. Let the younger

[1] Lenton's Letter.

women marry, was the best advice, that they might not be led into temptation. And that they might not forget what he taught them, he drew up his judgement in three sheets of paper, and sent it them home that they might dress themselves by that glass, and learn not to think of human nature above that which it is, a sea of flowings and ebbings, and of all manner of inconstancy." [1]

Dr. Jebb, on the contrary, says that "when their reverend diocesan had declared himself, without anybody's seeking to him, ready to accept a vow (not absolute and unconditional, as it were, in spite of heaven and hell, but)—a vow of sincere endeavour, if God should continue to them the grace, in a single state to withstand the temptations of the world, the flesh, and the devil, the foremost of them all in any of their generous and religious undertakings was not forward to take any such engagement upon her, but kept the middle way between vowing and slackness, arriving at that which St. Paul calls steadfastness of heart, and power over her own will." [2]

Of these opposite accounts Hacket's would seem, from the characters of the persons concerned, the most likely to be true, and it also bears more clearly

[1] Hacket, "Life of Archbishop Williams," part ii. p. 52.

[2] "Life of Nicholas Ferrar," by Dr. Jebb, p. 66. The manuscript "Life" by Bishop Turner omits all mention of the circumstance.

the stamp of personal acquaintance with the matter; Jebb's account appearing to be founded, not on John Ferrar's narrative, in which no mention is made of the proposal, but on recollections which he had gathered from various sources, and which he adds to his "Life" as a kind of appendix. His further statement, that Ferrar in some of his papers declared himself against vows of single life, is difficult to reconcile with the generally received impression among his personal friends that he had himself made such a vow, as well as with the solemn resolutions which he unquestionably sanctioned in his nieces.[1]

Anna and Mary Collett lived on like the veiled virgins of early Christian ages[2] in the house of their

---

[1] "Mary and Anna ——, who had both steadfastly, by the help of God, taken long ago resolutions of living in virginity."—"Life of Nicholas Ferrar," by his brother.

[2] "First in rank and responsibility stood the deaconess, . . . next to the deaconess were the consecrated virgins, who had been solemnly blessed by the bishop during the celebration of the Holy Eucharist, and had received the consecrated veil from his hands. . . . The third class of the virgins consisted of those who, though living to some extent in the world, yet by the adoption of a dark and simple dress, the practice of certain devotions, and the profession of a vow of celibacy, had placed themselves in relation with the members of the two higher ranks. . . . The circumstances of the first Christian ages did not admit of establishing convents for women, . . . and the deaconesses, the veiled virgins, and the professed, necessarily resided in their own homes."—"Religious Communities of Women in the Early

parents and kinsfolk, and their young sisters gathered round them, sharing in their rule of prayer and work, till each in succession passed from Gidding to a home of her own. At first the girls were under the special charge of their grandmother, but in 1632 Mrs. Ferrar, though still active both in mind and body, felt that the daily supervision of so many young people was a burden too heavy for her declining years. She resigned her post, and on St. Luke's day in that year her granddaughter, Mary Collett, was chosen to replace her.

Mrs. Ferrar had formed the sisters into a little society, which assumed the name of "Academy;" the members took the names of different virtues, thus turning a fantastic fashion of the day into what was no doubt meant as a continual reminder of the special grace which each should strive to attain. The "Academy" was composed of two "combinations." Mary Collett was "Chief" of the first "combination," and with her were associated Anna, under the name of "the Patient," and two other sisters, probably Hester and Margaret, who were respectively called "the Cheerful" and "the Affectionate." The "second combination" consisted of the younger girls and children down to little three-years-old Ann Mapletoft, who bore the name of "the Humble."

Church," reprinted from the *Ecclesiastic*, and understood to be written by the late Dr. Littledale.

Nicholas Ferrar was the " Visitor" of this so-called Academy; John Ferrar, "Guardian;" and Mrs. Collett, " Moderator."

They held frequent meetings for the discussion of subjects chosen by the " Visitor."   Nicholas Ferrar seems to have supplied much of the matter for these discussions, or "Conversations," as they were called, which the speakers themselves put into shape, their speeches being sometimes read, sometimes extempore or repeated by heart.

The plan of these "Conversations" reminds us somewhat of the Oratorian method, and gives reason to think that Ferrar must have sometimes, during his stay in Italy, attended the exercises of the Fathers of the Oratory in Padua, or elsewhere.   The members spoke in turn, expressing their opinion apparently with some freedom.   Appropriate hymns were sung (of which those that have come down to us are singularly unmelodious), and stories told from history, ancient and modern, or the lives of the saints, illustrating the truth which the discussion was intended to bring out.   These stories were often prepared beforehand, but sometimes told on the spur of the moment, as we learn from a little incident which has been preserved.

The young people were assembled as usual in the "sisters' chamber," and had made their set speeches on the virtue of meekness, which was the appointed topic of the day, when the " Moderator," Mrs. Collett, asked for an example of this virtue, so specially needful in their sex. None was in readiness, and in the pause which ensued, one of the younger girls, who had as yet taken no part in the debates, looked eagerly up, evidently longing to say something, yet not daring to speak till she had obtained permission.

" The ' Submiss ' countenance," said the " Chief " (Mary Collett), "seems to mine eye to promise satisfaction of your desires."

" I am much troubled," says the kindly "Guardian," " that both she and the 'Obedient' have been so long left out. In regard the first attempt cannot be so perfect; let them have the liberty for a while of telling their stories as they can." And so the little "Submiss" makes her first speech in the Academy, with a beating heart no doubt, and much shy delight. A great number of these " Conversations " were written down, revised, and preserved in the family. Copies of many of them were made about the year 1735, by Francis Peck, Rector of Godeby, author of an unprinted life of Nicholas Ferrar mentioned by Peckard,[1] and fragments were printed by Hearne, and

---

[1] The manuscript was lent by Peckard, into whose hands it came, to Mr. Jones, and by him lost. Peck's copy of some part of the Conversations is still in existence. See "Two Lives," Appendix, p. 294.

subsequently (from Peck's copy) by the Rev. J. B. Mayor.[1]

The originals, which are stated in a note left by Peck,[2] to have been at that time "at Mr. Mapletoft's at Bifield, near Daintry, in Northamptonshire," disappeared from public view for many years, but they were carefully treasured and reverently handed down by successive representatives of their original owner, Susannah Mapletoft. Their last possessor was Mrs. Hodges, of Tiverton, Devon, who inherited them from a cousin, Miss Ann Mapletoft. On Mrs. Hodges's death in April, 1888, they passed together with a Concordance and some other family relics,[3] to Mr. Mapletoft Davis, a gentleman residing in New South Wales; and in that far-off land these curious and interesting volumes find their present resting-place.

Before they were sent from England, copies of part of the first volume of "Conversations" (there are four),[4] and of the entries in the Concordance, were

---

[1] "Two Lives of Ferrar," Appendix.

[2] Ibid., p. 301.

[3] Among these relics is a cabinet said to have been given to the family by Charles I., and a lawn handkerchief marked "C. R." in gold thread. The Concordance is described Chap. VIII. II.

[4] In Peck's list of the papers at Bifield only three "Conversation" books are mentioned. In one of the four belonging to Mr. Mapletoft Davis is the following note: "N.B.—This No. 3 is a copy of the first part of No. 2, Elizabeth Kestian, given me by my dear aunt Legatt" (Margaret Collett married Thomas Legatt,

made by Mrs. Hodges' great-niece, Miss Cruwys Sharland, who with great and ready kindness has placed them at the disposal of the writer. Prefixed to the first volume are four letters, of which the first has already been printed by Hearne,[1] and the last by Peckard.[2] The second and third have never before appeared. They are here given in their proper order.

The first is addressed to Mrs. Ferrar by her two elder granddaughters.

"MOST DEARE AND HONOURED GRANDMOTHER,

"The finishing of this book in the return of the selfsame Festival in which it began, having amongst many other considerations brought to remembrance the love you that day showed in Bestowing ye Best of yor Roomes and Furniture upon us, for the performance of this and other good excercises, hath made us judge, that the first fruits of our labours in every kind, are due to you, by whose bounty we have received the opportunity of beginning and continuing in them. We most humbly beseech you therefore favourably to accept now in writing, that

she is especially mentioned in old Mrs. Ferrar's will); "I desier it to be given to my dear cosen Dr. John Mapletoft."

[1] "Caii Vindiciæ," p. 782.

[2] Peckard incorrectly states that it was sent to Mrs. Mapletoft with a Concordance.

which you so favourably was pleased to approve in the rehearsing; and together with it, our Faithful acknowledgement, that we owe to you, as the great instrument of God's mercy, not only the conveniency and opportunitie, but even y⁰ very abilities in themselves that are in us, towards the performance of this or any other good thing. Considering that the Vacancie of Time, the Means of Instruction, and all other necessary concurrent helps have had their prime and daily Rise from and by means of your Love; and on your Love and Life do at this present mainly depend. Besides, for that whereunto this Excercise is chiefly intended, the discovery of those false opinions wherewith the world misleads all mankind, especially our weaker sex, we have received both by your precept and example, if not the greatest and weightiest, yet surely the most proper and effectual arguments and motives that could have been brought. You have forsaken all those Affections, Imployments, and Delights, wherein the world perswades the chief content of Women's minds should lie and you have censured them as *vanities* at the best, as sins, and great ones, as they are commonly pursued. You have taught us often that which we hope shall ever remain as firm written in our Minds as in this book, *that there is nothing but the practise of Virtue and Religion that can in the end yield comfort; all other things will turn to Bitterness at the last.* We know your Experience hath been more large and full than most others in these matters ; and therefore cannot but beleive your Judgment to be right, and upon this ground have been the rather encouraged to the contempt of that which is indeed contemptible, and to the endeavouring after those things which are alone worthy of Love and Honour.

"We are bold, dear Grandmother, to refresh these things upon this occasion, the rather as it were by the recording thereof to oblige ourselves to the following both of your example and advice, the benefits whereof in the continuance of your life wee most humbly beseech God of His infinite mercy to continue to us and to your whole Family.

" Your most bounden daughters,

" The Sisters,

" MARY & ANNA COLLET.

" 2 Februarie, 1631."[1]

Next comes Mrs. Ferrars's reply.

" MY DEARE CHILDREN,

" What I have taught is true.   Use carefully therefore now and ever y^o time and Opportunities y^t God offers for ye attainement of wisedome and encrease of Vertue.   As for matters of Huswifery,

[1] 1631-32.

when God puts them upon you, it would be sin either
to refuse them, or to perform them negligently, and
therefore the ignorance of them is a great shame and
Danger for women that intend Marriage. But to
seek these kinds of Businesses for pleasure, and to
make them yor delights, and to pride yo^rselves for
yor care and curiositie in them, is a great vanitie and
Folly at ye best, and to neglect better things and
more necessarie by pretence of being imployed in
these things, is surely, though a common Practise,
yet a peice of sinfull Hypocrisie. Doe them therefore, when God puts them upon you, and doe them
carefully and well, and God shall reward you, however ye things themselves be but meane, accepting
them at yor hands, as if they were greater matters,
when they are done and undergone out of obedience
to his Command. But let yor Delight bee onely in
ye better part. As for yor Book, I kindly accept it;
and although I have heard you very Jealously deny
the Communicating it with any, yet because I suppose
you esteeme yor Sister Mapletoft all one with yor-
selves, I would have you send her this Book, which
I doubt not will bee both of Profit and Comfort to
her. God continue and encrease you in every good
way and thing, till you come to Perfection in Christ
Jesus.

"Yo^r Mother,

"MARY FARRAR."

The two following letters are addressed to Mrs. Mapletoft :—

"To our dearest Sister,

"With the same love y* is given by our most Honoured Grandmother, doe wee make y* Conveyance of this Book unto you, our Dearest Sister, Professing faithfully, y* wee esteeme our Paines as well Imployed in thus parting with it to you, as wee should have done in keeping it for ourselves, so much doe wee love and praise the Grace of God y* is in you, and the Gracious Benediction of God which wee have received by yo* meanes, a most worthy and Faithful Brother, to whose good judgment wee doe freely submitt this Little work, Beseeching him to give us Notice of what hee shall there find amisse. And so beseeching God to perfecte his goodnes in you by y* full Restitution both of Inward and Bodily Health wee rest

"Your Faithfull
"Sisters,
"Mary and Anna Collet.

"2 Februarie, 1631."

(The following note [1] is appended in another hand : "Who both dyed Virgins, Resolving so to live when

---

[1] This note is given by Mr. Mayor, Appendix, p. 301.

they were young, by the grace of God.   My much
honoured Aunt Mary, who took care of me and
my Brother Peter and Sister Mary after the death of
our Reverend and pious Father, Mr. Joshua Mapletoft, dyed in y* 80th year of her age.

" JOHN MAPLETOFT.

"Jan. 22, 1715.")

" MY DEARE AND WORTHY NEICE,

  " The Equall joy and Benefitt w^h I have in
and by you, make mee as gladly give you my part,
as yor Sisters have done theirs of this Book, and to
add my further promise, which their joynt consent
doth ratifie, that of every good thing y^t God shall
impart to us, y^u shall ever have as liberall and free a
Communication, as wee can possibly make you.
Which not onely our love but your own desert binds
us to whilest you continue what y^u are by the performance of yor Duty, ye great comfort and Ornament
to our Familie.   God make you to encrease in all
his graces and blessings.   Amen.

" Yo^r Unkle,

" NICHOLAS FERRAR."

The touching inscription in the beginning of the
book shows that it was left by Mrs. Mapletoft to her
eldest brother, Thomas Collett, and was given by him
to his son John ; it is as follows :—

> " JOHANNES COLLET
> Filius
> THOMAE COLLET
> Pater
> Thomas, Gulielmi, & Johannis,
> Omnium Superstes
> Natus
> Quarto Junii 1633,
> Denasciturus
> Quando DEO visum fuerit,
> Interim hujus proprietarius
> John Collet. "

The childless man left the treasured volume to his cousin Elizabeth, the daughter of Hester Collett and Francis Kestian, and below his signature is a note presumably in her writing.

" Elizabeth Kestian. Given me by my dear cosen John Collet. I desier it to be given to my dear cosen Dr. John Mapletoft."

Her wish was carried out, for after Nicholas Ferrar's letter to his niece follows a note by Dr. Mapletoft.

" This book was presented by my Great Grandmother, my honoured Mother's two Sisters (the daughters of John and Susannah Collet) and their Unkle Nicholas Farrar to my ever honoured Mother, Susanna Mapletoft, the same year in which I was born. And I desire my Son, to whom I do give it, with the great Concordance and the other story Books, that they may be preserved in the family as long as may be.

" JOHN MAPLETOFT.

" Jan. 23, 1715."

Dr. Mapletoft died in 1720, and Mr. Mapletoft, of Bifield, in whose hands the books were when Peck wrote in 1735, was probably his son.

The book opens with an account of the origin of the "Conversations" and the uses which they were intended to serve.

"It was at the same time when the Church celebrates the great festival of the Purification, that the maiden sisters, longing to be imitators of those glorious Saints by whose names they were called (for all bore Saints names, and she that was elected Chief, that of the blessed Virgin Mary, having entered into a joint covenant between themselves and some others of nearest blood, which, according to their several relations, they stiled Founder, Guardian, and Visitor, for the performance of divers religious exercises, lest— as sweet liquors are often times corrupted by the sourness of the vessels wherein they are infused— there should arise in their hearts a distaste or abuse, of those excellent things which they purposed), they therefore resolved, together with the practice of devotion, to intermingle the study of wisdom, searching and enquiring into those things which appertain to their condition and sex : finding in themselves and observing in others that do sincerely pursue virtue, that the greatest bar of perfection was ignorance of the truth, whereby through misapprehension, many prejudicial things were embraced, and many most behoveful to their ends, and most delightful in performance, were not only neglected, but abhorred."

The stress laid by Nicholas Ferrar on mental cultivation as a needful aid to devotion, is noteworthy. With this object, they agreed "every day at a sett houre to conferre together of some such subject, as should tend either to ye information of ye understanding, or to ye exciting of ye Affections, to ye more ready and fervent prosecution of vertues, and better performance of all such duties, as in their present or other Course of Life hereafter should be required of them."

Some of the discussions are very interesting, from the light they throw on the manners and ways of thought of the family. Thus, when Mrs. Collett has related the story of John the Almoner, showing "y^t hee that sows Almes on earth shall reape Treasures in Heaven," John Ferrar, in reply, denounces the folly of those who spend their substance on themselves, and who, at the Day of Judgment, must either "stand silent or, at best, show forth hounds and horses, and Idle droanes fatt crammed with continuall surfetts in the Hall, when ye question shall bee of feeding ye hungry. Will ye bringing forth of Liveries for Pages and footmen, and costly hangings for ye very walls, or ye dayly visits of ladies and great men bee accepted for answers touching ye clothing of ye Naked, and visiting ye sick? I need not goe over y^e

other particulars; you know what GOD will ask, you
see what men can say.   If you venter yo'selves upon
such answeares with them, so will not I.   My simple-
ness, I confesse, reacheth not to understand how
these Allegations will serve their turne.   I meane,
therefore, by GOD's grace, to keep on y° plaine way,
fulfilling y° letter as much as may bee.   And both mine
own body and my children must excuse mee if I take
lesse pleasure to myselfe, or leave lesse wealth to
them by this meanes."

"For mee not to be of the same mind," says Mary
Collett, "were double folly, inasmuch as my Virgin-
estate equally excludes y° care of both of worldly
pleasure and children;" and she then begs her sisters,
the "Patient" and the "Affectionate," to relate stories
of Saints, "whose riches and prosperity have gone on
multiplying by the distribution of them in pious uses."
And the "Patient," "having a little conferred with y°
'Affectionate,'" the two relate stories of the generosity
of Cosimo de Medicis and Gonsalvo Ferrante, the
"Great Captain," strangely chosen examples of
saintly life; Mrs. Collett, the "Moderator," having
first warned them that "The examples of Saints
work little, but upon those y° endeavour to become
Saints, or find themselves plain sinners, . . . but
worldly men, that think themselves Christians good
enough for Heaven, whilst none can tax them with
open enormities, make but a jest of the Example

or Authority of holy men, when they are alledged to prove or persuade them that which they please not to believe or follow."

These discourses may now appear dull and ponderous, but their quaint pedantry was in the taste of the day, and they seem to have greatly interested their hearers, to whom they were intended to serve, not only for instruction, but as a substitute for the idle and often coarse masques and interludes which then formed a favourite amusement. In the report of the Conversation on St. John's Day, 1631, we read that "the remembrance of the former day's pleasure having carried up most of the family (though after a dinner of more than ordinary cheer) into the sisters' chamber, the 'Guardian' (seeing himself and only one or two more left in the dining-room) said, smiling to his mother, 'Madam, you may now see that young people may be brought to take as great delight in things good and profitable, as in others which are vain and useless; for I do not think any gamesters were hardly ever more earnestly bent on their play than our family are upon their stories.'"

When Mrs. Ferrar resigned the personal super-intendence of her granddaughters, the sisters met together to elect a successor. A portion of the Conversation which followed is worth quoting.[1]

[1] The following Conversation is taken from Peck's copy, as printed in Mr. Mayor's Appendix, pp. 373-376.

The " Guardian," John Ferrar, begins by suggesting, " not for the excercise of misrule,[1] but the maintenance of good order," that a lord should be chosen among them for the ensuing Christmas. To which the " Affectionate " answers that they should choose, not a lord, but a lady, " as you have resolved, and as the constitution of our family requires, it being the female sex which exceeds among us, not merely in number, but in faultiness."

Moderator. " That we may not seem to usurp authority, I pray you, let the approbation of our dearest mother be first made known to the company."

Guardian. " She hath, not only out of love to us, and desire of our satisfaction, but out of her own judgment, given both consent and approbation in this matter."

Patient (Anna Collett). " Since the authority we are now establishing is derived from her, methinks the new title should not any way exceed the old, nor the translation may be more large and lofty than the original. I should counsel, therefore, that, waiving the ambitious stile of Lady, we should content our-

---

[1] An allusion to the custom of choosing a chief (sometimes called the " lord of misrule ") for the Christmas revels. " I was elected one of the comptrollers of the Middle Temple Revellers, as the fashion of the young students and gentlemen was, the Christmas being kept this yeare with great solemnity."—" Diary of John Evelyn : " December 15, 1642.

selves for our 'Chief' with one of those twain of Mother or Mistress, which our 'Guardian' ended with."

.   .   .   .   .   .

Affectionate. "For this regard, as also with regard to the virgin estate whereof our 'Chief' has made profession, as there is nothing more necessary than humility, both for ornament and protection, I suppose not only the swelling stile of Lady may be better waived than used; and that, with more grace to the office and satisfaction of all parties, we shall name her Mother, which virtually includes the authority of Mistress."

Here followed a conversation about the comparative merits of married and single life, which is closed by the "Cheerful" and the "Affectionate," whose views of life differed from those of their elder sisters.

Cheerful. "Though we cannot with so much ease as you" (Mary and Anna) "may, yet with no less desire, by God's grace, shall we follow after that which is excellent in every kind. Your virgin state serves better than wedlock to the attainment of perfection, but doth not more necessarily require it. We would not, with the whole world to boot, take husbands, to have less interest with God by that means. It is the hope of serving God better, and of our firmer union unto Him, which inclines our judgements to the married condition. We have made up the accompt and find it clear that there is no gain of worldly comforts to be got by marriage, except to them who look no higher than the earth, no farther than this life."

Affectionate. "For industry, therefore, worthy Chief, take what part you please for yourself, and you shall see a double charge belongs to us, who are by you and our other friends designed for wives."

In a further conversation, held on All Saints Day, Mary Collett was formally inducted into her office, and gifts are offered to her on this occasion, which she refuses, until a note from the "Visitor" (Nicholas) is handed to her, desiring her to accept them.

The new Mother begins by warning her sisters how she intends to exercise the authority confided in her. "You may cashier me if you please, but if you hold me in you must give me leave to govern as becomes my profession. It must be a very sober table that a virgin sits at the head of; and they must be sober cates that are of her providing."

Then the "Patient" arose, "and, kissing it, presented a rich Bible to the ' Chief,' " who, after receiving it, said, "I salute it with a kiss" (here she kissed it) "in token of love, and put it on my head" (here she put it on her head), "and lay it up in my bosom" (here she laid it in her bosom) "as an incomparable treasure. I have applied the letter without ; do Thou, O my God (here she lifts up the book) "apply the spirit of this book within."

The "Cheerful" gave a bell, inscribed, *The bell tolls to prayers and rings out for the dead.*

The "Affectionate" gave a watch light.

Then the "Moderator," Mrs. Collett, arose, and taking three of her children by the hand, led them up to the "Chief," saying, "I give you these now for children whom, at the first, I brought forth brothers and sisters to you."

The "Guardian" (John Ferrar): "The extent of her motherhood is by no means to be confined within those bounds, but must enlarge itself to the generality of this whole family, and in particular to my three" (Nicholas, John, and Virginia) "whom I likewise now set over to her motherhood."

"To make the gift more proportionable," Susannah Mapletoft offered a seventh child (her own little Ann), "seven being the number of perfection, and by the Pythagoreans more particularly attributed to virginity."

The curious mixture of playfulness and affectation in these formalities does not conceal the deep religious enthusiasm which they express—a strong and true enthusiasm, not suffered to burn away in excited feeling, but fed, instructed, and exercised in Christian learning and the practice of fixed and active duties.

CHAPTER VII.

SOME FAMILY LETTERS.

" No empty hopes, no courtly fears *her* fright,
No begging wants *her* middle fortunes bite,
But sweet content exiles both miserie and spite.

    .   .   .   .   .   .

Her life is neither tost in boisterous seas,
Of troublous world, nor lost in slothfull ease ;
Pleased and full blest *she* lives, when *she her* God can please."
PHINEAS FLETCHER, 1584–1650.

MRS. COLLETT'S letters,[1] full of good sense and affection, show under what careful tender guidance her children lived. Many are written from Margetting, where her daughter frequently claimed her care. She spent some months with Mrs. Mapletoft in the summer of 1628, and, when she returned to Gidding, left her daughter Hester to assist in the care of the baby grandchildren, Nan and Mary. This arrangement, it seems, could not be concluded without the permission of Nicholas, whose position in the

[1] The letters of Mrs. Collett that appear in this volume are all taken from those printed by the Rev. J. E. B. Mayor in the Appendix of " Two Lives of Ferrar."

house appears to have resembled that of the recognized Superior of a religious community.

"Even in this absence," Mrs. Collett writes to her brother in September, "your love hath been confirmed to us under many seals. For your agreement upon Hester's stay here for a while longer, as also myself in especial, give you many thanks, for as it will be a great comfort to my dear Su, so I hope by God's mercy, He giving her health, it will be no less content to Hester to show kindness than to receive it. For our resolutions what time to take our journey, we never concluded upon it, but desired that you would not only advise but determine of it. Only, by the way, at my husband's last being here he spake of setting forth from hence as on Monday next, because my son desired to begin our journey on a Monday that he might reach Lincolnshire the Friday after, but what Monday, he is very indifferent. It was only fear of foul weather and Essex bad ways made us think of going so soon, but we expect the resolution from you, for as yet we have made none. We all here beseech you to present our most humble and bounden duties to my most dear mother, our dearest love remembered to yourself, my good brother Ferrar and brother Richard (who I hope is yet with you), my sister, and all other friends."

In November Mrs. Collett is again at Gidding, having safely traversed the muddy Essex roads; and

we find her writing to Nicholas, who has been called
to London on "troublesome and weighty affairs," to
beg him to undertake some commission, apparently
relating to one or other of her sons.   In the following
March, Nicholas went to visit his niece at Margetting,
who was still far from strong.   His reports were
eagerly looked for, and the postal arrangements of the
time must have kept up a continual excitement on
the subject of letters.   Mrs. Collett writes—

" March 1, 1630.

"My most dear Brother,

        " Your letters were most gladly read, they
confirming us in that hope of your health, which, by
the carrier's negligence, we could the last week
receive no other testimony of than by his own report.
And now I beseech you to accept of my most hearty
and affectionate thanks for your so constant perseverance in the manifestation of your unparalleled love
and care of me and mine, and in particular that you
have been pleased not only to visit but to afford them
your company so long at Margetting when I doubt
not but, by God's help, the joy to see you and the
good counsel you have left with them, will be a
means of my dearest Su's speedier recovery of health.
For your letters also my husband and myself acknowledge ourselves bound and do still desire that you
will be pleased to take the like course with any that

shall come hereafter. But though time may per-
chance hardly permit it, yet the necessity of the case
makes me bold to entreat from you a full and ample
advice how to carry that business, which, as it seems,
can now no ways be avoided. My dear brother
Ferrar (John), who, as he best can, will sufficiently
inform you of every particular of our estate here,
only I cannot pass over the acknowledgement of
God's mercy to us all in that which is so main a
pillar of our comforts, the health of our dearest
mother, which I beseech Him long to continue and
make us truly thankful for it. Let me entreat you to
remember my most kind love to my good cousin
Arthur[1] and all other friends. With my prayers to
God for your health and prosperous success in all
your affairs, I commit you to God's protection."

No detail of the household at Margetting is too
minute for the consideration of the mother and uncle,
and in February, 1631, Mrs. Collett puts down in
writing her answer to several household difficulties
which her son-in law had brought to her for solution.

"Gidding, February 12, 1631.

"That which must be considered is, as I think,
what is best for her[2] to do, the things in question

[1] Mr. Arthur Woodnoth. Nicholas Ferrar was evidently
going on to London.
[2] Mrs. Mapletoft.

being such as tend either to easing her of trouble, avoiding of pain, or procuring some pleasure and content to her mind. Now, my opinion is, that if she shall purchase any of these with the displeasure either of God, her husband, or her friends, she will with much bitterness repent the bargain. Therefore my counsel in general is that she be most wary not to foil herself in this kind.

" Now, for the three first positions, I conceive them to be such as, should they be yielded unto, would in themselves be in no way displeasing to God, but as they have relation to others, and chiefly her husband, whose liking or dislike will make that either good or evil which simply in itself is not so. And first, for her going to see her brother and sister, I cannot see any harm likely to have ensued thereof; but should rather have hoped the quite contrary, and that their kind visitations and conversing together at times convenient might be a means to increase such love between them as might prove of good consequence to them both. For keeping another maid, I am not able to say what is best, but shall rather wish her to try the uttermost of her own strength, which, by God's blessing, may be increased into her that she shall not have such need of a maid as may now be feared she will. Concerning one of her sisters going unto her; though it might for the time be a great comfort to her, yet, considering that it may please God and is most likely that she may often have as great need of such helps in the same kind, and no probability that she shall often enjoy their company, I think it as good for her to satisfy herself with these comforts that she may have nearer hand, and not to be troubled in longing after that which is so doubtful she might. But for the nursing of her child, when it shall please God to send it to her, I would advise her not so much as to think of doing it by any but herself, but to resolve to do what possibly she may, though it should be with some pains, and leave the issue to God, for I cannot doubt but the putting of it forth would prove to her a matter of so much grief and trouble of mind that, though she were sure by that means to enjoy it, yet she would think her health bought at too dear a rate. Thus, according to my ability, you have my advice ; but I leave the solution to better judgements, and shall heartily beseech God to direct in the choice of what is best." [1]

The brother and sister whom Mrs. Mapletoft wished to visit were probably Thomas Collett and his wife, who had now left Gidding and settled in a home of their own. The following letter is to this son, and probably refers to the "Concordance of the Holy Gospels" made for him :—[2]

---

[1] With this letter was sent a copy of a prayer used at Gidding on behalf of the young couple.

[2] Chap. VIII., II.

"Gidding, November 22, 1630.

"The book which your sister sent you in the last week I doubt not but you have read before this (though in your letter to your grandmother you mention it not), which upon a diligent survey I am assured you cannot but read in it the character of a most unparalleled love and unwearied pains and carefulness in the contriving thereof for your benefit. God, for His mercy's sake, grant you may in some measure answer them all, the first in a return, the other in imitation ; and that you may with all speed resolve and constantly put in execution the practise of that which is contained therein."

Mrs. Collett's heart was filled with heavier anxieties than the number of Mrs. Mapletoft's maids, or the regulation of her visits to her family. Her youngest son Edward had been placed in some business in London ; Mrs. Collett writes to him a letter full of earnest advice in November, 1628, apparently shortly after his first leaving home.

"It would trouble me much if I had but a thought that you would forget those psalms that you have learned. Nay, I hope you will not content yourself in the only keeping of them in your memory, but learn much more, and in particular that book of the Proverbs, which both I desired, and you promised me to do ; and do not say with the sluggard, *There is a lion in the way*, you have now so much business that you

can intend nothing else, without the neglect of per-
forming your service to your master, which God
forbid you should do. No, my son; that time which
you shall spend in this kind, borrow it from those
hours that others take, and yourself may have liberty
to spend, in their own pleasures. But if you will say,
there is none such allowed you, though I can hardly
believe that, then take it from those that are allowed
for your rest, and assure yourself, if with a good heart
you shall do so, undoubtedly you shall find your mind
much strengthened for the performance of all your
duties, and the strength of your body no whit impaired. I might say much more, but I assure myself
and praise God for it, you shall not want better
counsel than I can give you ; for your dear uncle will
see you shortly."

The young man flung his mother's exhortations to
the winds. He is continually in trouble. His
master complains of him ; for a whole year he does
not write home, in spite of repeated admonitions. It
is no doubt of this son that Mrs. Collett speaks in a
letter from Margetting, where she had again gone to
watch over Mrs. Mapletoft's health.

"June, 1631.

" I am confident that by God's assistance you are
the best able to judge both of his disposition and of
what might be likeliest in such an uncertainty, to

bring him to a greater sense of his own ill case, and serious endeavours as much as possibly he may, to regain first pardon of God for his sin against Him, and so the assurance of the safety of his soul, and if God shall please to see it good for him, the repair of his now seeming lost hopes for the things of this life."

Thomas, now a barrister in London, and Nicholas Collett, who was learning the goldsmith's trade under Mr. Arthur Woodnoth, were both exhorted to do their utmost for their brother.   Thomas took him to live with him, but the youth seems to have been irreclaimable, and in despair his parents, with Mr. Woodnoth's aid, determined to send him abroad, a resolution of which her brother Nicholas did not wholly approve.

" *To my dear Brother Nicholas.*

"Oct. 21, 1631.

" MY MOST DEAR BROTHER,

" Since I entreated your help for a draught of a letter to Mr. B., I have gathered that by your denial and by your speeches (and the more at the receipt of my cousin Arthur's letter) that you do not well approve of my son's going to the Indies, which before that time I did not conceive that you disliked of the course as but only by reason of the difficulties that we are like to meet with in procuring his entertainment and his insufficiency to discharge any place of that kind. . . . The only hope I have of his well doing is only in God's mercy, who can give wisdom to the simple and grace to them that are most unworthy, even when in men's judgement they are most uncapable of the receiving of it, and my trust is that He will hear the prayers of so many as I hope will continually be intercessory for him. Besides, I do conceive well of the means, that the length of the voyage, the danger of peril in the way, the good orders that are kept in the ship, the necessity of forcing him to be obedient to so many that are in authority above him, the discretion he shall see in others in applying them-selves to perform their charge, may by God's grace work the like care in him, and bring him to a more feeling apprehension of his past faults, and so to a more hearty repentance and endeavour of amend-ment every way, Mr. Buckridge thinking it abso-lutely the best way we could set him in. . . . Mr. Bateman and my cousin Massenberd . . . gave instances of some but ill-disposed before their going thither, to have come home sober and discreet men. Yet notwithstanding perceiving now some opinions of such great danger of evil, I shall humbly beseech yours whether upon these grounds we may not still desire this for him, and have as good hope of his well-doing in this, as in any other course we shall be able to set him in, for, I profess, [for] my own part, I would not hazard a more imminent danger to his soul for a

more certainty of his temporal preferment. If you
therefore will please give me your opinion and counsel
herein, I shall by God's grace endeavour to follow it,
and shall ever acknowledge it for an addition to those
many favours and that obligation wherein myself and
all mine stand bound to you in the height of all love
and duty.

  " Your loving sister to you much obliged,

          "S. C."

Nicholas's answer is dated October 28, 1631.

" DEAR SISTER,

  " As I am partner in your cares, so shall I,
God willing, in your prayers to God for the good
success of the business, but counsel is too late to ask
when the business is brought almost to upshot. Your
reasons do not satisfy me, my own and others fears
trouble me. I cannot, therefore, be a setter forward
by my approbation, nor will be a hinderer of it,
because I have no certainty of exception against the
employment itself, and I see your husband's and your
own mind strongly bent to the going forward of it, to
which I shall never make any exception in any matter
touching your children but upon evidence of error
on your parts, and that in the very substance and
essence of the business; but as for circumstantial
errors (God willing), I will not stand upon them;

some such have been committed in this matter, but I freely pass them over, as much as concerns me; only one, out of the same love which makes me forget the rest, I am bound to remember, that is, burdening your son Thomas with Edward's diet, which I did not suspect you had intended, till my mother told me it. I am afraid, nay, I am almost assured, it will prove every way of evil consequences; if you doubt so too, you have for the making him satisfaction one of your £10 remaining of the £20, and also your husband hath free liberty to dispose of the twenty nobles a year overplus which remain of the £20 rent, besides your own and sister's allowance. I desire it to be reserved for the exercise of your bounty towards a son; if you will use it for the benefit of a couple, I shall not hold it an alteration but an improvement of your first resolution. I have no more to say in this business, but that you hearken diligently what God saith unto you in it and follow His direction, and all shall, I hope, prove to the best; He will not fail to instruct you if you call upon Him faithfully. To His good grace I commit you, and by His grace continue

> "Your faithful loving brother,
>
> "N. F."

The answer to this rather harsh letter, in which Nicholas betrays evident annoyance at finding that Mr. and Mrs. Collett had for once ventured to act on their own responsibility, is not given. Edward Collett sailed for the East Indies in the following March, with promises of amendment, which we may hope were kept. " I give you in charge not only the reading but the putting in practice those precepts contained in the written book I send you," Mrs. Collett wrote to him in 1634. " I send you also three books of Mr. Herbert's which are held (and worthily) in great esteem ; if they shall prove so with you, you shall please some of my friends." " The Temple " must have been one of the books sent out to the boy in India.

One more letter of Mrs. Collett's must be here given.

" *To my dearest Brother Nicholas.*

"March 2, 1631.

" MY MOST DEAR BROTHER,

" Since your first offer to me (of that which in all reason should have been either my suit or my want),—that is to give me your best assistance upon the revealing thereof, to the attaining of my own desires,— I have, I confess, had many conflicts within myself, to what bounds to limit them. But upon a strict examination of what hath passed in all my life hitherto, I have found that those hopes and expectations which I had fancied to myself would in the fruition prove most happy, they have not seldom deceived me. I have therefore now resolved by God's grace, not to make any choice for myself, but commit myself wholly to Him to dispose of my future estate which He hath hitherto so graciously provided for me. And for the things of this life my greatest desire is, that I may desire nothing but to rest content and fully satisfied with what estate soever He shall place me in, and with all thankful acknowledgment of His unspeakable mercy towards me to endeavour the performance of those duties which He requires of me, both to Himself and to all those to whom I have special reference of duty or love, and that I may be the more strongly conformed in this purpose, by framing my actions as is most befitting my present condition, I not only beseech your prayers but your counsels and directions. And for my daughter Betty,[1] my desire is that she may be trained up in the true fear of God and exercise of humility and obedience, and set in a course whereby she may attain such wisdom for the right ordering of her mind, that howsoever it may please God to settle her, she may by a right use make either a prosperous estate happy, or a mean contented. And if you shall please to assist me with your counsel for the effecting of this both in myself and her, I shall ever acknowledge it

---

[1] Elizabeth Collett afterwards married her cousin, Benjamin Woodnoth, of Shavington,

among the greatest of those many benefits, which it has pleased God to make you the instrument of to me and all mine, who shall ever rest in all due acknowledgment.

"Your most bounden and much-obliged sister,

"SUSANNAH COLLETT."

This letter appears to refer to some arrangement with regard to the family property. It may well be that among those hopes and expectations which Mrs. Collett desired to leave wholly to the disposal of God, were the vocation of Mary and Anna to the single life "for the better giving themselves to fasting and prayer," and the devotion of her son Ferrar to the priesthood. In the Conversation for the Feast of the Circumcision, 1632, she says, "I will give now by way of recipe to my son, whom my prayers and vows have set apart to this holy calling, that he keep himself pure and undefiled from this evil usage of the world, and whenever he is invited to a tavern or ale-house, let him answer, *his mother gave him charge to the contrary.*"

Two of the little grandchildren from Margetting were by this time added to the household at Gidding. Mrs. Mapletoft's health seems to have been unequal to the care of her increasing family. She accepted her sister's offer to take charge of Nan and Mall, and Nan was formally made over to Mary's care, as mentioned in the last chapter, and bore the name of "the Humble" in the Academy of Gidding. Three little boys followed one another quickly in the Margetting parsonage, but of these, one was soon taken to a more lasting home.

In 1635 Mr. Mapletoft died, greatly regretted. "I am truly sensible of the loss of such neighbours," a friend wrote to Mrs. Collett; "the loss of that glorified saint doth reflect double on me, not only in him, but in them likewise. I am so sorry for their going from hence, that truly I think the worse of my dwelling. I think there will come a supply to the parsonage, but none so endeared to me as these gentlewomen."

After a time Susannah was married again to a Mr. Chedley, but her daughter Mary and the two surviving boys, John and Peter, remained at Gidding in charge of her sisters.

CHAPTER VIII.

DESCRIPTIVE CATALOGUE OF THE CONCORDANCES MADE AT GIDDING.

"Prosper Thou, O Lord, the work of our hands: O prosper
Thou our handyworks."

"Innocency is never better lodged than at the sign of labour."
—*Inscriptions on the Wall of the Concordance Room at Gidding.*

THE Harmonies, or, as they are always called in the
family manuscripts, the Concordances, made at
Gidding, are so numerous and interesting that their
history requires a chapter to itself.[1]

It would be a misapprehension to regard these
unique works as mere curiosities, the laborious toys
of an unoccupied mind. They were the fruit of a
close and thoughtful study of Holy Scripture, an
earnest desire to learn and to teach its lessons.
Nicholas Ferrar's love for the Bible resembles that
of his friend Herbert.

[1] This chapter is taken from John Ferrar's (imperfect) list of
the works done at Gidding, printed by the Rev. J. E. B. Mayor,
and the very full and interesting catalogue published in the
Archæologia for 1888, vol. ii., by Captain Acland.

"O Book ! infinite sweetness ! let my heart
    Suck every letter, and a honey gain,
    Precious for any grief in any part,
To clear the breast, to mollify all pain.

.   .   .   .   .   .

Oh, that I knew how all thy lights combine,
    And the configurations of their glory !
    Seeing not only how each verse doth shine,
But all the constellations of the story."

During Ferrar's lifetime, the arrangement of the Harmonies seems to have been entirely his own, but all the members of the family, from Mrs. Ferrar down to the little girls, assisted in the manufacture. The method of their construction has been already described. The following extract from John Ferrar's account of the one originally made for their own use will show how much study must have been bestowed on the arrangement :—

I.

"Glory be to God on high.

"The actions, doctrines, and other passages touching our blessed Lord and Saviour Jesus Christ, as they are related by the four Evangelists, reduced into one complete body of history; wherein that which is severally related by them is digested into order, and that which is jointly related by all, or any of them, is first expressed in their own words, by way of comparison ; secondly, brought into one narration, by way of composition ; thirdly, extracted into clear context, by way of collection; yet so as whatsoever was omitted in the context, is inserted by way of supplement in another print, and in such a manner as all the four evangelists may easily be read severally and distinctly, each apart and alone, from first to last. Done at Little Gidding, anno 1630."

In each page throughout the book were sundry exquisite pictures added, expressing either the facts themselves, or other types and figures, or matters appertaining thereto, "much to the pleasure of the eye and delight of the reader."

This volume is lost, destroyed probably in the pillage of Gidding.

II.

Another Concordance was made apparently on the occasion of Thomas Collett leaving Gidding for a home of his own. This book is a "Harmony of the Four Gospels," bound in red parchment. On the first blank page are the following inscriptions :—(The first is the same as that in the Conversations.)

" Johannes Collet. Filius Thomæ Collet, Pater Thomæ, Gulielmi, and Johannis, omnium superstes. Natus Quarto Junii 1633. Denasciturus—Quando Deo visum fuerit. Interim hujus proprietarius.— JOHN COLLET."

"This was the book of my honoured Aunt, Mrs. Mary Collet, compiled at Little Gidding by the direction of her Uncle, Mr. N. Ferrar, and bound, I believe, by herself. It was given to me by my good and dear Cosin, Mrs. Elizabeth Kestian, who died Aug., 1715. I give it to my son, and if he dyes without issue to my daughter, Elizabeth Castrell, and to her son Robert, and I desire that it may be preserved in my family as long as may be. There were never above two more of the form that I ever heard of, one of which was presented to Charles the First, by his desire, when he was pleased to honour the Family at Little Gidding with a visit, when he went from London into the North; and the other to King Charles II. at his restoration, 1660, by John Ferrar,[1] who is now owner of Little Gidding, from the aforesaid Mrs. Mary Collett, who, as I think, bound both the said books in purple velvet and richly gilded.

"That to King Charles the First was sent to him soon after he had been there.—JOHN MAPLETOFT, Jan. 23, 1715" (1715–16).

This book remained in the Mapletoft family, and is now the property of a descendant, Mr. Harold Mapletoft Davis, residing in New South Wales, Australia.[2]

---

[1] Only surviving son of John Ferrar, author of "Memoir of Nicholas Ferrar." He died in 1719 in his eighty-ninth year.—Inscription in Gidding Church.

[2] Further note on the Harmonies, 1889, Captain Acland.

It is characteristic that in these elaborate works Nicholas Ferrar seems to have had no end in view beyond the instruction of his own family. It was only by accident that he was induced to extend their usefulness.

In 1631 the king, having heard—by what means we are not informed, but very probably through Cosins, one of the royal chaplains—that an extremely curious and interesting book had been compiled at Gidding, despatched a gentleman from Apthorpe, where he was then staying, to request that this choice volume might be sent for his inspection.

"The tidings were much unexpected, and Nicholas Ferrar at London." Apparently no one ventured to take any decided step in his absence; for they begged leave to defer sending the book for a week, adding a message that it "was wholly unfitting every way for a king's eye, and those who had given him any notice of such a thing had much misinformed his Majesty; and when he should see it, he would con[1] them no thanks, the book being made only for the young people in the family."

But the gentleman was not to be put off, declaring that if he went back without it, he knew he should be sent again that night. "So necessity enforced the delivery," and the book was carried off with a promise

[1] "'To con thanks,' an old expression for 'to thank;' it is the same with *sçavoir gré*."—Johnson.

that it should be returned when the king left Apthorpe; but three months passed before the gentleman came back to Gidding, and then he arrived empty-handed.

The king, he said, took such pleasure in that book, that he would not part with it unless the family would make him another for his daily use, "for in the midst of his progress and sports he spent one hour in the perusing of it, and that would apparently be seen by the notations he had made upon the margins of it with his own hand." Some months later, the volume was restored, and the many notes found in the margin proved how diligently Charles had studied it. "In one place, which is not to be forgotten to the eternal memory of his Majesty's superlative humility (no small virtue in a king), having written something in one place, he puts it out again very neatly with his pen. But that, it seems, not contenting him, he vouchsafes to underwrite, *I confess my error, It was well before* (an example to all his subjects), *I was mistaken.*

III.

The Ferrars hastened to obey the king's command, and another Harmony was at once put in hand.[1]

---

[1] From John Ferrar's narrative, it would appear that the first Concordance made for the king was finished in 1632 or 1633, but the date in the book itself is 1635. If this is correct, it was not presented till *after* the royal visit to Gidding.

So greatly was Charles interested in this book and its makers, that in 1633, on his progress into Scotland to be crowned at Holyrood, he stopped to visit Gidding. Strangely enough, the Ferrar memoirs make no mention of this honour; and it is only from Rushworth's "Progress" that we learn that on May 13 in that year the king "stept a little out of the way to view a place at Gidding, near Stilton, in Northamptonshire, which by the vulgar sort of people was called a *Protestant nunnery*." [1]

The king's description of this Protestant family, who "outdid the severest monastics abroad," kindled the curiosity of the queen, who perhaps fancied the account exaggerated. She sent a gentleman to Little Gidding, with commands to bring her an exact account of what he saw there; and she wished to have visited the place herself, but this was prevented by the state of the roads, which seem to have enjoyed a reputation for superior badness, and which proved impassable for her coach.

When the Concordance was finished it was sent to the king through Cosins, who was chaplain-in-waiting that month, and was received by Charles with expressions of pleasure which meant more than merely royal courtesy.

"It shall be my *vade mecum*," he said to Cosins,

[1] "Rushworth," vol. ii. p. 178, quoted by the Rev. J. E. B. Mayor.

and added to Laud, who stood by, " How happy a king were I if I had many more such workmen and women in my kingdom! God's blessing on their hearts and painful hands !"

This Concordance remained in the royal library at Windsor till it was presented by George III. to the British Museum, where it now remains.

IV.

The king was so much pleased with the work, that he asked Laud if he thought "these good people" would be willing to take some further trouble.

" I often," he said, " read the Books of Kings and Chronicles, as is befitting a king, but in many things I find some seeming contradictions, and one book saith more, and the other less, in many circumstances the latter being a supply to the former. Now I, seeing this judicious and well-contrived book of the four Evangelists, gladly would have these skilful persons to make me another book, that might be so ordered that I might read these stories of Kings and Chronicles so interwoven by them as if one pen had written the whole books." He added that he had often spoken to his chaplains about such a work, but that they had excused themselves on the ground of its difficulty.

Cosins informed the family of his Majesty's wish,

and in a year's time a Harmony of the Books of Kings and Chronicles, arranged with great care and skill, was ready for the king's use.

It was presented by John Ferrar, who gives a most graphic account of its reception, though with characteristic reticence he omits all mention of himself in the relation.

The book was first shown to Laud, who viewed it with great admiration, saying that the name of Gidding, where such works were produced, should be changed from *Parva* to *Magna*. He then introduced John Ferrar into the royal presence. The interview must be given in Ferrar's own words.

"At their coming into the room where the king was, he, seeing my lord of Canterbury to have a stately great book in his two hands, presently rose out of his chair where he was sitting, many lords then standing round about him.

" *What*, said he, *shall I now enjoy this rich jewel I have thus long desired? Have you, my lord, brought me my book?*

" *Yea, sir*, replied the Bishop of Canterbury. *Give it me, give it me*, said the king. *Your expectations, sir*, said he, *are not only performed, but out of doubt many ways surpassed. For my own part, I wonder at the work and all the parts of it.*

" *Let me have it*, said the king. So, smiling, he took it and carried it to the table.

" Then, first seriously viewing the outside of the book, which was bound in purple velvet, and that also most artificially gilt upon the velvet in an extraordinary manner, he said, *My lords, the outside thus glorious, what think you will be the inside and matter of it?* Then, untying the stately string, he opening it read the frontispiece and contents of the book. Then, turning to my lord of Canterbury, he said, *You have given me a right character of the work, truly it passeth what I could have wished. . . . I will not part with this diamond for all those in my jewel-house. For it is so delightful to me, and I know the virtues of it will pass all the precious stones in the world. It is a most rare crystal glass, and most useful and needful and profitable for me and all kings. It shows and represents to the life God's exceeding high and great mercies to all pious and virtuous kings, and likewise his severe justice to all ill and bad. It shall, I assure you, be my companion in the daytime, and the sweetest perfumed bags that can lay under my head at night.*

" He then sent his hearty thanks to the makers of the book. *I know,* he said, *that they look for none, neither will they receive any reward. Yet let them know, as occasion shall be, I will not forget them, and God bless them in their good intentions.* And so, after some more talk the lords had of Gidding, the king took the book, and went away with it in his arms."

This Concordance is also in the British Museum,

having been sent, like the first, from Windsor. It bears the date 1637, the last year of Nicholas Ferrar's life.

"Some while after," says John Ferrar, " Dr. Cosins gave notice that the king, the more he perused both books given him the more he liked them ; and had conference with him about the printing of them, that, as he said, all his people might have the benefit of them. And Dr. Cosins told the king it was a kingly notion, and by his Majesty's favour they should be put out, as at his command, and the latter as done by his directions."

The coming troubles, no doubt, caused this project to be laid aside, and these Harmonies have never been printed.

V.

Another Concordance, dated 1635, seems to have been made originally for Sir R. Cotton, founder of the Cottonian Library,[1] from whom it came by marriage into the possession of the Bowdler family. It was presented by the Rev. John Bowdler to the late Arthur Acland Troyte, Esq., of Huntsham Court, Devon. His son relates in the *Archæologia*, that the gift was made because, in the pious ordering of his family, the master of Huntsham recalled to mind the founder of Little Gidding.

[1] The Cotton family lived in the neighbouring parish of Denton.

This book is now in possession of Captain Acland, and is in daily use for the instruction of his children.

After the death of Nicholas Ferrar in 1637, the work was carried on by his favourite nephew and godson, Nicholas Ferrar the younger, who had long been his assistant. The story of this young scholar belongs to a later chapter, but it will be convenient to give here the list of his works.

VI.

"The Monotessaron; or, The Four Evangelists," in English, Latin, French, and Italian, "to which are, in all the pages of the book, added sundry of the best pictures that could be gotten, expressing the facts themselves, or their types, figures, or other matters pertaining thereto."

This was presented to Charles Prince of Wales, it having been made at his request.

It is now in possession of the Earl of Normanton, and is a magnificent book, 2 ft. 1 in. in height, richly bound in green velvet stamped with fleur-de-lis and sprays of oak.

VII.

"The Holy Gospels" in eight languages.

VIII.

The same in twenty-four languages.

IX.

" The Gospel of St. John " in twenty-one languages, each several language being accompanied by a Latin or English translation.

These three books were presented to the king, in the hope, probably, that he would assist in getting them printed.

Their subsequent history is unknown.

X.

" Acts of the Apostles and Revelation of St. John," bound in leather gilt. The title-page curiously decorated with pictures. Presented to the king, and remained in royal library at Windsor till lent by George II. to the British Museum.

XI.

A square folio, illustrated throughout, containing the Five Books of Moses. Presented by Archbishop Laud to St. John's College, Oxford, dated 1640 ; and now in the library of St. John's College.

After the death of the younger Nicholas, the surviving members of the family still continued the work.

XII.

" The Four Gospels," bound in purple velvet, stamped with a pattern of acorn sprigs of oak and fleur-de-lis. No date. Probably the volume made for the Duke of York, and never presented owing to the outbreak of the civil war.

It is now in possession of the Marquis of Salisbury.

XIII.

" The Pentateuch," a splendid volume 2 ft. 4½ in. by 1 ft. 8 in., bound in purple velvet stamped in patterns of small crowns. Profusely illustrated. No date. Contents : the Five Books of Moses, corresponding passages from the New Testament, also long extracts from a work entitled " Moses Unveiled," and papers on a variety of other subjects, including holy men, types of our Lord, etc. Evidently the second book made for Prince Charles, and seen by the King at Gidding in 1642, but never presented.

In 1776 this book belonged to Jacques Bourdillon, who bought it from the Harleian Library. It was found at the beginning of the present century, walled up at Brookman's Park, and is now in the library of Captain Gaussen, Brookman's Park, Hatfield.

XIV.

" Four Gospels," bound in light brown leather, illustrated throughout, dated 1640.   On the title-page is written—

" This book was the work of two ladies, nieces of Mr. Ferrar of L. Gidding, who, according to Ward's account in the Gresham professors, devoted themselves to a single life. . . .

" The said Mr. Ferrar was great-uncle to Dr. John Mapletoft, some time Phisic professor of Gresham College, and afterwards Vicar of St. Laurence Jewry, London; which Dr. Mapletoft was great-uncle to the present possessor of this book.

" J. MAPLETOFT, M.A.,
" Chaplain to the Right Hon. John, Lord St. John
" of Bletsoe.

" July 16, 1764."

Now in possession of Miss Heming, Hillingdon Hill, Uxbridge.

XV.

The Concordance " of an inferior kind and sort " sold to Lord Wharton for £37, mentioned by John Ferrar in letter to Dr. Basire; of which the history is unknown.

These, with (XVI.) the volume already mentioned

as belonging to the Harvey family, and the unfinished Concordance in the treasure trove at Magdalene College, are the whole of the works known [1] to have been executed at Gidding. All are bound by the hands of the family, who were also in the habit of binding other books [2] for their own use, for friends, and possibly for sale with a view to provide funds to carry on their costly work. Their friend Dr. Isaac Basire, sending to his betrothed a copy of St. Francis de Sale's " Devout Life," tells her that " it was bound by those devout virgins I told you of. Who knows but the prayers they may have bestowed on the binding may do you good in the reading thereof."

NOTE.

A specimen of the arrangement of these Harmonies may be found interesting ; it is taken from the great Concordance made for Charles I., now in the King's Library, British Museum. The words in italics are written, the rest printed, the slips of paper, often exceedingly small, being fitted together and pasted down on large folio paper with the utmost neatness. The words of the Evangelists are distinguished in the " Composition " by their initials, in the " Collection " by the marginal letters A, B, C, D. I have given only a portion of the " Comparison " and " Composition " of the passage chosen, which is selected on

---

[1] Others are said to have been made for Herbert and Dr. Jackson.

[2] A Bible, bound at Gidding for Charles I., is in the library at Cardiff Castle.

account of the close interweaving of the three sacred narratives in the compass of a few verses. The whole occupies a single page of the folio.

The Rubbing of the Ears of Corn.

COMPARISON.

ST. MATTHEW.	ST. MARK.	ST. LUKE.
At that time, Jesus went on the Sabbath day through the corn ; and his Disciples were an hungred, and began to pluck the ears of corn, and to eat. But when the Pharisees saw it, they said unto him, Behold, thy Disciples do that which is not lawfull to do upon the Sabbath day.	And it came to pass, that He went through the corn fields on the Sabbath day : and his disciples began as they went to pluck the ears of corn. And the Pharisees said unto him, Behold, why do they on the Sabbath day that which is not lawfull ?	And it came to pass on the second Sabbath after the first, that He went through the corn fields ; and his disciples plucked the ears of corn, and did eat, rubbing them in their hands. And certain of the Pharisees said unto them, Why do ye that which is not lawfull to do on the Sabbath days

COMPOSITION.

M And it came to passe *Mk* at that time *Mk* that *M* Jesus *Mk* went through the cornfields on the Sabbath day, *L* the second Sabbath after the first, *M* and his disciples were an hungred *Mk* and began as they went to pluck the ears of corn, *L* and did eat, rubbing them in their hands. *M* But when *L* certain of the Pharisees *M* saw it, they *L* said unto them, Why do ye that which is not lawfull to do on the Sabbath dayes ? *Mk* And the Pharisees said unto him, Behold, why do they on the Sabbath day that which is not lawfull ? *M* Behold Thy disciples do that which is not lawfull to do on the Sabbath day.

COLLECTION.

A. 12, 1. **At that time Jesus went on the Sabbath day thorowe the corne** and his disciples were an hungred and began to pluck the ears of corn and to eat.

B. 6, 1. And it came to passe on the second Sabbath after the first that he went thorowe the cornfields, and his disciples plucked the eares of corn and did eate, rubbing them in their hands.

2. And certain of the Pharisees said unto them, Why doe ye that which is not lawfull to doe on the Sabbath dayes?

A. 2. But when the Pharisees saw it, they said unto him, behold thy Disciples doe that which is not lawful to doe upon the Sabbath day.

3. But he said unto them, Have ye not read what David did when he was an hungred and they that were with him?

4. How he entered into the house of God and did eate the shewbread, which was not lawfull for him to eate, neither for them which were with him, but only for the priests?

C 2. And Jesus answering unto them, said, Have ye not read so much as this, what David did when himself was an hungred and they that were with him?

4. How he went into the house of God, and did take and eat the shewbread, and gave also to them that went with him, which is not lawful to eat but for the priest alone?

5. And he said unto them, That the Son of Man is Lord also of the Sabbath.

B. II. 23. And it came to pass as he went through the cornfields on the Sabbath day, and his disciples began as they went to pluck the ears of corn.

24. And the Pharisees said unto him, Behold, why do they on the Sabbath day that which

25. Is not lawfull? And he said unto them, Have ye never read what David did when he had neede and was an hungred he and they that were with him?

26. How he went into the House of God in the days of Abiathar the high priest and did eat the shewbread, which is not lawfull to eate but for the priests, and gave also to them that were with him.

A. 5. Or habe ye not read in the lawe how that on the Sabbath dayes the Priests in the temple profane the Sabbath and are blamelesse?

6. But I say unto you that in this place is one greater than the temple.

7. But if ye had knowen what this meaneth, I will habe mercy and not sacrifice, ye would not habe condemned the guiltlesse.

8. For the Son of Man is Lord even of the Sabbath day.

B. 27. And he said unto them, The Sabbath was made for man, and not man for the Sabbath.

28. Therefore the Son of Man is Lord also of the Sabbath.

CHAPTER IX.

" No longer shall our churches frighted stones
 Lie scattered like the dead and martyred bones
 Of dead devotion, nor faint marbles weep,
 For their sad ruins."
　　　R. CRASHAW, *Lines prefixed to*
　　　　Shelford's " Five Discourses."　1635.

A.D.—1628-1633.

THOUGH Nicholas Ferrar's chosen work lay in his
own family, his interests were not wholly confined
within its bounds.

George Herbert, while yet a layman, was presented
by Bishop Williams to a prebend at Lincoln, which
carried with it the patronage of Leighton Ecclesia, a
parish about six miles from Gidding.　This living he
earnestly pressed on his friend.　Ferrar was firm
in his resolve to remain a deacon, and to accept of
no preferment; but though he would not undertake
the charge of the parish, he became much interested
in its condition.　Leighton had shared in the neglect

which fell on so many parishes in the close of the sixteenth and beginning of the seventeenth centuries. Its " fair church " was in ruins. It " was fallen down a long time, and lay in the dust, the vicar and parish fain to use my lord duke's[1] great hall for their prayers and preaching."

The parishioners had collected some money for the restoration of their church, but they could not get together enough to begin building. Ferrar described the state of things to Herbert, and " earnestly assaulted " him to do what he could towards so good a work. He did not confine himself to exhortations, but gave liberally, and also undertook that " his brother John Ferrar should very carefully prosecute the business, if once began, by three times a week attending the workmen, and providing all materials." It is only in this incidental way that John lets us know how fully he entered into his brother's interests.

Ferrar's representations roused Herbert to active exertion. He " set upon it to solicit his friends, and spared not his own purse." Between them the church was rebuilt, " not only to the parishioners much comfort and joy, but to the admiration of all men." A steeple was afterwards added by the Duke of Lenox, " to the memorial of his honour."

Among those who assisted in the restoration, both with money and personal trouble, was Mr. Arthur

[1] James, fourth Duke of Lenox.

Woodnoth.   His name occurs so frequently in the history of the Ferrars, that Walton's short account of him,[1] though well-known, may not be out of place here.

"He was a man that had considered overgrown estates do often require more care and watchfulness to preserve than get them, and considered that there be many discontents that riches cure not, and did therefore set limits to himself, as to desire of wealth. And having attained so much as to be able to show some mercy to the poor, and preserve a competence for himself, he dedicated the remaining part of his life to the service of God, and to be useful to his friends."

This excellent man undertook to manage the accounts of the building, and paid many visits to Gidding during its progress.

The following letter was addressed to Ferrar by Herbert during the progress of the work :—

"MY EXCEEDING DEAR BROTHER,

        "Although you have a much better pay-master than myself, even Him whom we both serve, yet I shall ever put your care of Leighton upon my account, and give you myself for it, to be yours for ever.   God knows I have desired a long time to do the place good, and have endeavoured many ways to

[1] Walton's "Life of George Herbert."

find out a man for it.   And now my gracious Lord
God is pleased to give me you for the man I desired,
for which I humbly thank Him, and am so far from
giving you cause to apology about your counselling
me herein, that I take it exceeding kindly of you.   I
refuse not advice from the meanest that creeps upon
God's earth, no, not though the advice step so far as
to be reproof: much less can I disesteem it from you,
whom I esteem to be God's faithful and diligent
servant, not considering you any other ways, as
neither I myself desire to be considered.   Particularly I like all your addresses, and, for aught I see,
they are ever to be liked."   (Here follow particulars as
to the building of the church, in such form as Nicholas
Ferrar advised, and the collecting of the money.)
" You write very lovingly, that all your things are
mine.   If so, let this of Leighton Church the care
be among the chiefest also; so also have I requested
Mr. W.[1] for his part.   Now God, the Father of our
Lord Jesus Christ, bless you more and more, and so
turn you all, in your several ways, one to the other,
that ye may be a heavenly comfort, to His praise, and
the great joy of

" Your brother and servant in Christ Jesus,

" GEORGE HERBERT.

" Postscript.—As I had written thus much I re-

[1] Mr. Arthur Woodnoth.

ceived a letter from my brother, Sir Henry H., of
the blessed success that God had given us by moving
the duchess's heart [1] to an exceeding cheerfulness, in
signing £100 with her own hands, and promising to
get her son to do as much, with some little apology
that she had done nothing in it (as my brother writes)
hitherto.   She referred it also to my brother to name
at first what the sum should be ; but he told her Grace
that he would by no means do so, urging that charity
must be free.   She liked our book well, and has given
order to the tenants at Leighton to make payment of
it.   God Almighty prosper the work.   Amen." [2]

John Ferrar gives a fragment of another letter from
Herbert on the same subject.

"MY DEAR BROTHER,—

        "I thank you heartily for Leighton, your
care, your counsel, and your cost.   And as I am
glad for the thing, so no less for the heart that God
has given you and yours to pious works.   Blessed be
my God and dear Master, the Spring and Fountain
of all goodness.   As for my assistance, doubt not
through God's blessing, but it shall be to the full ;
and for my power, I have sent my letters to your
brother, investing him in all that I have."

[1] The Dowager Duchess of Lenox.
[2] "Life of Nicholas Ferrar," by his brother, p. 72.

Nicholas himself wrote a short account of the restoration of Leighton, in his preface to Herbert's "Temple," but not even his natural wish to link his name with that of his beloved and honoured friend could induce him to mention his own share in the work. He only tells us that the reparation was successfully effected by Herbert with the aid of "some few others' private freewill offerings."

From this time there seems to have been a constant interchange of letters between the friends, and it is said that Herbert contemplated exchanging his living of Bemerton for one in the neighbourhood of Gidding, "merely for the situation, as being nearer to his dear brother, though in value much inferior to his own ; but he said *that he valued Mr. Ferrar's near neighbourhood more than any living.* And truly there was no loss of affection between them ; Nicholas Ferrar prizing him as a most precious friend, and with whom he could live and die, if God saw it so good for both. And as Nicholas Ferrar communicated his heart to him so he made him the peruser, and desired the approbation of what he did, as in those three translations of Valdesso, Lessius, and Carbo." [1]

Though Ferrar seems to have written much, the greater part of his work was intended solely for the use of his own family, and the translations above

[1] "Life of Nicholas Ferrar," by his brother.

named are the only writings which he prepared for the press.

One of these, a treatise "On the Instruction of Children in the Christian Doctrine," by Ludovico Carbone,[1] was "well approved" by Herbert, but when it was sent to Cambridge to be licensed the authorities, for some unexplained reason, took a different view, and, as Oley says quaintly, "would not suffer that Egyptian jewel to be published."

The works of Juan de Valdés, whose Spanish name Ferrar translates as "John Valdesso," and Lessius, met with more favour.

The "Hundred and Ten Considerations" of Juan de Valdés have been already mentioned.[2] The book, though written in Spanish, was first printed in an Italian translation, published at Bâle in 1550, and this was soon followed by translations in French[3] and Dutch.

[1] The manuscripts have disappeared. The title is given in the Middle Hill manuscripts, 9527, among a list of books and manuscripts belonging to Mr. John Mapletoft. It is described as "a work very profitable and necessary for every Christian. Printed at Venice by John Guarigli, 1596." And the translation is said to have been finished in June, 1634, at the request of Edmund Duncon, so that the rough draft only can have been shown to Herbert.—Rev. J. E. B. Mayor, "Two Lives," Appendix.

[2] See Chap. II.

[3] A French translation of Valdés, dated 1563, is now in the Bodleian. It contains the following inscriptions: "This booke was the Right Reverend Father in God, Austin, Lord Bishop

" John Valdesso," says the Italian editor (the English is Ferrar's), " was by nation a Spaniard, of noble kindred, of honourable degree, and a resplendent chevalier of the Emperour,[1] but a much more honourable and resplendent chevalier of Christ. True it is he did not much follow the Court after Christ had revealed Himself to him, but abode in Italy, spending the greatest part of his life at Naples, where, with the sweetnesse of his doctrine and sanctity of his life, he gained many disciples unto Christ; and especially among the gentlemen and cavaliers, and some ladies ; he was very eminent and praiseworthy in all kinds of praise ; it seemed that he was appointed by God for a teacher and pastour of noble and illustrious personages ; although he was of such benignitie and charity that he accounted himself debtour of his talent to every mean and rude person, and became all things to all men that he might gain all to Christ. And not this alone, but he gave light to some of the most famous preachers of Italy, which I very well know, having conversed with them themselves."

Among the distinguished persons who gathered

of Hereford ; " and below, " Given to the Publique Library in Oxford by Mr. John Farrar, of Huntingdonshire. September 8, 1642."—" Two Lives," Appendix.

[1] He was Chamberlain to Pope Adrian VI., and brother to Alonzo de Valdés, Latin Secretary to the Emperor Charles V. —See " Life of Valdés," by Benjamin Wiffen, Esq.

round Valdés in his Neapolitan retreat, we find the names of Bernardino Ochino, the great Capuchin preacher, and Peter Martyr Vermiglio, afterwards Dean of Christchurch, of Marc Antonio Flaminio, of Giulia Gonzaga, and Vittoria Colonna, the friend of Michael Angelo.

A letter has been preserved, written soon after his death, in 1540, which shows how highly these friends regarded him.

"If you were now at the window of that turret so often praised by us," wrote Jacomo Bonfadio to his friend Monsignor Carnesecchi, secretary to Clement VII., "while the eyes were cast by turns all round those sunny gardens, and then stretched along the spacious bosom of that shining sea,[1] a thousand vital spirits would multiply about the heart. I remember your lordship said many times before leaving, that you wished to return, and as often invited me there. May it please God that we may return. Yet, thinking on the other side, where shall we go now that Signor Valdés is dead? This truly has been a great loss for us and the world, for Signor Valdés was one of the rare men of Europe, and those writings he has left on the Epistles of Paul and the Psalms of David most amply show it. He was, without doubt, in his actions, his speech, and in all his conduct, a perfect man. With a particle of his soul he governed his

---

[1] The Bay of Naples.

P

frail and spare body ; with the larger part, and with his pure understanding, as though almost out of the body, he was always raised in the contemplation of truth and of divine things." [1]

Valdés has been called a Protestant, and some of those who came under his influence, notably Ochiro and Vermiglio, afterwards left Italy and openly joined the Reformers ; but he himself never separated from the Roman Church.

Much of his teaching is said to be based on the " Christian Institutes " of Tauler.[2]   Its merits and defects are brought out in the letter which George Herbert, after careful study of the translation, addressed to Ferrar, and in the notes that follow.

"MY DEAR AND DESERVING BROTHER,

"Your 'Valdesso' I now return with many thanks, and some notes, in which perhaps you will discover some care, which I forbare not in the midst

[1] Quoted in "Life of Valdés" by Benjamin Wiffen, Esq. Carnesecchi was burnt by the Holy Office on suspicion of heresy, in 1567.   Both he and Flaminio were friends of Cardinal Pole.   Mr. Wiffen gives a letter of Pole, in which he says "the remainder of the day was spent in the holy and profitable society of Signor Carnesecchi and our Marc Antonio Flaminio.   I call it profitable because in the evening Marc Antonio gave me and most of my family a supper of that bread which perishes not, in such a manner that I know not when I have felt greater consolation or greater edification."

[2] McCrie, "Reformation in Italy."

of my griefes; first, for your sake, because I would do nothing negligently which you commit unto mee; secondly, for the author's sake, whom I conceive to have been a true servant of God; and to such, and all that is theirs, I owe diligence; thirdly, for the Church's sake, to whom, by printing it, I would have you consecrate it. You owe the Church a debt, and God hath put this into your hands (as He sent the fish with money to S. Peter) to discharge it; happily also with this (as His thoughts are fruitful), intending the honour of His servant the author, who, being obscured in his own country, He would have to flourish in this land of light and region of the Gospel among His chosen. It is true there are some things which I like not in him, as my fragments will express, when you read them; neverthelesse I wish you by all means to publish it, for these three eminent things observable therein: First, that God in the midst of Popery should open the eyes of one to understand and express so clearly and excellently the intent of the Gospel in the acceptation of Christ's righteousness (as he sheweth through all his Considerations) a thing strangely buried and darkened by the Adversaries, and their great stumbling-block. Secondly, the great honour and reverence which he everywhere beares towards our deare Master and Lord, concluding every Consideration almost with His holy Name, and setting His merit forth so piously; for which I doe so love him, that were there nothing else, I would print it, that with it the honour of my Lord might be published. Thirdly, the many pious rules of ordering our life, about mortification, and observation of God's kingdom within us, and the working thereof, of which he was a very diligent observer. These three things are very eminent in the author, and overweigh the defects (as I conceive) towards the publishing thereof.

> " From his Parsonage of Bemmorton, near Salisbury,
> " September 29, 1632."

" A copy of a letter written by Mr. George Herbert to his friend the translator of this book."

Though Ferrar thought with Herbert that the book contained expressions "at which not only the weak reader may stumble, and the curious quarrel, but also the wise and charitable reader may justly blame," it was contrary to his scrupulous sense of the duty of a translator to omit or alter the offensive passages ; the altering of ancient authors is an "ill example," and one of the "greatest causes of the corruption of truth and learning," he says, in his preface to the Considerations.

He was equally unwilling to make the needful corrections himself. He placed Herbert's letter in the beginning of the book, and his notes in the margin of the passages to which they refer, and, thus recommended and safeguarded the " Hundred and

Ten Considerations of Signior John Valdesso . . . translated out of the Italian copy into English, with notes," was made ready for the press. His own name nowhere appears.

It was perhaps the death of Herbert which caused the finished book to be laid aside till 1638, when it was published at Oxford. It was reprinted at Cambridge in 1646. In this second edition the text is somewhat altered, and some of Herbert's notes omitted. The book is now so rare that those who would like to know something of an author whom Herbert loved, and Ferrar felt profitable to his soul, will pardon the length of the following extracts.

The two first treat of Mortification, and of the demands made by God on the soul of man.

"CONSIDERATION XLIV.

"In what manner a man shall know what fruit he hath made in Mortification, and what is the cause that they who apply themselves to piety, are tempted by affections and appetites with which they were never before tempted.

"I consider that when a person *would understand the profit that he hath made in Mortification*, that is, what affections and appetites he hath mortified, he shall know it by examining himself thoroughly what affections and appetites he hath found alive in himself, having been tempted by them. And considering what, and which of them, are now dead and mortified, he shall understand what profit he hath made in mortification.

"For I understand that he who hath never felt the shame to speak of the Justice of Christ, hath not mortified the affection of shame, which is proper and naturall unto man ; and he that hath felt the shame, and now no more feels it, he it is that hath mortified it; as St. Paul had mortified it, as he shows, saying *that he was not ashamed to preach the gospel*, and I understand that if he had never been ashamed, he would never have gloried in not being ashamed. In like manner I understand the affection of the honour of the world, and of his own proper esteem, that he that having been tempted thereunto, and having concluded with it, is now no more tempted. . . . Understanding that he only may say that he is mortified in these appetites when having been tempted and molested by them, and having combated with them, is now reduced to such terms, that either he feels them not, or is so much master of them, that with ease he overcomes them whenever they molest him. And because none dies but he that hath lived, it being necessary that, in them who are to be quickened, all that which is according to the flesh should die, as well touching affections as appetites, I understand that all this being to die in the regenerated, it is the work of God that presently when a man sets himself to pietie, he should be molested and tempted, not only from those affections and appetites with which he was formerly tempted, but moreover with others, which he never before felt, being different, yea, and very strange ones ; to the intent that feeling them alive he may kill them, and killing them, his regeneration should be made perfect, as appertains to them that are members of the Sonne of God, Jesus Christ our Lord."

"Consideration LXXX.

"What God's intent is in demanding of men that which of themselves alone they cannot give Him ; and why He gives them not at once all that which He will give them.

Extract.—" From the knowledge which the Spirit of God hath of God's being, it comes to passe that not judging of Him as one of the Princes of the world, it knows, that He demanding of men that which they cannot give Him, He doth it not to condemn them, but to save them ; and that from the knowledge which the Holy Spirit hath of the being of man it proceeds, that knowing that man in himself is so arrogant, that if God should demand of him for his salvation things that he could easily give of himself, he would enter into such pride when he had given them, that by the selfsame way whereby he thought to obtain salvation, he would get condemnation.   By this he comes to know, that the intent with which God demands of men that which of themselves they cannot give Him, is not to condemn them, as human wisdom judgeth, which hereupon holds God for unjust, and for cruell; but it is to save them, and to further their salvation; God doing this to the intent that men assaying and trying *to love God with all their heart,* and to believe in Him, and finding themselves altogether unable thus to love and believe, they should have recoarse unto God, and beg those graces of Him, and by those gifts and graces of His they may obtain that felicity which they desire, not for that which they are of themselves, but for that which they are through God. . . .

"I would say, that as He demands of them that which they cannot give Him, to the intent they should not grow proud, as they would if He should demand of them that which they could give Him, and so their salvation would be hindred; so He doth not let them entirely comprehend spiritual things, which He sometimes makes them feel, to the end they should not pride themselves, and so hinder their salvation.

"God knows our evil lump, and desiring our salvation He deals with us, as He sees it convenient we should be dealt with; herein doing that with us, which we do with a child, when we would have him to love us and depend on us, as I would say, that as we give not the child at one time all that which he would have from us, and which we mean to give him ; nay, rather some things we give him altogether, others in part, and others we only show unto him, so much as to breed in him a desire to them, and to enamour him of them, to the end he may go en-amouring himself in us, may follow and depend on us, knowing that if we gave him at once all that we have to give him, he would grow proud, and would not love us, nor depend on us. So God giveth not unto us at once all that which we would have from Him, not that which He will give us, but some things He gives altogether, and others in part, and others He lets us see so much as sufficieth to breed a longing in us for them, and to enamour us of them ; to the intent we may follow Him, love Him, and depend on Him. This He doth, because He knows us to be such that if He should give us at once all that which He hath to give us, we should become proud, and so He should not have from us what He would, that is, *that we should love Him with all our hearts*, and that for the obtaining of eternall life, firmly believing we may make ours the justice of his only begotten Sonne Jesus Christ our Lord."

The three passages which follow are among those condemned by Herbert. The first and last of his notes here given, only appear in the first edition of

Valdesso, and are not to be found in Pickering's edition of "Herbert's Remains," in which the notes are reprinted from the second, or Cambridge edition.

"Consideration III.

" In what the sonnes of God differ from the sonnes of Adam.

" *Extract.*—In the purity and holinesse, which is the health of the soul, the sonnes of God growing daily in grace, and perfecting themselves in holinesse, as they of Samaria (John iv. 42) said unto the woman, *Now we believe, not because, of thy saying: for we have heard Him ourselves;* so they say of the Holy Scriptures, Now we live and grow in spiritual strength, not by the letter or outward relation of the Scriptures, but by the inward teaching and anointing of the Heavenly Spirit of truth, this is that which ruleth and governeth us in the ways of holinesse and righteousness, and so long as He abideth in us and we in Him, we need no other guide, because we are hereby led unto God our Father in Heaven."[1]   The sons of

[1] Compare " The Imitation of Christ," book iii. ch. ii., " That the Truth speaketh inwardly without noise of words," and Tauler's "Sermon for Whit-Sunday," "In the school of the Spirit, man does not learn through books, which teach through outward image addressed to the senses, but here the truth, which of its nature does not speak by means of images, is spoken into the soul itself."—"Life of the Reverend Dr. John Tauler, with Twenty-five of his Sermons," translated by Susannah Winkworth.

God likewise " make use of some rules to preserve the health of their soules. This they do rather to conform themselves outwardly with the sonnes of Adam, than because they feel themselves to stand in need of such observations, forasmuch as they being governed by God alone, observe the will of God and wholly depend on it."

MARGINAL NOTE BY G. HERBERT.—" I like none of it, for it slights the Scriptures too much. Holy Scriptures have not only an elementary use, but a use of perfection, and are able to make the man of God perfect. And David (though David) studied all the day long upon it; and Joshua was to meditate therein day and night.

" All the saints of God may be said in some sense to have put confidence in Scripture; but not as a naked word severed from God, but as the Word of God, and in so doing they do not sever their trust from God. But by trusting in the Word of God, they trust in God."

Again, in Consideration XXXII., " On the abuse and the right use of the Holy Scriptures," Valdesso writes : 'The unlearned man that hath the Spirit serveth himself with images, as with an alphabet of Christian piety; for as much as he so much serves himself with the *picture* of Christ crucified, as serves to imprint on his mind that which Christ suffered,

and to taste and feel the benefit of Christ. And
when he hath imprinted Him, and tasteth and feeleth
Him, he cares no more for the *picture*, leaving it to
serve for an alphabet to other beginners. . . . In like
manner, a learned man that hath the Spirit, serveth
himself of *Holy Scriptures*, as of an alphabet of
Christian piety . . . until such time as it penetrates
into his mind, . . . afterwards leaves them to serve
for the same effect to other beginners, he attending
to the inward inspiration.' . . . And so as well in
the unlearned with the Spirit as in the learned with
the Spirit, is fulfilled that which was prophesied of
the time of the Gospel, where it is said, *They shall all
be taught of God.*"

Note in Margin, G. Herbert.—" I much mislike
the comparison of images and Holy Scriptures, as if
they were both but alphabets, and after a time to be
left. The Holy Scriptures have not only an elementary
use, but a use of perfection ; neither can they ever be
exhausted (as pictures may by a plenary circum-
spection), but still, even to the most learned and
perfect in them, there is somewhat to be learnt more,
therefore David desireth God, in the 119th Psalme, *to
open his eyes that he might see the wondrous things of
His law,* and that he *would make them his study ;*
although, by other words of the same Psalme, it is
evident that he was not meanly conversant in them.
Indeed, he that shall so attend to the back of the

letter as to neglect the consideration of God's work in his heart through the Word, doth amisse; both are to be done, the Scripture still used, and God's work within us still observed, who works by His Word, and ever in the reading of it. As for the text, *They shall all be taught of God*, it being Scripture, cannot be spoken to the disparagement of Scripture; but the meaning is this; that God in the dayes of the Gospel will not give an outward law of ceremonies as of old; but such an one as shall still have the assistance of the Holy Spirit applying it to our hearts, and ever out-running the teacher, as it did when Peter taught Cornelius. There the case is plain, Cornelius had revelation, yet Peter was to be sent for; and those that have inspirations must still use Peter—God's Word. If we make another sense of the text, we shall overthrow all means, save catechising, and set up enthusiasmes."

"Consideration VI.

"Two depravations of man, the one Naturall, the other Acquisite.

"Of these two depravations I understand that the naturall cannot be repaired but by grace, and that they only are free from it who enter into the Kingdom of God by faith, and come to be the sonnes of God by the Holy Spirit, which abideth in them; in such sort that in them, who knowing Christ by Revelation, and accepting the covenant which He made between

God and man, believe and because they believe, are baptised; the natural depravation is repaired, and they remain only with that which is acquisite; from which they go on freeing themselves by little and little, the Spirit of God helping them therein, and whilst they go on freeing themselves of it, that wherein they offend is not put to their account of sin; because they be incorporated in Christ Jesus : for St. Paul sayeth, *There is no condemnation to them which are in Christ Jesus.*"

NOTE IN MARGIN, G. HERBERT.—" The doctrine of this passage must be warily understood : First, that it is not to be understood of actual sins but habitual, for I can no more free myself from actual sins, after baptisme, than I could of originall, before and without baptisme; the exemption from both is by the grace of God. Secondly, among Habits, some oppose Theological virtues, as Vncharitablenesse opposes Charity; Infidelity, Faith; Distrust, Hope : of these, none can free themselves of themselves, but only by the grace of God. Other habits oppose moral virtues, as Prodigality opposes Moderation, and Pusillanimity, Magnanimity. Of these the heathen freed themselves only by the general Providence of God, as Socrates and Aristides, etc."

The second work of these two friends was not completed till after Herbert's death. The preface of

"The Temperate Man" bears date December 7, 1633. It consists of three treatises "On the right way of preserving life and health, together with soundness of the senses, judgement, and memory unto extream old age." The first of these is Ferrar's translation of the " Hygieasticon," published in 1613 by Leonard Lessius, a Jesuit of Louvain ; the other two are translated by Herbert from the Italian of Ludovico Cornaro and another author unnamed.

Complimentary verses, in the fashion of the day, are prefixed to the little book, written by young Cambridge friends of the Ferrars, some of whom became noted men in their day. Among these are Barnabas Oley, afterwards well-known as the editor of " The Country Parson," a Fellow and tutor of Clare ;[1] Peter

---

[1] Oley was ejected from his fellowship in 1644. After the Restoration he became Vicar of Great Grandsden, Huntingdonshire. He left an endowment of £20 a year to the school, which was built during his incumbency. His recollections of Ferrar are to be found in his " Life of George Herbert," published as a preface to the first edition of the " Country Parson " in 1652. He was much beloved and respected. " I'm told that this day your friend, Mr. Barnabas Oley, is to be buried. His parishioners are already extreme sensible of their loss of that reverend and eminently worthy good man."—Letter to Dean Granville, quoted by Rev. J. H. Overton, " Life in the Church of England, 1660—1714." Oley was also Prebendary of Worcester, and was the means of establishing a weekly Celebration in the Cathedral.

Gunning, the future Bishop of Ely, then a youth of twenty, who had just taken his degree ; and Richard Crashaw, the poet, still an undergraduate at Pembroke. Crashaw's verses are to be found among his collected poems, but they are more interesting when read in connection with the book to which they refer :—

> " Haste hither, reader, wouldst thou see
> Nature her own physician be ?
> Wouldst see a man all his own wealth,
> His own music, his own health ?
> A man whose sober soul can tell
> How to wear her garments well ;
> Her garments that upon her sit
> (As garments should do), close and fit ;
> A well-clothed soul, that's not opprest,
> Nor chokt with what she should be drest ?
> Whose soul, sheathed in a crystal shrine,
> Through which all her bright features shine,
> As when a piece of wanton lawn
> A thin ærial veil is drawn
> O'er beauty's face ; seeming to hide,
> More sweetly shows the blushing bride ?
> A soul, whose intellectual beams,
> No mists do mask, no lazy steams ?
> A happy soul, that all the way
> To heaven rides in a summer's day ?
> Wouldst see a man whose well-warmed blood,
> Bathes him in a genuine flood ;
> A man whose tuned humours be
> A set of rarest harmony ?
> Wouldst see blithe looks, fresh cheeks beguile
> Age ? Wouldst see December smile ?

> Wouldst see a nest of roses grow
> In a bed of reverend snow ?
> Warm thoughts, free spirits, flattering
> Winter's self into a spring ?—
> In sum, wouldst see a man that can
> Live to be old, and still a man ;
> Whose latest and most leaden hours
> Fall with soft wings, stuck with soft flowers,
> And when life's sweet fable ends,
> His soul and body part like friends ;
> No quarrels, murmurs, no delay ;
> A kiss, a sigh, and so away ?
> This rare one, reader, wouldst thou see ?
> Haste hither, and thyself be he."

Crashaw is said by the editor of his poems to have himself practised "an almost Lessian temperance," and Ferrar's preface bears witness that the severe rules prescribed in these treatises spurred on his little community to greater austerities than they had at first attempted.

"Master George Herbert of blessed memory," he says, "having at the request of a noble personage translated it" (Cornaro on Temperance) " into English, sent a copy thereof, not many months before his death, unto some friends of his, who a good while before had given an attempt at regulating themselves in matter of diet ; which, although it was after a very imperfect manner, in regard of that exact course therein prescribed, yet was of great advantage to them, inasmuch as they were enabled, through the good example that they had thus made, to go immediately to the practise of that pattern which Cornarus had set them and so have reaped the benefit thereof in a larger and eminenter manner than could otherwise possibly have been imagined in so short a space.

" Not long after, Lessius his book, by happy chance, or, to speak better, by gracious providence of the Author of health and all other good things, came to their hands ; whereby receiving much instruction and confirmation, they requested from me the translation of it into English. Whereupon hath ensued what you shall now receive. . . . As for the practitioners they forbid any more to be spoken of them than this, that as they find all the benefits which are promised by Cornarus and Lessius most true and real, so by God's mercy they had no difficulty at all in the observation of this course. They are sufficient witnesses in their own affairs, and I hold them to be faithful, and therefore making no doubt of the truth of the latter part of their statement, as I can abundantly give testimony to the verities of the former, I commend both to thy belief and consideration, and so commit thee to God's grace."

Herbert's translations have been reprinted in his " Remains." The work of Lessius is now to be found only in the edition of " The Temperate Man," published in 1678.[1]

[1] A copy of this edition is in the Library of Pembroke College, from which, by the kindness of the librarian, the following ex-

The author begins his work with an apology for the subject which he has chosen. "The search into and consideration of this business," he writes, "is not altogether physical, but in great part appertains to divinity and moral philosophy.

"And over and above, the end which I aim at herein, is indeed most befitting a Divine. For that which I principally intend, is to furnish religious persons and those who give themselves to piety, with such a way and manner of living, as they may with more ease, cheerfulness and fervency apply themselves to the faithful service of the great God, and our Saviour the Lord Jesus Christ."

The author then proceeds to give a graphic picture of the evil effects of intemperate eating, and of the gain to mind and body of a strict rule of temperance, illustrated by examples from the lives of the Fathers of the Desert, and other ascetics.

The gluttony which he denounces, and the abstinence which he recommends, are both on a scale too heroic for our feebler times; yet since the spirit of an ordered life is the same in all ages, a few paragraphs from his "Seven Commodities of Temperance," may be worth inserting.

"The Fourth Commodity is the vigour of the wit

tracts have been taken. It is not marked on the title-page as a second edition, and it is possible that the Ferrars may have circulated the work in manuscript only.

in excogitating, reasoning, finding out, and judging of things, and the aptitude and fitness that it hath for the receiving of Divine illuminations.   And hence it comes to pass, that men given to abstinence are watchful, circumspect, provident, of good forecast, able to give counsel, and of sound judgement, and for matters of learning, they do easily grow to excellency in these things whereunto they apply themselves.   As for prayer, meditation, and contemplation, they do perform them with great facility, pleasure, and spiritual delight.

" The ancient Fathers and those that lived in the deserts prove this by their example, who being most abstinent, were always fresh in their minds, and spent whole nights in prayer, and in search and study of divine matters, with so great solace of mind, that they deemed themselves to be in Paradise as it were, and perceived not the passage of the time.   And by this means they came to that great measure of holinesse, and familiarity with God, and were adorned with the gifts of prophesie and miracles, and became admirable to all the world. . . . There are very many also now-adays, who tend unto the highest pitches of wisdom and vertue by the selfsame way of abstinence, whereof some are very admirable in all men's eyes through the abundance of their writings, and their surpassing learning. But no man without the assistance of sobriety can perform any such matter, and if he obstinately attempt it, be shall kill himself long before his time. . . . All the Saints who have gone about the building up the High Tower of Evangelical Perfection, have made their beginnings from this vertue, as from the foundation of their spiritual fabrick."

Besides these works, Nicholas Ferrar translated from the Spanish the " Life of Tho. Sanquay of Cordova, a gentleman by birth, and very learned in law and divinity, one who led a very holy and strict life. He died in 1612." [1]   This translation was never published.

[1] Peckard.

CHAPTER X.

A.D. 1633.

> " The day is spent and hath his will on mee :
>   I and the sunn have run our races,
>   I went ye slower, yet more paces :
> For I decay, not hee.
>
> . . . . . .
>
> O let my soule, whose keys I must deliver
>   Into the hands of senceless dreames,
>   W^{ch} know not Thee, suck in Thy beames,
> And wake with Thee for ever."
>   G. HERBERT, *printed by* Dr. GROSART, *from*
>   *the " Williams' Manuscript."*

THE griefs of which Herbert speaks in the letter prefixed to the " Considerations " are perhaps the trials of his failing health.   Through the winter of 1632–33 he became increasingly feeble.

His friends at Gidding prayed constantly for him during those weary months when he was obliged to forego the public services of the Church which he loved so much.

"O most mighty God," so runs their supplication, "merciful Father, we most humbly beseech Thee if it be Thy good pleasure to continue to us that singular benefit which Thou hast given us in the friendship of Thy servant, our dear brother, who now lieth on the bed of sickness. Let him abide with us yet awhile for the furtherance of our faith. . . . Lord, Thou hast willed that our delights should be in the saints on earth, and in such as excel in virtue ; how then should we not be afflicted and mourn when Thou takest them away from us ! Thou hast made him a great help, and furtherance of the best things amongst us. . . . If it be Thy good pleasure restore unto us our dear brother."[1]

This affectionate and tender desire was not granted. The time had come for fulfilment of the longing of Herbert's fervent soul—

> "O that I now past changing were,
> Safe in Thy Paradise, where no flower can wither."

On a certain Friday, of which the date is not given, but which must have been at the end of January or February, 1633, Mr. Mapletoft, arriving at Gidding on a visit to his wife's relations, brought the grievous news that Herbert was ill past hope of recovery. The blow was unexpected, they had not realized that the danger was so pressing.

[1] " Life of Nicholas Ferrar," by his brother, p. 74.

It was now, probably, that Nicholas Ferrar sent Mr. Edmund Duncon to Bemerton to learn how his friend did, and to bear him loving assurances of prayer and sympathy.

The history of that holy death-bed is too well known for repetition, yet since Herbert's last gift to the Church was made through Ferrar's hands, it must be told, how "with so sweet a humility as seemed to exalt him," he bowed down to Mr. Duncon, saying, with a thoughtful and contented look, "Sir, I pray deliver this little book to my dear brother Ferrar, and tell him he shall find in it a picture of the many spiritual conflicts that have passed between God and my soul, before I could subject mine to the will of Jesus my Master, in Whose service I have now found perfect freedom; desire him to read it, and then, if he can think it may turn to the advantage of any de-jected poor soul; let it be made public, if not, let him burn it; for I and it are less than the least of God's mercies."[1]

The book so humbly given was the manuscript of "The Temple."

When the precious legacy was brought to Ferrar, he read it many times over, kissing again and again the pages on which his beloved friend had poured out his inmost soul. "He could not," he said, "sufficiently admire it, as a rich jewel and most

----

[1] Walton, "Life of Herbert."

worthy to be in the hands and hearts of all true Christians that feared God and loved the Church of England." [1]

His prompt action with regard to his friend's poems is a great contrast to the tardiness with which his own works were brought out. Within three weeks of Herbert's death a few copies of " The Temple " were printed, apparently for private distribution. A little delay in publication was caused by the Chancellor's refusal to license the book [2] unless the lines

> " Religion stands on tip-toe in our land,
> Readie to pass to the American strand,"

were omitted. Ferrar stoutly refused to alter a line or word of the work entrusted to his charge, but the difficulty was got over in some way, and two editions, in neither of which any license appears, were brought out in the course of the year. They came out with no dedication, and unaccompanied by the com-

---

[1] " Life of Nicholas Ferrar," by his brother, p. 51.

[2] The manuscript copy sent to Cambridge for license is now in the Bodleian. Herbert's original manuscript is lost, destroyed probably in the plunder of Gidding, but a very interesting manuscript, partly in his handwriting, containing about one-third of " The Temple," with some additional poems, is in the Williams' Library. It is in a Gidding binding, and was once the property of one of the Mapletofts, who probably received it from Nicholas Ferrar. See " Dict. Nat. Biog.," article " Herbert," and Dr. Grosart's preface to the collected edition of " Herbert's Poems," published by Messrs. G. Bell and Sons.

plimentary verses so often prefixed to books of the period.

"The dedication of this work," Ferrar wrote in the preface, which has been retained in each succeeding edition, "having been made by the authour to the Divine Majestie only, how should we now presume to interest any mortall man in the patronage of it! Much lesse think we it meet to seek the recommendation of the Muses, for that which himself was confident to have been inspired by a diviner breath than flows from Helicon. The world therefore shall receive it in that naked simplicitie with which he left it, without any addition either of support or ornament more than is included in itself. We leave it free and unforestalled to every man's judgement, and to the benefit that he shall find by perusall."

No such record of spiritual experience had yet appeared in the English language, and the book at once took a place only to be compared to that of the "Christian Year." It was reprinted in 1634, in 1635, again in 1638, and six more editions followed in the course of the century. It was the treasured companion of the most dissimilar people. It was among the books from which Charles I. sought consolation in his prison. "Next to the Scripture poems" Richard Baxter found "none so savoury" as these. It brought comfort and light to the sick-bed of Henry Vaughan, who in the preface to his "Silex Scintillans" speaks

of "the blessed man, Mr. George Herbert, whose
holy life and verse gained many pious converts, of
whom I am the least." Crashaw wrote in a copy
which he sent to a friend the lines beginning—

> "When your hands untie these strings,
> Think you've an angel by the wings."

And he named his own poems "Steps to the Temple."[1]

It was probably at Gidding that the younger poet
first learnt to know and admire the works of the
elder. Crashaw came up to Pembroke a boy about
sixteen, the year before Herbert's death. He soon
became acquainted with the Ferrars, for we find him
writing the verses prefixed to the "Temperate Man,"
in 1633; and it is evident that his tender, affectionate,
enthusiastic spirit was at once attracted by their life
of devotion. At Gidding he found his ideal, "Religious
House," in a visible shape.

> "Walks and unshorn woods, and souls, just so
> Unforced and genuine ; but not shady tho' ;
>
> .   .   .   .   .
>
> Our lodging hard, and homely as our fare,
> That chaste and cheap as the few clothes we wear.
>
> .   .   .   .   .
>
> A hasty portion of prescribed sleep,
> Obedient slumbers that can wake and weep,
> And sing, and sigh, and work, and sleep again,
> Still rowling a round sphear of still returning pain.
> Hands full of hearty labours. . . .
>
> .   .   .   .   .

---

[1] See Dr. Grosart's preface to "Herbert's Poems."

> Reverent Discipline, and religious fear,
> And soft obedience find sweet hiding here,
> Silence and sacred rest ; peace and pure joys.
>
> .   .   .   .   .
>
> The self-remembering soul sweetly recovers
> Her kindred with the stars, nor basely hovers
> Below, but meditates her immortal way
> Home to the original source of light and intellectual day."

There seems to be an allusion to the employments of Gidding in another poem, sufficiently marked to warrant the conjecture that the " Lines on a Prayer-book " may have been originally addressed to one of the Ferrar family.

> "Lo, here a little volume, but greate booke,
>   *A neste of new-borne sweetes,*
>   *Whose native fires disdaining*
>   *To lie thus folded and complaining*
>   *Of these ignoble sheetes,*
>   *Affect more comely bands*
>   *Fair one from thy kinde handes,*
>   *And confidently looke*
>   *To find the reste*
>   *Of a rich binding in your breste.*[1]
>
> .   .   .   .   .
>
> " It is an armoury of light ;
>   Let constant use but keep it bright,
>   You'll find it yields
>   To holy hands and humble hearts,

---

[1] The lines printed in italics do not occur in the first edition of the poems, printed in 1646, but they are found in those of 1648 and 1652.—Dr. Grosart, "Fuller Worthies," ed. of Crashaw.

More swordes and shields,
Than sinne hath snares, or hell hath dartes.

" Only be sure
The hands be pure
That hold these weapons, and the eyes
Those of turtles, chast and **true**,
Wakeful and wise ;
Here is a friend shall fight for you ;
Hold but this book before your heart,
Let prayer alone to play its part.

" But, oh ! the heart
That studies this high art
Must be a sure housekeeper,
And yet no sleeper.

  .   .   .   .   .

" Dear soule, be strong.
Mercy will come ere long,
And bring its bosome full of blessings,
Flowers of never-fading graces,
To make immortal dressings,
For worthy soules, whose wise embraces,
Store up themselves for Him who is alone
The spouse of virgins and the Virgin's Son."

If we may suppose that lines five to ten in the above ode refer to the work done at Gidding, it seems to follow that a companion poem, "Counsel to a Young Lady Concerning her Choice," addressed to the same lady, "Mistress M. R.,"[1] is an exhortation to follow the path already marked out by Mary and Anna Collett.

[1] May not this unknown "M. R." be MaRgaret Collett or MaRy Mapletoft ?

> " 'Tis time you listen to a braver love
>   Which from above
>   Calls you up higher,
>   And bids you come
>   And choose your roome
>   Among His own fair sons of fire.
>
>   .   .   .   .
>
>   " It was His heavenly art
>   Kindly to cross you
>   In your mistaken love,
>   That at the next remove
>   Thence he might toss you,
>   . And strike your troubled heart
>   Home to Himself, to hide it on His brest,
>   The bright ambrosial nest
>   Of love, of life, and everlasting rest."

Crashaw's sympathy with the life of Gidding was not expressed in words alone. He was himself often to be found among those

> " Holy hands and humble hearts "

of whom he sings; delighting to join in their prayers and watchings, and when in Cambridge his leisure time was spent "in the temple of God, under His wing" in " St. Marie's Church near St. Peter's College ; there he lodged under Tertullian's roof of angels, there he made his rest more gladly than David's swallow near the house of God, where, like a primitive saint, he offered more prayers in the night than others in the day."[1]

---

[1] Preface to first edition of " Steps to the Temple.'

When Crashaw was made Fellow and Tutor of Peterhouse, Ferrar Collett, one of the "towardly youths" who loved to share the watch-nights of their Uncle Nicholas, became his pupil, and the friendly intercourse continued till Crashaw, with two hundred other resident Fellows, was ejected by Cromwell for refusing to sign the Covenant.

There were many who, like Crashaw, loved to withdraw themselves for a while from the world and refresh their souls in the peaceful atmosphere of Gidding, so that it became a house of retreat, to which "many of the clergy that were more inclined to practical piety and devotion than to doubtful and needless disputation, did often come," [1] not to disturb the strict order of the household, but to make themselves for a time "a part of that happy society," sharing in the daily hours of prayer, and often assisting Mr. Ferrar and his family in keeping up the night watch.

[1] Walton's "Life of Herbert."

CHAPTER XI.

A.D. 1633-1637.

> "Our all is from Thy gracious throne,
>   We nought can style our own,
>   And when to Thee we offerings bring,
>   They drops are of Thy boundless spring."
>
> BISHOP KEN, 1637-1711.

MANY visitors came to Gidding besides the sympathetic friends who looked upon it as an oasis of peace and refreshment. The peculiarities of the family life attracted attention from all kinds of people; and, the house, being easy of access from the Huntingdon high-road, a visit to Gidding seems to have become a favourite amusement with leisurely travellers, mildly interested in Church matters, who happened to find themselves in the neighbourhood. One such self-invited guest, a lawyer from Gray's Inn, named Lenton, chronicled his experience in an extremely interesting and amusing letter,[1] which has already been referred to in these pages. He was received by Nicholas Ferrar with great courtesy, presented to his mother and sister, and hospitably offered "a glass of sack, a sugar-cake, and a fine napkin, brought by a mannerly maid."

On the strength of this kind reception, Mr. Lenton catechised his host with an unabashed curiosity, which proves that the "interviewer" is not of modern growth. He inquired how long a time they spent in prayers, and what they did besides, whether it was true that some of the young ladies were vowed to celibacy, at what hour they rose in the morning, how they furnished their chapel, and if they did not consider that their habits and customs savoured of popery and superstition. All these remarks and many more Nicholas Ferrar heard "very civilly and with much humility," and answered them "with mildness and moderation," as Lenton, who seems quite unconscious that he had been making himself extremely disagreeable, assures his correspondent.

After accompanying his host to the morning service, he asked for his horse, hoping inwardly that he would be invited to remain and dine with the family, "that he might have gained more time to

---

[1] Lenton to Hetley, 1634. This letter is to be found in Peckard's "Life of Nicholas Ferrar" and Mr. Mayor's Preface to "Two Lives," p. xxvi.

R

have seen and observed more of their fashions;" but Ferrar, whose patience must have been somewhat outworn, instead of making him stay, helped him in calling for his horse, and the inquisitive gentleman rode away musing on the "many more questions" which he "thought on when it was too late."

Some persons pushed their curiosity so far that they left their horses and servants at a neighbouring inn, and wandered in the dark to Gidding, pretending to have lost their way, and begging for a night's lodging, merely that they might see something of the customs of the house.

Nicholas Ferrar treated all who came with kindness, never refusing to see them, however busy he might be. "He well hoped," he would say, when called from his study to receive some uninvited guest, "they came for his good or their own, and the whole design of his life was to make himself or others better." Often, we may believe, his grave and kindly words were blest to these chance comers, who carried away with them the lasting recollection of a home in which the service of God was visibly set before all other objects and duties; but there were some whose dislike and contempt for what they considered Roman ways, blinded them to the beauty of a life of piety and charity. Such persons were not appeased by the declaration with which Ferrar had silenced Lenton, that he "believed the Pope to be Antichrist, as firmly as any article in his creed." They pointed to the "I.H.S." constantly used in the letters and papers of Gidding, and asked if that sacred monogram were not the symbol of the Jesuits; they found fault with the cross on the altar, and with the lengthy devotions of the family. The Ferrars "rose at midnight for prayer," writes Fuller, "and other people much complained of it, whose heads, I dare say, never ached for want of sleep." [1]

The critics even accused Nicholas of harshness to his family, of overbearing ways, and the enforcement of a severe rule—ridiculous accusations enough, since John Ferrar and Mr. Collett were free agents, and could have broken up the joint household at any time, if they had been so minded. So much was said that Mrs. Collett actually felt compelled to write a letter to her brother exculpating him from these charges, and also replying to some objections which seem to have been made to the " Conversations " with which her daughters amused themselves.

The letter is written from Gidding, and undated.

"My most dear Brother,

"As you desire a free, so I make no doubt but a brief, declaration will give you satisfaction in those two things wherein you require an answer. And first for letters, those you have been pleased to

[1] Fuller, "Worthies of Huntingdonshire."

give me any assistance in, I think myself much beholden, and if hereafter upon entreaty and occasion you shall afford me your help, I shall thankfully acknowledge it for a great favour. Then, for the matter of storying, I have accounted the most part of them to be delivered by way of relation of the actions and opinions of good and virtuous men and women, and such as for the substance ought to be taken for patterns of imitation, and so for all other passages that are intermingled with them, and do heartily desire that whatever is contained in them, that is the will and command of God, that we in our own particular should do, we may both consent and conform unto all points. For any corporal exercise, there is none imposed, nor (as I conceive) expected from me, but what I both may and do willingly perform, and therefore I shall not need to say any more to that, nor, I hope, at all in these matters, but humbly beseech God that whatever shall be done or said further may prove to His glory and our comforts.

" Your loving Sister,

"S. C."[1]

Nicholas was painfully sensitive to these unkindly criticisms. He told his friend Barnabas Oley "that to fry a faggot was not more martyrdom than con-

---

[1] "Two Lives," Appendix.

tinual obloquy."[1] The thirst for battle was not in him, and, were it but possible, he would fain have lived at peace with all men, though he could hold his own with spirit when a controversy was forced on him, as happened occasionally when Roman missioners, thinking perhaps that a man who was so obnoxious to the Puritans must be ripe for submission to the Pope, found their way to Gidding.

Meanwhile the practices of the family found firm support in a quarter where such help could hardly have been looked for. In the same year in which Nicholas Ferrar, with joy and thankfulness, began that retired course of life for which he had long prepared, his old acquaintance Williams, the late Lord Keeper, came, a most unwilling exile, to take up his abode at Buckden, the country house of the Bishops of Lincoln, distant only a few miles from Gidding. When the Great Seal was taken from him, he "having now no more to do with civil distractions, bethought him instantly of the Duty of his Pastoral Staff,"[2] and paid his first visit to the diocese over which he had already presided four years. He comforted himself for the loss of court favour by

[1] "Life of G. Herbert." Oley adds that his friend was "torn asunder as with mad horses, or crushed betwixt the under and upper millstone of contrary reports; that he was a Papist, and that he was a Puritan."

[2] Hacket's "Life of Archbishop Williams."

laying out the neglected grounds of Buckden with a lavish magnificence which recalls the visionary gardens of Bacon's essay, and there lived with splendid hospitality, making all comers welcome, and receiving with equal kindness the nobles and rich gentry, the clergy, of whom he had " commonly a coovy" about him, the neighbouring townsmen, and the poor.

Nicholas Ferrar must have known his future diocesan at least by sight as one of the proctors at Cambridge, and he may have formed one of the crowd of gownsmen in St. Mary's on the occasion when, in his examination for the degree of Bachelor of Divinity, Williams defended the characteristic thesis that, "though the end of Theology is to gain souls, the end of the Theologue, subject to the first and Architectonical end, is for an honest maintenance and sustentation :" but his real acquaintance with him began during the long debates held at the council board on the Virginian affairs, while Williams was Lord Keeper.

This acquaintance was continued in Huntingdon-shire ; and one of the most amiable points in the character of the world-loving bishop is the uniform kindness and consideration which he showed to the unworldly family at Gidding, through good and evil days.   He could admire the strict life, which he had no wish to imitate, and he seems to have felt for these simple and single-hearted people a regard which was almost affection. He made himself acquainted with their rule of prayer and discipline, and gave it his full approval, undisturbed by the plain-spoken opinion of the Huntingdonshire Puritans, that a house so conducted could be none other than "a convent packed together of some superstitious order beyond seas, or a nunnery, and that the sufferance of it looked towards a change in religion." His friend and biographer, Hacket, shared his admiration for Gidding; "Let this history,"[1] he says, "give glory to God in their behalf, showing in a touch on what religious grounds their policy was founded. . . . All their practice was heavenly; a great deal of it had some singularity, by the custom of our corrupt ways, who do not strive to enter in at the strait gate to come to Blessedness," and he indignantly repudiates the idea that their rule was in any respect alien to the spirit of the English Church. "Speak, Sir Censurer," he cries, "we, the true children of the Church of England, were we not, without departing from our own Station, capable of Mortification? of vowing ourselves to God? of renouncing the World? of Fasting? of Vigils? of prayer limited to Canons, and Hours, as any that say, and do not, that call themselves from St. Basil, St. Bennet, or such other institution? Not our Reformation, but our slothfulness

[1] "Life of Archbishop Williams," part ii. p. 51.

doth indispose us, that we let others run faster than we in Temperance, in Chastity, in Scleragogy, as it was called."

Some little time after her arrival at Gidding, Mrs. Ferrar discovered that a portion of the estate had formerly been glebe, which had been enclosed for pasture by a former lord of the manor, he having compounded with the vicar for a payment of £20 a year, to be paid for ever, in lieu of glebe and tithes. She felt this arrangement insufficient, and having with some trouble made out the extent of the ancient glebe, in 1633 she restored the whole to the Church. Hacket gives extracts from the letter in which she announced her intention to the bishop.

" Right reverend Father in God—the expectation of opportunities, having some years whealed me off from the Performance of this Business, I now think it necessary to break through all Impediments, and humbly to present to your Lordship the Desires and the Intentions, of my Heart. Beseeching you, on God's behalf, to take them into your Fatherly Consideration, and to give a speedy accomplishment to them, by the Direction of your Wisdom, and the Assistance of your authority. . . ."

The paper ends with the prayer subjoined.

" Be graciously pleased, LORD, now to accept from Thy Handmaid the Restitution of that, which has been unduly heretofore taken from Thy Ministers.

And as an earnest and pledge of the total Resignation of herself and hers to Thy Service, vouchsafe to receive to the use of Thy Church this small portion of that large Estate, which Thou hast bestowed on her, the unworthiest of Thy Servants. LORD, redeem Thy right, whereof Thou hast been too long disseized by the world, both in the Possessions, and in the Person of Thy Handmaid. And let this outward seizure of Earth be accompanied by an inward Surprizal of the Heart and Spirit into Thine own Hands ; So that the Restorer, as well as that which is restored, may become and be confirmed Thine inheritance. . . ."

Williams, who was not himself in the habit of voluntarily resigning any possession which he had once acquired, and who held so many and various preferments that he was said to be "a whole diocese in his own person," prized this generous gift at its fullest worth. " It was the joy of his heart," he said, " to live to see such an act done, in honour of God and the Church of England. Many had taken from it, and the coal from the altar had consumed many of their inheritances ; yet the rest feared not. But to restore, as is now done, the glebe land to the Church of their own accord, request, and seeking, which was no less than to give so much to it ! Here's an example to all the gentry of England."

To do honour to this liberality, and to give a public mark of his approval to the family, the bishop, at his next visitation, administered Confirmation and preached in the church at Gidding.

It was a great day at Gidding, and the family spared no pains to show their respect for the bishop, and to give him pleasure. Williams loved music, and the choir of Peterborough Cathedral, where Ferrar's old friend Augustine Lindsell was now bishop, and his successor, Dr. Towers, dean, came over that the musical part of the service might be worthy of the occasion. The little church was crowded with the neighbouring gentry and villagers, many of whom brought their children to be confirmed together with the younger Ferrars and Colletts. In the midst of the press the bishop, scarce raised above their heads in the low pulpit, spoke, in words which must have sounded strangely from his lips, of the contempt of the world, of the cutting off of the right hand and the right eye, and all fleshly contentments, that so they might enter into life eternal.[1] The sermon was meant, and understood, as an eulogium of the Ferrars, and must have been a little trying to the venerable lady who sat by, in the midst of her children, listening to these veiled praises, but it may be hoped that it had at least some temporary effect in silencing the criticism of the neighbourhood.

After the service the bishop dined at the house, and went over it, noticing and approving all the arrange-

---

[1] "Life of Archbishop Williams," part ii. p. 51.

ments, and before his departure he gave his solemn benediction to the assembled family. A crowd of people gathered about the gates to see him ride away, and before them all he embraced Nicholas Ferrar with the words, "*Deus tibi animum istum et animo isti tempus longissimum concedet*" ("God keep you in that mind, and grant that mind of yours a long continuance here on earth ").[1]

Williams paid several visits to Gidding. He took great delight in the conversation of Nicholas Ferrar ; and John, with evident pleasure in the recollection, tells how on one occasion it seemed good to the bishop "to enter into the pleasantness of telling stories," and "he would have Nicholas Ferrar to parallel them with some of the like nature, and so the time passed away to the great delight of the present company." "I must confess," said the bishop afterwards to a mutual friend, "I thought myself pretty good at storying, but never met with my match till then. . . . Commend me to him, and tell him, the next time I come, we will have another game at storying."

The opportunity never came. In July, 1637, Williams was committed to the Tower. He was permitted to receive his friends freely, keeping open house in the prison rooms, and here, mindful of old kindness, Nicholas Ferrar came to see him. This time

---

[1] "Life of Nicholas Ferrar," by his brother, p. 63.

there was no gay encounter of wits.   The bishop was conscious of some change in the countenance and manner of his visitor, some marks of infirmity, or a look more withdrawn and spiritual ; his farewell words had the ring of prophecy.

They talked long together, and then Nicholas asked the bishop's blessing and took his leave gravely, with a sad foreboding in his heart.   "Your brother made me much to wonder," said Williams afterwards, describing the interview to John Ferrar, " for he said to me, that I should come out of this place, and rise to greater dignity, but the times would be dangerous.   I thought, when he was gone, the more upon them, as from a dying man's words, for so he seemed to me, and I feared I never should see him again." [1]

[1] "Life of Nicholas Ferrar," by his brother, p. 58.

CHAPTER XII.

DEATH OF MRS. FERRAR—LAST YEARS, ILLNESS, AND DEATH OF NICHOLAS FERRAR.

A.D. 1634–1637.

" Since I am coming to that holy room,
   Where with Thy quire of saints for evermore
   I shall be made Thy music, as I come
   I tune my instrument here at the doors
   And what I must do then, think here before."
Donne (1573–1630).

In the spring of 1634 a heavy blow fell on the household of Gidding. Mrs. Ferrar had always been the prop and centre of her family. Her daughter's letters are full of tender allusions to her. Mrs. Collett speaks of " God's mercy to us all in that which is so great a pillar of our comforts, the health of our dearest mother, which I beseech Him still to continue, and make us truly thankful for it ; " and again, in writing to a cousin, she dwells on " the perfect health, and (I may well say and bless God for it) the great strength and ability both of body and mind, of my dearest mother."   Early in 1634 Lenton saw her, "tall, straight, and clear complexioned," going on her son's arm to the daily prayer, at the head of her children and grandchildren, but in the May of that year her strength failed, and she was taken from the home which she had founded and guided, going before her children to the perpetual worship of Paradise, as she had so often gone before them to the sanctuary which she had prepared for their constant prayers on earth.

"Though of so great age, at her dying day she had no infirmity, and scarce any sign of old age upon her. Her hearing, sight, and all her senses were very good. She had never lost a tooth; she walked very upright, and with great agility. Nor was she troubled with any pains or uneasiness of body. While she lived at Gidding, she rose, summer and winter, at five o'clock, and sometimes sooner. In her person she was of a comely presence, and had a countenance, so full of gravity that it drew respect from all who beheld her. In her words she was courteous, in her actions obliging. In her diet always very temperate; saying she did not live to eat and drink, but ate and drank to live. She was a pattern of piety, benevolence, and charity. And thus she lived and died, esteemed, revered, and beloved of all who knew her."[1]

After his mother's death Nicholas Ferrar increased his austerities. He would no longer go to bed, but

[1] John Ferrar, quoted by Peckard.

lay, wrapped "in a great shag black freize gown," on a bearskin on the floor, for the few hours sleep which he allowed himself; and in the coldest weather he would scarce ever sit by the fire. His faithful old friend, Bishop Lindsell, remonstrated with him in vain. Nicholas answered by reminding his former tutor of his lessons on the ascetic lives of the ancient fathers. To other friends he declared "that he knew that whosoever, upon what pretence so ever did by these means infringe their healths, did sore amiss and sin; for that it is found by daily experience that sickly, infirm, and weak healths make men subject to many ill passions and distempers, and the pains of the body disquiet the mind not a little, and make us not so apt and fit, neither to perform our duties to God in that station He hath appointed us, nor to execute our duty to our neighbour."

But he seems to have found by experience that, however little such a way of life might appear suited to the powers of ordinary men, to him at least it was not injurious, for his brother affirms that "it is known to all, that he never had so much health, together with ability of bodily strength and mind, as in the last seven years of his life, when he was as they thought most strictest in these things."

Nicholas Ferrar wrote much during this period, and often on his knees. The whole of the manuscripts thus composed — to the number it is said of five folio volumes—are lost; destroyed probably in the plunder of Gidding. The result of those last years of prayer and fasting can be traced only in the tender memories of his friends, and the life lived by the children of his training. Bishop Lindsell never ceased to regret that he had shrunk from the priesthood. He was a better scholar and an abler divine than himself, he would say, and of all men he knew he would have chosen him to be his confessor. The venerable bishop willingly accepted reproof from his old pupil, who "never heard his tutor say or do amiss at any time, but he would before they parted, in some sweet good way, let him know his mind, which was commonly by way of story."[1]   And many other friends long remembered the affectionate pains with which he would advise them in their spiritual distresses, until he had, "as it were, begotten them anew to God."

Meanwhile the shadows deepened on his own spirit, and his last year of life was passed in sad and bitter forebodings. The time was one of great outward prosperity both in Church and State. "What a halcyonian calm, a blessed time of peace, this Church of England had for many years, above all the churches in the world beside, when the King, St. Charles of blessed memory, and the good Archbishop of Canterbury, with others, were endeavouring to perfect the

---

[1] "Life of Nicholas Ferrar," by his brother, p. 76.

clergy in regularity of life, uniformity of officiating, and all variety of learning !" So wrote Barnabas Oley in his old age, looking back across forty troubled years to the prosperous days of youth.[1] But already below the fair and shining surface a listening ear might catch the murmur of the rising storm.

Gidding lay within the bounds of the most Puritan region of England, the counties which afterwards formed the "Eastern Association,"[2] "the Torres Vedras lines of the early Civil War." In the fen-lands about Huntingdon and Peterborough, Cromwell, now peacefully employed in farming at St. Ives, afterwards found and formed his famous Ironsides. The flame which was to break forth so soon, was already smouldering, and it is easy to imagine with what a troubled heart the pupil of Lindsell and White, the friend of Sandys, the once eager member of the "country party," must have watched the signs of coming strife, all his keen sympathies, his early associations going with the cause of liberty, while yet he felt that the religion which was dearer than all, would be dragged in the dust by the men who were ranged on the popular side.

As early as 1636 he perceived that trouble was at

[1] Preface to second edition of the "Country Parson," published 1671.

[2] The Associated Counties were Cambridgeshire, Norfolk, Suffolk, Essex, Hertfordshire, Huntingdonshire, and Lincoln

hand.   Some of his tenants applied for leases of fifteen years at the old rent.   John Ferrar objected to the proposed arrangement, saying that the land was under rented, and the leases much too long. "Content yourself, I pray," said Nicholas.   "Let the men have ten years time, and a good pennyworth, so that they may be contented, and pay you honestly at your day of payment, for I tell you that before those times come out, you will see other days, and think yourself happy that you may receive, and they pay you, that rent in quiet."

In the following year, 1637, Nicholas had the interview with Williams in the Tower which has been already mentioned.   From that visit he returned to Gidding weighed down by sadness, the depression of failing health adding to his prophetic sorrow for the coming troubles of his country.

John Ferrar remembered and wrote down long after the words in which he gave expression to these feelings.

The brothers were walking up and down in the great parlour, when Nicholas told John that he felt the hand of death drawing near.   "My dear brother," he said, "I am now shortly to appear before our good Lord God, to whom I must give account of what I have said and taught you all of this family in the ways and service of God.   I have, I tell you, delivered unto you all nothing but what is agreeable to His holy law, will, and word, that you should love Him, serve Him, and have showed you the right good way . . . it is the right old good way you are in ; keep in it. God will be worshipped in spirit and truth, in soul and in body ; He will have both inward love and fear, and outward reverence of body and gesture. . . . There will be sad times come, and very sad; you will live to see them, but be courageous, and hold you fast to God with humility and patience, rely upon His mercy and power ; you will suffer much . . . and you will be sifted, but be you steadfast and call upon God. Keep to your daily prayers, and let all be done in sincerity, setting God always before your eyes."

And then, " weeping and grasping his brother by the hand," he went on, " Ah, brother, my brother, I pity you, I pity your care and what you may live to see, even great alterations. God will bring punishments upon this land, but I trust not to the utter ruin of it, but in judgment He will remember mercy, and will yet spare this sinful and unthankful land and nation. But if you should live to see the Divine service and worship of God by supreme authority brought to nought and suppressed, then look and fear that desolation is at hand, and cry mightily to God : His wrath will be then hot against the land. God in His infinite mercy, whose mercy is above all, divert such a judgment." [1]

Nicholas had been engaged on some work, the

---

[1] " Life of Nicholas Ferrar," by his brother.

subject of which we are not told. He now laid it aside, and began to write a meditation on death, of which the following fragment has been preserved :—

" The remembrance of death is very powerful to restrain us from sinning. For he who shall well consider that the day will come (and he knoweth not how soon) when he shall be laid on a sick-bed, weak and faint, without care and almost without strength, encompassed with melancholy thoughts and over-whelmed with auguish ; when, on one side, his dis-temper increasing upon him, the physician tells him that he is past all hope of life, and, on the other, his friends urge him to dispose of his worldly goods and share his wealth among them, that wealth which he procured with trouble and preserved with anxiety, that wealth which he now parts from with sorrow ; when again the priest calls on him to take the prepa-ratory measures for his departure ; when he himself now begins to be assured that here he hath no abiding city, that this is no longer a world for him, that no more suns will rise and set upon him, that for him there will be no more seeing, no more hearing, no more speaking, no more touching, no more tasting, no more fancying, no more understanding, no more remembering, no more desiring, no more loving, no more delights of any sort to be enjoyed by him ; but that death will at one stroke deprive him of all these things, that he will speedily be carried out of that house which he had called his own, and is now become another's, that he will be put into a cold narrow grave, that earth will be consigned to earth, ashes to ashes, dust to dust;—let any man duly and daily ponder these things, and how could it be that he should dare——"[1]

The paper here breaks off unfinished, and these solemn words seem to be the last that ever fell from the pen of Nicholas Ferrar. On Friday, November 3, he went to church and said the service, according to his custom, but on coming home he sat down and complained of faintness. He rested awhile by the fire and took some broth which was brought to him, but felt no better, and when some one expressed a hope that in God's mercy the weakness would pass, replied "that he thought not so," and presently desired that Mr. Groose, the Vicar of Great Gidding, might be sent for. He was an old friend, having already held the living for seventeen years, and Nicholas now begged of him that he would keep up the daily services at Little Gidding.

"It is my first care," he said, "that the service of my God be not one day neglected by those that can go to church. We owe much more than any our continual serving God; for his favours to us are above what we can express, and the performances of our dutiful thankfulness can have no end. I shall

---

[1] " Life of Nicholas Ferrar," by his brother, p. 88.

not, I know, be any more able to perform my duty to Him at church, but come I pray you daily, and perform there my part."

The next morning Nicholas rose again, but felt unable to go out, and had prayers in his chamber, sending the family to church at their usual hours. That evening he moved into another room, larger perhaps and more suitable to a sick man than his own, and there took to his bed, where he remained for two or three days, and then "he willed a pallet to be made on the floor, unto which he removed, and came no more off it." On this lowly couch he lay for nearly a month, feeling no pain, but a constant faintness and decay of strength.

From the first he felt an inward conviction that this illness was his last. "In all former sickness I have had a strong desire to live," he said to the troubled friends who watched him, "and an earnestness to pray to my God to spare me, which He hath to this day done, and I may further say, to the glory of His great Name, that I never earnestly set myself to beg of God anything, but He fulfilled the petition of His most unworthy servant. But now, and of late, I do not find in my heart any inclination to beg longer life of God. Nay, I rather desire to be dissolved with St. Paul, and to leave this life for one eternal in heaven, through the merits of my Saviour Jesus Christ, now wholly and fully submitting myself to the blessed will of my good Lord, to do with me for life or death as He sees best for me."

Sunday, November 5, Mr. Groose gave him the Holy Communion. Before receiving it he "made a most solemn and comfortable confession of his faith," according to the Church of England, acknowledging his salvation to depend only upon the sweet and infinite mercies and sufferings of his most dear Lord and Saviour Jesus Christ, renouncing all other dependencies, "saying when men had done all they could, they must wholly acknowledge and confess themselves most unworthy servants," and so "with great desire and devotion, he received the Blessed Sacrament with much joy."

Throughout his illness he constantly exhorted his family whom he had so carefully taught and trained, to continue in "the good old way" which he had pointed out. "Be constant, be steadfast, do not shrink." These are the constant tenor of his last instructions ; the fear of coming trouble is always before his dying eyes. "Adhere to the doctrine of the Church of England," he repeats, with prophetic consciousness of the evil days to come.

He recommended the young people to continue working at the Concordances, as he had taught them. "I hope God will send you ways and means and helps to go forward with them," he said. "You may grow to perfection of something, by such helps as

God will send. Leave not the thought of them, though I be gone."

The care of the little Community was constantly in his thoughts. He would send for them all from time to time, down to the little ones, ten-year-old Virginia and her brother John, and the Mapletoft children, and bid them remember all he had taught them, and keep in heart diligently the Psalms and Gospels which they had learnt, and remember ever that the fear of God is the beginning of wisdom, and then would dismiss them with his blessing, kissing them tenderly, and calling on God to protect them, for he only was safe whom God kept.

His most earnest advice and special care was for his brother's eldest son, his own godson, Nicholas. "This youth he loved dearly, and looked upon as him to whom Gidding, by God's blessing, would in the end descend; and desirous he was, that he might continue in that virtuous and pious course he had by his love and care been trained up in from his cradle."

He shrank with horror from anything that implied praise; all the eager vehemence of his youth breaks forth in the sick man if he hears any utterance of overmuch sorrow, of too great regret for the loss of his guiding hand. He reproved his brother for saying " in his exuberance of grief," " What shall become of us poor sheep, if the shepherd be now thus taken from us?" " Do you know what you say?" he asked with startling severity. "Go, I pray you, go to church and fast this day, and beg of God to forgive you your undue speeches and expressions; it much grieveth me to hear them. God forgive you them, I beseech Him."

He was "much offended and displeased" when Mr. Groose spoke of his sickness as a punishment to his family, as well as a trial to his own patience, and, "with great vehemency and a loud voice," begged "that he would not let such a word proceed out of his mouth;" and to another clergyman who spoke to him of the comfort he must now feel in his alms-deeds, he replied, "Mass, I am to ask my God forgiveness for my great neglect in that my duty. It had been but my part to have given all that I had, and not to have scattered a few crumbs of alms here and there. The Lord God forgive, I most humbly beseech Him, my too much carnal love to my friends in this kind."

Thus, growing more and more feeble in body, but still lively and vigorous in mind, he spent the month of November on his pallet bed on the floor, advising, exhorting, planning for the continuance of the life of work and devotion which he had built up round him, preparing with passionate self-humiliation for the account which he was soon to render.

He had still one possession which had once, perhaps, been a source of temptation to him—the collection of plays and poems, which he had packed away before quitting London. They had remained at Gidding unopened. Early in the winter morning (it was about the first of December) he called his brother and sister and his nieces to him. "Brother," he said, "I would have you go to the church, and measure seven foot to the westward from the door where we go into church, and at the end of that seven foot let my grave be made;" his brother, looking very sadly at him, with his eyes full of tears, (and so all the standers-by did). He went on saying, "Brother, that first place of the length of seven foot I leave for your own burying-place, for you are my elder; God, I hope, will let you there take up your resting-place till we all rise again in joy." And then, speaking with some vehemency and passion of indignation, he bade that the great hampers of books, which he had kept so long, should be carried to the place of his grave and there burnt. "Go," he cried, "let it be done, let it be done, and then come again, all of you, to me."

The smoke of this strange bonfire rose high above the leafless trees, visible to all the hamlets round, and men left their work in the fields and came running to see what was the matter at Gidding Hall. The burning of so many books created a not unnatural awe among the simple villagers, and it was told through all the country-side that Mr. Nicholas

Ferrar lay dying, but could not die till he had burnt his conjuring books.

He had destroyed the last relics of the worldly life which he had never loved, and had long since renounced; and for three days more he lay tranquil, calmly awaiting the end.

On the morning of Advent Sunday he found his strength declining. "This Sunday was the first Sunday in the month, the constant usual day for their monthly Communion. He acquainted the minister that, after he had celebrated it at the church, he would come home and give It to him; for now it was that heavenly food was his only stay, strength, and joy to receive. As for earthly food, he had now done with it; God would ere long hear his prayers, and the humble requests of his poor soul. To this end and like effect he spake, but in far better expressions. When the minister came to give it him, he desired absolution, having made again a most full and lively expression of his faith. The minister said, 'Shall I give it you in the words of the book?' 'Ay, ay,' said he, 'nothing better, nothing better.' Then he received, in most devout manner, the Sacrament; which done, gave Almighty God most humble and hearty thanks for this inestimable benefit and favour, and used very effectual words to that purpose, and so awhile lay very silent and still.

"And afterwards being demanded, 'how he felt

himself?' he would say he was very well, blessed be God, but hoped to be better ere long. As his friends, brother, sister, nieces, etc., stood about him with sad looks, he would bid them 'be cheerful, for part we all must. It was the common portion for all men to die. Be of good comfort, be of good courage; we shall meet again in heaven at last, I doubt it not (and some of you ere long). It will be the best wisdom and only happiness to prepare all for it; for who can be too ready for death?' He more particularly directed his speeches to his dearly beloved two nieces, Mary and Anna (whom, as formerly related, he most entirely loved; who had both steadfastly, by the help of God's assistance, taken long ago resolutions of living in virginity, and in such and such ways and course of life as they had chosen, with the advice and assistance of their good uncle Nicholas Ferrar, whom he most tenderly affected, and highly esteemed of), that 'they should be steadfast, and commit themselves to the good guidance of their gracious Lord God and Master, Jesus Christ, to whom they had, more than in an ordinary manner, given themselves, each in their station;' assuring them that 'they should in the end have cause to rejoice in their good resolutions.'

" Being demanded, ' if the ministers should be called,' who not long before were gone out of the chamber, all supposing he had been asleep, he said,

' Entreat them to come in and pray together.'   Which
being done, he desired them to say that prayer for
a dying man; which ended, he being by them
demanded, ' how he did,' said, " Pretty well, I thank
my God and you ; and I shall be better.'   And
then he lay very still half an hour and more, all
standing by him, supposing him to be in a fine
slumber.   But afterwards he, on a sudden, casting
his hands out of the bed with great strength, and
looking up and about, with a strong voice and
cheerful, said, ' Oh, what a blessed change is here !
What do I see ?   Oh, let us come and sing unto the
Lord, and magnify His holy Name together.   I have
been at a great feast : Oh, magnify the Lord with
me.'   One of his nieces said presently, ' At a feast,
dear father ? '   ' Ay,' replied he ; ' at a great feast,
the great King's feast.'   And this he uttered with as
sound and perfect voice as in time of his health.
While all stood somewhat amazed and loth to inter-
rupt him, if he should say more, he laid himself down
most quietly, putting his hands into the bed, laid
them by his side, and then shut his eyes, and in this
posture laid, his legs stretched out, most sweetly and
still.   The ministers went again presently to prayers,
and after awhile they said that prayer again (that God
would be pleased to send His angels to carry his soul
to heaven), all kneeling round about his pallet.
While these words were saying, he opened his lips

and gave one gasp; and so, not once moving or
stirring hand, foot, or eyes, he rendered up his soul,
to be carried in their hands unto his Lord Jesus
Christ's bosom, which was that he so often prayed for.
And at that instant the clock struck *one*, the hour that
he constantly rose up every morning to praise God
and to pray unto Him. That very hour and time
God, you see, called him to His heavenly kingdom, to
praise Him everlastingly with the blessed angels and
saints above, and, as one of the company said, ' he
ended the sabbath here on earth, to begin the everlasting sabbath in heaven.' " [1]

No word can be changed or added to this history
of a saintly death-bed, told by the brother who
stood by.

Till the Thursday following his body rested in the
care of his loving friends—a most fair and sweet
corpse. It was observed that the right hand and
fingers remained " lithe and flexible, as if they were
of a living man." "Well," said one who saw it,
" may that hand not grow stiff, that was so often, day
and night, lifted up to God; and was so liberal in
continual giving alms to the poor and needy in
several kinds ! "

On December 7, 1637, he was laid in a vault of
brick, made, as he had desired, in the midst of the
path, a few feet from the west door of the church.

[1] " Life of Nicholas Ferrar," by his brother, pp. 78–92.

The funeral service was said by his cousin, Robert Mapletoft,[1] afterwards Master of Pembroke and Dean of Ely, "whom he loved exceeding well, who often came to Gidding, and was most welcome to him."

A short notice of Nicholas Ferrar was published in 1652, in the anonymous preface to the first edition of the "Country Parson." He is there commemorated, together with its author, George Herbert, and their common friend, Dr. Jackson, the president of Corpus. "All three holy in their lives, eminent in their gifts, signal Protestants for their religion, painful in their several stations, precious in their deaths, and sweet in their memories." "Methinks Dr. J. had somewhat like the spirit of *Jeremy*, Saint *James*, and *Salvian;* Master Herbert like *David*, and other Psalm-men, Saint *John* and *Prudentius;* Master F. like *Esay*, Saint *Luke*, and Saint *Chrysostom*."

"What is so well compiled by that worthy learned man (whoever he be)," says John Ferrar, "it's but my poor pains to write it out of the book, that can never too often read or meditate upon that discourse, that so nearly concerns me, as of such a brother, whom the world never could show a better brother to any brother, nor a more true lover, and one that did more for his family than he did, in all kinds and ways— for their temporal welfare, in preservation, augmenta-

---

[1] Brother to Joshua and Solomon Mapletoft, who married two of his nieces.

tion, and maintenance of their civil estates and affairs, and that, which is the superlative of all goodness and benefit, his never-ceasing care and pains for their spiritual well-being, everlasting happiness, and bliss."

The unknown writer was their old friend Barnabas Oley, and in his hyperbolic phrase he expresses Ferrar's warmth of sympathetic affection, his tender charity, and his ready and persuasive speech. He tells us also that Ferrar was no controversialist; " he would scarcely opine." He carried his respect for authority, for the established order of things, to an extent which seems extreme. He would not allow his nieces to teach the Catechism in their Sunday school, because this would trench on the prerogatives of the parents and the parish priest. And when Dr. Morison, the Chancellor of Lincoln, told him that the only thing wanting in his chapel was a painted window with the crucifix, he replied, that had he found such a thing, he would have preserved it, but he would not set one up where none had been before."

He must have inherited this conservative turn of mind from the good old merchant, his father. He inherited also his straightforward sincerity and honesty of purpose, together with some touch of his choleric temper, for (as we may gather from some of his utterances) Nicholas could be overbearing and very hot on occasion. He was affectionate, home-loving, dutiful, simple and sober in his tastes. He had all the making of an excellent man of business; he was acute, clear-headed, prompt, observant, with a gift for organization, and a great power of adopting and assimilating new ideas, whenever his respect for precedent did not come in the way.

From his mother he inherited a strong will, and that faculty of ruling others which he was tempted to use at times, perhaps too absolutely. His portrait shows that he also inherited her delicate and refined features, and suggests that to her he owed the graceful speech and manner which won him so much popularity. The picture is at Magdalene College, near those of his parents. The likeness to Mrs. Ferrar is in feature only; the serene calm of her fair countenance is replaced in that of her son by an expression of deep and almost melancholy gravity.

He had a vivid, bright, restless intellect, practical, not speculative; he does not seem to have indulged in any flight of original thought; but everything he reads or sees is remembered and turned to account, whether it be the ascetic example of the Fathers of the Desert, the skill of German artificers, or the admirable provision made in Holland for the necessities of the poor.

His practical law-abiding spirit is shown in his religion. He was thoroughly English, a dutiful son of the Reformed Church as it was understood by the

T

school of Andrewes.   In this way of thinking he had
always been brought up, and his mind took the mould
and kept it.   He was not insular; his acquaintance with foreign devotional writings appears to
have been extensive, but so far as the objects of
his study were Roman rather than Catholic, he does
not seem to have been even transiently influenced
by them.

His extreme austerity grew out of this dutiful nature.
He had been taught to study the lives of the saintly
ascetics of primitive times.   To these times the
Church of England appealed for its standards of
doctrine; and if of doctrine, then surely of life also.
For what purpose had these models been set before
him, if not that he might copy them?   And he did
copy them, so far as circumstances permitted, with
the eager warmth with which he did everything.

He was a firm Protestant, as his friends, nettled by
the frequent accusations of Romanizing, were never
tired of repeating.   He hated popery with the solid
hatred which was nourished by Foxe's "Book of
Martyrs."   He believed that the Pope was Antichrist;
when asked what he would do if by any chance the
Mass was celebrated in his house, he is said to have
replied that he would pull that room down and build
another.

This is strong language; but Churchmen were
accustomed to use strong language on the subject in

those days. To them the supremacy of Rome meant the destruction of all their liberties, civil and religious; it meant foreign invasion and the Holy Office. Laud dreaded the "grim wolf" who, "with privy paw, daily devours apace," as much as Milton, and put down all leaning to distinctive Roman doctrine with as firm a hand as he used to the recalcitrant Puritans. When he heard of the publication of an English translation of St. Francis de Sales's "Introduction to the Devout Life," which had not received his sanction, a translation which had not been "adapted," he "gave present orders to seize upon all the copies and burn them publicly in Smithfield,"[1] and eleven or twelve hundred copies were destroyed accordingly.

It must not be supposed from the startling language which Ferrar is reported to have used with regard to the Mass, that he denied the holy and awful Presence in the Eucharist. It is from the material view of the mystery that his mind revolts—the view which shaped such legends as that of the Miracle of Bolsena. For the positive side of his faith, in the absence of any writings of his own, it is perhaps not unfair to quote those of the friend whose name is most closely entwined with his. Herbert's view is clearly expressed in the poem entitled; "The Priesthood."

---

[1] Archbishop Laud to the Vice-Chancellor of Oxford, "Autobiography," p. 228.

" When God vouchsafeth to become our fare,
　Their hands convey Him who conveys their hands :
　Oh what pure things, most pure, must those things be
　　Who bring my God to me ! "

It seems the more permissible to take Herbert's words as showing Ferrar's thought, because, where Ferrar wants doctrine clearly laid down (as in the notes to Valdesso) he appeals to Herbert to do it for him.

His own cast of mind was mystical and devotional, rather than theological. Throughout his life, underneath his busy, practical nature, lay the keenest sense of the supernatural. He is ever conscious of a mission, a call, of some special vocation. He goes through an agony of doubt and ecstasy in his childhood, of which the memory never leaves him. He has moments of sharp struggle through his boyish days at Cambridge. He rushes away impulsively from Leipzig or Padua, to bury himself for weeks together in lonely villages. In the hurry and strain of London life, he retires for prayer and fasting so often that his family cease to notice it.

As the spiritual element in him gained full sway, it conquered alike the desire of action and the love of learning. Thenceforth he had no wish, no aim, no ambition, but to offer himself wholly to the worship of God, and to teach those around him to do the same.

LITTLE GIDDING CHURCH AND GRAVE OF NICHOLAS FERRAR.

To face page 277.

It was this entire singleness of purpose, rather than his intellectual vigour, which gave him so great a mastery over those with whom he came in contact. They felt themselves in the presence of one, every fibre of whose soul was purified and spiritualized by the flame of Divine Love.

The value of his life and work is not of a kind that can be tested by visible results.

> "Think'st thou the spires that glow so bright
>   In front of yonder setting sun,
> Stand by their own unshaken might ?
>   No ; where the upholding grace is won
> We dare not ask, nor Heaven would tell,
> But sure from many a hidden dell,
> From many a rural nook unthought of there,
> Rises for that proud world the saints' prevailing prayer."

The grass grows over the site of Gidding Hall, and sheep feed on the slopes which once were covered with orchards and gardens. The oft-trodden path which led to the churchyard gate is now only a green ridge across the meadow ; but the church itself, and the churchyard, are not greatly altered. In the centre of the path, a little way from the west door, under a plain altar tomb, without name or date, Nicholas Ferrar lies in the place of his choice, at the feet of his elder brother.

CHAPTER XIII.

A.D. 1637—1642.

> " Dear, beauteous Death ; the Jewel of the Just !
>   Shining nowhere but in the dark ;
> What mysteries do lie beyond thy dust,
>   Could man outlook that mark !
>
> " He that hath found some fledged bird's nest may know
>   At first sight if the bird be flown ;
> But what fair dell or grove he sings in now,
>   That is to him unknown."
>
> H. VAUGHAN (1621–1695).

THE Community, if so it may be called, at Gidding appears to have suffered little change from the death of the founder. The same charitable works were carried on. We know that the aged widows were still cared for. The poor, no doubt, were relieved, and the Psalm-children taught, as before. The Harmonies were continued, with even increased zeal, under the charge of young Nicholas.[1]

His cousin, Ferrar Collett, was already at Peterhouse, under Crashaw's tutorship, and it seems strange that Nicholas, with his remarkable abilities, should not have enjoyed the same advantage. Perhaps the delicacy of his constitution made his father unwilling that he should change the invigorating breezes of Gidding for the damp Cambridge air.

This same delicacy of health, combined with an impediment in his speech, which seems to have been sufficiently marked to be a hindrance in any pursuit which required much intercourse with his fellows, doubtless conduced to the boy's extraordinary devotion to learning.

He possessed the great powers of attention and application which had distinguished his uncle, but he does not seem to have shared his restless and versatile temper. The elder Nicholas divided his attention among a multiplicity of studies; the younger seems to have given his mind wholly to one branch of learning—the knowledge of languages. His acquisitions in this way are amazing, and his aims far-reaching and noble. Among the papers found in his study after

---

[1] This chapter is taken from a memoir by John Ferrar, published in Wordsworth's "Ecclesiastical Biography," and again by Rev. J. E. B. Mayor, in the "Two Lives of Ferrar." The original manuscript is in the Lambeth Library.

his premature death is a scheme for translating the New Testament into fifty languages; and underneath the list of these languages he had written, " This, by the help of God, I intend to effect, and also to translate the Church Catechism into these languages, so likewise the 117th Psalm, 'Praise the Lord, all ye heathen : praise Him, all ye nations,' and present them to the king, that he may print them and send them to all nations."

The amount of work of this kind which he actually executed is truly astonishing.

In 1640, at the age of twenty-one, he went, accompanied by his father, to London, taking with him no fewer than six Concordances, all arranged and carried out by himself, with the help of the ladies of the family.   Of these books, one was a " Harmony of the New Testament in Twenty-four Languages." [1]   On the way they stayed at Cambridge, where the books were shown to many learned persons, and were greatly admired.   The father and son arrived in London shortly before Easter, and were received with great kindness by Laud, to whom they presented themselves.   When Nicholas knelt to ask his blessing, the archbishop " embraced him very lovingly," and, having examined the books, was warm in his commendations. " They were truly jewels for princes," he said; and

[1] For a fuller account of these Concordances see Chapter VIII., where they are numbered VI., VII., VIII., IX., X., XI.

he desired Nicholas to attend at Whitehall on the following day, Maundy Thursday, that he might present him to the king.

At the time appointed the youth came with his father to the palace, and took his place among other applicants for royal favour, waiting the archbishop's leisure.

The great man came in. " Follow me," he said to Nicholas, and led the way into the next room, where the king stood by the fire, with many nobles about him.

We have here a glimpse of one of the last peaceful days of that stately Court, the home of art and of learning. Laud led the young scholar by the hand into the royal presence, and Charles received him with the kindliest grace. The book, made for the prince, was first exhibited—a splendid volume, bound in green velvet.

" Here," said the king, " is a fine book for Charles indeed. I hope it will soon make him in love with what is within it, for I know it is good. I like it in all respects exceedingly well, and find Charles will have a double benefit by the contrivement of it, and not only obtain by the daily reading of it a full information of our blessed Saviour's life, doctrine, and actions, but the knowledge of four languages. A couple of better things a prince cannot desire, nor the world recommend to him."

Nicholas then begged his Majesty's permission to carry the book to the prince. "My learned and religious wise uncle," he said, "under whose wings I was covered, gave me among other rules, this one, that I should never give anything, though never so good and fitting, to any person whatever that had a superior over him, without his consent and approbation first obtained."

"I like the rule well," said the king; and then, turning to the archbishop, he desired that the young gentleman should carry the book next day to the prince, then staying at Richmond, adding, "It is a good day, and a good work should be done on it."

Nicholas then produced, one after the other, three more books, one being the New Testament in twenty-four languages. The king turned them over with delighted interest, happy no doubt to forget for a few moments his troubles with the rebellious Scotch, and his anxiety as to the conduct of the short-lived parliament which he had unwillingly summoned at the advice of Strafford, while he examined these efforts of precocious scholarship. "Here we have more and more rarities," he exclaimed. The great Polyglott was surely "the emperor of all books." He called the nobles round him to look and wonder, and appealed to Laud if it were possible that a young man of twenty-one could have acquired the knowledge of so many languages.

Nicholas had prepared a little surprise as an answer to this expected question. He took from the bottom of the box in which he had brought his great works a fifth book, in which he had written out the Gospel of St. John in twenty-one languages, each verse being accompanied by a Latin or English translation made by himself.

"Lo," said his Majesty, "here is ample proof, and I am fully satisfied in all things."

He then dismissed Nicholas "with a cheerful royal look," desiring him to attend the prince next morning, and afterwards to wait on the archbishop, who would acquaint him with his further pleasure.

On the next morning, Good Friday, provided with a letter to Bishop Duppa, the prince's tutor, Nicholas and his father repaired to Richmond. Prince Charles received the book with many expressions of pleasure, and the little Duke of York, delighted with the pictures and the fine binding, begged earnestly that such another might be made for him. "How soon will it be ready?" he cried, with royal and boyish impatience. "Pray tell the gentlewomen at Gidding I will heartily thank them if they will despatch it."

Nicholas dined with Bishop Duppa, and some of the young lords, the prince's companions, among whom was the boy Duke of Buckingham, receiving compliments enough to turn an older head; it must have been a strange Good Friday for a youth bred at

Gidding. After dinner the prince somewhat disconcerted him by offering him a handful of gold pieces. The scholar stepped back, perhaps a little affronted, but Charles, with graceful courtesy inherited from his father, assured him that it was not meant as a recompense for the work, which he prized far above gold, but only as a testimony of his esteem ; and so, amid many kind words, Nicholas took his leave, attended to his coach by my lord bishop's own secretary.

On the following morning, Easter Eve, he went to Lambeth, by the archbishop's order, to let him know what had passed at Richmond. The interview is worth transcribing at length as a picture of the great archbishop on his gentler side. Laud, who could be so hasty and sharp of speech, who took so little pains to court popularity, that "few excellent men ever had fewer friends to their persons,"[1] had yet an under-current of tender feeling which breaks out in frequent entries in his diaries and private letters. He treated Nicholas with fatherly kindness. He had "much longed to know what entertainment was given to the book and person, and was right glad that things went as he hoped ; he should acquaint the king with all."

"Then, taking Nicholas Ferrar's father aside, he said, ' Let your care now cease for your hopeful son, or for his future preferment, or estate, or present main-

[1] Clarendon.

tenance. God hath so inclined the king's heart, and his liking to your son, and the gifts God hath endued him with ; and having been informed of his virtuous, pious education, and singular industry and Christian deportment, and of his sober inclination, that he will take him from you into his own protection and care, and make him his scholar and servant; and hath given me order, that, after the holidays being past, I should send him to Oxford, and that there he shall be maintained in all things needful to him at the king's proper charge, and shall not need what he can desire, to further him in the prosecution of those works he hath begun in matter of languages, and what help of books or heads or hands he shall require, he shall not be unfurnished with ; for the king would have this work of the New Testament in twenty-four languages to be accomplished by his own care and assistance ; and to have the help of all the learned men that can be had to that end. Assure yourself he shall want for nothing. In a word, the king is greatly in love with him, and you will, and have cause to, bless and praise God for such a son.'

"So John Ferrar, being ravished with joy, in all humble manner gave thanks to my lord's grace. And they, returning to Nicholas Ferrar, my lord embraced him, and gave him his benediction. Nicholas Ferrar, kneeling down, took the bishop by the hand and kissed it. He took him up in his arms, and laid his hand on his cheek, and earnestly besought God Almighty to bless him and increase all grace in him, and fit him every day more and more for an instrument of His glory here upon earth and a saint in heaven, 'which,' said he, 'is the only happiness that can be desired, and ought to be our chief end in all our actions. God bless you! God bless you! I have told your father what is to be done for you after the holidays. God will provide for you better than your father can. God bless you, and keep you!' So they parted from his grace."

The archbishop's words were fulfilled, but not in the sense in which they were spoken. Nicholas Ferrar was never to become the king's young scholar and servant. At the moment when his hopes were at the flood, a summons came which could not be put by. His name lives in no roll of famous scholars; it is inscribed on the forgotten list of the "inheritors of unfulfilled renown."

Happy they if their thread of life, in the quaintly beautiful phrase of Herbert, is "wound up and laid ready for work in the New Jerusalem."

It may be that the eager brain of the young student, "like a sharp penknife in a narrow sheath," had worn his strength away, and that excitement and over-fatigue made him an easy prey to the foul air of the narrow London streets, so different to the fresh breezes on the heights of Gidding. On the same afternoon on which he received the king's promise of protection, the Saturday in Holy Week, he felt unwell, but he rose early on the Easter morning, and received the Holy Communion at St. Paul's Cathedral. On his return he could scarce eat anything, and by the following day he became so ill that the anxious father called in two physicians. Nicholas grew worse and worse, but bore his sickness with brave submission and cheerfulness.

Bishop Williams was still in the Tower, but their old friend Dr. Towers, first Dean and then Bishop of Peterborough, who had known Nicholas from his childhood, and loved him dearly, was in London, and came to minister to him. He confessed and absolved him, and bade his father be of good comfort, for the instructions of his pious uncle had taken mighty root in his soul, and now sprang up not "only with leaves and fair blossoms, but with good and ripe fruit." "He is too good, he is too good," said he, "to live longer in these ill-approaching times. For there is much fear now that the glory of Church and State is at the highest."

Nicholas prepared himself to resign his young life, and the bright future which seemed opening before him, with touching submission. "I am too young to be mine own judge what is best for me," he said to a friend who asked if he were not grieved to leave the world in the flower of his youth ; "let all be, as God's will is. If I live, I desire it may be to His further glory, and mine own soul's good, and the comfort and service that I intend to be to my father, that loves me so dearly, and in his old age to be his servant. If I die I hope my father will submit all to God's will and pleasure, and rejoice at my happiness in heaven, where, by the merits of my blessed Lord and Saviour, I know I shall go out of this wretched life."

Had he lived he would have met with bitter disappointment. The peace of this calm sick-room seems the deeper for its contrast to the growing storm without. On the Monday after Low Sunday the "Short Parliament" began its sittings. On May 6 the king dissolved it in hot indignation at its refusal to aid him against the Scotch. "Things must go worse before they go better," was the ominous comment of Cromwell's cousin, Oliver St. John, when he found himself thus abruptly unseated.

Placards were posted inciting the mob to sack Lambeth Palace. On May 11 it was attacked by a mob of Anabaptists, Brownists, and other sectaries, five hundred strong. Laud had notice, and fortified his house as well as he could, and the rabble, finding itself unable to make any impression on the solid walls of Lambeth, turned its attention to Convocation, which was still sitting, and the trainbands had to be called out to protect the bishops. Several arrests were made, but the prisons were broken open in broad daylight, and the rioters set free.

The news of these outrages disturbed even the stillness of the sick-chamber. The dying youth was deeply moved. "Alas! alas!" he said, "God help His Church and poor England! I now fear, indeed, what my dear uncle said before he died, that evil days were coming, and happy were they that went to heaven before they came. . . . God amend all! Truly, truly, it troubles me."

By this time it drew towards Ascensiontide. He lingered yet a few days longer. Bishop Towers came again, and found him "most cheerful to die and to be with God." He "gave him absolution, and with many tears departed, saying to his father, 'God give you consolation, and prepare yourself to part with your good son; . . . be of good comfort; you give him back again to Him that gave him you for a season.'"

On the Tuesday before Whit-Sunday, May 19, 1640, at the age of twenty-one, Nicholas Ferrar the younger was taken away from the evil to come.

The stricken father comforted himself by writing a short memoir of these closing days. He says no word of his own sorrow. He forgot himself in his promising son, as completely as he had forgotten himself in his distinguished brother. It is only from a word here and there, from the entry, very touching in the light of what was to follow, that he was "ravished with joy" when Laud told him of the king's proposed care of young Nicholas, that we learn that John Ferrar was present throughout; but the tender pride with which he chronicles every detail of his son's brief success, and the careful treasuring of his last sayings, tell the tale of the father's love and grief more clearly than any words.

Mr. Ferrar went sadly home along the ways which he had travelled so joyfully but a few weeks before in company with his son, and bravely began the old life afresh. He found consolation and pleasure, no doubt, in watching his little daughter's industrious fingers, as she learnt to take her share in the family work. The book belonging to the Bishop of Bath and Wells, made by "Virginia Ferrar, aged twelve," is dated 1642, and must have been begun about this time. The Concordance which Nicholas had promised to the little Duke of York was also taken in hand.

The miserable winter of 1640–41 brought new trouble to Gidding. The enemies of the Church were not satisfied with attacking the Archbishop. They desired to give battle all along the line, and even this peaceful family, carrying on their quiet pursuits in the midst of their own fields and woods, were not safe from annoyance. A tract was published called "The

Arminian Nunnery," [1] containing a scandalous attack on Gidding, " such stories told as the devil himself would be ashamed to utter." A false air of truth was thrown round this publication by the free use of passages in the letter written seven years earlier by Lenton to his friend Sergeant Hetley, describing his visit to Gidding, which letter seems to have been shown about.

John Ferrar wrote at once to Mr. Lenton, apparently (for his letter is not forthcoming), inquiring if he had taken any share in putting forth the pamphlet.

Lenton indignantly disclaimed all responsibility, and was evidently extremely annoyed at finding that his kindly gossip had been turned to such malicious use.

" I should much degenerate," he writes, " from my birth (being a gentleman), my breeding (well known to the world), and the religion I profess, if having, upon something a bold visit, been entertained in your family with kind and civil respects, I should requite it with such scorn and calumny as this libellous

---

[1] " The Arminian Nunnery, or a Brief Description and Relation of the late erected Monasticall Place called the Arminian Nunnery at Little Gidding in Huntingdonshire, humbly recommended to the wise consideration of this present Parliament. The Foundation is by a Company of Ferrars at Gidding. Printed for Thomas Underhill, 1641, London."

pamphlet seems to insinuate. . . . I am so far from being the author, infuser, or countenancer of this fable, that by it I take myself to be as much abused, and that there is as much aspersion cast upon me as upon your family, by a sly and cunning intimation (my letter being his groundwork), to make me thought (by such as know me not well) to be the author and divulger of his lies and scandals, which (by God's mercy) my soul abhors." [1]

But, however groundless, the pamphlet was spread abroad in all directions; copies were put into the hands of members of parliament as they went into the House, and dispersed among the soldiery who passed near Gidding on their way to the army in the north, apparently with the hope of stirring the Puritans to attempt some violence; but, for the present, no actual injury was done to the family or their property.

In the midst of this annoyance they were cheered by a visit from Bishop Williams. That time-serving but kindly prelate had been released from the Tower in the autumn of 1640, and for a short time his star was again in the ascendant.

"The Bishop of Lincoln rides his visitation, and begins in October, and for security he hath an order from the Lords at his own motion," wrote Dr. Busby, the famous and loyal head-master of Westminster, to

---

[1] Lenton to Ferrar, Oct. 27, 1641. Preface to "Two Lives," p. 23, printed also by Hearne and Peckard.

a friend in the country. "The bishop hath not yet left us at Westminster, remaining alone of all the bishops ; a stout defender of his order and discipline ; not without the envy and broad censures of the people. Pray for the Church, as it concerns us all, and pray for me." [1]

The bishop went the round of his diocese, diplomatizing, persuading, preaching to congregations of "ignoble sectaries and high-shone clowns," as Hacket uncivilly calls the Puritans of Lincolnshire and Huntingdonshire ; doing his best "to heal the maladies of brainsick distempers," and draw his people to attend the ministrations of their lawful pastors, instead of following after "coachman-preachers, watchmaking-preachers, barber-preachers, and such addle-headed companions," with very limited success. "So long as he was in place, and for a while that his words were remembered," says the admiring Hacket, he "brought those counties to a handsome state of quietness ; " [2] but the bishop himself confided to John Ferrar that he "was used but coarsely" by the people of Boston, from which place he came to Gidding.

---

[1] Dr. Busby to Dr. Isaac Basire, Vicar of Egglescliffe, and one of the royal chaplains.—"Life and Correspondence of I. B." (Isaac Basire). Twelve bishops, including the Ferrars' friend, Dr. Towers, had spent a considerable portion of this year in prison, for protesting against their exclusion from the House of Lords.

[2] "Life of Archbishop Williams," part ii. p. 156.

From his prison in the Tower, Williams had inquired with much interest for Mary and Anna Collett, after their uncle's death; telling Ferrar that he "had now well studied the case of his virgin nieces," and was "armed to maintain their good resolutions," which he prayed God to keep them in.[1]

He now exerted himself to vindicate the household from the charge of Popery, saying publicly that "they were of his flock," and he "knew they did practise nothing but what was according to the law of the Church of England," but to the family he counselled prudence, and an avoidance of all that might give offence "seeing whither the stream is turning." He advised them to take down the tablet which Mrs. Ferrar set up in the parlour, and which one would think was harmless enough. " Not that I dislike it," said the bishop, but " the times, as you see, grow high and turbulent; I counsel as your friend only."

His advice was taken, "and the old gentlewoman's tablet taken down out of the common parlour, whereinto, indeed, not very long after, came men of another garb than the bishop, and of other minds."

We have one more record of Gidding in its peaceful days; a memorable and touching incident.

In March, 1642, on his way from Newmarket to York, the king slept at Huntingdon. Next morning, as, accompanied by his son, his nephew the Elector

---

[1] " Life of Nicholas Ferrar," by his brother.

Palatine, and a train of nobles and county gentlemen, he rode towards Stamford, he observed the roof of a great house among the still leafless trees. "What house is that," he asked, "that stands so pleasingly?" And on hearing that it was Little Gidding, he expressed a desire to visit the place again.

The family having heard that he was passing, came loyally down to a little bridge, near the place where the way to Gidding turned out of the main road, and on his approach, "they all knelt down and prayed God to bless and preserve his Majesty, and protect him from the fury of his enemies." Then one by one they came up to the king, and kissed his hand as he sat on his horse. Prince Charles then came galloping up, and gave his hand likewise to be kissed, and he and the Palsgrave, who was in the company, proposed that the ladies should mount their horses, and ride behind them up the hill. This invitation was declined, and the ladies hastened up the steep fields as quickly as they could, the king courteously keeping his horse at a foot pace, as he rode beside them up the grassy track toward the house.

Before entering the house, he went to look at the church; the accusations of Popery put forth in "The Arminian Nunnery" had probably reached his ears.

"Where," he said, "are those images so much talked of?" He was told that everything had always been as his Majesty now saw it. "I knew it full well that never any were in it," he answered, smiling; "but what will not malice invent?"

One of the lords present said that he had been told there was in one of the windows a cross in painted glass.

"The lion that supported the king's arms (in the west window) had on the crown he wore on his head a little cross," was the answer.   There was no other painted glass or picture in the church.

"Envy is quick-sighted," said the Duke of Lenox.

"Nay, it can see what is not," the Palsgrave answered.

From the church they went past Nicholas Ferrar's grave, across the garden to the house, and the king asked to see the book which was being made for Prince Charles. It was brought, the tallest of tall folios, more than two feet high, magnificent in purple velvet.[1]

"Sir," said the Duke of Lenox, "one of your strongest guard will be but able to carry this book."

It was laid on the table before the king. He read over the title and frontispiece "very deliberately," and then proceeded carefully to examine the book. "Charles," he said to the prince, who stood by, "here is a book that contains excellent things; this will make you both wise and good." He was much

---

[1] Probably the one now in possession of Captain Gaussen. See Chap. VIII., No. XIII.

interested in the engravings with which the book was illustrated, and pointed them out to his nephew, who seems to have had some share of his brother Rupert's knowledge of such matters, naming the engravers.

The king sat for hours turning over the book, reading and asking questions, while the younger members of his suite roved about the house, winding up with a visit to the buttery, whence they emerged with their hands full of apple-pie and cheesecakes. They were full of gaiety and laughter, as was natural, the Prince of Wales the gayest of them all. To them the ride to York was no doubt a holiday expedition, and the struggle with the Parliament a matter which would soon be put to rights, scarce worth a moment's serious thought; but to Charles what thoughts must have come as he sat turning the leaves of the great Pentateuch, glad, no doubt, of leisure and quiet, of the calm unworldly atmosphere of the devout house. How much he had passed through since, two years before, with Laud at his side, he had received John Ferrar and his lost son at Whitehall. Now Laud was in the Tower, and he himself had quitted his palace, never again to return as king. He had broken with his Parliament; only a few days before he came to Gidding he had ridden along the cliffs of Dover to watch, as long as the sails remained in sight, the ship that bore his beloved wife to her refuge in France.

He was roused at last by the Palsgrave, who begged him to come and see the alms widows' rooms, which he said he would like well. Charles went through them, "looking well about him." "Truly," he said, "this is worth the sight. I did not think to have seen a thing in this kind that so well pleaseth me. God's blessing be upon the founders thereof," and taking from his pocket five pieces of gold, he directed that they should be given to the poor widows, adding, "and will them to pray for me."

Before his departure, he looked round on the peaceful landscape—the house set deep in budding orchards, the sheep feeding in the meadows. "Gidding is a happy place in many respects; I am glad I have seen it," he said.

The sun got low, and Stamford, their destination for the night, was still far away. The horses were brought to the door, and, while the king mounted, all the family, men and women, knelt down and prayed God to bless and defend him, and give him a long and happy reign. He, lifting his hand to his hat, replied, "Pray, pray for my speedy and safe return."[1]

He rode away through the gathering twilight with the young princes and his attendant nobles, a gallant train, making a splendid appearance in the country lanes; away to Stamford and the North; to be

[1] "Life of Nicholas Ferrar," by his brother, pp. 130-136; and Appendix, p. 253.

repulsed from the gates of Hull; to gather a loyal remnant of his Parliament at York; to raise, before the summer was out, his standard at Nottingham; to meet his rebellious subjects in open field at Edgehill.

Once again, after four weary years, he came to Gidding, disguised, almost alone, in the shadows of night and failure.

CHAPTER XIV.

GIDDING DURING THE CIVIL WAR — JOHN FERRAR
PLANS ANOTHER POLYGLOTT—THE KING'S LAST
VISIT — SACK OF GIDDING — RETURN OF THE
FAMILY—DEATHS OF JOHN FERRAR AND MR. AND
MRS. COLLETT.

A.D. 1642—1660.

"We can see
The Church thrive in her misery,
And like her Head at Bethlehem, rise,
When she oppressed with trouble lies.
Rise?　Should all fall, we cannot be
In more extremities than He.

.　　　.　　　.　　　.　　　.

" But stay ! what light is that doth stream
And drop here in a gilded beam ?
It is Thy star runs page, and brings
The tributary Eastern kings.
Lord, grant some light to us, that we
May find with them the way to Thee !

" Behold what mists eclipse the day !
How dark it is !　Shed down one ray,
To guide us out of this dark night,
And say once more, 'Let there be light.' "

H. VAUGHAN, *from " Verses on the Nativity*
of our Lord, written in 1656."

THE chronicles of Gidding end with the outbreak of the Civil War. We have only scattered notices, a brief note on the margin of a manuscript, an occasional sentence in a letter, to show how the Ferrars and Colletts lived through these years of distress and disaster.

Through the summer of 1642 armed men were passing continually along the lanes which lie below the Gidding fields. The distant tramp of horse, the flash of arms among the trees, must have become familiar sounds and sights to the inhabitants of Gidding from the earliest period of the war. The house stood alone on its green hill, an unwarlike stronghold of loyalty and Churchmanship, in the midst of a hostile country.

Here, perhaps, Barnabas Oley came for shelter when the college tutor, roused from his steady work at Clare by the excitement of the hour, rode, with a few trusty friends, " through bypaths in the night," to carry a contribution of plate from loyal Cambridge to the aid of the king at Nottingham,[1] slipping triumphantly, in the darkness, past Oliver Cromwell himself, who, " with a train of townsmen and rustics," lay in wait to intercept him not far from Huntingdon.

Except for such chance visitors as may have taken

[1] Dr. Worthington's Diary, quoted by Mr. Mullinger, " Cambridge in the Seventeenth Century."

Gidding in their way to join the Royalist armies, or to exchange secretly a few words of sympathy on the troubles which came thicker every year, the lives of John Ferrar and his family must have become more and more isolated.   Their school was apparently broken up, for little John Mapletoft was sent to be educated at Westminster, where Dr. Busby calmly carried on his work throughout the turmoil, with un-diminished energy, and a special regard for the children of Royalists.   He seems to have been personally acquainted with the Ferrars.   " Certify me when and how I may pay my respects to your friends in Huntingdonshire," he writes to Basire, in September, 1642.

The wreck of Peterborough Cathedral, in 1643, must have struck all lovers of the Church—it might almost be said, all true lovers of the worship of God— with heart-sickness.   Such outrages soon became too common ; but the beautiful church which rises among the waters of the Nen valley was the first to suffer.

" In this place," says Gunton, " began that strange kind of deformed Reformation which afterwards passed over most places in the land, by robbing, rifling, and defacing churches."

The troopers (they were under the command of Cromwell's son) dragged down the altar screen, and being unable to reach the painting of our Saviour in glory, which hung above, *fired* at it until it was riddled by shot. They carried off the silver candlesticks from the altar, tore up all the Common Prayer-books that could be found, pulled out the Apocrypha from the great Bible, and destroyed the whole of the carved decoration of the choir stalls.

Their wrath was specially hot against the organs, of which there were two pair. These were "stamped, trampled on, and broken in pieces, with such a strange, furious, and frantic zeal, as cannot be well conceived but by them that saw it."

When a "well-disposed person" who was present offered some protest against this fearful sacrilege, the officer in command merely remarked, "See how these poor people are concerned to see their idols pulled down."

The soldiers stayed a fortnight in Peterborough, and "went to church daily to do mischief." [1]

In December of the same year the storm broke on Cambridge. "We went to Peterhouse," writes one of the spoilers, evidently rejoicing in his work, "and pulled down two mighty great angels with wings, and divers other angels, and the four Evangelists, and Peter, with his keies, over the chapell dore, and about a hundred cherubims and angels, and divers superstitious letters in gold." [2] At Little St. Mary's, close

---

[1] Gunton's "Peterborough."

[2] Quoted in Dr. Grosart's introduction to "Fuller Worthies," edition of Crashaw.

by, the church in which Crashaw spent so many hours in prayer, "sixty superstitious pictures" were destroyed.

Next year the heads and fellows of colleges were required to sign the Covenant. Upwards of two hundred refused compliance, and were ejected in consequence.

Among those who went out was Crashaw. His tender and sensitive spirit was well-nigh broken by the desolation of the holy places he had loved so well, the ruin which seemed falling on the University and the Church. His version of the 137th Psalm is perhaps an expression of his feelings during this time of bitter pain.

> "Sing ! play ! to whom, ah ! shall we sing or play
>   If not, Jerusalem, to thee ?
> Ah ! thee, Jerusalem, ah ! sooner may
>   This hand forget the mastery
>   Of music's dainty touch, than I
>   The music of thy memory.
>
> "Which when I lose, oh ! may at once my tongue
>   Lose this same busy-speaking art ;
> Unperched, her vocal arteries unstrung,
>   No more acquainted with my heart,
>   On my dry pallat's roof to rest,
>   A withered leaf, an idle guest."

He lacked the courage and patience to wait for better days. "Upon an infallible foresight that the Church of England would be quite ruinated by the untimely fury of the Presbyterians,"[1] he left England, joined the Roman Church, and, after long wandering and much poverty, died in 1650, at the age of thirty-five, having enjoyed for a few weeks some small office at Loretto. There, in the great church which encloses the "holy house," he lies buried, far from his early friends.[2]

Through loneliness, and loss, and anxiety, the Ferrars kept bravely on with their life of prayer, of charity, and steady industry. The labours of the Concordance room were continued as before, and John Ferrar, with courage unabated by bereavement and straitened circumstances, still cherished the hope of carrying out some of the lofty designs of his dead son.

He formed a scheme, probably with the assistance of Ferrar Collett, for a Polyglott on a still more extensive scale than those presented to the king. It was to consist of the New Testament in twenty-six languages, Chaldee and Samaritan being added to the twenty-four employed by young Nicholas. To these were to be added twelve several English translations, twenty various Latin translations, three in Italian, etc., besides a comparison between the authorized and the Rhemish versions of the English Testament,

---

[1] Preface to first edition of " Poems."

[2] See Dr. Grosart, "Fuller Worthies," ed. of Crashaw's Poems.

the two being placed side by side; together with a defence of the Authorized Version against the slanders of one Gregory Martin.

The following letters relate to the preparation of materials for this gigantic undertaking. They are undated, but the mention of the "stately Bible of the King of France," as lately printed, seems to prove that they were written some time in 1645, in which year a magnificent Bible in Hebrew, Samaritan, Chaldee, Greek, Syriac, Latin, and Arabic, was published in Paris in nine folio volumes.

John Ferrar to Dr. Basire.

" At your best leisure.

" WORTHY SIR,

" That you will please to favour me with your help and advice, how and where to procure these ensuing things, by your own and friends' assistance.

" 1. All the several translations that have been since Henry VIII.'s time of the Holy Bible in the English tongue."

(Here follows a list of translations.)

" 2. And all the several translations of the New Testament."

(Here follows a list of desiderata in various languages.)

" 3. To inquire if the great and stately Bible of

the King of France in the seven several languages, be come yet into England, and the price of it; if not, how it is at Paris sold, and if the New Testament is not to be had single. I suppose the French preachers in London can inform you at full of it."

(Here follows an inquiry for further translations, among others Armenian and Persian, which " are to be had at Venice, so that Signior Burlamac, the Postmaster at London, spoken to by any friend, would easily send for them to come in the first ship that comes from Venice.")

.   .   .   .   .   .

" If so be our dear brother Thristcross [1] should desire, or you so think good, that he take a copy of the titles of these books in the other paper, which were done at Gidding, he may. For it may be some of his acquaintance of noble personages, may desire some of them to be made for them; yea, some rich divines, as deans, or prebends, etc. And it may be there may be more occasion to show them, upon this libel, [2] which makes as if there were no work done at Gidding, but all the time spent in contemplation, as it would make the world believe : that they may see this cost hath time and much labour every way ; and it may do us much right in that thing."

[1] Chaplain to the Duke of Lenox.
[2] " The Arminian Nunnery."

Second Letter.

"At your best and spare leisure, and when there is fitting time and opportunity for it.

" SIR,

"I have now further taken the presumption to send you herein enclosed the titles or frontispieces of some of those works and books done at Gidding; the inventions and patterns left us by our dearest brother.

"The intent and end I have in it (submitting all this and other my desires to your better judgement) is, that if you think so good to show them to my lord of Durham,[1] or to some other worthy noble personages; if his lordship or they might desire to have any of these made for their uses, and would bestow their money upon them, if not for their own use, yet it may be for some library, as rarities in their kinds and the handiwork of women (for their manufacture, I mean, and labour of putting together by way of pasting, etc.), we should be glad of the employment for our younger and elder people; and it may be if noble personages and learned knew of them, they would be casting away money upon them as well as upon other things. My Lord Wharton, upon the sight of King's Concordance, desired to have one in an inferior kind and

---

[1] Dr. Morton, Bishop of Durham.

sort, for the king's stands us in above £100; but my lord Wharton's cost him but £37; and so much he gave us for it willingly; but it was deemed of all that saw it to be of more worth.

"Well, sir, I know you love us, and would be glad in any good way to promote our affairs and employments; if shall find that the times settle, and men grow out of these fears and doubts; I hope in God, if the bishops and Book of Common Prayer be established, all will settle shortly in a good end; which God Almighty grant, unto whom I recommend this and yourself, and am

"Yours,

"J. F.

" To Dr. Basier at his best leisure and fitting time." [1]

The answers to these letters are not given, and we do not know whether Dr. Basire took any steps to procure the books. Probably not, for " the sad times coming on amain, gave an obstruction to these proceedings." In the following year, Basire was a prisoner for his loyalty in Stockton Castle, and on his release, his living of Egglescliff being sequestrated, he thought "that it was better to turn his steps towards Italy than towards Newgate," and went abroad to seek subsistence as tutor to the sons of some royalist gentlemen. Finding, after a time,

[1] Rev. J. E. B. Mayor, Appendix to " Two Lives of Ferrar."

employment in Eastern Europe, he did not return to England till after the Restoration.

After the crushing defeat at Naseby, the fall of one royalist stronghold after another, the surrender of Astley and of Hopton, the most sanguine of royalists could hardly dare to hope that bishops or other noble personages could soon be in a condition to assist in the production of costly and learned works.

John Ferrar had other reasons, besides the imprisonment of Dr. Basire, and the difficulty of procuring the rare and costly books he needed, for postponing his grand project. He had already seen most of his friends driven from their homes. His own turn was now close at hand.

On April 27, 1646, the king, in despair, left Oxford secretly. He wandered from place to place in disguise, attended only by his trusty chaplain, Dr. Hudson, and Mr. Ashburnham. At length he came to Downham, in Norfolk. In his desolation, the remembrance of the religious house in which he had spent some peaceful hours on the eve of the war recurred to his mind. Very privately, in the darkness of night, he came once more to Gidding. The steep field, to the southwest of the church, up which he is said to have come, is still called the King's Close. " Having an entire confidence in the family, he made himself known to Mr. John Ferrar, who received his Majesty with all possible duty and respect. But fearing that Gidding, from the known loyalty of the family, might be a suspected place, for better concealment he conducted his Majesty to a private house at Coppingford, an obscure village at a small distance from Gidding, and not far from Stilton. Here the king slept, and went from thence, May 3, to Stamford, where he lodged one night, stayed till eleven the next night, and from thence went, on May 5, to join the Scotch army."[1]

On the 16th, Charles wrote from Newcastle, to Sir Edward Nicholas at Oxford, the despairing words, "Know that you are not to expect releefe, so that I give you leave to treate on good condic'ons."[2]

Perhaps, in spite of all precautions, the king's visit to Gidding became known to some parliamentary officer in the neighbourhood, for the blow which had long been threatened fell on Gidding at this crisis.

"Not long before the real tragedy of King Charles was perpetrated, active soldiers of the Parliament party resolved to plunder the house at Gidding. The family being informed of their intended approach, thought it prudent to fly, and, as to their persons, endeavour to escape the intended violence.

[1] Peckard, on authority of a manuscript account by J. Ferrar. No mention of Charles's visit to Gidding at this time is made in the inquiry instituted by the Commonwealth into the particulars of his journey, but Dr. Peckard considers that it took place during an evening which that inquiry leaves unacco ted for.

[2] The king to Sir E. Nicholas, "Diary and Correspondence of John Evelyn."

"These military zealots, in the rage of what they called reformation, ransacked both the church and the house. In doing which they expressed a particular spite against the organ. This they broke in pieces, of which they made a large fire, and thereat roasted several of Mr. Ferrar's sheep, which they had killed in his grounds. This done, they seized all the plate, furniture, and provision which they could conveniently carry away. And in this general devastation perished those works of Mr. Nicholas Ferrar which merited a better fate." [1]

It does not appear whether the ejection of Ferrar Collett from his fellowship at Peterhouse had any connection with this attack on Gidding, but it took place in the same year—on November 6, 1646.

Where the Ferrars took shelter in their trouble we are not informed, no letters or journals belonging to this time of distress having come to light. We may be sure that they suffered much. The universal poverty which overwhelmed the royalist party had touched its lowest point, and out of all their many friends few indeed could have been in a position to offer them shelter or help in their need. Mrs. Basire's letters to her husband give a pathetic description of her efforts to bring up her children on the scanty and ill-paid "fifths," which were allowed for the maintenance of the families of the sequestered clergy.

[1] Peckard.

She writes to say that her "frend busbe" (Dr. Busby) had offered to educate their eldest boy free of cost, if she could pay for his board, but even this she cannot manage. Dr. Basire, now at Rouen with his pupils, can do little to help her. "I advise every one interested in the English desolation, to read the Book of Lamentations," he writes to her, apparently by way of consolation.

In the following summer the hopes of the royalists began to revive. On July 7, 1647, Sir Edward Nicholas wrote, full of hope in the pending negotiations between Charles and the parliament, "I hope it will not now be long before we heare that peace in England is in soe good forwardness as that honnest men may return with comfort to their homes. Dr. Hammond preached, Sunday was se'ennight, before the king, when service was said according to the English Liturgy. God will, I trust, finish the good work which he hath so wonderfully begun for the peace and good of England." [1]

During this breathing space, Mr. Ferrar brought his family back to Gidding.

On July 27 Dr. Busby communicates the news to their mutual friend, Basire : " A dead numnes hath these many years fall'n on my spirits, as upon the nation ; join with me in the versicle, 'O Lord my

[1] Sir E. Nicholas to Dr. Basire, "Life and Correspondence of Isaac Basire."

God, lighten mine eyes that I sleep not in death !'
All things at this time are in so dubious a calme, that
the fear is greatest when the danger is less. . . .
Mr. Thuscrosse is again settled in Yorkshire, Mr.
Ferrar with his family at Gidden, long since Mr.
Mapletoft hath a good living. All remember you, the
Joseph in affliction."

The calm lasted a few months longer. In October,
Nicholas could still write, with unconquerable hope-
fulness, " I do not despair but before the spring,
the king may yet be resetled on his throane. . . . All
now expect to heare whether his Ma'ts pious over-
ture for a personall treaty for an accomodation
wil be yielded unto, and then what will be the
yssue of that treaty, which I trust wil be a happy
peace."

The king's flight from Hampton Court, his re-
capture, the renewed outbreak of civil war, dashed
all these hopes to the ground.

We know nothing of the Ferrars during the sad days
that followed. They must have shared fully in the
awestruck and amazed horror with which the country
heard of the king's death sentence, " that horrid act
of which noe age ever heard the like." " I look for
nothing after this but the destruction of the kingdom,"
wrote the Dean of Bristol to his brother, Sir E.
Nicholas.[1] " The sad news," says Basire, " had almost

---

[1] " Nicholas Papers," edited by Mr. Warner.

spoyled my life ; yet his blood lives, and cries loud I fear."

In one respect, the Ferrars were more fortunate than most of their friends. They were never deprived of the services of the faithful friend and pastor, who had ministered to them ever since the first years of their coming to Gidding.

The living of Great Gidding was very poor, and was perhaps not considered worth sequestrating, for Mr. Groose held it undisturbed throughout the Civil War, and into the first years of the Restoration.[1]

It may surely be viewed as a special blessing, granted to their continual prayer, that even in the darkest years of the Commonwealth the family of Gidding were never deprived of the Sacraments of the Church.

"Where shall we now receive the Viaticum with safety ? How shall we be baptized ?[2] For to this pass is it come, sir," wrote John Evelyn, in 1655, to his "ghostly father," Jeremy Taylor. "The shepherds are smitten, and the sheep must of a necessity be scattered, unlesse the greate Shephearde of Soules oppose, or some of His delegates reduce and direct

---

[1] This appears from the registers of Gidding Church. See Mr. Mayor, Appendix.

[2] Sir Ralph Verney writes to his wife in 1647, "Now for the christening. I pray give noe offence to the State ; should it bee donn in the old way perhapps it may bring more trouble uppon you then you can immagen."—"Memoirs of the Verney Family."

us. Deare Sir, we are now preparing to take our last sad farewell (as they threaten) of God's service in this citty or anywhere else in publique. I must confesse it is a sad consideration, but it is what God sees best, and to what we must submitt. My comfort is, *Deus providebit.*" [1]

In the tiny church at Gidding, hidden by its sheltering woods, the edict of " Julianus Redivivus," as Evelyn terms Cromwell, could perhaps be safely disregarded ; if it were not so, at least in the great parlour, or the oratories sanctified by years of nightly intercession, the holy Mysteries might still be celebrated by the faithful friend who for so many years had fed that little flock with the Bread of Life.

The remaining members of the family still clung together.

" My dear Swete Sister," writes Susannah Chedley (formerly Susannah Mapletoft) to Virginia Ferrar, in 1650, " the blessed Psalm saith, it is a joyful thing when brethren dwell together in unity, as I am sure you do."

Virginia, now grown to womanhood, seems to have been a great joy and delight to her family, " making a sunshine in the shady place." Among the Magdalene College manuscripts are numerous letters to her from Susannah Chedley, and from Jane Collett, wife to her

[1] John Evelyn to Dr. Taylor, London, March 18, 1655, " Diary and Correspondence."

cousin Richard. " Your noble and free sperrit . . . hath satisfide me beyond expression," writes Jane in one of her affectionate ill-spelt epistles, which present a great contrast to Susannah's careful writing.

It is pleasant to think that John Ferrar's declining years were brightened by the presence of this beloved child. He occupied himself in writing the Memoirs from which this book is drawn—and still the vision of his great Bible flitted before his eyes.

" It hath lain still till this year, 165— " [1] (they are the closing words of " Observations on the Works done at Gidding ") ; " and now it hath so fallen out, that (to the honour of those worthy learned men that have, by their great care and diligence, set it on foot) the printing of the Holy Bible in eight several languages is designed here in England ; [2] the which work in many respects is like to pass that Bible both of the King of Spain's, and the aforenamed King of France's : in which regard it is now thought fitting to defer this model and intended work, till that our Bible be finished. And then, by the good blessing of God, and the help of some of those active hands, that are yet alive, who were instruments of the other many precedent works, as you have heard, this may in a good hour be begun, and by the help of God and good

[1] Year omitted or illegible in manuscripts.
[2] The printing of Bishop Walton's Polyglott was begun in 1653, and completed 1657.

friends brought to light' and finished. . . . A book it will be that hath not its parallel or match in the whole world, and may well become, as many learned men say that have seen the model of it, the best library in the Christian world, and a jewel not unbeseeming the greatest potentate's study. God Almighty give both means and heads and hands to effect it : to whom must be the glory, praise, and honour! Amen, amen, amen." [1]

In the September of the year in which the English Polyglott was published—1657—the earthly remains of John Ferrar were laid in Gidding churchyard, and his noble conception was left a dream unrealized.

On the memorial brass, which still remains in Gidding church, is inscribed, beneath his name and arms, the same text which, on his first coming to Gidding, was engraved over the door of the house : " Flee from evil, and do ye the thing y[t] is right, and dwell for ever-more."

His sister, Mrs. Collett, survived him little more than a week, dying on the 9th of October, at the age of seventy-six. She had been a widow seven years, Mr. Collett having ended his quiet life in 1650. Both husband and wife lie in the churchyard at Gidding, and near them rests their daughter, Susannah Chedley, " who exchanged this life for a better on the 31st day

[1] " Observations on Works done at Gidding," printed with " Two Lives," by Mr. Mayor.

of October, in the year of our Lord 1657, and of her pilgrimage fifty and five," [1] but three weeks after her mother.

The inhabitants of Gidding Hall were by this time but few. The family now consisted of John Ferrar's only surviving son, also named John, with his wife and children, and his sister Virginia, Mary and Anna Collett, their brother Ferrar, and the young Mapletofts—the children of Susannah Chedley by her first marriage. Mrs. Collett's younger daughters were all married, and the sons long since established in their various trades and professions. The great house must have been far too large for the diminished numbers and lessened means of the household. At what time they removed from it, and suffered it to fall into decay, is not known. A note from Ferrar Collett to his brother Nicholas in town,[2] containing a list of small commissions for their sister Mary, proves that they were still at Gidding in 1660. At some later date John Ferrar, with his wife and sister, removed to Old Park, but the connection with Gidding remained unbroken, for the brother and sister were both buried among their kindred. Virginia died in 1668. John survived till 1715, when he passed away at the age of eighty-nine. Two small brasses in Gidding church preserve his memory and that of

[1] Inscription on her tomb in Gidding churchyard.
[2] Magdalene College Manuscripts.

his wife.   He left a large family, of whom some
descendants yet remain.   His grandson, Thomas, was
buried at Gidding in 1748, and the baptism of the
little daughter of a cousin, Henry Ferrar, is noted in
the Gidding Register in 1753.   After this date the
estate seems to have passed out of the hands of the
Ferrars.[1]

[1] For these dates the writer is indebted to Mr. Mayor's
Appendix.

CHAPTER XV.

A.D. 1660-1720.

> " How brave a prospect is a traversed plain,
>   Where flowers and palms refresh the eye,
> And days well spent like the glad East remain,
>   Whose morning glories cannot die."
>   H. VAUGHAN.

WHEN the home at Gidding was broken up, Mary and
Anna Collett seem to have left the neighbourhood,
for their names are not to be found among those who
sleep in that peaceful churchyard. Of Anna, indeed,
we have no further knowledge except such as is contained in the few words written by John Mapletoft
under the sisters' names in the " Conversation Book."

"Who both died Virgins, resolving (so) to live
when they were young, by the grace of God."[1]

A slight and uncertain glimpse of the surroundings

---

[1] Chap. VII.

Y

of Mary in her later years, may be gathered from a few words written in a copy of the *Eikon Basiliké*, given by her to a friend.

"This book was bound at litle Giding in Huntingdonshire by ye much celebrated Mrs. Mary Colet, ye beloved Neece of ye famous Mr. Nicolas Farar, who honoured her with ye title of Chief of his most pious Society.

"I leave ye Book as a valuable jewel to my Son, who in his childhood was very dear to ye S[t] who presented me ye book and who bound it with her own hands.

"ANNE GRIGG, March,
"1678."[1]

Anne Grigg is probably the Mrs. Grigge to whom Bishop Ken addressed, in 1691, an interesting letter (given in Dean Plumptre's Life of Ken), written in terms which imply friendship and confidence.

"God of His infinite goodnesse," it concludes, "multiply His blessings on yourself and on my good friends with you, and enable us to doe, and to suffer, His most Holy Will.

"Your very affectionate friend,
"THOS. BATH AND WELLS."

---

[1] Rev. J. E. B. Mayor, Appendix. The book belonged, in 1858, to the Rev. T. H. Tcoke, who showed it to Mr. Mayor.

The "good friends" were Francis Turner, the nonjuring Bishop of Ely, and his mother, in whose family Mrs. Grigge was living, apparently as governess to the bishop's daughter.

We may suppose, therefore, that it was through this lady, or perhaps direct from Mary Collett herself, that Bishop Turner obtained the materials for his life of Nicholas Ferrar.

The link between Mrs. Grigge and Mary Collett is easily found. Mrs. Grigge was cousin to the celebrated John Locke, to whose constant kindness she and her son (she was early left a widow) seem to have been much indebted; and one of Locke's earliest and closest friends was John Mapletoft. The friendship extended to the members of their respective families. "And now I come to you, beloved, first, with a word of information, that your cousin Collett is well," Locke writes to Mapletoft in 1672,[1] and Mapletoft in return sends messages of remembrance to Mrs. Grigge.

A short account of Mary Collett's adopted son may form a not unfitting close to this imperfect sketch of the family to which he owed his training.

John Mapletoft[2] was originally intended for Holy Orders, but the troublous times in which he grew up

---

[1] Fox Bournes' "Life of Locke."

[2] See "Life of Dr. Mapletoft" in Ward's "Gresham Professors," and Rev. R. F. Secretan's "Life of Robert Nelson."

long prevented the fulfilment of his desire. Following the footsteps of his great-uncle Nicholas, he proceeded, after graduating at Trinity College, Cambridge, to Italy, and there devoted himself to the study of medicine. On his return to England he settled as a physician in London. He still cherished a desire for ordination, but when all difficulties were removed by the Restoration, he was long withheld from carrying out his wish by a sensitive dread lest his change of profession should seem to be actuated by worldly views. It was not until 1678, when he had attained to high distinction as a physician, and had become Professor of Medicine at Gresham College, that he gave up practice, quitted London, and retired into the country to prepare himself in quiet for Holy Orders.

"I cannot tell how to blame your design, but I must confess to you, I like our calling the worse since you have quitted it," Locke writes, on hearing his friend's decision.

Two letters from Robert Nelson, then a youth of twenty-three, with whom the physician of eight and forty had already formed a friendship that lasted through their lives, show that part of this season of retirement was spent at Hemel Hempstead, in Hertfordshire.

"Dear and honoured Sir," writes Nelson in 1679, "as soon as I came to town, which was about ten days ago, I made a strict inquiry concerning your welfare, which I counted myself not a little concerned in, by reason your many favours and obligations, besides the just value of your person, have engaged me in a particular respect and esteem to yourself."

Mary Collett seems to have lived just long enough to rejoice in her nephew's ordination. We learn from the " Conversation Book " that " My much honoured Aunt Mary, who took care of me and my brother Peter and sister Mary, after the death of our reverend and pious father, Mr. Joshua Mapletoft, died in the 80th year of her age."

As she was thirty-two in 1634,[1] this would place her death in 1682, the year in which Dr. Mapletoft was appointed to the living of Braybrooke, in North-amptonshire. At Braybrooke he remained only three years, but in that space of time he effected much good. He prevailed on his parishioners to repair their fine old church, and to furnish the altar with suitable Communion plate. He brought many of the people to their religious duties, and took pains to supply them with good books; he was also careful to provide employment for the poor (often setting them to work at his own expense), and instruction for the children. To this day the schools at Bray-brooke benefit by his generosity.

[1] " His nieces had lived, one thirty, the other thirty-two years, virgins."—Lenton's Letter.

In 1685, at the request of several of the London clergy, he was appointed to the living of St. Lawrence Jewry, " but would never advance farther, to avoid the suspicion of having left one profession and taken up another, to enrich himself and his family." [1]

It was a time of reviving life in the Church. Under the Commonwealth a generation had grown up without teaching and without sacraments ; such a population formed an evil soil in which the wild license of the Restoration spread and flourished ; but a strong reaction had now set in. In 1678 a few young laymen formed themselves into a society, bound to meet frequently for prayer, for religious conferences, and for the reception of the Holy Communion ; in a few years similar societies were spread throughout London, and had been founded in many provincial towns. These religious societies strengthened the hands of the parochial clergy, they supported daily services, they collected alms among themselves for various charitable purposes, and by their exertions and example did much to purify and reform the neighbourhoods where they lived and worked.

Dr. Mapletoft entered zealously into the work which was going on round his new cure, showing a special interest in the increase of Church services and the spread of Christian education.

The Holy Communion was celebrated in St. Law-

' Ward, " Lives of Gresham Professors."

rence Jewry at six o'clock every Sunday morning.
He took much pains with the religious instruction
of his people, seeing that every house in the parish
was supplied with good books.   He assisted in Dr.
Bray's schemes for the establishment of parochial
libraries, and was an early member of the Christian
Knowledge Society. "I depend upon your usual
goodwill for some considerable encouragement,"
Nelson writes, when announcing that the society proposes to set up at once fifty libraries.   His interest
in the cause of foreign missions must have been first
awakened in his childish days, when he was taught
no doubt to join in the intercessions of his family
for the cause of the Church in Virginia.   When the
desolate state of the American missions began once
more to engage the attention of Churchmen in
England, Dr. Mapletoft came forward at once.   He
joined in the foundation of the Society for the Propa-
gation of the Gospel, and was one of its first vice-
presidents.   His interest in it continued when he had
become too infirm to attend its meetings.

"I will to-morrow communicate your letter to the
society, who are very much disposed to encourage
the mission in the East," writes Robert Nelson to him
in 1710. "I despair of finding any of that sort of
zeal among us as will carry our clergy to such distant
places, where they are exposed to so many hardships ;
the business of party takes up all our zeal."

The "business of party" had indeed made sad
havoc in the Church; but though Dr. Mapletoft did
not join the ranks of the Nonjurors, the difference of
opinion led to no breach with those of his friends
whose conscience compelled them to take a different
line.   Nelson writes to him in 1701, suggesting that
he should visit Lord Weymouth; "you will find him
(Dr. Bray) and Bishop Ken both there."

In 1710, after an illness which seems to have
occasioned much anxiety to his friends, Dr. Mapletoft resigned his living.   As a farewell to his
parishioners, he gave to each householder a book
which he had written specially for that purpose—
" The Principles and Duties of the Christian Religion
Considered and Explained, in order to Retrieve and
Promote the Christian Life, and that Holiness without
which no man shall see the LORD."

The book contains a clear and practical exposition
of the Creed, and the duties of the Christian life as
taught in the Beatitudes, with instructions on self-
examination, prayer, and the Holy Communion.
A few paragraphs from the "Short Discourse on
Prayer" will show its tone.

"Prayer is that homage we owe and pay to our
Creator for having made us men in His own image "
. . . it " will unlock our souls from that clod of earth
to which they now grow, and in which they lose
themselves; it will raise our thoughts, and desires,

and aims above the smoak and dust, the petty cares,
and worthless trifling designs of this lower world. . . .
They therefore that have any, though but the least,
trace of that image of GOD in which man was first
created, remaining in their souls, and who understand
anything of that religion which chiefly distinguishes
man from the beasts that perish, will never pass any
one day of their life without making devout and
solemn application to the Father of their spirits, the
GOD of all grace, and the only Giver of all good
things. . . . Nor can he be presumed to have any
great desire or to be in any measure fit to enjoy GOD
in heaven to eternal ages, who can be usually hindred
by any vain amusements, or business at that time
unnecessary, from employing an hour or two in each
day in attendance upon and doing open honour to
his Creator, Redeemer, and Sanctifier, in those as-
semblies and performances which make the best
representation and performance of the heavenly
state, which we are now capable of. . . . We ought,
whenever we are about to pray, to labour to possess
our minds with an actual awful apprehension of the
great and tremendous Majesty we approach to, with
a deep sense of the importance of those things we
ask, which are of no less consequence to us than the
life of our immortal souls, with that humility which
becomes sinners, and yet with that faith and trust in
GOD which becomes His children."

"Such truly pious and Christian discourses must particularly affect your friends and acquaintances, because your own example preaches to them at the same time," Nelson writes, in acknowledging a copy sent to him. "This a very acceptable legacy to your friends and parishioners."

Dr. Mapletoft spent his last years under the roof of his daughter and her husband, Dr. Gastrell, Bishop of Chester. He had, as Nelson wrote, "a soft and gentle old age," preserving to the last the gaiety and cheerfulness of his temper, seeming always desirous "to gain the affections of those about him that he might engage them to virtue and religion."

"His body decayed gently, but his mind not at all."[1] He clung affectionately to the recollections of his early years. "I desire that it may be preserved in my family as long as may be," he writes in 1715, in a Gidding Concordance, which he gives to his son.[2]

In 1720, in the ninetieth year of his age, the latest survivor of the household of Nicholas Ferrar entered into "the rest that remaineth to the people of God."

His life covers an era in the history of the English Church. In his youth he saw it trodden down by the Commonwealth. He lived through the time of its

---

[1] Ward.

[2] See Chap. VIII., No. II.

revival, with energies quickened and renewed by suffering. When he passed away, it was already sinking into the strange sleep of the eighteenth century, the sleep of the chrysalis, full of unknown forces and unconscious growth.

THE END.

PRINTED BY WILLIAM CLOWES AND SONS, LIMITED,
LONDON AND BECCLES.

A Catalogue of Works

IN

THEOLOGICAL LITERATURE

PUBLISHED BY

Messrs. LONGMANS, GREEN, & CO.

39 Paternoster Row, London, E.C.,

Abbey and Overton.—THE ENGLISH CHURCH IN THE EIGHTEENTH CENTURY. By Charles J. Abbey, M.A., Rector of Checkendon, Reading, and John H. Overton, M.A., Rector of Epworth ; Rural Dean of Isle of Axholme. *Crown 8vo. 7s. 6d.*

Adams.—SACRED ALLEGORIES. The Shadow of the Cross —The Distant Hills—The Old Man's Home—The King's Messengers. By the Rev. William Adams, M.A. *Crown 8vo. 3s. 6d.*

The Four Allegories may be had separately, with Illustrations. *16mo. 1s. each. Also the Miniature Edition. Four Vols. 32mo. 1s. each.*

Aids to the Inner Life.

Edited by the Rev. W. H. Hutchings, M.A., Rector of Kirkby Misperton, Yorkshire. *Five Vols. 32mo, cloth limp, 6d. each ; or cloth extra, 1s. each.*

With red borders, 2s. each. Sold separately.

OF THE IMITATION OF CHRIST. By Thomas à Kempis.

THE CHRISTIAN YEAR.

THE DEVOUT LIFE. By St. Francis de Sales.

THE HIDDEN LIFE OF THE SOUL.

THE SPIRITUAL COMBAT. By Laurence Scupoli.

Allen.—THE CHURCH CATECHISM : its History and Contents. A Manual for Teachers and Students. By the Rev. A. J. C. Allen, M.A., formerly Principal of the Chester Diocesan Training College. *Crown 8vo. 3s. 6d.*

Barry.—LIGHT OF SCIENCE ON THE FAITH. Being the Bampton Lectures for 1892. By the Right Rev. Alfred Barry, D.D., Canon of Windsor, formerly Bishop of Sydney, Metropolitan of New South Wales, and Primate of Australia. *8vo.*

Bathe.—Works by the Rev. ANTHONY BATHE, M.A.

A LENT WITH JESUS. A Plain Guide for Churchmen. Containing Readings for Lent and Easter Week, and on the Holy Eucharist. *32mo, 1s.; or in paper cover, 6d.*

AN ADVENT WITH JESUS. *32mo, 1s.; or in paper cover, 6d.*

WHAT I SHOULD BELIEVE. A Simple Manual of Self-Instruction for Church People. *Crown 8vo. 3s. 6d.*

Bickersteth.—YESTERDAY, TO-DAY, AND FOR EVER: a Poem in Twelve Books. By EDWARD HENRY BICKERSTETH, D.D., Bishop of Exeter. *One Shilling Edition*, 18mo. *With red borders,* 16mo, 2s. 6d.

The Crown 8vo Edition (5s.) may still be had.

Blunt.—Works by the Rev. JOHN HENRY BLUNT, D.D.

THE ANNOTATED BOOK OF COMMON PRAYER: Being an Historical, Ritual, and Theological Commentary on the Devotional System of the Church of England. *4to. 21s.*

THE COMPENDIOUS EDITION OF THE ANNOTATED BOOK OF COMMON PRAYER: Forming a concise Commentary on the Devotional System of the Church of England. *Crown 8vo. 10s. 6d.*

DICTIONARY OF DOCTRINAL AND HISTORICAL THEOLOGY. By various Writers. *Imperial 8vo. 21s.*

DICTIONARY OF SECTS, HERESIES, ECCLESIASTICAL PARTIES AND SCHOOLS OF RELIGIOUS THOUGHT. By various Writers. *Imperial 8vo. 21s.*

THE BOOK OF CHURCH LAW. Being an Exposition of the Legal Rights and Duties of the Parochial Clergy and the Laity of the Church of England. Revised by Sir WALTER G. F. PHILLIMORE, Bart., D.C.L. *Crown 8vo. 7s. 6d.*

A COMPANION TO THE BIBLE: Being a Plain Commentary on Scripture History, to the end of the Apostolic Age. *Two vols. small 8vo. Sold separately.*

THE OLD TESTAMENT. *3s. 6d.*   THE NEW TESTAMENT. *3s. 6d.*

HOUSEHOLD THEOLOGY: a Handbook of Religious Information respecting the Holy Bible, the Prayer Book, the Church, etc. etc. *Paper cover,* 16mo. *1s.* Also the Larger Edition, 3s. 6d.

Body.—Works by the Rev. GEORGE BODY, D.D., Canon of Durham.

THE SCHOOL OF CALVARY ; or, Laws of Christian Life revealed from the Cross. *Small 8vo. 3s. 6d.*

THE LIFE OF JUSTIFICATION. *16mo. 2s. 6d.*

THE LIFE OF TEMPTATION. *16mo. 2s. 6d.*

Bonney.—CHRISTIAN DOCTRINES AND MODERN THOUGHT: being the Boyle Lectures for 1891. By the Rev. T. G. BONNEY, D.Sc., Hon. Canon of Manchester. *Crown 8vo. 5s.*

Boultbee.—A COMMENTARY ON THE THIRTY-NINE ARTICLES OF THE CHURCH OF ENGLAND. By the Rev. T. P. BOULTBEE, formerly Principal of the London College of Divinity, St. John's Hall, Highbury. *Crown 8vo. 6s.*

Bright.—Works by WILLIAM BRIGHT, D.D., Canon of Christ Church Oxford.

MORALITY IN DOCTRINE. Sermons. *Crown 8vo.*

LESSONS FROM THE LIVES OF THREE GREAT FATHERS: St. Athanasius, St. Chrysostom, and St. Augustine. *Crown 8vo. 6s.*

THE INCARNATION AS A MOTIVE POWER. *Crown 8vo. 6s.*

Bright and Medd.—LIBER PRECUM PUBLICARUM EC-CLESIÆ ANGLICANÆ. A GULIELMO BRIGHT, S.T.P., et PETRO GOLDSMITH MEDD, A.M., Latine redditus. [In hac Editione continentur Versiones Latinæ—1. Libri Precum Publicarum Ecclesiæ Anglicanæ ; 2. Liturgiæ Primæ Reformatæ ; 3. Liturgiæ Scoticanæ ; 4. Liturgiæ Americanæ.] *Small 8vo. 7s. 6d.*

Browne.—AN EXPOSITION OF THE THIRTY-NINE ARTICLES, Historical and Doctrinal. By E. H. BROWNE, D.D., formerly Bishop of Winchester. *8vo. 16s.*

Campion and Beamont.—THE PRAYER BOOK INTER-LEAVED. With Historical Illustrations and Explanatory Notes arranged parallel to the Text. By W. M. CAMPION, D.D., and W. J. BEAMONT, M.A. *Small 8vo. 7s. 6d.*

Carter.—Works edited by the Rev. T. T. CARTER, M.A., Hon. Canon of Christ Church, Oxford.

THE TREASURY OF DEVOTION : a Manual of Prayer for General and Daily Use. Compiled by a Priest. *18mo. 2s. 6d. ; cloth limp, 2s. ; or bound with the Book of Common Prayer, 3s. 6d. Large-Type Edition. Crown 8vo. 3s. 6d.*

THE WAY OF LIFE : A Book of Prayers and Instruction for the Young at School, with a Preparation for Confirmation. Compiled by a Priest. *18mo. 1s. 6d.*

THE PATH OF HOLINESS : a First Book of Prayers, with the Service of the Holy Communion, for the Young. Compiled by a Priest. With Illustrations. *16mo. 1s. 6d. ; cloth limp, 1s.*

THE GUIDE TO HEAVEN : a Book of Prayers for every Want. (For the Working Classes.) Compiled by a Priest. *18mo. 1s. 6d. ; cloth limp, 1s. Large-Type Edition. Crown 8vo. 1s. 6d. ; cloth limp, 1s.*

[continued.

Carter.—Works edited by the Rev. T. T. CARTER, M.A., Hon. Canon of Christ Church, Oxford—*continued.*

 SELF-RENUNCIATION. 16mo. 2s. 6d.

 THE STAR OF CHILDHOOD: a First Book of Prayers and Instruction for Children. Compiled by a Priest. With Illustrations. 16mo. 2s. 6d.

Carter.—MAXIMS AND GLEANINGS FROM THE WRITINGS OF T. T. CARTER, M.A. Selected and arranged for Daily Use. *Crown 16mo.* 1s.

Chandler.—THE SPIRIT OF MAN: An Essay in Christian Philosophy. By the Rev. A. CHANDLER, M.A., Rector of Poplar, E., *Crown 8vo.* 5s.

Church's Seasons (The), and other Verses. BY YOLANDE. *Crown 8vo.* 4s. 6d.

Conybeare and Howson.—THE LIFE AND EPISTLES OF ST. PAUL. By the Rev. W. J. CONYBEARE, M.A., and the Very Rev. J. S. HOWSON, D.D. With numerous Maps and Illustrations.
  LIBRARY EDITION. *Two Vols. 8vo.* 21s.
  POPULAR EDITION. *One Vol. Crown 8vo.* 3s. 6d.

Copleston.—BUDDHISM—PRIMITIVE AND PRESENT IN MAGADHA AND IN CEYLON. By REGINALD STEPHEN COPLESTON, D.D., Bishop of Colombo. 8vo. 16s.

Devotional Series, 16mo, Red Borders. *Each 2s. 6d.*
 BICKERSTETH'S YESTERDAY, TO-DAY, AND FOR EVER.
 CHILCOT'S TREATISE ON EVIL THOUGHTS.
 THE CHRISTIAN YEAR.
 FRANCIS DE SALES' (ST.) THE DEVOUT LIFE.
 HERBERT'S POEMS AND PROVERBS.
 KEMPIS' (À) OF THE IMITATION OF CHRIST.
 WILSON'S THE LORD'S SUPPER. *Large type.*
 *TAYLOR'S (JEREMY) HOLY LIVING.
 *——— ——— HOLY DYING.
    * *These two in one Volume.* 5s.

Devotional Series, 18mo, without Red Borders. *Each 1s.*
 BICKERSTETH'S YESTERDAY, TO-DAY, AND FOR EVER.
 THE CHRISTIAN YEAR.
 FRANCIS DE SALES' (ST.) THE DEVOUT LIFE.
 HERBERT'S POEMS AND PROVERBS.
 KEMPIS' (À) OF THE IMITATION OF CHRIST.
 WILSON'S THE LORD'S SUPPER. *Large type.*
 *TAYLOR'S (JEREMY) HOLY LIVING.
 *——— ——— HOLY DYING.
    * *These two in one Volume.* 2s. 6d.

Edersheim.—Works by ALFRED EDERSHEIM, M.A., D.D., Ph.D., sometime Grinfield Lecturer on the Septuagint Oxford.

THE LIFE AND TIMES OF JESUS THE MESSIAH. *Two Vols.* 8*vo.* 24*s.*

JESUS THE MESSIAH: being an Abridged Edition of 'The Life and Times of Jesus the Messiah.' *Crown* 8*vo.* 7*s.* 6*d.*

PROPHECY AND HISTORY IN RELATION TO THE MESSIAH: The Warburton Lectures, 1880-1884. 8*vo.* 12*s.*

TOHU-VA-VOHU ('Without Form and Void'): being a collection of Fragmentary Thoughts and Criticism. *Crown* 8*vo.* 6*s.*

Ellicott.—Works by C. J. ELLICOTT, D.D., Bishop of Gloucester and Bristol.

A CRITICAL AND GRAMMATICAL COMMENTARY ON ST. PAUL'S EPISTLES. Greek Text, with a Critical and Grammatical Commentary, and a Revised English Translation. 8*vo.*

1 CORINTHIANS. 16*s.*	PHILIPPIANS, COLOSSIANS, AND
GALATIANS. 8*s.* 6*d.*	PHILEMON. 10*s.* 6*d.*
EPHESIANS. 8*s.* 6*d.*	THESSALONIANS. 7*s.* 6*d.*
PASTORAL EPISTLES. 10*s.* 6*d.*	

HISTORICAL LECTURES ON THE LIFE OF OUR LORD JESUS CHRIST. 8*vo.* 12*s.*

Epochs of Church History. Edited by MANDELL CREIGHTON, D.D., LL.D., Bishop of Peterborough. *Fcap.* 8*vo.* 2*s.* 6*d. each.*

THE ENGLISH CHURCH IN OTHER LANDS. By the Rev. H. W. TUCKER, M.A.

THE HISTORY OF THE RE-FORMATION IN ENGLAND. By the Rev. GEO. G. PERRY, M.A.

THE CHURCH OF THE EARLY FATHERS. By the Rev. ALFRED PLUMMER, D.D.

THE EVANGELICAL REVIVAL IN THE EIGHTEENTH CENTURY. By the Rev. J. H. OVERTON, M.A.

THE UNIVERSITY OF OXFORD. By the Hon. G. C. BRODRICK, D.C.L.

THE UNIVERSITY OF CAMBRIDGE. By J. BASS MULLINGER, M.A.

THE ENGLISH CHURCH IN THE MIDDLE AGES. By the Rev. W. HUNT, M.A.

THE CHURCH AND THE EASTERN EMPIRE. By the Rev. H. F. TOZER, M.A.

THE CHURCH AND THE ROMAN EMPIRE. By the Rev. A. CARR.

THE CHURCH AND THE PURITANS, 1570-1660. By HENRY OFFLEY WAKEMAN, M.A.

HILDEBRAND AND HIS TIMES. By the Rev. W. R. W. STEPHENS, M.A.

THE POPES AND THE HOHEN-STAUFEN. By UGO BALZANI.

THE COUNTER-REFORMATION. By ADOLPHUS WILLIAM WARD, Litt. D.

WYCLIFFE AND MOVEMENTS FOR REFORM. By REGINALD L. POOLE, M.A.

THE ARIAN CONTROVERSY. By H. M. GWATKIN, M.A.

Fosbery.—Works edited by the Rev. THOMAS VINCENT FOSBERY, M.A., sometime Vicar of St. Giles's, Reading.

VOICES OF COMFORT. *Cheap Edition. Small 8vo. 3s. 6d.*
The Larger Edition (7s. 6d.) may still be had.

HYMNS AND POEMS FOR THE SICK AND SUFFERING. In connection with the Service for the Visitation of the Sick. Selected from Various Authors. *Small 8vo. 3s. 6d.*

Garland.—THE PRACTICAL TEACHING OF THE APO-CALYPSE. By the Rev. G. V. GARLAND, M.A. *8vo. 16s.*

Gore.—Works by the Rev. CHARLES GORE, M.A., Principal of the Pusey House ; Fellow of Trinity College, Oxford.

THE MINISTRY OF THE CHRISTIAN CHURCH. *8vo. 10s. 6d.*

ROMAN CATHOLIC CLAIMS. *Crown 8vo. 3s. 6d.*

Goulburn.—Works by EDWARD MEYRICK GOULBURN, D.D., D.C.L., sometime Dean of Norwich.

THOUGHTS ON PERSONAL RELIGION. *Small 8vo, 6s. 6d. ; Cheap Edition, 3s. 6d. ; Presentation Edition, 2 vols. small 8vo, 10s. 6d.*

THE PURSUIT OF HOLINESS : a Sequel to ' Thoughts on Personal Religion.' *Small 8vo. 5s. Cheap Edition, 3s. 6d.*

THE CHILD SAMUEL : a Practical and Devotional Commentary on the Birth and Childhood of the Prophet Samuel, as recorded in 1 Sam. i., ii. 1-27, iii. *Small 8vo. 2s. 6d.*

THE GOSPEL OF THE CHILDHOOD : a Practical and Devotional Commentary on the Single Incident of our Blessed Lord's Childhood (St. Luke ii. 41 to the end.) *Crown 8vo. 2s. 6d.*

THE COLLECTS OF THE DAY : an Exposition, Critical and Devotional, of the Collects appointed at the Communion. With Preliminary Essays on their Structure, Sources, etc. *2 vols. Crown 8vo. 8s. each.*

THOUGHTS UPON THE LITURGICAL GOSPELS for the Sundays, one for each day in the year. With an Introduction on their Origin, History, the Modifications made in them by the Reformers and by the Revisers of the Prayer Book. *2 vols. Crown 8vo. 16s.*

MEDITATIONS UPON THE LITURGICAL GOSPELS for the Minor Festivals of Christ, the two first Week-days of the Easter and Whitsun Festivals, and the Red-letter Saints' Days. *Crown 8vo. 8s. 6d.*

FAMILY PRAYERS compiled from various sources (chiefly from Bishop Hamilton's Manual), and arranged on the Liturgical Principle. *Crown 8vo. 3s. 6d. Cheap Edition. 16mo. 1s.*

Harrison.—Works by the Rev. ALEXANDER J. HARRISON, B.D., Lecturer of the Christian Evidence Society.

PROBLEMS OF CHRISTIANITY AND SCEPTICISM ; Lessons from Twenty Years' Experience in the Field of Christian Evidence. *Crown 8vo. 7s. 6d.*

THE CHURCH IN RELATION TO SCEPTICS : a Conversational Guide to Evidential Work. *Crown 8vo. 7s. 6d.*

Holland.—Works by the Rev. HENRY SCOTT HOLLAND, M.A., Canon and Precentor of St. Paul's.

> PLEAS AND CLAIMS FOR CHRIST. *Crown 8vo.*
>
> CREED AND CHARACTER : Sermons. *Crown 8vo. 3s. 6d.*
>
> ON BEHALF OF BELIEF. Sermons preached in St. Paul's Cathedral. *Crown 8vo. 3s. 6d.*
>
> CHRIST OR ECCLESIASTES. Sermons preached in St. Paul's Cathedral. *Crown 8vo. 3s. 6d.*
>
> LOGIC AND LIFE, with other Sermons. *Crown 8vo. 3s. 6d.*

Hopkins.—CHRIST THE CONSOLER. A Book of Comfort for the Sick. By ELLICE HOPKINS. *Small 8vo. 2s. 6d.*

Howard.—THE SCHISM BETWEEN THE ORIENTAL AND WESTERN CHURCHES. With special reference to the addition of the *Filioque* to the Creed. By the Rev. G. B. HOWARD, B.A., sometime Scholar of St. John's College, Cambridge. *Crown 8vo. 3s. 6d.*

Ingram.—HAPPINESS IN THE SPIRITUAL LIFE; or, 'The Secret of the Lord.' A Series of Practical Considerations. By the Rev. W. CLAVELL INGRAM, M.A., Vicar of St. Matthew's, Leicester. *Crown 8vo. 7s. 6d.*

INHERITANCE OF THE SAINTS, THE ; or, Thoughts on the Communion of Saints and the Life of the World to come. Collected chiefly from English Writers by L. P. With a Preface by the Rev. HENRY SCOTT HOLLAND, M.A. *Crown 8vo. 7s. 6d.*

Jameson.—Works by Mrs. JAMESON.

> SACRED AND LEGENDARY ART, containing Legends of the Angels and Archangels, the Evangelists, the Apostles. With 19 etchings and 187 Woodcuts. *Two Vols. Cloth, gilt top, 20s. net.*
>
> LEGENDS OF THE MONASTIC ORDERS, as represented in the Fine Arts. With 11 etchings and 88 Woodcuts. *One Vol. Cloth, gilt top, 10s. net.*
>
> LEGENDS OF THE MADONNA, OR BLESSED VIRGIN MARY. With 27 Etchings and 165 Woodcuts. *One Vol. Cloth, gilt top, 10s. net.*
>
> THE HISTORY OF OUR LORD, as exemplified in Works of Art, Commenced by the late Mrs. JAMESON, continued and completed by LADY EASTLAKE. With 31 Etchings and 281 Woodcuts. *Two Vols. 8vo. 20s. net.*

Jennings.—ECCLESIA ANGLICANA. A History of the Church of Christ in England from the Earliest to the Present Times. By the Rev. ARTHUR CHARLES JENNINGS, M.A. *Crown 8vo. 7s. 6d.*

Jukes.—Works by ANDREW JUKES.

THE NEW MAN AND THE ETERNAL LIFE. Notes on the Reiterated Amens of the Son of God. *Crown 8vo.* 6s.

THE NAMES OF GOD IN HOLY SCRIPTURE : a Revelation of His Nature and Relationships. *Crown 8vo.* 4s. 6d.

THE TYPES OF GENESIS. *Crown 8vo.* 7s. 6d.

THE SECOND DEATH AND THE RESTITUTION OF ALL THINGS. *Crown 8vo.* 3s. 6d.

THE MYSTERY OF THE KINGDOM. *Crown 8vo.* 2s. 6d.

Keble.—MAXIMS AND GLEANINGS FROM THE WRITINGS OF JOHN KEBLE, M.A. Selected and Arranged for Daily Use. By C. M. S. *Crown 16mo.* 1s.

SELECTIONS FROM THE WRITINGS OF JOHN KEBLE, M.A. *Crown 8vo.* 3s. 6d.

King.—DR. LIDDON'S TOUR IN EGYPT AND PALESTINE IN 1886. Benig Letters descriptive of the Tour, written by his Sister, Mrs. KING. *Crown 8vo.* 5s.

Knowling.—THE WITNESS OF THE EPISTLES : a Study in Modern Criticism. By the Rev. R. J. KNOWLING, M.A., Vice-Principal of King's College, London. *8vo.* 15s.

Knox Little.—Works by W. J. KNOX LITTLE, M.A., Canon Residentiary of Worcester, and Vicar of Hoar Cross.

SKETCHES IN SUNSHINE AND STORM: a Collection of Miscellaneous Essays and Notes of Travel. *Crown 8vo.* 7s. 6d.

THE CHRISTIAN HOME. *Crown 8vo.* 6s. 6d.

THE HOPES AND DECISIONS OF THE PASSION OF OUR MOST HOLY REDEEMER. *Crown 8vo.* 3s. 6d.

CHARACTERISTICS AND MOTIVES OF THE CHRISTIAN LIFE. Ten Sermons preached in Manchester Cathedral, in Lent and Advent. *Crown 8vo.* 3s. 6d.

SERMONS PREACHED FOR THE MOST PART IN MANCHESTER. *Crown 8vo.* 3s. 6d.

THE MYSTERY OF THE PASSION OF OUR MOST HOLY REDEEMER. *Crown 8vo.* 3s. 6d.

THE WITNESS OF THE PASSION OF OUR MOST HOLY REDEEMER. *Crown 8vo.* 3s. 6d.

THE LIGHT OF LIFE. Sermons preached on Various Occasions. *Crown 8vo.* 3s. 6d.

SUNLIGHT AND SHADOW IN THE CHRISTIAN LIFE. Sermons preached for the most part in America. *Crown 8vo.* 3s. 6d.

Lear.—Works by, and Edited by, H. L. SIDNEY LEAR.

FOR DAYS AND YEARS. A Book containing a Text, Short Reading, and Hymn for Every Day in the Church's Year. 16mo. 2s. 6d. *Also a Cheap Edition, 32mo. 1s.; or cloth gilt, 1s. 6d.*

FIVE MINUTES. Daily Readings of Poetry. 16mo. 3s. 6d. *Also a Cheap Edition. 32mo. 1s.; or cloth gilt, 1s. 6d.*

WEARINESS. A Book for the Languid and Lonely. *Large Type.* Small 8vo. 5s.

THE LIGHT OF THE CONSCIENCE. 16mo. 2s. 6d. 32mo. 1s.; cloth limp, 6d.

CHRISTIAN BIOGRAPHIES. *Nine Vols. Crown 8vo. 3s. 6d. each.*

MADAME LOUISE DE FRANCE, Daughter of Louis XV., known also as the Mother Térèse de St. Augustin.

A DOMINICAN ARTIST: a Sketch of the Life of the Rev. Père Besson, of the Order of St. Dominic.

HENRI PERREYVE. By A. GRATRY.

ST. FRANCIS DE SALES, Bishop and Prince of Geneva.

THE REVIVAL OF PRIESTLY LIFE IN THE SEVENTEENTH CENTURY IN FRANCE.

A CHRISTIAN PAINTER OF THE NINETEENTH CENTURY.

BOSSUET AND HIS CONTEMPORARIES.

FÉNELON, ARCHBISHOP OF CAMBRAI.

HENRI DOMINIQUE LACORDAIRE.

DEVOTIONAL WORKS. Edited by H. L. SIDNEY LEAR. *New and Uniform Editions. Nine Vols.* 16mo. 2s. 6d. each.

FÉNELON'S SPIRITUAL LETTERS TO MEN.

FÉNELON'S SPIRITUAL LETTERS TO WOMEN.

A SELECTION FROM THE SPIRITUAL LETTERS OF ST. FRANCIS DE SALES.

THE SPIRIT OF ST. FRANCIS DE SALES.

THE HIDDEN LIFE OF THE SOUL.

THE LIGHT OF THE CONSCIENCE.

SELF-RENUNCIATION. From the French.

ST. FRANCES DE SALES' OF THE LOVE OF GOD.

SELECTIONS FROM PASCAL'S THOUGHTS.

Library of Spiritual Works for English Catholics. *Original Edition. With Red Borders. Small 8vo. 5s. each. New and Cheaper Editions. 16mo. 2s. 6d. each.*

OF THE IMITATION OF CHRIST.

THE SPIRITUAL COMBAT. By LAURENCE SCUPOLI.

THE DEVOUT LIFE. By ST. FRANCIS DE SALES.

OF THE LOVE OF GOD. By ST. FRANCIS DE SALES.

THE CONFESSIONS OF ST. AUGUSTINE. *In Ten Books.*

THE CHRISTIAN YEAR. 5s. *Edition only.*

Liddon.—Works by HENRY PARRY LIDDON, D.D., D.C.L., LL.D., late Canon Residentiary and Chancellor of St. Paul's.

LECTURES AND ESSAYS. *Crown 8vo.*

THE EPISTLE TO THE ROMANS. *8vo.*

SERMONS ON OLD TESTAMENT SUBJECTS. *Crown 8vo.* 5*s.*

SERMONS ON SOME WORDS OF CHRIST. *Crown 8vo.* 5*s.*

THE DIVINITY OF OUR LORD AND SAVIOUR JESUS CHRIST. Being the Bampton Lectures for 1866. *Crown 8vo.* 5*s.*

ADVENT IN ST. PAUL'S. Sermons bearing chiefly on the Two Comings of our Lord. *Two Vols. Crown 8vo. 3s. 6d. each. Cheap Edition in one Volume. Crown 8vo. 5s.*

CHRISTMASTIDE IN ST. PAUL'S. Sermons bearing chiefly on the Birth of our Lord and the End of the Year. *Crown 8vo.* 5*s.*

PASSIONTIDE SERMONS. *Crown 8vo.* 5*s.*

EASTER IN ST. PAUL'S. Sermons bearing chiefly on the Resurrection of our Lord. *Two Vols. Crown 8vo. 3s. 6d. each. Cheap Edition in one Volume. Crown 8vo. 5s.*

SERMONS PREACHED BEFORE THE UNIVERSITY OF OXFORD. *Two Vols. Crown 8vo. 3s. 6d. each. Cheap Edition in one Volume. Crown 8vo. 5s.*

THE MAGNIFICAT. Sermons in St. Paul's. *Crown 8vo.* 2*s.* 6*d.*

SOME ELEMENTS OF RELIGION. Lent Lectures. *Small 8vo.* 2*s.* 6*d.* ; *or in paper cover,* 1*s.* 6*d.*
  The Crown 8vo Edition (5s.) may still be had.

SELECTIONS FROM THE WRITINGS OF H. P. LIDDON, D.D. *Crown 8vo.* 3*s.* 6*d.*

MAXIMS AND GLEANINGS FROM THE WRITINGS OF H. P. LIDDON, D.D. Selected and arranged by C. M. S. *Crown 16mo.* 1*s.*

DR. LIDDON'S TOUR IN EGYPT AND PALESTINE IN 1886. Being Letters descriptive of the Tour, written by his Sister, Mrs. KING. *Crown 8vo.* 5*s.*

Luckock.—Works by HERBERT MORTIMER LUCKOCK, D.D., Canon of Ely.

AFTER DEATH. An Examination of the Testimony of Primitive Times respecting the State of the Faithful Dead, and their Relationship to the Living. *Crown 8vo.* 6*s.*

[*continued.*

Luckock.—Works by HERBERT MORTIMER LUCKOCK, D.D. Canon of Ely—*continued.*

THE INTERMEDIATE STATE BETWEEN DEATH AND JUDGMENT. Being a Sequel to *After Death. Crown 8vo. 6s.*

FOOTPRINTS OF THE SON OF MAN, as traced by St. Mark. Being Eighty Portions for Private Study, Family Reading, and Instructions in Church. *Two Vols. Crown 8vo. 12s. Cheap Edition in one Vol. Crown 8vo. 5s.*

THE DIVINE LITURGY. Being the Order for Holy Communion, Historically, Doctrinally, and Devotionally set forth, in Fifty Portions. *Crown 8vo. 6s.*

STUDIES IN THE HISTORY OF THE BOOK OF COMMON PRAYER. The Anglican Reform—The Puritan Innovations—The Elizabethan Reaction—The Caroline Settlement. With Appendices. *Crown 8vo. 6s.*

THE BISHOPS IN THE TOWER. A Record of Stirring Events affecting the Church and Nonconformists from the Restoration to the Revolution. *Crown 8vo. 6s.*

LYRA GERMANICA. Hymns translated from the German by CATHERINE WINKWORTH. *Small 8vo. 5s.*

MacColl.—CHRISTIANITY IN RELATION TO SCIENCE AND MORALS. By the Rev. MALCOLM MACCOLL, M.A., Canon Residentiary of Ripon. *Crown 8vo. 6s.*

Mason.—Works by A. J. MASON, D.D., formerly Fellow of Trinity College, Cambridge.

THE FAITH OF THE GOSPEL. A Manual of Christian Doctrine. *Crown 8vo. 3s. 6d. Also a Large-Paper Edition for Marginal Notes. 4to. 12s. 6d.*

THE RELATION OF CONFIRMATION TO BAPTISM. As taught in Holy Scripture and the Fathers. *Crown 8vo. 7s. 6d.*

Mercier.—OUR MOTHER CHURCH : Being Simple Talk on High Topics. By Mrs. JEROME MERCIER. *Small 8vo. 3s. 6d.*

Molesworth.—STORIES OF THE SAINTS FOR CHILDREN : The Black Letter Saints. By Mrs. MOLESWORTH, Author of 'The Palace in the Garden,' etc. etc. With Illustrations. *Royal 16mo. 5s.*

Mozley.—Works by J. B. MOZLEY, D.D., late Canon of Christ Church, and Regius Professor of Divinity at Oxford.

ESSAYS, HISTORICAL AND THEOLOGICAL. *Two Vols. 8vo.* 24*s.*

EIGHT LECTURES ON MIRACLES. Being the Bampton Lectures for 1865. *Crown 8vo.* 7*s. 6d.*

RULING IDEAS IN EARLY AGES AND THEIR RELATION TO OLD TESTAMENT FAITH. Lectures delivered to Graduates of the University of Oxford. *8vo.* 10*s. 6d.*

SERMONS PREACHED BEFORE THE UNIVERSITY OF OXFORD, and on Various Occasions. *Crown 8vo.* 7*s. 6d.*

SERMONS, PAROCHIAL AND OCCASIONAL. *Crown 8vo.* 7*s. 6d.*

Mozley.—Works by the Rev. T. MOZLEY, M.A., Author of 'Reminiscences of Oriel College and the Oxford Movement.'

THE CREED OR A PHILOSOPHY. *Crown 8vo.*

THE WORD. *Crown 8vo.* 7*s. 6d.*

THE SON. *Crown 8vo.* 7*s. 6d.*

LETTERS FROM ROME ON THE OCCASION OF THE ŒCUMENICAL COUNCIL 1869-1870. *Two Vols. Cr. 8vo.* 18*s.*

Newbolt.—Works by the Rev. W. C. E. NEWBOLT, M.A., Canon and Chancellor of St. Paul's.

THE FRUIT OF THE SPIRIT. Being Ten Addresses bearing on the Spiritual Life. *Crown 8vo.* 2*s. 6d.*

THE MAN OF GOD. Being Six Addresses delivered during Lent at the Primary Ordination of the Right Rev. the Lord Alwyne Compton, D.D., Bishop of Ely. *Small 8vo.* 1*s. 6d.*

THE VOICE OF THE PRAYER BOOK. Being Spiritual Addresses bearing on the Book of Common Prayer. *Crown 8vo.* 2*s. 6d.*

Newnham.—THE ALL-FATHER: Sermons preached in a Village Church. By the Rev. H. P. NEWNHAM. With Preface by EDNA LYALL. *Crown 8vo.* 4*s. 6d.*

Newnham.—ALRESFORD ESSAYS FOR THE TIMES. By Rev. W. O. NEWNHAM, M.A., late Rector of Alresford. CONTENTS :—Bible Story of Creation—Bible Story of Eden—Bible Story of the Deluge—After Death—Miracles : A Conversation—Eternal Punishment—The Resurrection of the Body. *Crown 8vo.* 6*s.*

Newman.—Works by JOHN HENRY NEWMAN, B.D., sometime Vicar of St. Mary's, Oxford.

PAROCHIAL AND PLAIN SERMONS. *Eight Vols. Cabinet Edition. Crown 8vo. 5s. each. Popular Edition. 3s. 6d. each.*

SELECTION, ADAPTED TO THE SEASONS OF THE ECCLE-SIASTICAL YEAR, from the 'Parochial and Plain Sermons.' *Cabinet Edition. Crown 8vo. 5s. Popular Edition. 3s. 6d.*

FIFTEEN SERMONS PREACHED BEFORE THE UNIVERSITY OF OXFORD. *Cabinet Edition. Crown 8vo. 5s. Popular Edition. 3s. 6d.*

SERMONS BEARING UPON SUBJECTS OF THE DAY. *Cabinet Edition. Crown 8vo. 5s. Popular Edition. Crown 8vo. 3s. 6d.*

LECTURES ON THE DOCTRINE OF JUSTIFICATION. *Cabinet Edition. Crown 8vo. 5s. Popular Edition. 3s. 6d.*

THE LETTERS AND CORRESPONDENCE OF JOHN HENRY NEWMAN DURING HIS LIFE IN THE ENGLISH CHURCH. With a Brief Autobiographical Memoir. Arranged and Edited by ANNE MOZLEY. *Two Vols. 8vo. 30s. net.*

*** *For other Works by Cardinal Newman, see Messrs. Longmans & Co.'s Catalogue of Works in General Literature.*

Osborne.—Works by EDWARD OSBORNE, Mission Priest of the Society of St. John the Evangelist, Cowley, Oxford.

THE CHILDREN'S SAVIOUR. Instructions to Children on the Life of our Lord and Saviour Jesus Christ. *Illustrated. 16mo. 2s. 6d.*

THE SAVIOUR-KING. Instructions to Children on Old Testament Types and Illustrations of the Life of Christ. *Illustrated. 16mo. 2s. 6d.*

THE CHILDREN'S FAITH. Instructions to Children on the Apostles' Creed. *Illustrated. 16mo. 2s. 6d.*

Oxenden.—Works by the Right Rev. ASHTON OXENDEN, formerly Bishop of Montreal.

PLAIN SERMONS. *Crown 8vo.*

THE HISTORY OF MY LIFE : An Autobiography. *Crown 8vo. 5s.*

PEACE AND ITS HINDRANCES. *Crown 8vo. 1s. ; sewed, 2s., cloth.*

THE PATHWAY OF SAFETY ; or, Counsel to the Awakened. *Fcap. 8vo, large type. 2s. 6d. Cheap Edition. Small type, limp. 1s.*

THE EARNEST COMMUNICANT. *New Red Rubric Edition. 32mo, cloth. 2s. Common Edition. 32mo. 1s.*

OUR CHURCH AND HER SERVICES. *Fcap. 8vo. 2s. 6d.*

[continued.

Oxenden.—Works by the Right Rev. ASHTON OXENDEN, formerly Bishop of Montreal—*continued.*

    FAMILY PRAYERS FOR FOUR WEEKS. First Series. *Fcap. 8vo.* 2s. 6d. Second Series. *Fcap. 8vo.* 2s. 6d.

        LARGE TYPE EDITION. Two Series in one Volume. *Crown 8vo.* 6s.

    COTTAGE SERMONS; or, Plain Words to the Poor. *Fcap. 8vo.* 2s. 6d.

    THOUGHTS FOR HOLY WEEK. 16mo, cloth. 1s. 6d.

    DECISION. 18mo. 1s. 6d.

    THE HOME BEYOND; or, A Happy Old Age. *Fcap. 8vo.* 1s. 6d.

    THE LABOURING MAN'S BOOK. 18mo, *large type, cloth.* 1s. 6d.

Paget.—Works by FRANCIS PAGET, D.D., Dean of Christ Church, Oxford.

    THE SPIRIT OF DISCIPLINE: Sermons. *Crown 8vo.* 6s. 6d.

    FACULTIES AND DIFFICULTIES FOR BELIEF AND DIS-BELIEF. *Crown 8vo.* 6s. 6d.

    THE HALLOWING OF WORK. Addresses given at Eton, January 16-18, 1888. *Small 8vo.* 2s.

PRACTICAL REFLECTIONS. By a CLERGYMAN. With Prefaces by H. P. LIDDON, D.D., D.C.L., and the Bishop of Lincoln. *Crown 8vo.*

Vol. I.—THE HOLY GOSPELS. 4s. 6d.	THE PSALMS. 5s.
Vol. II.—ACTS TO REVELATION. 6s.	THE BOOK OF GENESIS. 4s. 6d.

PRIEST (THE) TO THE ALTAR; or, Aids to the Devout Celebration of Holy Communion, chiefly after the Ancient English Use of Sarum. *Royal 8vo.* 12s.

Pusey.—Works by the Rev. E. B. PUSEY, D.D.

    PRIVATE PRAYERS. With Preface by H. P. LIDDON, D.D. 32mo. 1s.

    PRAYERS FOR A YOUNG SCHOOLBOY. With a Preface by H. P. LIDDON, D.D. 24mo. 1s.

    SELECTIONS FROM THE WRITINGS OF EDWARD BOUVERIE PUSEY, D.D. *Crown 8vo.* 3s. 6d.

    MAXIMS AND GLEANINGS FROM THE WRITINGS OF EDWARD BOUVERIE PUSEY, D.D. Selected and Arranged for Daily Use. By C. M. S. *Crown 16mo.* 1s.

Reynolds.—THE NATURAL HISTORY OF IMMORTALITY. By the Rev. J. W. REYNOLDS, M.A., Prebendary of St. Paul's. *Crown 8vo.* 7s. 6d.

Sanday.—THE ORACLES OF GOD : Nine Lectures on the Nature and Extent of Biblical Inspiration and the Special Significance of the Old Testament Scriptures at the Present Time. By W. SANDAY, M.A., D.D., LL.D., Dean Ireland's Professor of Exegesis and Fellow of Exeter College. *Crown 8vo.* 4s.

Seebohm.—THE OXFORD REFORMERS—JOHN COLET, ERASMUS, AND THOMAS MORE: A History of their Fellow-Work. By FREDERIC SEEBOHM. *8vo.* 14s.

Stanton.—THE PLACE OF AUTHORITY IN MATTERS OF RELIGIOUS BELIEF. By VINCENT HENRY STANTON, D.D., Fellow of Trinity Coll., Ely Prof. of Divinity, Cambridge. *Cr. 8vo.* 6s.

Stephen.—ESSAYS IN ECCLESIASTICAL BIOGRAPHY. By the Right Hon. Sir J. STEPHEN. *Crown 8vo.* 7s. 6d.

Swayne.—THE BLESSED DEAD IN PARADISE. Four All Saints' Day Sermons, preached in Salisbury Cathedral. By R. G. SWAYNE, M.A. *Crown 8vo.* 3s. 6d.

Tweddell.—THE SOUL IN CONFLICT. A Practical Examination of some Difficulties and Duties of the Spiritual Life. By MARSHALL TWEDDELL, M.A., Vicar of St. Saviour, Paddington. *Crown 8vo.* 6s.

Twells.—COLLOQUIES ON PREACHING. By HENRY TWELLS, M.A., Honorary Canon of Peterborough. *Crown 8vo.* 2s. 6d.

Welldon. — THE FUTURE AND THE PAST. Sermons preached to Harrow Boys. By the Rev. J. E. C. WELLDON, M.A., Head Master of Harrow School. *Crown 8vo.* 7s. 6d.

Williams.—Works by the Rev. ISAAC WILLIAMS, B.D.

A DEVOTIONAL COMMENTARY ON THE GOSPEL NARRA-TIVE. *Eight Vols. Crown 8vo.* 5s. *each. Sold separately.*

THOUGHTS ON THE STUDY OF THE HOLY GOSPELS.	OUR LORD'S MINISTRY (Third Year).
A HARMONY OF THE FOUR GOSPELS.	THE HOLY WEEK.
OUR LORD'S NATIVITY.	OUR LORD'S PASSION.
OUR LORD'S MINISTRY (Second Year).	OUR LORD'S RESURRECTION.

FEMALE CHARACTERS OF HOLY SCRIPTURE. A Series of Sermons. *Crown 8vo.* 5s.

THE CHARACTERS OF THE OLD TESTAMENT. *Crown 8vo.* 5s.

THE APOCALYPSE. With Notes and Reflections. *Crown 8vo.* 5s.

SERMONS ON THE EPISTLES AND GOSPELS FOR THE SUN-DAYS AND HOLY DAYS. *Two Vols. Crown 8vo.* 5s. *each.*

[*continued.*

Williams.—Works by the Rev. ISAAC WILLIAMS, B.D.—*continued.*

PLAIN SERMONS ON CATECHISM. *Two Vols. Cr. 8vo. 5s. each.*

SELECTIONS FROM ISAAC WILLIAMS' WRITINGS. *Cr. 8vo.* 3s. 6d.

THE AUTOBIOGRAPHY OF ISAAC WILLIAMS, B.D., Author of several of the 'Tracts for the Times.' Edited by the Venerable Sir GEORGE PREVOST, as throwing further light on the history of the Oxford Movement. *Crown 8vo. 5s.*

Woodford.—Works by J. R. WOODFORD, D.D., Bishop of Ely.

THE GREAT COMMISSION. Addresses on the Ordinal. Edited, with an Introduction, by H. M. LUCKOCK, D.D. *Crown 8vo. 5s.*

SERMONS ON OLD AND NEW TESTAMENT SUBJECTS. Edited by H. M. LUCKOCK, D.D. *Crown 8vo. 5s.*

Woodruff.—THE CHILDREN'S YEAR. Verses for the Sundays and Holy Days throughout the Year. By C. H. WOODRUFF, B.C.L. With an Introduction by the Lord Bishop of SOUTHWELL. *Fcap. 8vo. 3s. 6d.*

Wordsworth.

For List of Works by the late Christopher Wordsworth, D.D., Bishop of Lincoln, see Messrs. Longmans & Co.'s Catalogue of Theological Works, 32 pp. Sent post free on application.

Wordsworth.—Works by ELIZABETH WORDSWORTH, Principal of Lady Margaret Hall, Oxford.

ILLUSTRATIONS OF THE CREED. *Crown 8vo. 5s.*

ST. CHRISTOPHER AND OTHER POEMS. *Crown 8vo. 6s.*

Wordsworth.—Works by CHARLES WORDSWORTH, D.D., D.C.L., Lord Bishop of St. Andrews, and Fellow of Winchester College.

ANNALS OF MY EARLY LIFE, 1806-1846. *8vo. 15s.*

PRIMARY WITNESS TO THE TRUTH OF THE GOSPEL, to which is added a Charge on Modern Teaching on the Canon of the Old Testament. *Crown 8vo. 7s. 6d.*

Younghusband.—Works by FRANCES YOUNGHUSBAND.

THE STORY OF OUR LORD, told in Simple Language for Children. With 25 Illustrations from Pictures by the Old Masters. *Crown 8vo.* 2s. 6d.

THE STORY OF GENESIS, told in Simple Language for Children. *Crown 8vo. 2s. 6d.*

THE STORY OF THE EXODUS, told in Simple Language for Children. With Map and 29 Illustrations. *Crown 8vo. 2s. 6d.*

Printed by T. and A. CONSTABLE, Printers to Her Majesty, at the Edinburgh University Press.

20,000/10/92.